AF527693

BRINK

S.L. BHYRAPPA

TRANSLATED BY
R. Ranganath Prasad
FROM THE KANNADA NOVEL *ANCHU*

THORNBIRD

NIYOGI BOOKS

Published by
NIYOGI BOOKS
Block D, Building No. 77
Okhla Industrial Area, Phase-I
New Delhi-110 020, India
Tel: 91-11-26816301, 26818960
Email: niyogibooks@gmail.com
Website: www.niyogibooksindia.com

Original text © S.L. Bhyrappa
Translated text © R. Ranganath Prasad

Editor: Sukanya Sur
Design: Shashi Bhushan Prasad
Cover Design: Misha Oberoi

ISBN: 978-93-89136-58-6
Publication: 2020

All rights are reserved. No part of this publication may be reproduced or transmitted in any form or by any means, electronic or mechanical, including photocopying, recording or by any information storage and retrieval system without prior written permission and consent of the Publisher.

Printed at: Niyogi Offset Pvt. Ltd., New Delhi, India

PREFACE

Brink is the translation of *Anchu* (1990), a Kannada novel by renowned philosopher-historian-litterateur Padmashri Dr S.L. Bhyrappa. It is a prominent work that deserves to be reckoned alongside his other works – *Vamshavriksha, Niraakarna, Daatu, Parva, Nele, Sakshi, Tantu, Saartha, Mandra, Aavarana,* and *Uttarakaaṇda* – most of which are translated into English besides pan-Indian languages. His autobiography *Bhitti* is as engrossing as his novels.

Brink deliberates on the nature of male–female love from physical, moral, and philosophical angles. Dr Amrita[1], the female character, repeatedly suffers from the severest urge to commit suicide, and the male counterpart Mr Somashekhar[2] anchors her to life each time. She nevertheless revolts, and he inevitably becomes the target of her unrelenting anger, torture, and blackmail – emotional and moral. With great personal suffering, perseverance, and sacrifice, he brings her back to normalcy.

Ostensibly, *Brink* is a love saga between a widower and an estranged woman. Obviously, it borders on adultery, but on the part of the man, it is not adultery. His empathy is genuine, and it morphs into love. As would a guru, he assumes responsibility to make her realize a value expounded in the *Bhagavadgita,* that is, *nirlipti*[3]

1 Paradoxically, 'Amrita' means 'ambrosia'.

2 'Soma-shekhar' is a synonym of Lord Shiva, whose anthropomorphic form is adorned in the head (*shekhar*) by a moon (*soma*). In a mythological event, Shiva swallowed poison to save the universe.

3 Its roots are traceable to the Upanishads, but delineation and prescriptiveness is lucid in *Bhagavadgita*.

(selfless conduct/ unaffectedness) vis-à-vis her estate usurped by her kin in particular and vis-à-vis the familial injustice perpetrated by them in general. Compliance to his wisdom equips her with the means to overcome depression. Such leverage and his compassion for her go on to serve as her emancipation, thereby doing away with the need for a psychiatrist. The remedial nature of this traditional canon makes human distress bearable. *Brink* would like to know if such values of Indian tradition appeal to the readers as worthy of inculcation.

The aforementioned constitutes the philosophical undercurrent of the novel. What equally matters in a work of fiction is its linguistic vehicle, and the creative narrative of *Brink* is enthralling to say the least. Employing techniques such as flashback, stream of consciousness, internal drama, and tension, this novel is verily quick-paced. Considering that there isn't much of interconnected 'events' in this tale, to be able to pen these many pages of anatomized emotional catharsis between two lovers – actually entirely the abreaction of one of them – and still make it engrossing is nothing short of ingenuity.

TRANSLATOR'S NOTE

In relating the thoughts of the characters in this novel – and his other novels as well – it is typical of Dr S.L. Bhyrappa to script contiguously within a single sentence the seemingly disparate thoughts as they occur in their minds. Though the constituent parts of this 'stream of consciousness' are almost complete semantically, they are mostly incomplete syntactically, except possibly the last in the series. While translating sentences thus structured, care has been taken to strike a balance between retaining the 'stream' per se and splitting it into several sentences with a view to ironing out the impediments to comprehension. I have ensured that the former instances are sustainable within the ipseity of English language, wherefore there shall neither be confusion in the minds of the readers nor loss of import. A maximal example is the passage in pages 62 and 63.

Also typical of the literary narrative of this author is synthesis of actuality, author's take, and characters' thought/speak[1] in the same sentence. Here too, I have been selective in retaining such script per se. Wherever retained, it is not at the cost of comprehension.

I am aware that such structuring is not legit, but I feel it to be kosher here for two reasons: one, this is not a work of science, and two, it serves to impart aesthetic experience to the reader in the manner the original endeavours to.

Typically, glossary is suffixed to a literary work, but those are treatises all. This is fiction, and it would be a breach of relish to *take*

1 The three types of literary expressions distinctly defined in Indian poetics.

a break for referring to the glossary. Listed below (alphabetically) are terms typical to Indian traditions and culture (to the exclusion of contextually comprehensible ones), which the readers outside of the subcontinent might be unfamiliar with. It is therefore suggested that the readers familiarize themselves with these few before embarking on an exhilarating journey of poring over the tale.

- **Bheema** (p. 270) is a physically robust Pandava sibling in the epic *Mahabharata*, and **Hidimba** is his wife from a marriage of convenience. She belonged in the rakshasa (demon) clan.
- **Draupadi** (p. 270) is the polyandrous wife to the five Pandava siblings in the epic *Mahabharata*. Dr S.L. Bhyrappa surmises that polyandry was in vogue in India till the era preceding *Mahabharata*, and that Draupadi could be one of the last victims of it for it came to be looked down upon thereabouts. The marriage institution's perpetual subjection to experimentation the world over is one of the synopses that induced Dr S.L. Bhyrappa to study *Mahabharata*; Draupadi thereat. The results of his expeditious scholastic research are handed over to all posterity in *Parva*.
- **Dussehra** and **Ramnavami** (p. 91) are annual festivals. The former is typically a *Kṣatriya*[2] festival, and continues to be celebrated in a grand way by the royal family of Mysore (southern India) and communally all over Bengal (eastern India). The latter is in celebration of the birth of Lord Rama and is held

2 *Brāhmaṇa*, *Kṣatriya*, *Vaiśya*, and *Śūdra* are 'varṇas', the four pragmatic leagues, and every individual was reckoned as belonging in a certain varṇa in consonance with one's societal obligations. The design is congenial for migration through the varṇas, and there have been quite some instances, a prominent one being that of *Viśvāmitra*. A pertinent proposition is also featured in this author's novel *Parva*, the recreation of the epic *Mahabharata*. In consonance with the successive advancements and diversity in science and technology over the eons, this skill-based system of categorization has been uneventfully withering with endorsement from the inherent anthropological adaptability of Indian traditions.

communally across India. Both festivals are also celebrated in homes. Cultural events – especially classical vocal/instrumental music – are integral to communally celebrated festivals.

- **Ekalavya** (p. 218): In the epic *Mahabharata*, Droṇa is the preceptor to the Pandavas and Kauravas. He vowed to groom the Pandava sibling Arjuna into a pre-eminent archer and tutored him accordingly. Eventually surfaces an obscure hunter called Ekalavya, who attained parity with Arjuna in archery. Ekalavya had aspired to get tutored by Droṇa, but the latter rejected him. Without getting disheartened, he installs a Droṇa statue, hones his warfare skills (that were default in him by virtue of he being a hunter) on his own in the spirit of having learned it from the statue, and pays obeisance to it. When Droṇa gets to know of his achievement, he is disturbed that his pet pupil Arjuna is no more the only one at the top. He sets the situation right by requisitioning an unreasonable tuition fee from the doctrinally devout Ekalavya – his severed proper thumb so that he can no more wield an arrow! This is featured intricately and extensively in Dr S.L. Bhyrappa's *Parva*.
- ***Gokulāṣṭami*** (p. 110) is an annual festival held in celebration of the birth of Lord Krishna. Gokula is the place where he was born, and *Aṣṭami* (eighth) is the day of the lunar month in which he was born.
- **Hanuman** (p. 166), a character in the epic *Ramayana*, is the most ardent providential devotee in all of Indian classical literature. His devotion to Lord Rama is unparalleled. His master would be present in his heart every single moment. There is an anecdote about him peeling off his chest to reveal his master's presence there.
- ***homa*** (p. 156) is a rite that necessarily entails assorted offerings into *agni* (p. 176), the sacrificial fire, accompanied by iterative chanting of mantras to invoke blessings of the gods on auspicious

occasions such as wedding, christening, *upanayanam* (threading ceremony), house-warming etc. It is also done as part of funeral rites with distinct chants/ procedures.

- ***Kālabhairava*** (p. 63) is a reincarnation of Lord Shiva, the leveller among the triad (the other two being Brahma, the creator, and Viṣhṇu, the sustainer). As is typical in Indian mythology for every god to have a unique carrier, *Kālabhairava* rides a dog. In Indian mythology, dog is allegoric of past life too.
- ***kesaribhāt*** (p. 162) is a simple sweet pudding made from semolina.
- ***masurpāk*** (p. 248) is a crispy sweet made from chickpea (*masur*) flour. It is pronounced (and in the marketplace invariably spelled) 'Mysorepak', a queer result of its popularity – and possibly its genesis – in Mysore, South India.
- **pallu** (p. 37) is the decorative fringe of sari worn over the shoulder after the rest of it is used up for draping.
- **puja** (p. 156) is ritualistic worship wherein God is symbolically served as would a guest[3] actually be.
- **royal jasmine** (p. 16), *Jasminum grandiflorum*; **jasmine** (p. 215), *Jasminum officinale.*
- **Sri** (p. 96): The honorific masculine prefix *Śrīmān* abridged in usage.
- **thirteen years** (p. 151) is the duration of the forestial exile imposed on the Pandavas in the epic *Mahabharata* (for losing a game of dice), including going underground during the last year,

3 The Indian tradition recognizes two types of guests: the invited (*abhyāgata*) and the walk-in (*atithi*). The invited is by default venerable, for s/he has merited invitation. The walk-in is accorded greater veneration in Indian tradition and is ascribed a place among the godly – mother, father, teacher, and *atithi*. There is no bigger charity than opening up our private time and space to others, more so to the unacquainted, for it will sometime be our turn to be one! An aspect of Indian tradition in serving an *atithi* is evidenced in the conversation among Dr Amrita, her brother, and her aunt (p. 371). Another aspect of it is delineated in this author's novel *Sakṣhi* (*Witness*).

with the condition that they shall go through another thirteen-year-cycle if uncovered during that last year.

- ***uppiṭṭu*** (p. 65), also known as *upma*, is a popular South Indian breakfast dish prepared from semolina. There are several variants of *uppiṭṭu*, and the recipe ranges from simple to motley.
- ***Vaikuṇṭha*** (p. 86), colloquial for *Vaikuṇṭha samārādhanā*, is a religious oblation for the departed held on the thirteenth day of death. The preceding twelve days witness funeral rites, but this thirteenth is festive.
- **weekly victuals guest** (p. 110): In the not so distant past preceding the Indian IT revolution, there was a system wherein one moving to a nearby city to pursue higher academics would enquire, seek recommendations, and arrange with seven households (normally of the same/related caste that one belonged in) to provide him with the day's food on corresponding days of each week.

Somashekhar wasn't so haughty as to think it befitting of an architect functioning from a panelled office to only conceive and design new buildings, not counsel in the matter of refurbishing old ones. Not until now though had someone sought him out for a maintenance job. Seemingly decrepit, the large oldish Madras-roofed bungalow with no upper stories stood amidst a sprawling turf on Lalitamahal Road on the outskirts of Mysore. Apparently, it wasn't repainted since construction, and by the very fact of its antiquity, one could aver that the wood used for doors and windows was pure teak. Only in the good old days was timbering synonymous with teak. One glimpsing the fifteen-feet-high roof can't help reflecting on its suitability for suicidal lynching. Two cracks have developed right in the middle of the roof, causing water to seep and pool on the floor below when the skies opened up. Soaked and stained in the rainwater, the exquisite mortar floor was unsightly. Landlady Dr Amrita's car was old too, an early model Fiat weathered by sun and rain and appearing antiquated, but as sturdy as the house. 'This leakage has to be plugged. Entire house has to be repainted. How much will it cost totally? You have to get this done, please.'

He mulled over and said, 'The upper concrete layer along the crack has to be chipped off and laid afresh. This costs nine thousand. Scraping the old paint on all walls and laying fresh distemper will cost thirty thousand.'

Her face showed anxiety on hearing the colossal quote. She said, 'Should think about it. Be back.' But she did not revert for about a month. One evening, she visited him and said diffidently, 'I have to forego the repainting. Right now, even the nine-thousand-rupee repair job is beyond me. Is there no other economical way? Monsoon is around the corner. Repairs can't be foregone. The thought of the dribbling rainwater is scary. But now….' Demurely, she stopped short of restating her pecuniary constraints.

He empathized with her plight, pondered, and said, 'There is another way – chipping along the crease and sealing the cleft with tar. It however protects through one monsoon only. If the tar melts during the ensuing summer, rainwater will seep. Costs five or six hundred. Painting the house with just primer will cost one thousand only.'

She mused for a moment and said, 'For now, get the tar filled. After two months, I will go for the primer work.' Somashekhar summoned a mason, climbed up a tall ladder, gave instructions to him, and got the work done. He understood that some time back this was a flourishing household; in a bad shape now. 'Though a minor work, you have gone through it earnestly. Please state your fee,' she said.

'When I handle a full-fledged job, I will charge fee on percentage or other basis. Now, no.' He gently but firmly resigned her offer. A mother of two sons, a seven-year-old and a four-year-old, a well-educated woman, astute of intellect, of tall build with attractive facial features, among them keen eyes, and a university lecturer holding a doctoral degree in Kannada literature. She handles everything herself; her husband's not around. She hasn't spoken a single word about him yet. Enquire about him? He abandoned that thought. Now that I have got her work done, there will be no contact anymore. Nevertheless, she lingered in his mind for a few days.

Not just she, even that house hung on. Quite a few times he contemplated as to what was intriguing in that old big Madras-roofed bungalow that presented no noticeable architectural speciality. One day, it crossed his mind. Behind the house, reaching out to the sky was the Chamundi Hill. With foliage or without, this hill has an enigmatic existence of its own – a bridge to the mysterious sky. What other periphery does a house with such a hill as its background need! Even as he framed that picture in his mind, he recalled his bland career at Bombay. Such spacious site is non-existent in that titanic city. Such individually characteristic independent house did not belong in that city. Only multi-storied – of late, fifteen- to twenty-storied – lacklustre edifices, wherein an architect's enterprise is limited to the adaptation of latest equipments developed in Europe and America to the congested environ at hand. The thought of moving to Mysore dawned after four years' ennui of the career and life in Bombay. If nothing else, the possibility of constructing unique and individualistic, albeit small, buildings was appealing. Not just that, whatever the present growth and density of Mysore, the open sky can be watched unobstructed. The old Kukkarahalli Lake is very much there. Though vegetation is deplete in patches, no factory has devoured the Chamundi Hill. The childhood obsession of climbing the hill alone at dusk or dawn, beholding the panorama from the peak, and watching at length – till sweat dried up – the serenely dignified but un-arrogant expanse of the township of Mysore surfaced and began to haunt. He recalled that on moving here, abandoning his work many an evening, he had scaled the hill at dusk and was absorbed in gazing the canvas of the horizon fostered by the glistening crimson white radiance of the receding sun. A desire arose in him to identify, on his next visit to that quarter of the hilltop, the house he got repaired.

One day, on a Monday evening at 4, she called him. 'I am frittering away your time alright, but my mind needs solace. Next Sunday you are joining me for tea in my house. Please do not dodge me.'

He was delighted on hearing the voice and for being invited. Instantly, he understood the treat as gratis for having got the work done without receiving any fee. He recalled that it had rained heavily the day before – the first showers of the monsoon. The roof would not have leaked. Was this tea party in expression of gratitude! He enquired, 'Did the roof leak in yesterday's rains?'

'To be frank, I was not sure that the repair work would so effectively plug the leakage. Not a single drop seeped. I do not know how to express my gratitude. Sunday, please visit without fail.' He felt glad, but on second thoughts, attempted to evade. She, however, persisted till he consented.

He felt ecstatic that in six days, he would visit her and spend about an hour conversing face-to-face with her over tea. All his spare time, his mind would be in anticipation of that event. But by the evening of Wednesday, he thought of backing out by offering some excuse. Why? What is wrong with visiting her? Though no clear reason emerged, the desire to back out turned out to be irresistible. The next morning offered a pretext for visiting elsewhere on Sunday. One Bopanna of Virajpet had consulted him to construct a house in his new coffee estate. He set the site inspection for the very Sunday and made arrangements to leave Mysore on the eve. He mailed a postcard to her residence on Friday so that it would reach her on Saturday. He just wrote, 'I have to leave station on some professional work. I am unable to visit tomorrow. Sorry, please excuse.' But while strolling in the Kaveri estate of Bopanna, beholding its topography and periphery, and assessing the length and breadth of the proposed building, he began repenting why did I pointlessly resign her cordial invitation? Shouldn't I rather have visited her today and appointed this for tomorrow? Glancing at his watch while returning to Mysore, he reflected that he would presently have been leisurely chatting with her.

It was one week since. He had almost forgotten her. Work pressure was excessive too. Mind was fully engrossed in giving suitable form to the Virajpet barn. On Monday, at about 1 pm, she called him. Assistant Neelakanthappa had just left for lunch.

It was his regular practice to break for lunch after Neelakanthappa returned. She enquired, 'Mr Somashekhar?'

'Yes, good afternoon.'

'This is Dr Amrita. Good afternoon. I owe you fee for fixing the roof of my house. How shall I remit? Shall I come over myself? Or shall I send in a cheque?'

'What fee? For what profound job? Wasn't the matter settled then and there?' he was surprised.

After a moment's silence, she said, 'Extensive work or not, I am obligated to pay. It is one thing if we were friends.'

'Aren't we already?'

'How can one who has reservations about accompanying at tea be considered a friend?' her question embarrassed him.

'I had to leave town urgently.'

'You had to go to Virajpet. You could have scheduled it for another day. That apart, you could have called me directly and said, "I can't visit on Sunday, will drop in another day." You washed your hands off by dropping a postcard with a message of the tenor "*can't visit. Nothing else.*" What feelers will such a message send out?' When she'd finished, he felt guilty of misdemeanour. He was at a loss to find an excuse. At the other end, she was intently waiting with the receiver in hand. She resumed her speak, 'Care to know what my feelers were on seeing your letter? I am a damsel in distress who can't afford to fix the leaking roof. Therefore, you refused fee. My invitation to tea was in expression of my gratitude, and you dodged even that. Right?'

'My! Madam, I had no such thoughts; not even now. Please do not misunderstand me. I will visit some day and … yes, have lunch.' He was plainly apologetic.

'Well then, tomorrow at 1 pm, you are coming over for lunch, okay?' He readily accepted the invitation. She has understood that I dodged her that day. Regrets about that act pervaded his mind. She has thought of it as my disdain towards her destitution. She is genial. Why did I pointlessly spurn her cordiality, get spurned rather? Have I but one confidant in this place? The thoughts comforted him. He was levitated by spirits that soared and permeated the expanse of the sky.

In that forlorn and sparsely populated part of the town to the left of the hill, whose tor seemed to mark the altitude of the sky, she awaited him at the appointed hour by the door of her old lonely house that stood amidst vast vacant surroundings. Even as he took off the helmet and rang the doorbell, the door flung open and the clock in the drawing space struck 1 pm. 'Welcome,' she greeted with a smile, led him to a section of the house that could be called a lounge, and showed him to a big old patchy sofa.

'No college today?' he launched the conversation.

'Social Sciences classes are held from 7:30 am to 11:30 am. Till we move to own premises, I will be home by 11:45.' She seated herself on a sofa opposite him.

He continued, 'Said you are an academician in Kannada literature. While in Mysore earlier, I used to read Kannada fiction, used to croon odes. After moving to Bombay, I lost touch. I now aspire to read during my leisure time. In fact, that is one of the reasons I relocated from Bombay to Mysore. Will you lend from your collection?' Both chatted happily for half an hour. She then led him to the big old dining table, appointed his salver, and took a seat opposite him. No one else was in the house. He surmised that both her sons were away in school. She had prepared vegetable pulao, rice, plain curry, vegetable stew, and fruit salad. Chiding his moderate ingestion, she filled his cup of fruit salad again and again, threatening to spill on his shielding hands. Lunch over, they retreated to the lounge and, as before, positioned themselves on the facing sofas. The gentle aroma of the royal jasmine flowers that she had worn in her plait pervaded. He inhaled subtly but deeply, and relished the aroma.

He recalled that he had earlier noticed her fancy for royal jasmine flowers. She prefers mild colours to the gaudy. The colour additive in the fruit salad was a golden mean between plain and tinge. So were the hues and motifs on the saris she wore. He deduced that she would shy away from the garish red and yellow of the Tamils, as also the blood red and wild Holi colours of the Punjabis. Imprudently, he even expressed it. 'You prefer royal jasmine to jasmine for its aroma is milder, right?' Delighted that he has noticed and noted her taste for the flower she preferred, she blushed. Guarding himself, he spoke up as if his words were commonplace. 'I say so having noticed the tastes of my clients. Highly educated people prefer mild hues and gentle aroma. The less educated are overindulgent in matters of colour, smell, and taste. Inclination to spicy foods that instantly incite the palate and flare the nostrils is characteristic of the illiterate. Your cuisine was in all ways moderate. Hone taste.'

She was happy that he once again spoke appreciatively of her. It mollified her mind. She said, 'You too do not like intense colours and intense flavours, wherefore you are appreciative of those who follow suit.'

He enthusiastically added, 'So we share a specific wavelength.'

They talked away till 4:30. In between he said, 'Your house is finely positioned against the background of the hill. There is ample front yard. Please nurture a garden. The portico would be aesthetic if adorned by dense royal-jasmine creeper. A floral courtyard is very invigorating. The Horticulture Department has supplies of all saplings, seeds, and shoots. Monsoon has set in. Sowings will germinate without fail.'

She felt that this was a genial suggestion. She acknowledged, 'I am from the Ghats. Belong in coffee plantations. I love greenery.' When he took leave of her, she handed him four Kannada novels and two poetry collections that she brought from her study and said, 'Take your time. I have no need for these now. When you are finished with these, you will get more.'

Engrossed in his work that he was, he could not read the novels. During his leisure, he read the verses, few at a time. He discerned seeds, saplings, and shoots of plant species, which, when fully grown, would gel well with the house and the backdrop hill, and procured them for her. On her part, she indulged in gardening earnestly and in gratitude. Having planted the royal-jasmine shoot, and irrigating it regularly so that it would grow and swell across the portico, she would reminisce him, him that had whetted her tastes. And thus they met some fifteen times within the month. Twice they had together driven up the hill in her car and roamed amidst clouds on the hilltop. Vistas and words that transcended the images of the sky, cloud, greenery, and horizon bred familiarity between them. When it was explicitly clear to him that the feelings were beyond just familiarity, he would get anxious and contemplate backing out.

~

Though he was preoccupied in designing Bopanna's and another proposed building in Mysore, his mind was entangled in her. Not just in him, he firmly understood that the feeling of love was greater in her. Experience told him that his comprehension was not unfounded. This history vetoed him from proceeding any further in the matter. Nevertheless, his mind would secretly relish pleasurable thoughts. Though his mind desired to reach out for her, he would refrain. A phone call, a short drive on the scooter was all. But drive was lacking. He thus spent one week. One afternoon at 2:30, when the phone on his desk rang, endorsing his intuition that it was her call, he picked it up. It was. 'Well, I have understood that you have deliberately abstained from visiting. Cordiality is not earned abegging. Such cordiality has no value either. I am calling now to seek your help for urgent repairs to the old kennels to the fore and backyard of my house. Lonely house on the outskirts of the town, surrounded by vegetation, bordered by the hill, and a lone lady with two young children! To alert us about robbery attempts at nights, I bought two pups recently. If you are inclined, please note down my phone number. Don't cede to my compulsion.'

Though weary of her spiky words and squabble, not inclined to terminate the conversation he said, 'I have the number. I am coming in half an hour.'

'I won't say thanks just for the heck of it. Half an hour translates to thirty minutes. Isn't it now 2:31 pm by your watch?' she said.

'Yes, bye.' For the first time, he got to know a trait of hers – that she was excessively termagant. All these days, squabbles aside, there was no trace of brusque words or altercation. The genesis of these corresponded to the onset of mutual intimacy. Are these the mandatory elements of love? Or is it anger resulting from anguish towards my inept apathetic response to her ardour? I, too, am at fault. He calmly surmised that his distancing and abrupt silence had but annoyed her. It is just eleven or twelve minutes' drive from here. If I reach within fifteen minutes, she will feel happy. He informed Neelakanthappa that he would return by 4:30 and started on his scooter.

Holding two pups by the chains and stationed at the doorstep, she spotted him at a distance, opened the gate, and ushered him straight in. Though young, the two seemingly well-grown, sharp, and brave Alsatian pups tugged at the chain and howled menacingly at him. He parked his scooter. While she closed the gate and comforted the pups, he said, 'I have arrived a quarter hour ahead of the appointed time.'

She replied with a triumphant smile, 'I knew. I therefore received you at the right moment.'

He neared and began observing the pups. Though fierce-eyed, they were cute. He developed a liking for them. Aware that they would apply their teeth on a novice pending introduction and acclimatization, he abstained from fondling them and watched from a distance. Having anchored them by the doorstep, they receded to the lounge. The canines fell silent. He took his usual seat on the sofa. Noticing that she was about to take her seat across from him, he said, 'Should sit here,' and motioned with his eyes to his side.

'Why?' she snapped back.

'In proximity, we can converse freely,' he said.

'What to talk about?' she queried.

'If you come to think of it, there are volumes.'

'If I think there's nothing?'

'That negative is false.'

'I think there surely is nothing.' She resolutely sat on the opposite sofa.

'Get up and come here,' he scoffed at her.

'Don't command me. I give a damn for orders,' she retorted.

He strode towards her and, in a brisk flurry of his arm, slapped her shoulder. Her face and eyes were instantly ablaze with feral anger. She too raised her arm. But then, she controlled herself and hung her head. He felt guilty. 'Sorry,' he lost no time in seeking pardon. She did not lift her head. He repeated, 'Sorry. Pardon me.' She looked up at him. Her eyes were squirting fury. She ogled as if she would defeat him in a match of sights. His gaze was fixed too. He stood staring into her eyes without batting an eyelid. He had resolved not to lose this conflict. Two minutes after the two sights kept pushing each other, he said, 'Sorry, excuse.' Instantaneously, she lifted her proper hand and struck him hard on his left arm. He stood still. In her eyes that pierced his sight, tears welled up. In four seconds, she began sobbing, neared him, and rested her head on his shoulder. He held her firmly in a cuddle.

She wept till her tears soaked the yoke of his shirt and then said, 'I hit you because you said sorry. You should never ever say so.' He was observing the interlacing along her long sumptuous braid that meandered unto the small of her back. Presently, the gentle whiff of the royal-jasmine string that she wore in her plait at the nape entered his conscious. Not just the tenderness of the royal jasmine, he was doused in the quintessence of her tender, un-grating, un-discordant physique leaning against him up to his ears. Aware that any utterance would disrupt the accord of emotions, he kept quiet.

After a while, she gently freed herself from his arms and went into the kitchen. Returning five minutes later, she said, 'Invited here to repair the kennels, architect sahib has chosen to beat up the landlady. Who to complain to against this rowdy?' With a chiding smile, she added, 'At least, have you brought the measuring tape?'

Extracting a retractable measuring tape from his trouser pocket, he said, 'Without this, there is no life for us architects. Pray, what the job is?'

Second day since, at 1 pm, when Neelakanthappa had left for lunch, he telephoned her. 'Hello,' came her voice. He spoke, 'It is me. Got me or should I declare my name?' She replied, 'Announce your name if you must. I will not pronounce it.' He felt at home.

'All yesterday had you lost my phone number?' she continued.

'No. I wasn't sure what time you would be home. I surmised you would be away even now.'

'Were you disappointed?'

'Yes, for being wedged at the hands of a Calamity Jane.'

'It has been quite some time since you got trapped. Can't redeem yourself another seven births and more. Why keep chatting over phone? Come over. Let's lunch together.'

'Neelakanthappa has left for lunch. I will start after he returns.'

'Well then. I will wait for you with two platters served. If I can't stand hunger, I will have just a glass of diluted lemon juice. Okay?'

On his arrival and subsequent lunch together, she played a ritual host devoid of any jest and bonhomie. Though embarrassed, he silently munched. Cooked rice, curry, vegetable stew, and curd. After he had finished, he washed and returned to his seat on the sofa. She appeared there in a short while and asked, 'If you do not have any pressing work, shall we drive to the hilltop? I have three hours' time left to fetch the children.'

'In this sun?'

'Are evening breeze and milky moonlight a must for visiting a hilltop? Why not visit in the sun? I do not like your ilk, the pleasure-seekers,' she paused some. 'If you are not inclined, let's not. Shall I turn on the fan for you?' Though it was quite cool, she walked up to the regulator. He felt embarrassed and discomfiture showed in his face. Noticing it, she felt ashamed of her bad temper. After evading his sight for a lengthy minute on the pretext of checking the regulator, she turned and neared him. 'Now I will really plead pardon. You should not slap me. If you don't permit me to apologize for a fault, I'll have to hang my head.' Repentance and apology were writ large on her face. The distension on his face disappeared. 'Let's go,' he pulled himself up. She rationalized her proposition, 'The reason I chose this hour for the visit is that, viewed from the hilltop at noon, you will notice the surrounding world thaw and the horizon distort. Moreover, under the sweltering sun, stillness pools intense and is more veritable than dusk and moonlight. Have you ever experienced it?' He recalled that once he had watched the surroundings from atop the Shivagange Hill at midday. He felt that her prophecies were true. 'True,' he neared her, touched her back, and prompted, 'Let's go.'

When the car moved out, the dogs started yelling. After clearing the fence, he shut the heavy, discoloured, old wooden gate, latched it, boarded the car from the left side, and sat beside her. 'You drive?' she queried.

'I used to in Bombay. There was the office car. After moving here, I haven't held the steering. Shall I? Your driving is very smooth.'

She chuckled on hearing the appreciation. Then she said, 'If you keep guiding me without losing your patience, my driving may stay smooth.'

In a short while, the car was scaling the hill. Exuberance showed in her face. She drove slowly, drawing his attention to the surroundings. 'Look here ... there.... Well, I am from the Ghats. This is nothing compared to the terrain and greenery there. Yet, uphill attribute is inimitable. Look to your left. How much we have scaled! Left please, you are looking rightward!' she guided his observation. He complied. After scaling a little more, she pulled up, parked at an even spot, and said, 'Look to your left now. The higher you go, wider the view becomes. We feel that some emotion from within holds us aloft. Is this transformation not real? What say thou?' She killed the engine, opened the door, and exited. He too got out from the other side. They paced a few steps, stood close to each other on a rock, and solemnly regarded the still eastern ravine. The sun scorched his skull. She was oblivious of the same. Unless instructed by her, he did not move his feet even half an inch. For a while, she kept intently observing the undulating heatwaves among the rocky parts to the other side of the gorge. She then said, 'The sweltering sun has brought the boulders to melting point. Don't you think so?' He agreed. After a while, she again spoke, 'Shall we go a little further?' He joined her on her way back to the car and got in from the left side. After a short distance, she suddenly brought the car to a halt and said, 'Doesn't the entire valley appear like a triangle perceived by an exorcist?' 'True, true,' he agreed and began looking at it intently. She added, 'I have visited this place very many times, but it had never appeared to me so.' She turned off the humming engine saying that it disturbed the stillness around. After observing the scenery for a little while from within the car, she drove further on. While she scaled the hill, she resumed drawing his attention to the surroundings, herself partaking with childlike eagerness. But when they encountered a woody section that should have instilled greater enthusiasm in her, reticence befell her. 'Look at the lush,' he said. Though she heard it, she gave an expression of rebuff. Half a minute later, she said, 'Look, you should visit my coffee estate. There is the Jenkal mound near it. We should trek it together. From there, we should swoop down and drive up the Bisale grade. Beyond Sringeri, there is the Tunga Hillock. We should trek it and see around from the peak. We should visit and stay for about a week in Mullayyanagiri and Kemmannugundi. Are you game?' Continuing to drive, she proffered her right palm, seeking his assurance. He covered it with his right palm and said, 'Of course.' She noticed matching eagerness on his face. 'Same wave....' Halfway through, she bit her tongue.

She then drove straight atop the hill. Though she knew that the sanctum sanctorum would be closed, she went to a nearby store and got herself a small urn of flowers, coconut, incense sticks, turmeric powder, and vermilion. She deferentially applied the turmeric and vermilion to the threshold rung of the sanctum sanctorum, placed the coconut there after splitting it in half, and, holding the lighted incense sticks, ritually lustrated her arms in the direction of the deity. She then closed her eyes, reverentially pirouetted thrice, and prostrated before the deity. Then, having prayed for a while with her eyes shut, she drew a pinch of vermilion from the sachet and applied it between his eyebrows. Eyes shut, he welcomed it. Then she stood still, completely blanked out. Amiss, he too stay put silent. Two minutes, three, a little more. All of a sudden, her face was livid with rage. She said, 'Sorry. This visit is erroneous.' At a loss, he was embarrassed. 'Why?' he asked. She said, 'Let's go. I'll drop you by your office. Oh, your scooter is in my parking. I'll take you there. You may retrieve it.'

His embarrassment only increased. 'What can I make of it if you just go wild? If you state reasons, I can correct myself.'

'I am not a beggar to state reasons, tender application forms, and obtain grants. Let's go.'

'Well then, I'm not joining you. I will return on foot. I may even get a bus or taxi that comes by.' She left instantly. The urn of consecrated elements stayed behind.

He saw no point, except that she was wont to flare up. He felt that this tough nut was not acquiescent to amity. He thought of descending the stairs on foot and reach Mysore. He recalled that his shoes were in the car. Can walk barefooted once. On reaching office, have Neelakanthappa fetch the scooter. But he felt arrested as if tied by invisible strings, and was rendered immobile. He sensed an anonymous suggestion that if he disentangled himself by shredding the strings, bondage would be lost with no possibility whatsoever of convergence again. His mind couldn't brace itself against such loss. He sat right there by the urn of consecrated elements. Flies were buzzing around the coconut that she had split for consecration. He covered it with his hanky and then sat silently. About half an hour passed. 'She has left. What am I doing here?' He was agitated by the irrelevant question. Still, he could not pull himself up and leave. 'How did I get myself into such a predicament?' he thought. With nothing to lean upon, squatting trouser-clad on the sod in a single posture, back pain set in. Yet, the resolve to get up and leave did not concretize.

By that time, she returned there. Her face showed repentance and defeat. Her natural cerise complexion had blanched. She neared him and said, 'You were right in saying that instead of suddenly going wild, I should have told you the reason for my dissidence so that you can make amends. By now, you would be aware that I am bad-tempered. But isn't a self-inspired act more meaningful than a request granted?'

Her return reassured him anew. All the frustration and despair that he suffered till then seemed to dissipate. 'Tell me what?' he asked.

'I applied vermilion to your forehead, right? Didn't it occur to you that you should do the same?'

'Sorry,' he not only said but felt too. He reached for the sachet of vermilion on the floor, took a pinch of it, and applied it on her forehead. Her face relaxed. He sensed the incarnation of a new rhythm to his feelings. 'Really sorry,' he said.

She lifted her hand, 'Your sorry will invite thrashing.' Almost instantly, she withdrew and said in cadence, 'This is a temple, a public place. Possible public attention has saved your clavicle.' His mind turned even more upbeat. They both exited. With unexpressed concurrence, they together drew to a roadside vendor of tender coconuts and sipped the cordial. Later, when they headed towards the car, an elderly florist at a distance to his right caught his attention. He bounded up to her and checked. Royal jasmine! He bought arms' length of the string. Her face swelled on seeing it. 'This is zest,' she said, voluntarily extended her hand, took it, and placed it at her side in the car. Getting into the car, he retrieved it and, while she gunned the engine, tucked it in her plait. The serenely beautiful, aromatic, and tender royal jasmine matched her sumptuous braid. Turning the ignition on, she sat still in the idling car, eyes open but unfocussed. After a while, she said, 'Shall we go to a point from where we can spot my house?'

'I was about to say the same,' he said.

'Truly?'

'Truly.'

'It is now convenient for you to further your wavelength theory,' she said and, throwing a mischievous glance at him, engaged the transmission.

She drove in the direction of Lalitamahal Extension, down the road running east-west in the northern section of the hill, and parked under a tree. At least ten times she would have visited that spot and watched her house. Besides, on umpteen other occasions, she had been to that place and surveyed the ravine below, the township of Mysore to the north, paddy fields, Srirangapatna, and Sangama. She had prided in the fact that her ancestral house was at the foot of her favourite quarter of the hill. After they both got down from their respective sides, she locked the car, neared him, and said, 'Can you see that black even ledge thirty feet below? Obscured by the wild mango trees, it is not clearly visible from here. I have explored. Come, let's go there. Nice place to lounge.' They both trekked the distance amid the thorny shrubs and rubble.

The black granite slab seemed made to order for relaxing. Two intertwined jungli mango trees provided shelter from the sun above, and to the other side were like a green canopy above the road. 'You have identified an ideal spot,' he said and came to a halt. Ambling up to his right, she said, 'Spot my house, in a second. Quick.'

'I, too, am looking. There! Yonder,' he aimed with his finger.

'I can even see your scooter,' she said.

'Your eyes are sharper than mine alright, but the scooter is not visible from this altitude,' he looked her in the face.

'Henceforth, we should carry a binocular with us to notice whether the gate is closed and such.' She sat on the granite floor. He sat down beside her. Their shoulders made contact. The gentle whiff of royal jasmine was playing hide-and-seek with his nostrils. Beyond them, the scorching sun had brought the boulders, canyon, houses, lanes, and localities below to the echelons of the heatwaves. Intently observing the same, she asked, 'What do you feel on seeing the world thaw in this heat?'

'I have seen higher temperature than this. I have been in work spots in Nagpur, Aurangabad, and Rajasthan.'

'I asked what your feelings are, not your experience.'

'If I keep viewing it, I feel morose.'

'Precisely.' Placing her left palm on his right wrist and clinging to it, she said, 'It is satisfying to see that you share my feelings. It brings solace, too. Want to know my feelings ? The whole world, plants and trees, rivers and oceans, the moon and the sun, the constellation of stars, and the vast sky are all melting under sweltering grief.'

'Those are Buddha's words,' he instantly said.

His words hurt her and the harm morphed into a thwarted voice. 'The Buddha having declared it first does not render my experience redundant. This disregard of yours !'

'Not disregard,' he freed his wrist from her hands, held her hands, and said, 'Presuming that you cited from the Upanishad, I said so.'

'I will never cite others' prophecies. The miseries that I have undergone are ample enough to provide fare for the philosophers who have propounded lofty prophecies.' Eyes ajar, she perceived an invisible blaze in the abyss of the sky. He felt greater closeness towards her. Taciturn, he surveyed the colours in the same sky turn blue and then thaw under extreme heat. Her hand was still in his right. She was deeply introspecting. A little later, she firmly cupped his right hand with her left palm and said, 'Look. I think we should mutually share our inner truth. Ignorant of it, it would be improper to further our camaraderie.'

'Inner truth ? Which ? The feeling now on our minds ?' he enquired solemnly.

'Both fully know what the current feelings are. No need to express. My desire is to unveil and express everything that is deep within us. Let me relate first. I just told you that I have enough stockpile of miseries to provide ample fare for those that propound lofty prophecies. I shall always hoard them. This is the truth of my inner recesses. There is no meaning in living. Rather, I think many a time, death brings about cessation to distress. Not just a thought, a deluge of feelings.'

'Why so ?' he was upset.

'I do not know. There may be a few reasons, but the reasons for the basic disposition of life are but inconsequential. Someday, I will deliberate upon them. You should not slight me saying that they are commonplace and I am not to fret about them. Well, let me know the truth inside of you.'

He began introspecting. Which shall designate as the truth inside of me? Education? Career? Industrial enterprise in Bombay in the association of friends? Retreat to Mysore from an insipid Bombay? Can these be called inner truths? Weighing his thoughts, he kept looking down the ravine. After a while, she said, 'If you do not want to, don't. Don't cede to compulsion.' His right hand was in the warm grasp of both her palms.

'I was married and had a child too. Both died four years ago,' he said.

'I know. Anybody would know that.'

'There is something else, which nobody knows. Nobody. I haven't shared it even with my friend and business partner, Shah. I feel like disclosing it to you. I had befriended a lady in Bombay. This when my wife was still alive. For more than two years, we were dating twice a week; on each occasion, in five to six hours' seclusion. Seclusion meaning, in undisturbed physical conjugation with all the windows and doors of the house shut. When in concert, she used to articulate our romance by quoting verses from ghazals – intense romantic songs. Together we attended many ghazal concerts. I had thought of life as a cruise on the ripples of such romance and passion. Those two years she bestowed upon me uninterrupted sensuous physical contentment, contentment meaning thrill. Later, abruptly, the relationship ceased.'

He did not notice Amrita's grip on his right hand slacken while she listened to this. Oblivious to himself, he had related all this in a fit of excitement.

'Why did it end?' she asked in a faint voice devoid of any feeling.

'Once I paid a visit to her at about 7 in the evening. Holding the doorknob, I shook free of my footwear. The door yielded; I went inside and was taken aback by the sight. A student of music that she was, I knew that she practised in the company of a percussionist. Presently, they were in each other's arms! I couldn't help feeling relieved that I had not arrived a little later. The air smacked of whisky. She saw me enter. I saw her too and hurriedly retreated. Later, I did not communicate with her. Neither did she.'

'Well, did she belong in the danseuse clan?' Now her hands had completely let go of his.

'No. A Madrasi woman. My age, then thirty-five. Mother to three daughters. Husband a high-flying federal government bureaucrat. She held a Doctoral degree from an American university and was Reader in a postgraduate department.'

She sought no more details. In a mood to relieve himself by spilling out everything if queried, her stillness cut him off from relating any further. By such time, her hands had retreated away from his. He gathered that she was perturbed by his declarations. Beyond the shade of the mango tree beneath which they were sitting, the static touch of the sun seemed to mutually repel all and sundry. He sat silently. With a facial expression that increased the intensity of the stillness around, she looked up to the skies. After a short while, she was on her feet. 'I am leaving. If you come along, I will drop you.'

He felt dejected. 'You may leave yourself.' She now turned towards him. Her eyes were feral. He chose not to face her sight. Reflecting that she merited neither eyeing nor being eyed, he turned to the ravine that was being ravaged by Helios. After half a minute, she said, 'And that's all?' He turned to her. With both her hands, she removed the royal-jasmine string from her plait and flung it with all her might onto the scorching rock. Then she looked at him. He continued to be mute. Fuming with rage, she spun around and hastily headed to the car, caring none to patiently mark her path between the thorny shrubs. He even heard the sound of her sari tear, contacted by thorn. She neither slowed down, nor cared to untangle the sari from the shrub. Sick of surveillance, he retrieved his craned neck and began watching the ravine below thaw in the sun. In three minutes, he heard the door of the car slam shut and thereafter the gunning of the engine and the movement of the car were also heard. His mind decreed that this lady wasn't just short-tempered or bad-tempered; she was arrogant. His intellect decreed that he saw her no more. His mind was filled with agony and self-contempt for being attracted towards such a woman. In fact, I had distanced myself. She came after me again and asked to visit her. Now having flung the flowers that I had decked her plait with … pain surfaced deep in his mind. Pain that she possibly has spurned me? That question popped up shortly. Why should I be pained by her denunciation? He tried consoling himself. In a short while, he was weary of sitting there alone. Impossible. He pulled himself up. Down there was her house – which she said she could see from here – and within the compound was his scooter. He meticulously traced his path between the shrubs and reached the road. When he considered that it was three to four hours' walk in the scorching sun to Mysore town limits, the thought about the scooter returned. He set out, discerning an autorickshaw or a bus, intending to hand the keys to Neelakanthappa with instructions to fetch the scooter. In the scorching receding sun, he headed to the steps to climb down the hill.

Neelakanthappa hired an autorickshaw onwards and drove back his scooter. He reported, 'Sir, she has reared two pups. They tugged at the chains and leapt menacingly at me. Madam held them back by the chains and allowed me to retrieve the scooter.' He wanted to know if she had said something. If she had, Neelakanthappa would have reported it. Besides, what if she enquired or didn't? He ignored the thought and tried to concentrate on his work. Sleep eluded him late unto night. Though he consoled himself that such incidents invariably muddled up the mind, he felt astonished as to why he had taken it so much to the heart. Got the house repaired.

Then got familiar. Would have exchanged a bit of fun. Why should that upset me? Though his mind rationalized, sleep evaded him. Two such sleepless nights troubled him, and when he retired the third night, deep sleep instantly overcame him, sound till daybreak. He felt relieved. On waking up, in a calm state of mind, he began ruminating. She compelled me to speak out my mind. But why did I disclose this matter that I had not shared with anyone, nor would be known by anyone ever? I am at fault. But when truth was solicited, would not holding back tantamount to perjury? This question assured him that his declaration was righteous. But why was I impelled to disclose this part of me that I had shared with none? He was astonished again.

~

Virajpet Bopanna's project was completed to his satisfaction. Not just designing, he was assigned the job of supervising the construction too. After the disturbing hilltop episode, wherein she had walked out on him, he could hardly concentrate on his work. In about a week's time, he applied himself though. Yet, the pain of rejection was smarting in a corner of his mind.

It was twenty days since his afternoon trek down the hill. At 1.30 pm, the phone on the desk in his office rang. He received the call, 'Hello.' She rambled on immediately, 'Now don't reason that I am shameless. Why didn't *you* call? Don't you know that I am short-tempered? That I will not act wise when irate? And that you should forever excuse me at that?' Her voice brought to him relief and anger at once. He did not say anything in reply. She waited half a minute before she said, 'Hello, hello,' and after eliciting a 'yes' from him, she continued, 'Neelakanthappa may be there. His presence has tongue-tied you. I must speak to you. You must come here. If you don't, I will come over myself and, in everyone's presence, beg at your feet.

Tell me when you can make it. I have much to talk. First, I have to ask pardon of you.'

In fact, Neelakanthappa had left for lunch. He understood that she had chosen to call at this hour because she knew this fully well. He said, 'Madam, I am busy. This is a workplace. Do not present yourself here to enact some feet-grabbing or unfolding drama. Nothing remains to be excused. Goodbye.' He placed the handset in the cradle. It rang again instantly. It was clear that it was she. He ignored it for a minute and more. Then he felt like lifting it and severing the call. But his mind assuaged. He lifted and said, 'Hello.'

She said, 'You have every right to punish me. But you should never slight me. I will not lunch until you come here. Not just now, until you come over and accept my apology, I will not drink even a spoonful of water. I give a damn to my life. I am not saying this to scare you. I am speaking out my mind.' She replaced the handset.

At first, he felt annoyed. Then his mind became muddled. A state wherein the *whats* and *whys* remained elusive, and his innards were completely shaken up. Thoughts like '*I and she in no way correlate*' and '*no possibility of contact any more*' melted as would a hunk of plastic that came in contact with intense thermal heat. She wants to talk to me, wants to earn back goodwill by repenting for her headlong behaviour. He suspected if she was pretending. The moment suspicion crept in, his determination began to steel.

In a short while, Neelakanthappa returned from lunch. Now he could leave. His lunch usually was two idlis or two slices of bread and coffee at the Welcome Café that he regularly visited. When he headed there, he felt like visiting her. Without much ado, he turned towards Lalitamahal. To the right, the sight of the blue-green wall of the hill that towered aloft and framed the sky brought cheer to him. He reflected that a cordial relationship with one, rather than a non-committal distancing resulting from ill will, made living sufferable. I never have severed communication with anyone till date, except that

Bombay madam. That thought reminded him that the intimate lingo that he had gotten used to in her company had given way to formal language in reminiscences about her, and he reflected that with such a person there was no possibility of any cordiality residual of rancour. By then, the hill filled the horizon to his right and he craned his neck to discern the spot that was witness to their rendezvous under the jungli mango tree twenty days before. He could not spot it readily. He applied the brakes and surveyed. When he aligned his sight along a line, recalling that it was twenty to thirty feet trek down the road, yes, that spot seems like it, from there the direction of her house, yes, that is it, most probably it is. Then on, he recalled the whole debate thereat, his declarations and her reactions. He thought of reversing the direction of his drive and returning. But deciding against abhorrence, neither abhorrence nor camaraderie, and deciding that today's visit be categorical, he moved on.

She was by the gate, awaiting his arrival. She seemed confident that he would visit. He felt a setback when he became cognizant that he had tritely fallen in place. But his feelings mellowed when he saw her blanched face. The bark of the pups was heard in response to the sound of the automobile. Entering and parking the scooter, when he turned towards her while she closed the gate, he caught sight of the big kennel by the gate inside the compound wall, which was recently fortified by steel railings on three sides. It was clear that she had sought help elsewhere. Thinking that she despised him, he mentally distanced himself. Having neared him by then, she held his arms and said, 'As a mark of my disgrace, this and the one at the back stand renovated. Umpteen times, I have felt like razing them myself. But I checked myself thinking that the daily morning sight of the result of my foolishness, foolishness from bad temper, will serve as a warning, deterring me from committing such misdeed again. Let's go in. I'll explain.' She took him into the lounge, secured the door, pulled him down on the sofa, sat contiguous to him, held both his hands, and said, 'You know that I am obstinate, am restless until I am finished with anything that crosses my mind. I solicited a mason's help, bought the steel and cement, and got this renovated. To tell you the truth, I was angry with you even as I went through the work. Anger subsiding, I am feeling ashamed, truly ashamed. Look in my face, straight.' When she cupped his face in both her palms, turned it towards hers, and rooted her gaze in his, he observed that her eyes were moist and displayed the spectrum. In another second, wail erupted and her face transformed into a ball of white humus. He drew her face to his chest and held her in a cuddle.

Beside him at lunch, she said, 'It is ten days since I realized that I was culpable. What with the weighing of right and wrongs, it is ten days since I realized that I couldn't live without your companionship. But preposterous that I was, I had forfeited my strength to bring you back into my fold. I would surely have died in the despair of this weakness. Believe me when I say that death is not at all a difficult proposition to me. I have a firm feeling that it is an easy and alleviating way out. Someday, I will pass through that vent. That aside, I was fasting these ten days. Whenever my stomach stung, I ate just a fistful of rice flakes swilled in water, without spice, jaggery, or salt to taste. And a cup of coffee. Today, resolving to invite you, I have prepared this cuisine for you. If you had not turned up, the cooked rice, curry, vegetable stew would have all....Well, didn't you once think of me? What sort of reminiscing? Tell me. Relief that the geek exhibited its trait sooner than later?'

He said nothing. His mind was pegged at her words that death was an alleviating vent. She continued, 'Didn't you think of me even once?' When he related to her the sorts of her disturbing memories, his inability to concentrate on work during day, and his sleepless nocturnal plight, her face showed some contentment.

After lunch, when they retreated to the lounge and sat together on the sofa, she held both his hands in hers and asked, 'Look, the other day I was angry. I flung the flowers that you so fondly adorned me with. In fact, I have not worn flower since. If you once again adorn me with it, I may resume wearing it ! Without so much as giving a thought as to how you would return in that scorching sun, with no conveyance available around, I simply returned home in my car. My ire that day was excessive alright. But must not there be a reason, albeit small ? Did you ever give a thought as to why I got angry ?'

'That one's beloved had an affair with another is not well tolerated. Peril to the feeling that "one is mine only" naturally begets anger,' he calmly intoned.

'Your words are true. But just that would not have brought about so much anger in me. Recall what you said. I sensed derision in the inner intent of your words. Look, I wished that we should lay bare our inner truths, strong truths on which our relationship should rest. I will, therefore, disclose my doubts. My inferences may be incorrect. Nevertheless, it is not untrue that they occurred to me. Rectify them if wrong. But you should not resent and shy away from my revelations. Fearing that you may quit, I am holding both your hands.' She squeezed and held on to his hands firmly.

'No, tell me. If I am wrong, I will correct myself,' he said sincerely.

'What was it that you said when asked to speak out your inner truth ? You had a girlfriend in Bombay, over two years you were in unbridled company with her twice every week, in five to six hours' seclusion on each such occasion, the notion that life was a buoyant ripple of romance and lust dawned on you in her association, those two years she gave you unrestrained physical contentment, contentment meaning thrill – isn't this what you said ?' she reiterated the question.

He confirmed by nodding.

She went on, 'Then you said that she was a married woman, a mother of three, a PhD and Reader in a PG faculty of a university. Why did you say all this ? I too am a married woman, a mother of two, a PhD holder, a college lecturer like her, and my husband too is a high-up bureaucrat. You suggested that you expected a similar relationship from me too. I should play the ripple that buoys you on romance and lust. You explicitly hinted that I should give you unbridled physical satisfaction – thrill. You made clear the truth of your inner aspirations from our relationship. I aspired for a sacrosanct relationship with you, but you fancied me at what level! Tell me, was I wrong in getting irate? That my contempt at the presence, in my plait, of the flowers gifted by such a person was unjust?'

While she said this, she was intently watching his face. Not just in his face and forehead, sweat beads appeared on his neck too. He was fully introspect. His vocal chords' muted state made it impossible to lend decibel to any reply. Marshalling as much supplication as he could, he squeezed out some sonic and spoke, 'I swear on God. I did not nurse any such feelings. I do not even now.'

'Granted. But such intent latent deep inside you could have prompted such words. Else, why would that alone have come out as the first inner truth of yours? Why didn't such aspiration, say, of envisioning a monument like the world famous Taj Mahal, manifest and emerge? That's okay. Tell me, do you believe in God?'

'I do not precisely know about the existence or otherwise of a persona or potence called God,' he replied, relieved at being provided a diversion from the ensnaring court-martial.

'In which case, why did you swear on God that hath no locus?' He choked on being trapped in an all the more inescapable spot. The sweat beads on his face, forehead, and neck swelled into droplets and dripped. 'Somu,' she let go of his hands, wiped clean the sweat from his face and neck with the pallu of her sari, and said, 'Do not presume that my contentions are intended to fault you. I haven't another confidant. Wherefore I aspired that our bond should rest on pure candour. Therefore, I dissected you. You too explore me. Now, recline here.' She moved to one end of the sofa, tugged at his shoulders, and pulled his head onto her thighs. 'Hesitation? Very bad! Or are you still angry? Somu, I desire to hold you this way, as I would my child and put you to sleep by caressing and patting. Thus reclined, you should keep talking, forever now on. Now, stretch your legs and sleep well.' She bent over, unlaced his shoes, removed them and the socks, and again mopped his face with the pallu of her sari. In a short while, confidence and contentment showed in his face.

~

Every day since, after Neelakanthappa's return from lunch, he visits her at 1 pm. Post lunch, he chats with her till 4 or 4:30, returns to his office, and slogs till 8. Though she insisted that he have supper daily in her house, he refrained either from vacillation or from the impossibility to talk unreservedly in the presence of her children. Winding up for the day, he sups at the Welcome Café, returns to his rented house in Jayalakshmipuram, and retires. During their afternoon siesta, there's just the two of them in that entire large bungalow within the spacious site and vacant surroundings. While chatting, they would at times recline on each other on the sofa, or lie down with the other's thigh serving as a pillow. At times, they would sleep on the old rattan divan in embrace. Though he would, at times, feel encouraged by the firm feel of her slender frame in tender skin, he refrained from expressing his feelings in any way, behaving moderately with a resolve to steer clear of any carnality with her. Neither is such desire absent in her, nor has duologue stayed from turning mellifluous, indicating pleasurable inclinations. But both are hesitant to breach the mutually unexpressed confines assumed by them.

On one of those days, while reclining in his arms, she asked, 'Now, that Bombayite. Where would you both convene?' He did not reply. Embarrassment showed in his face. When she repeated her question, he said, 'Why that now?'

'If you are not willing, don't. My behaviour in this matter has annoyed you much. I am still ashamed of it. Yet, for two full years, she has given you abundant satisfaction. I must be grateful to her. It is my duty to be gratuitous to anyone who has given solace and satisfaction to my beloved. Of late, this gratis of mine has become profound. Will you still not answer? If you don't, then you have not pardoned me.' She cheerfully hugged him and caressed his head. 'I am envious of her for reason of she having cared for you better than I have. Try as you may, you cannot hide that nostalgic glint in your eyes at the mention of her and those issues. Even now, you are unable to conceal the exuberance on your face. Speak up.' She massaged his back.

'Precisely what?' he asked.

'Where would you convene?'

'In her friend's apartment. The friend would be away in her bank from 9 in the morning till 6:30–7:00 in the evening. Manager of a big branch, I was told. She had the duplicate keys of the apartment. We would take the elevator to the apartment on the sixteenth floor of a twenty-storied building. Lonely apartments inhabited by alien neighbours. We never once spotted a single soul in the lift or in the corridors.'

'Was that friend who made her flat available aware of your meetings?'

'I think, yes. When I once enquired, she parried saying that it was an "arrangement between friends". I didn't ask again. In fact, I never saw that friend. On her part, she had no intent to introduce her or even reveal her identity.'

'What brought you together? And how did the acquaintance turn intimate?'

He felt hesitant. 'Why rake up that dead story now?' he asked.

'If it irritates you, don't. I want to get familiar with all the details of your life.' Sincere concern was writ large on her face.

'We met at a party. "Creative architect" was what the introducer told her I was. She shook my hands, saying that she liked creative persons and would not stand the company of naive nerds for more than two minutes. She had on a meticulous make-up, an arresting intoxicating sparkle to her eyes, thirty-three years young. We could not talk much there. You know these parties. Frequently accosting acquaintances – *hello, hello*. A very nimble woman that she was, she was eager to meet many people. I had left my card with her. Fourth or fifth day since, I received a call in my office, "Remember me? We had met at that party, Mrs....Shall we meet today? Dressed in a pink sari, I will be waiting by the Rajabhoi Tower so that you can readily recognize me. I, however, can recognize you even if you are guised." My business was a partnership. An architect frequented work spots. I took leave on that pretext. It was she. She greeted me with a smile and took my arms. While we strolled along, she zeroed in, "Tell me what you felt when you saw me that day?" "What shall I say?" "Nothing? If you got no feelings at first sight, you will never get any anytime later. Why, then, did you come now?" Her smile was vanquishing. "Know how handsome you are! Hence, you are haughty." She tugged at my arm and looked in my face. Shortly, she beckoned a taxi and we headed to her house. Nobody was in the house. I never could have imagined that with a well-educated, careerist, financially well-to-do wife of a well-placed man, I would get physically proximate, lustfully intimate so soon! Later, we met twice in her house. "Let us not meet in this house. Being a man, it is your duty to arrange an alternative hangout," she twice indicated. What arrangements shall I make? Are Bombay's hotels affordable? Besides, she made it clear that she would not go to a hotel. We could not, therefore, meet for two weeks. Eventually, she arranged for the keys of her friend's apartment and informed me. When I sought the details of her endeavour, she parried and said smiling, "I, the woman, am more resourceful than your masculine self."'

Her face and eyes suggested that she was intently listening and figuring out the details. Presently, her eyes were engrossed in his face. He, too, was disposed for colloquy and had his gaze rooted in her face without hesitation or discomfiture. After two minutes, she inquired, 'Was she very adept?'

'Not just adept. She was a woman of mental disposition that gets engrossed oblivious of the outer world. She would express many variations of such stimulating words as, "Som, any femme that you got in should beg of Eros serfdom to you for the next and following lives." In fact, her creativity bestowed such unheard of and hitherto unknown experiences that the man who got to know her would turn servile rather. I told you the other day that she sang ghazals well. Her creativity in rendering the manifold nuances of the ghazals revealed in her amorous acts and, in between, conversation in the tenor of ghazal. À la Aphrodite, the warp, and Adonis, the weft, she would weave a fantasy world that evoked body, mind, and soul. She would arrest time with the elucidation that life was just such intimacy, merriment, and lust and that any other deliberation was idiocy.'

'Did you love her that much?'

For a minute, he drew into introspection, as if to contemplate the meaning of her words. Then he spoke measuredly, 'Can't say if it was love. Or wasn't. I have read poets and philosophers say that pain is the essence of love, and anxiety the basal tone of love. Where anxiety is, there will be apprehension and pain. But neither in our conjugation, nor parting was pain or anxiety. When we met, we would relish four to five hours' uninterrupted pleasure. And there was always the certainty of meeting again in three or four days. We would take leave on that reassurance. In between, she was away in her hometown Madras for four weeks. Then I was not pained by the pangs of separation. I was rather bothered by the cupid's shaft. She had written three letters to me from Madras. Even therein were passionate words like, "Dearie, I'm coming soon, coming to get squashed, pulverized, and thawed in your robust masculine embrace."'

Her mind was rooted in the first two sentences thereat. In a quick motion, she propped herself up from her reclining position. Before he had finished his last sentence, she squatted, positioned his head on her lap, cuddled him, and said, 'Som, you! How well said! Despite being a PhD in Literature, I never could analyse the enigma of love like you have. *Pain is the essence of love. Anxiety is the basal tone of love. Where anxiety is, there will be apprehension and pain.* Somu, our love throbs in pain. It is not with intent to hurt you that I vent my ire on you. If you are ten minutes late, I get restless. Why is he not here yet? Injured by a brush with another automobile? Especially that leftward curve by the zoo! Oncoming cars and trucks swerve shallow and glide rightward. You will be to your left. Know how many times I keep watching the clock each minute anxiously? God! Why is he not here yet?' Tears welled up in her eyes and trickled onto his face. He was reflecting upon that Bombay friend, and weighed against the fact that she never once so cuddled me and wept for my sake, for my refuge, and that pain and anxiety were never in her disposition. But then, he reflected that it was improper to compare one with the other.

After a while, she asked, 'Hey dude, will you too get anxious about my well-being? Speak the truth. I know that you will never lie for the sake of pleasing. Still, speak out the truth.'

He noticed the dilution of her lingo to intimate. It only seemed natural to him in the circumstance. Without so much as a preamble, a comment, or assent that would bring it to consciousness, he responded in letter and spirit, 'In this sparsely populated locality on the outskirts of the city, where houses are not within hearing distance of each other, that you stay alone with two young children begins bothering me now and then, and I go sleepless during nights.'

'Truly?'

'Swear on you.'

'Then just drive your scooter and come over. So holding you in my lap, I will put you to sleep – *pat, pat*.' Her eyes got moist again.

~

Spending time at home was boring, and so they would go out on a two or three hours' drive in her car many a day after a quick lunch. Having understood that her financial situation was acute, he more than once indicated that riding his scooter would be more economical than the car. At first she consented, but later declined stating that the two together on a scooter would be very overt. Once, when he offered to pay the petrol bill, she took exception to it right in the presence of the pump attendant. 'Somu, I am pressed for money alright, but should you cause me such disgrace?' He abstained from it thence.

The most favourite pastime cherished by both was to visit the hill, the river capture Tirumakudalu Sangama, Brindavan Gardens, or someplace else, discern a bench beneath a tree, watch the sky, clouds, and greenery, and chat in the manner of the thin clouds jostled hither and thither by the crass wind. After such visits, their minds would be buoyant. Not that their every outing would dish up delight. Many a day, her mood would go melancholic. For no reason whatsoever, she would flare up in anger. If he went about consoling her, he would become both the cause and target of her ire. On several days, she would be simmering even as they embarked on their drive. If he said, 'Your mood is not chipper. Let's not go anywhere', she would say, 'You want a pretext to stay back. You put it on my moods. Instead of killing me by your devious ways, why not take a dagger and stab me? At least, be honest.' Dumbfounded, he would stay quiet, despondent. She would chide him, 'Mr Somashekhar, should I formally invite you with all fanfare to take a seat in my car?'

The formal deferential argot would convey to him that her ire had graduated to the second-degree boil. He would never know how long her anger would last. There wasn't the remotest possibility that *she* would know of it. Not a single word exchanged, the car would roll on for eight or ten miles. Once, in between, she would say, 'Why, sir, have you decided to stifle me to silent death by abstaining from uttering even a single word?' When he said, 'It is you who is silent, not I', she would gawp at him. 'You are driving. Watch out the road,' he would caution her. Giggling hysterically, she would chide him, 'Coward, afraid of death.' He would retort, 'Yes, I am afraid of leaving you and going too far.' 'Meaning, I should die too? Watch out, sir, I'll cause a crash so that both of us perish.' She would jack up the speed excessively. Though petrified, he would sit quiet without showing it. All of a sudden, she would step down the gas, pull up the car to the kerb, shuffle across to him, hug, and, with tears in her eyes, say, 'Somu, your patience towards me is boundless!' He would then gather that her ire has subdued, and his mind would ease. Not just serenity; post seethe, they would both feel that they have meld into each other greater than before. She would justify, 'Somu, my anger is not just tart. It is rather a furnace heat that welds us together more and more.' He would surmise, 'Possibly,' and would concur with a yes.

By now, good monsoon had set in, garnered clouds, cleared the sky of its monotony, and ushered in life. She more than agreed with his observation that sunshine sans clouds was insufferable. 'Tell that to me, one from the Ghats!' When clouds would overcast three-fourths of a mile above, the hill acquired a mysterious meaning and it would be their worthwhile indulgence to watch the same from the lawns of that house. The clouds would assume different designs every other second, whose secret import they would grasp according to their respective creative abilities, exchange, and mutually approve. One afternoon before lunch, while they both stood watching the overcast hill, she announced, 'Feel like penning a ghazal.'

'Does the innate nativity of Canarese champion the ghazal structure? It only goes well with Urdu.'

'Is it not in a litterateur's ingenuity to lend pliancy to language? I am no ingenuous poet though. Its – ghazal's – flashes are fine. Besides, it is nostalgic of your beloved companion. Somu, tell me the truth. I am not jealous, but haven't you once written to that girlfriend of yours? At least, will you not convey your well-being?'

There was a glint of mischief in her face. 'Shall I?' he asked. 'I haven't the least idea as to the wayward ways of the males or their clandestine links,' she kept up her mischievousness. She continued with her impishness through lunch. After lunch, seated on the divan in a snug embrace, she asked, 'Somu, tell me the truth. I behaved very rudely that day when you spilled the specifics of your relationship with your girlfriend, well ex-girlfriend, as the truth inside of you. Isn't it why you haven't since shared with me any bodily desire even once? Though manifest in body, you have withheld it by resolve. It is very unnatural that even while we are so intimate, you haven't once kissed me. Know how abashing and inhibiting it is for me to say so? Should come about naturally from the man. The woman should not be requesting. Aren't you bent on punishing me?'

'Good God! What say thou?' He cupped her mouth with his palm.

'Look, if I get wild I'll overtly express it. Like fire, I'll flare up and burn to a cinder. But you hold it within you and shove me to slow death.'

'Without accusing me, can you say anything at all? I restrain myself for if I don't, it would mean to use you as a sex toy. How will it mean punishing you?'

'Will it not hurt me if you allow yourself to be pained by restraint?' She held his face in both her hands, pressed her lips against his, and planted an intense kiss. Abashed, she then hid her face in his chest. Though he tried to lift her face with both his hands, she slackened not her tautly hung neck. 'Now then, you made a shameless creature of me. Is your ego satisfied?' By now, he comprehended the articulation in her speech. Articulation of speech or disposition, he couldn't figure out which. She will hold me guilty in any matter whatsoever. Although he had so much as understood that it was in her comportment to regard him blameworthy in any issue, despite the fact that he was in the dark apropos of, and was not a partaker consciously, purposefully, by drive, or otherwise, he had resolved rather to grasp the critical connotation or primary suggestion of her words and abstain from discerning distortions therein. He had convinced himself that the difference between connotation and distortion depended on the disposition of mind. Drawing his mouth near her face that she hid in his chest, he cooed in her ears a thought that had been forming in his mind for some days now. 'If physical attraction is prime, love is devoid of sanctity. If physical contact is suppressed, pleasantness and warmth are wanting.'

She remained silent for a while. Then she lifted her head and, gazing at him, said in an accusatory tone, 'Do you mean that our bond is parched of pleasantness and warmth?'

'If you go about digging up contorted meaning in every word I say, conversation gets strenuous. What I said is a simple subtlety,' he said in an exhortative tone.

'Somu, why did you allow this to drift to such a low point? Why did you keep me aloof? You are pretending love overtly, and within, you harbour disdain towards me.'

'Mind your language,' he bawled at her again.

'Shout at me, choose to beat me, but you *have* to agree with me,' she hugged him enticingly.

Neither resisting her embrace, nor responding to her incitation, irrigating her with compassion than with enamour, he murmured, 'Amrita, you aren't moving out, nor am I. I am yours. You are mine. Let us not hasten. We shall wait till tomorrow. Don't suppose that I

disappointed. No use even calling. Arriving in office, he fully applied himself to the work that Neelakanthappa had placed for his perusal, made a quick visit to a work spot that demanded his attention, sent Neelakanthappa to have a quick lunch at noon, then called her and apprised – look, this is what happened. She remained silent. 'I know that you are angry. I did not do so purposefully. Now tell me, shall I come over or not?' 'Why ask me when in your mind of minds, you want to stay back?' she questioned. 'Don't talk rot. Be there in half an hour.' Replacing the handset, he reflected, at times, though I am not erring, she delves into it and gives it a facade of iniquity. If, for once, I do go wrong, how could she be so magnanimous as to overlook it and be conciliatory and complaisant towards me? He couldn't regard her critically though. Immediately on Neelakanthappa's return, he started on his scooter, went to the marketplace, looked for a royal-jasmine string, bought an arms' length of it, and drove in the direction of Lalitamahal Extension. She wasn't by the gate. When he opened the gate himself and parked, the well-grown, six-month old puppy in the front kennel barked raucously. In response, the one at the hind joined and matched in decibel count. Is aware that I have arrived, yet has not opened the door for me. Shall I return just so? He instantly dismissed that thought. She is unable to control her anger. If I, too, conduct myself in bad temper, what distinction is there? He acquiesced and rung the doorbell. Just then, he discovered that she stood to the other side of the door; simply hadn't unbolted the door. He saw her through the windowpane. She too was eyeing him. Yet, she did not open the door. He rang the doorbell again. Though his voice would not carry through the glass, he admonished her warmly so that she could decipher his lip movement, 'Have your eyes gone sightless?' She opened the door; he stepped in. She stood her place like a dispirited doll. Neither was there any sign of welcome, nor an arm extended forward. But her face and body explicitly revealed that she had not ate or slept for the last five or six days. Having secured the door, when he held her in embrace, she wriggled and distanced herself. He strode to her and, this time holding her firmly, said, 'Now, don't be obstinate. Listen. You know my firm's name "Shah and Shekhar". Navin Shah, my partner, visited with his family for an excursion. We had started together our enterprise in Bombay. A close friend. I had to leave in a hurry. Couldn't inform you.'

'Friends from Bom-bay, but take me away from your mind,' she said, twirling the message.

He said as if he did not notice her contorted accusation, 'Was always reminiscing, but could not call. To call, I had to declare your name and number, and Navin was always beside.'

She led him to the kitchen and put the curry and stew, which she had removed from the fridge on receiving his call, on the burner. The rice cooker was done by then. He asked, 'Why haven't you eaten for the last five days?'

She replied, 'At least you could so much as grasp my condition! Thanks.' Then she placed a single salver and started serving to him only. 'Unless you eat, I will not even touch the food,' he persisted. She placed another salver and sat beside him. While dining, she volunteered, 'You reported your version. Now I will give an account of mine. Recall what we discussed that day. I didn't sleep that night. Sorts of delight, expectation, eagerness! Next morning, I got up early and lighted the divine lamp. You would be here by about noon. It is one thing that you visited every afternoon. But that day, I waited at the gate right from quarter past noon. Turning and craning my neck in the direction of your path, propped up on my toes, looking without batting an eyelid, only to be afflicted by neck pain, growing anxious why, why is he not here yet? God, some mishap en route, panicking at the thought of that curve by the zoo. The impact of a crash is first felt by the engine of the car. But the impact of a hit to the scooter is first felt by the rider. At 2 pm, I drew into the house and called your office. I asked if I may speak to Mr Somashekhar and when Neelakanthappa replied, "Madam, he is not in station, has left for Bangalore, will return on twenty-sixth night or twenty-seventh morning", swallowing the piercing shock, I said customarily, "On his return, please inform him that I wanted to consult him for erecting a two-feet fence on the compound wall." On replacing the handset, know how dejected I felt about myself? How can you ever know? I accosted you like a bitch in heat. "No haste, please," you warded me off by suggesting abstinence till the morrow and left with that Bombay friend, without any sensitivity whatsoever or even informing me. I am one hell of a dog and approached you like one, and thinking that you treated me much inferior to a dog, I ... ' the exhaled breath got stuck up and she started crying loud and drawn-out, putting him in consternation. He hugged her by his left arm, and she could be contained only after he consoled her much.

'Now you console me. But you abandoned me like you would a lesser dog and just walked away.'

He interrupted her, 'I told you why and in what circumstances I left.'

She retorted, 'Now you clarified. It is not untrue that such feelings assailed me then.'

'On knowing the truth, you have understood that those feelings were imaginary, ones induced by agitation. Why express it again?'

'If I don't, how will it reach unto you?'

'Why convey an unfounded feeling?'

'If you don't allow me to share my feelings, I will not speak a single word,' she shot up, went to the sink in the corner, and started washing her hands.

'Now, what are you doing?' he tailed her, checking. 'Okay then, I am finished too. Let me wash.' He held his hand under the tap while she stood still. He rinsed his mouth with water, dried his hands with a towel, and took his seat on the sofa in the lounge. She did not turn up there. He was weighed down by burdensome thoughts – what sort of a nature is this of hers, what sort of a situation is this of mine – and was rendered torpid. Entire house was suffocatingly calm. She was not even heard pacing.

After fifteen minutes, she appeared from nowhere, stood facing him, and said, 'Finished punishing me?' When he popped up his head with a questioning look in his eyes, she asked, 'Why did you give up your lunch?'

'Why did *you*?' he rejoined.

'If I resume now, will you too?' she asked. He chose to remain silent. Nearing, she hugged him, 'Somu, don't you remember that you have promised to regard me with tolerance, even if I behave rudely? Now, come on.' She kissed him on the forehead and head and tugged him by his arms. On tow, reaching the dining table, he noticed that she had removed the defile plates, placed a fresh plate of curd rice, a spoon in it, and beside it, a bowl full of ice cream. 'I had prepared the ice cream to share with you that day. Gave some to the children and stashed away the rest in deep freeze, wanting to share it exclusively with you.' She parked him on a chair, pulled another adjacent to his, sat on it, and with the spoon, fed him and herself morsels of the curd rice alternately.

She had noticed the royal jasmine that he had brought rolled in a kerchief, but had chosen to keep mum. On arrival, he had placed it on the sofa. Now, on finishing his dessert, he brought it from the lounge and adorned her locks with it. Head bowed, she welcomed it. At a loss for words, he was silent for a full minute. He then held both her shoulders and spoke softly, 'Amrita, I will not proceed without your consent.' She spoke not. He awaited her approval. After another minute, he said, 'Heard me? Don't if you are not inclined.'

She lifted her head, briefly stared at him with fierce eyes, put down her sight, and said, 'I have no need for the company of people who tread the precautious path of consent, covenant, and compliance.' He did not speak any. Hugging, he carted her, partly hauled up and partly dragging to the divan in the lounge, shed his inhibition, divested her of the same, and immersed in the warmth of togetherness. Though he was exploring the throb and tempo of the first union, as also submitting to the transcendental feel of embodied attainable nirvana, he was elated by a pleasant sense of blest when he clearly realized that, albeit silently, she was submitting and welcoming with full cognition. His empirical knowledge that not just he, she was imbibing it too and with greater relish, encouraged him and caused counter encouragement in her. The gamut of happiness of life thus fount, her face and body smacked of the blest awareness of her contributory role therein. Amidst intense happiness and upbeat excitement, an intense sensation pooled still within her that there was no room for even an iota of grief or disgrace. Life à la happiness! Having got hold of the font of truth that the elemental surge of life had the conjuring attribute of converting into bliss even pain that might show up at the core of all this, she aligned herself fervently, reflecting *let pain, pain let it, it nothing but is the portal that ushers happiness*. While her final vibes strummed, dousing, sousing, and dissolving in happiness all of life and self, the gentle aroma of royal jasmine coalesced, and as he swelled in the faith that in her there shall no more be distress, sorrow, and agitation, in her face showed a suppressive wrench, a plunge down a cavern, and depleting dying vigour. The lustre drained from her eyes and sent her sight astray and confused. The spirit of imbibition wore out and paved way for jab, dejection, and stiffness that unmistakably nudged the amalgam. Even before his reciprocity, which was as subtly grasping the nuances of tendencies in her, could get the full import of the transformed tang, it was apparent that she had slipped far away from his reach. He mumbled, 'Amrita, Amrita', as one groping in darkness would appeal. She was not there. Prodding her again and again, he compellingly called out to her, as if it were his unquestionable right to know of her whereabouts. Instead of softly cooing in a stimulating tone, she retorted in denigrating despise, 'Aren't you finished with your bestial crave yet?' At the moment, when he strove to steady himself from the imbalance caused by the sudden change in rhythm, she pushed him, rolled over, got up, picked up in one sweep all her clothes that lay rumpled below the divan, darted to her bedroom, slammed the door, and shut it from within. Owing to this sudden piercing sound in the house, the dogs started barking raucously.

While he sat cringed on that divan, trying to recover from the sudden onslaught, his mind surmised, 'What an astringent woman this!' Aware of his present state, he crouched and sank, stifled by disgrace. Instantly, he got up and dressed. He wanted to exit, board his scooter, and leave. He resolved never to step into this house again. A picture formed and crystallized in his mind that this was a truly selfish female animal. Eating from a common salver, her belly full, she, an obstinate woman, would just hurl the salver in mire, devoid of any sympathy towards the partner. He went up to the sofa and wore his socks and shoes. What with the etiquette of leave-taking, this beast doesn't merit even a tirade, or even a final declaration of calling it quits. Making for the lounge without causing any sound, he neared the door only to hear a faint sobbing from some cavern corner of the still house in the quiet purlieus. She? He walked up to the door of her bedroom and lent an ear. Yes, it is she. Sobbing. The dogs had ceased barking and calmness was intense, wherefore the weeping could be heard clearly. Now why is she crying? He could not understand. What befell her now? In a short while, he recalled that her ire flares up instantly and subsides only after it drains in the form of tears. So is the cry a sign of cessation of anger? And anger for what now? It is also in her nature to get angry for no reason whatsoever. Now, while she weeps, it would be inconsiderate of me to leave without offering a word of consolation. Immediately, he tapped the door and called out, 'Amrita, Amrita.' The sound of weeping ceased. But she replied not. He was sure that she had heard him. He appealed once again, 'Amrita,

Amrita, open the door.' No reply even now. He added, 'If you don't open, I will stand rooted here, however long.' Still no reply. He stood his place. In a short while, his legs ached. He felt like retreating to the lounge and sitting on the sofa. But he had committed to stand there, no matter how long. Stand he did. Legs ached more. He thought of pulling up a chair and slumping into it, but he remained still, recalling that he had declared he would be on his feet, any long.

Abruptly, she opened the door. The two found themselves positioned diametrically face-to-face with each other, the doorsill demarcating their precincts. She had untidily worn the clothes that she had picked up from the floor, but had not combed her dishevelled hair. The vermilion that had lost shape remained so. In no time after opening the door, she noticed that he was dressed. She imposed a sense of calm on herself and said, 'He who is dressed to the heel may leave. The dogs are tied. Won't harm.'

He felt a bit guilty for wearing the shoes, wherefore no explanation came to his mind. He said, 'Time to leave for office.'

'If time was up, you should have left. Nobody means anything to me,' she said. Though he felt maligned as if struck in the face, not even a normal quantum of anger brewed in him in requital. He stood motionless. She was facing him, her entire body held within the bounds of controlled ire. Wasn't even looking at him. Five minutes later, she said, 'Mr Somashekhar, I need to discuss some serious matter with you.' 'Speak up,' he mimed. Presenting herself in the same controlled bearing, she said, 'Said you have behind you the experience of having toyed with a married woman. Much of it, and a man's conscience gets blunted. While you messed with me, shouldn't you have given but a fleeting thought to discriminate between the aptness or otherwise of causing ethical damage to a woman, rendering her sacrilegious towards her husband, of damaging her authority over her children? Or did you for once presume that I too belong in the clan of that all-relinquishing Bombay woman?'

His ethical grit received a further setback. He felt what she said was right. Once chastity is lost, she loses the courage and composure to face her husband. When that is obliterated, how can there remain confidence in one's personality? I am an inept fellow, he chastised himself. His head whirled and, sensing that he would slump, he extended his arms and sought the support of the doorframe. He felt as if some unknown gas was streaming into his head. One minute, two, three, he knew not how many ticked away. But a while later, his head cleared, as also his conscious. He recalled everything. His confidence returned and he felt he could stand without the support of the doorframe. He stood firm and said, 'Whatever has happened was initiated by us both. I proceeded only after you firmly declared that you had "no need for the company of people who tread the precautious path of consent, covenant, and compliance". You too participated with application. Six days ago, it was I who advocated restraint, not you.'

'Yet, should it not occur to you that you should not touch, even mentally, a married woman?' she put the blame on him again.

'Awareness about marriage should have been yours, not mine,' he exhorted her in a raucous voice.

She was numbed. Colour drained from her face and she sensed a heavy fluid filling her head; her vision went blank. She took support of the door she had held open and steadied herself, eyes closed. *I belong nowhere. There is no confidant who shares my agony, no companion who can support me a wee bit.* Such thoughts filled her with intense loneliness. Head hung with eyes shut, the void within her swelled unobstructed. Observing her state, he reflected if his words were indeed harsh. But along came the justification that he had no alternative but to retort to her accusatory act of assigning a biting ethical dimension to the incident and holding him downright responsible for it. He stood his place, justifying to himself again that he had done nothing more than bring plain fact to her notice. He thought of departing, boarding his scooter, and leaving. But that, he reflected, would tantamount to ratifying her moralistic accusation and accepting defeat. He, therefore, stayed on with a resolve not to leave before she had accepted his contention.

By then, she lifted her head. She let go of the support of the door and stood upright. He saw in her eyes a hitherto unseen weird resoluteness, which, like a faint lamp, seemed to draw light instead of emitting it.

'You should stand your place. I warn you not to cross the doorsill,' cautioning him in a low but firm voice, she left the door open and receded into her bedroom. He could see that the mortar floor had faded, cracked, and dented in a few places. Inside was an old, bulky, opulent double bed with its fore aligned against a wall. She opened a chest beside the bed and took out a revolver. The way she held it in her proper hand, he understood that she was proficient at shooting without erring in any detail. Till now, he had no idea that she possessed one. Revolver in hand, as she neared him with firm steps, he was filled with fear that his life may not last more than a couple of seconds. *Duck, close the door, bolt it from outside, flee, board the scooter* ... but a section of his mind checked him from the reprehensible idea of instantaneously fleeing for life. After all, what if I die? Apathy and detachment spumed fortitude within him, and he reflected that life and death were both senseless occurrences. A thin coating of perspiration formed on his forehead and neck. Having neared him with resolute steps, she posted herself at the very spot by the open door where she had earlier stood and, staring at him, said, 'Yes, I should have been aware. You brought to my notice my position and my propriety. You edified me of the final doctrine that I have no moral right to live on. This revolver will relieve me. Without much ado and without wasting time, take your scooter and leave. Goodbye, a final goodbye.' She slammed the door and bolted it from inside.

A moment before, his forehead and neck perspired from the fear of death. Now his entire body transuded from dread. Not just the inner vest and brief, but also the insides of his shirt and trousers got wet and sticky. A shudder went up his spine. Involuntarily, he started banging on the door. She did not respond. Knocking a few more times, he pleaded aloud, 'Amrita, Amrita, here, open the door. Whatever's my fault, let's discuss. Open the door. My word.' No answer whatsoever from her. In response to his banging, the dogs started barking loudly. That slackened his tenacity further. 'Open the door, swear on me, on God, on you....' Groping for words, he pleaded again in all humility. More aloud, he implored further, 'Hear me, don't harm yourself. If you live, we can discuss everything. Hear me, if you die, I too will not live. Always remember that. Heard me, Amu?' The dogs responded by barking louder. Then, not only did his vocal chords subdue, it seemed that his active power to call out, to beg, and to implore was subdued too. He felt embroiled in a situation that outdid his willpower. He went silent. Seven or eight seconds' pin-drop silence. The dogs also stopped howling. Abruptly, a wail spewed from within him. Given to the knowledge that she, of the name Amrita, whom he loved, who, a little before, had with the gentle tenderness of royal jasmine, teemed *sap de vitae* into his body, mind, and soul, was eager to end her life by putting a bullet in her body, he came to know how much he loved her. He humbly appealed to God. God, instill wisdom in her, check her mind that is set to pull the trigger, let the chamber be empty; if perchance it isn't, let the aim fail and the bullet hurl out the window. His intellectual stance that he hadn't absolute belief in the existence of God took a backseat and a stream of faith oozed within him. That past, silence pervaded again. To understand what was going on in the room, he lent an ear. Calmness, dead calm, prevailed in the entire house. Dogs weren't barking. Alert that he might hear the bullet go off any moment in the room, his anxiety bubbled up. The pace, sound, and heave of his heartbeat shot up and could be heard by him. He glanced at his watch. The second hand expounded on every second that it scaled. Perceiving that within the span of one such second, a shot might be heard from inside, his every heartbeat pulsated like the thud of a revolver.

Suddenly, fear of a different order overcame him. If she did kill herself, the police who would eventually arrive apprehend me despite the fact that she had locked herself in. It wouldn't miss them that I visited here daily. Nor would it help to flee, for they would suspect me even more. The cause of death being gunshot notwithstanding, the postmortem would expose our conjugation of a few moments before. With stories rife that she died from the ignominy of rape inflicted by 'architect Somashekhar', my name would appear in every newspaper along with my handcuffed photo and then a plaint. What if she did shoot herself in vengeance to bring me to such state! It would have been a simple end if she had killed me rather. Sensing that it would be perilous, very perilous to leave now, he appealed again in a beseeching voice, 'Amrita, my Amrita, open the door, my word, I am very much here. Open the door.' He did not knock the door. The dogs did not bark. Unable to do anything else, he just stood and prayed. After a while, removing his shoes to shut out the sound of pacing, he opened the main door, passed through the garden, and neared her bedroom window. If it were open, he could see what she was up to; he was persuaded by the assurance that if she saw him in the face, he could possibly cajole her into opening the door. But the inch-thick teak windows of her bedroom were shut. The paint on them had peeled and crumbled due to exposure to the sun. She hadn't till date invited him into her bedroom. He too hadn't intruded, nor even sloppily expressed inclination to go there. He recalled that hugging, reclining, and all conversation were on the divan in the lounge. After lingering for a while by the bedroom window, his sight shifted to the window of the attached bathroom. It was closed too. The bottom half of it was wood, the upper half glass. He hesitated to approach it. What if she noticed! He felt sullied. Silently retreating through the garden without looking in the direction of the growling dogs by the gate, he re-entered the house, carefully closed the big door, neared the door of her bedroom, and wore his shoes. A sort of reassurance pervaded through him. If she intended to, she would have shot herself by now. By now, the intensity of her ire has subsided. He felt relieved and waited a little more. As his legs pained, he put his back against the wall by the doorframe and lowered himself to a sitting position. Calmed down, he started pondering. She hadn't told me about the revolver. When he had queried if it wasn't dangerous for her to dwell all alone in the big lonely house in the desolate outskirts of the city, without even a sentry, she said that she had faith in her bravery and didn't need any watch or ward. Hailing from a coffee estate, she is familiar with revolvers and rifles. Would have had enough practice in aiming and shooting. Yet, to spend nights alone in this house! She had said that the children slept in another room. Is this love for loneliness default in the coffee planters from the Ghats? As he started cogitating, his anxiety subdued and heartbeat came down to normalcy. His mind was insulated from any more worry. He still but sat.

A little later, a sound was heard from the room. It was the gush of water from the attached bathroom. He focused his audition in the direction of the sound and reflected that it could be the sound of shower. He opened the main door, walked through the garden, stood by the bath so that his shadow would not fall on the windowpane, and pricked up his ears. Yes, she is bathing. The inside of the pane is haze from the steam of the hot water shower. All his worries dissipated. He returned, locked the door, and posted himself at the earlier spot. He knew that this was not her usual bathing time, and save for the morning bath she did not bathe again. Did she bathe now because of sweat? Or is it to cleanse the muck consequent to the union? He felt that it was a sanitization process to shun him and their ardent relationship. He stood still, listening to the fizz of the shower. He decided to never step into that house again after such disgrace. Yet, he checked himself from leaving abruptly and waited. In a while, the sound from the bath ceased. He inferred that the hot-water boiler was used up fully. A little later, the opening of another door was heard. The wardrobe? He lost interest in the sounds coming from inside.

In ten minutes, she flung open the door and stepped out. Her face was spotless, she had worn a pressed pastel yellow sari, her sumptuous moist hair combed, a dot on the forehead to match the hue of the sari, and a handbag hanging from her left hand. She looked at him, but he did not contest her stare. She said, 'I have to fetch the children,' and shifted her sight. Without reacting, he skirted past her and went to the gate, gunned his scooter, and left without looking back.

~

The bed is smooth. The nozzle of the revolver held to the right temple is in a cold round contour. The right hand holds the revolver. The index finger has not yet hooked the trigger. When the doors and windows are closed, any outside sound is barred from coasting in. The thick curtains extending two feet below the windowsill shut out any residual sound and brought about an ambience just about ideal for death. This is not the ambiguous feeling that occurred hitherto many a time. This time, now, sure to pull the trigger and die, must die. What a torture life is! To think of the torment of cancer! Even that can be borne. This torment within! Why bear this harrowing agony that, without reason or warning, all of a sudden emerges from the void deep within and infuses an emptiness inside out? Half a second ample to position finger on the trigger and just jerk. The point at which to instantly, painlessly exterminate is the temple whereat the bullet pierces through the skull and, shredding the brain, foremost decimates the very font of pain and nothing is felt thereafter, the medics themselves opining that a shot elsewhere at the belly, heart, or neck not to be as trouble-free. This position is ideal, even half a second's hold-up is pointless, more the delay greater the agony before dying. Yes, forgot, I am the one who decided to depart, let not the police or anyone else irk or trouble none. How many times to write so in the suicide note? Aren't there umpteen notes enough? But important are the date and time of suicide. Get up and take the pad, no need to get up, it is here nearby in the chest where the revolver is kept, reach out a bit. Nobody is responsible for my death. In anguish, I shot myself through the skull at the right temple at 3:15 pm, precisely at 3:17½ pm. Many more such notes below this one, haven't the leisure to count them now, what with counting, a crap of a draft lacking individuality, recorded by anyone committing suicide. No need to write afresh, just affix today's date and time on one of the earlier notes. Why have I retained them without discarding? Who needs that record of how many times and over what period I was driven to suicide by escalating agony and acute void? Leave it on this very bed to be readily seen by the police when they break open the door. Yes, this is the right place, pen on the pad. He is knocking on the door, he who severed the ethical string that firmly bound me to life and inevitably paraded me to death is pleading in fear of what the police might do to him, bestowed on me, no, he derived uninterrupted, unique never-before pleasure; should have been aware that unbridled conjugation leads to void. Why this note? The sinner be apprehended by the police and hanged. But for him, wouldn't have got into this situation and didn't have to contemplate dying. Should be punished, is knocking on the door and pleading. Timorous coward. Let none suffer; at least with effort, he has enacted love. Let the note be, an unnecessary holdup, not even half a second to place the finger and let off, if I die intestate, my husband will get a share of my assets, nevertheless the father will be the administrator till the children attain majority, eleven more for Vijai to be eighteen, fourteen more for Vikas, who'll slog to repay the interest and borrowing and salvage the vast coffee estate for these children who, by then, would suck our blood dry. This void conquered and the desire to clench the revolver at bay. Without squandering the estate, which reliable person or institution is there that might rear the children? Somashekhar is undeserving, the rogue brought me to the point of pulling the trigger by severing the ethical string that linked me and life. However, he is honest in money matters, knocking again, why are these dogs barking their lungs out? Do the carriers of Lord *Kālabhairava*, the annihilator, sense death? At least should settle the estate rights, even if I didn't, he will educate and make wise men of them, the scoundrel loves children, will also educate them that I was wicked and undeserving, would wed again and sire, rascal. Today I lost my authority to call him so, irretrievably forfeited my rights, and slid into a chasm, has sculpted a smooth greasy slide that cannot be scaled back, rogue Somashekhar, to jail, to the gallows, silence. He has left, aches more than cancer, torture, only Yama, the God of Death, can relieve me, pounding inside the mind, a tranquilizer shot would pacify, not even half second, pull the trigger and before the sound is heard, all pain is alleviated, the switch of the pain spot shut off and a state of painless relief where even the susurrant silence is not heard, has definitely left, after having savoured pleasure, rogue, having sired progeny resembling him in eyebrow, nose, and chin, alienating them from me. What if the estate passed on to him or to some carnivore, wait for the apportionment and only suffer more. If nothing is done, it will still pass on to them, or to him. Consult lawyer and will so that none gets it, jerk the trigger. God, it is false that you be existent, if thou art whence my agony, the churning of iron thorn in my entrails, how much to bear, eyes shut tight and concentrating on the torment within. God, thou art not, none art, nothing art, only pain is, exterminating, thwarting peaceful death. Uh, stress, tears, shouldn't cry, if he is out there and hears, in the presence of none, no one's pity needed, grit jaw and restrain the mind, no one's sympathy, the deception called love, succour, grime, having vapourized the tears by silence, having shut the eyes in samadhi, having stifled the buzz of time, victory.

The forte of talking to him, towering over, head held high, is no more. She began crying aloud, sensing that she might never recover from the decadence. Apprehensive that he might hear if he was by the door, silently she got up. Having placed the revolver on the bed, she went to the bathroom, stood facing the wall, covered her face with her palms, and began weeping to her heart's relief. More uncontainable tears gushed forth. She reached for the towel on the peg, stuffed it in her mouth, and sobbed. At once, she felt like bathing and cleansing. Instantly, she mixed hot and cold water and slid under the shower, dressed as she was, just unfurling her braid. In a while, she felt contented and relieved, the consolation of impurity awash and hygiene returning. Removing the wet clothes, she stood, eyes shut under the shower that poured like rain, searching the void, the root of the void within. She felt some remission in the affliction. She continued to stand for some time, forgetting even to use soap. Even as the warm water in the boiler drained and cold water poured, the difference in temperature didn't appeal to her body, mind, or intellect. When the overhead tank drained fully and the shower ceased, she dried her face, body, and head with a towel and came out. The big, silent clock on the wall, oh, past the time to fetch the children. Hurriedly, she dressed and dried the tresses with a thick Turkish towel. Latching the revolver, she kept it and the suicide notepad in the closet and locked it, tied the key to the necklace, then slipped into her high heels, paced hurriedly amidst the potholes in the mortar floor, and opened the door. He still stood there. A part of her mind contented, but another part seething in anger and disdain. Without facing my sight, he left immediately in scorn when

I announced that I had to fetch the children, as though there would be no bond between us any more.

While she drove the car, she clenched her jaws and told herself, 'Let him get lost, my life is not dependent on anyone.' The Brindavan School and the crèche had both closed half an hour before. But an arrangement was in place whereby the teacher Susheelamma, who stayed thereabouts, detained in her house those children whose parents did not pick them up in time. On seeing his mother's car, the younger one Vikas trotted up and began tugging at the handle even before she could open it. Holding his bag, Vijai walked up leisurely and got in the car. By handing over the empty lunchboxes of the children, Mrs Susheelamma indicated, 'You have safely taken custody of your children.' Even as the car moved, radiating glee in her face, Amrita asked, 'What did my toddler play today?'

'Mom, why did you bathe at this hour, rinsing your head?' Vijai enquired.

'I took a morning bath,' she said. He noted, 'It is wet at the tip.'

Miffed for having been caught at lying, she quickly jumped to another matter, 'Said you had difficulty with your math. Did you seek clarification with your teacher?' At home, she positioned them both on her lap and, feeding them *uppiṭṭu* and ice cream, enquired about the new lessons and games taught at school. Then, unchaining the pups, she let the children play with the dogs. Balls were flung and the dogs had to fetch their respective balls. She, on conferring with the children, had named the identical male dogs Vikrant and Vishvas. Vikrant had to fetch the red ball, while the white ball was Vishvas' responsibility. Vikrant was fond of Vijai and Vishvas was close to Vikas.

Amrita didn't fail to consider the disadvantages of staying in the lonely house on the outskirts of the city. It was quite a distance for the cook and the domestic help to shuttle daily. No company for the children in studies and play. She was also aware that security-wise, this place was danger-prone. But to her who was bred in a forlorn house in a big coffee estate, this didn't seem too desolate. The cook Puttamma, who arrived at 8 am, would cook different cuisines for lunch and supper and store them in the fridge. She would also prepare for the kids different fare for lunch and for evenings. Once in a week, she would prepare deep-fried delicacies enough for the whole week. Domestic help Mahadevamma, who worked similar hours, broomed and mopped the floor, windows, and doors, washed the clothes, cleaned the garden, and irrigated it. One set of keys would be with Puttamma. Amrita paid them liberal wages and they worked sincerely without absenting themselves. Besides, Puttamma was an honest person. Of late, Amrita was in love with loneliness. The backdrop of the hill that framed the sky shored up feelings of solitariness and made it impossible for her to vacate this house and move elsewhere.

As a matter of routine, after supper, she would sit legs folded on the divan in the lounge with her children reclining on each of her thighs, and they would slip into sleep listening to the story. She would then lift them by turns and put them in their beds. Today, as she sat on the divan with Vijai and Vikas, drained of fortitude, her mind felt heavy. Why can't I recall any story on this divan? Stories needn't be necessarily those related and published by others. The children sometimes demanded a story that was told earlier. Or if she chose to characterize a bird, a tree, or a hill and expounded on an aspect of it, as would appeal to the minds of the children, they would surely get engrossed. The story needed no preface, prologue, body, culmination, or any such dimension or form. If she chose to talk about a bird that took off from the Chamundi Hill with Vijai on one wing and Vikas on the other, surveying around and flying over KRS, Srirangapatna, Somnath, Talakadu, and Nanjangud, and after a round over Mysore city return home by evening, the outline offered scope for incorporating the view that was beneath, what could be seen, and, in between, if asked what Vijai and Vikas did when the clouds gathered or the sun shone, the children would fill in the details enthusiastically. By the time the bird landed back on the hill, they would be asleep. But today, no subject came to her mind. Imagination was not soaring even so much as an inch. Felt as if she kept sliding into a greasy chasm; the more she tried scaling the more she slid, her efforts fruitless, her intellect blunted, and she went blank. Out of this divan, elsewhere, on the sofa, no, out of this lounge, she felt like shifting to the bench in the drawing room. But then, she wasn't sure that an alternative location would be any helpful. 'Viju dear, will you tell a story today? My head is aching.' 'Mm, no, you only should.' Vikas is adamant, 'If he tells, I won't listen.' 'Then why don't *you* tell one?' 'If he does, I won't listen too,' Vijai retorts. To pacify them both, she must tell something. 'What shall I tell?' she leaves it to them. 'One where the horse got itself wings,' they both make a compromise. As she started relating the story that was told many times before, Vikas says, 'Mom, you are not telling it properly today.' Nevertheless, they both slid into sleep listening to it.

Tonight, Amrita is extremely unenthusiastic. She is wont to retire late every night. Sleep doesn't come until after 1 am. She is habituated to sit on the sofa in her bedroom and read or press the kids' clothes or just sit silently in a lonely mood. Many a time, she would point the revolver at her temple or at her heart. At such times, she would bolt the door of the children's bedroom from outside. She is sensitive to the effect on their minds in case Vijai or Vikas emerged from their room and saw their mother holding a revolver. At times, the compulsion to pull the trigger gets irrepressible. Her mind would arrive at the threshold of the ultimate stage that adherence to such compulsion alone would mark the end of her agony and torture, no other way. Cometh the awareness of the final moments of her life. Along come the tears. Awareness of the inevitability of death as also the unbearable stress of fighting tears at the thought of death manifest simultaneously. She sets out to identify her emancipation. Subduing the impulse of death, she cannot. She can, at best, devise a simple method of dying. Though aware that it would be less painful to shoot through the temple than through the heart, at times the attraction of the bullet scraping through the heart reigns supreme. At other times, the revolver would turn out uninspiring; rather a dagger would become endearing. Unlocking the chest to the other side of the bed, among many shiny, sharp steel daggers stashed there, she retrieves the one that presently appealed to her the most, points it to her heart, and, like a statue, sits still on the sofa. Only a second, just hold the handle firmly and plunge it. Not enough just to plunge it; should pull it back so that the blood starts spilling out, and then the essence. Still, it is a torturous method, not as swiftly achieved as with a revolver. Nonetheless, the attraction of the dagger reigning supreme that day, she sits holding it firm without putting it down. In between, she gets up, opens the chest, retrieves the pad of suicide notes, and hurriedly drafts a new one with current date and time. The repeated drafting having ingrained the words into her memory, the account, date, and signature are finished in a jiffy. Having put away the pad on the bed, she returns, holds the dagger firmly by its grip, points its tip to her heart, and sits with eyes shut.

Today, after putting the children to sleep, she went to the lounge. Usually, she sits on the sofa or the divan for two or three hours. When she saw the divan, she recalled that she had just now occupied it with the children and felt like bathing again. If not the entire divan and the upholstery, she felt like washing at least the spreads. Have had bath once since. Coming to think of it, I have to bathe the children who too had occupied this divan. That deterred her from bathing again. She took the spreads to the bathroom, soaked detergent powder in a pail of water, and rinsed them in the solution. Then she brought a fresh set of spreads from the wardrobe, draped them properly over the divan, tucked the tails properly under the upholstery, and arranged the cushions. She then went to her bedroom, took out the revolver, and, placing it on her thighs, sat on the sofa. Depressing, depressing, depressing feeling! Though she didn't feel an intense urge to shoot, she was engrossed in fancying how comforting would it be if death was forthcoming on its own, what a solace of relief, and yearned for it. If ever I attain a state devoid of gloom, tribulation, or the need for a desire to die! Gazing at the wall with an unfocussed sight, she sat inert. Why doesn't it come to me naturally? How long do I have to wait in agony for that?

After a while, she got up, placed the revolver in the chest, and entered the children's bedroom. In the faint red light of the night lamp, she observed their faces. 'Both have the very same forehead, nose, and eyes. They are born with these features only to torture me,' she told herself and gritted. When an idea surfaced that all her worries would vanish if she shot them both and herself, her mind did not approve of it even in that state. No, this is not my cuppa. A sequent flashed: anyway I am dying, so why not invite him, shoot him, and then shoot myself? Consensus came from within. Yes, I can do this. But these thoughts have surfaced even before. None of these are occurring for the first time. Behind came the memory and disappointment that they were never executed. She held herself in contempt for being a coward, incapable of any act. Watching the children asleep, she chastised herself that she was a sinner who merited death penalty for contemplating murder of such charming kids. With brisk steps, she went to her bedroom, opened the chest, and again took out the revolver. Holding it, she stood by the window and lamented about her dithering. The strong suit of determination is lacking! Felt like crying, but compellingly suppressed and contained it. Subconsciously, she slid the window curtains. Dense darkness outside. Instantaneously, the hill came to her mind. Outstretched, it stood behind her house, death congealed and personified. Felt she must go there. Still holding the revolver and leaving the light on, she took the key bunch and went out. Vikrant, sleeping in the front kennel, growled. Vishvas in the hind kennel echoed. 'Eh, it's I.' In recognition, they started yodelling. Opening the garage door and the gate, she drove the car out, parked outside, shut the garage and the gate, boarded the car, and sped towards the hill.

Silence everywhere. The streetlights receded, darkness congealed, and the faint outline of the hill appeared like concrete death asleep. Only the gradient road was visible in the automobile light. After she had driven some distance so that the township was out of sight, she halted, put off the light, killed the engine, and sat quiet. Darkness and silence meld, she sensed death and felt that she was near the location she longed for. Having witnessed it several times in daylight, the ravine to the left and what lay beyond it appeared just in memory, the present ocular evidence being just darkness incarnate as void. And as she kept watching it, her mind felt a semblance of equilibrium. For some time, she stay put. Then she gunned the car and started scaling the hill. She felt annoyed at the disturbance caused by the strained sound of the uphill engine to the stillness around. The floodlight that flashed, as if to split the road, was irksome too. Nevertheless, she drove towards the peak, to the section facing her house. Parking the car, she took out the revolver and got out. It was pitch-dark where she stood, and scattered in the distance were the streetlights of the town. As she looked at them, the darkness at hand got more intense. Craning her neck, she saw a few random stars twinkling feebly in the sky, establishing the impregnable fort of darkness. The feeling that darkness and loneliness alone were the ultimate truths of life teemed within. She reflected that if she were to shoot herself through the temple and die here, in this lofty place, it would establish her self-respect. But the hand that held the revolver did not rise.

As she so stood for some time, her sight shot in the direction of her house. The light from the lamp at the rear appeared feebly. Is it from my house or someone else's? She stood watching it. A surge of fear crept into her. The children were alone, sleeping. What if they woke up and started crying, 'Amma, Amma', or if some robber broke in on seeing me leave in my car! She got in the car, put on the light, and glanced at her watch. Ten minutes to two. She recalled that earlier while she stayed in a rented bungalow in Yadavagiri, many a night she would leave the children at home and drive ten or twenty miles in the darkness. But ever since she moved to this own house on the outskirts of the city, this was the first time that she thus ventured out; this was the first time that she was so downcast. No more apathy. She gunned the engine and drove speedily down the hill. What if the car broke down in this jungle! Nervously, she arrived at her house. When she opened the gate, the dogs started barking. She lent her voice to let know of her arrival, then opened the garage door, parked the car inside, locked the gate, and walked up to the children's room. Both were asleep. She went to her bedroom, locked the revolver, placed it securely in the chest, and changed. After long, she fell asleep.

~

If it were just a muddle or an ordeal, he could have easily banished her from his mind and regained his poise in a couple of days. Try as he may to forget it, he discovered that the rending roots had proliferated far and wide, the extent of which he could not simply imagine. He felt that if he had to pull out the roots of her memory, he had to delve deeper than his own mainstay, meaning that he had to cave in and obliterate himself. Though he would clearly sense a warning that any day her association was perilous, very perilous, a section of his mind would, day and night, while at work or idle, while asleep too, summon her and get engrossed. He was not a specialist with women. God! No need for another. But his promiscuous friends opined that though a woman accosts a man on her own, and causes to be laid by her amorous suggestions and demands, in the end she accuses him of molesting a chaste one. Such a woman reasons that she would not, on her own, forfeit her chastity, and that she has to pass the sin on to the partner. 'Should it not occur to you that you should not touch, even mentally, a married woman?' she had devolved the sin ultimately on me. That other woman was right royal, never once raised the ethical question of our relationship. Never once mentioned as to who initiated the relationship or who first strung the cords of passion. She took upon herself fully her share of the responsibility of the association, thereby indicating that my share of the responsibility was fully mine. She had explicitly expressed that the very purpose of our union was to mutually give and take pleasure. During the union and later, other than the memory of the effervescent bliss, there wasn't even an iota of tart. Comparison would set in that in those two years, there wasn't a trace of acrimony. The way she faulted me at consummation, the way she scared the living daylights out of me! A whoop-it-up, exaggerated character. A clear conclusion would emerge that the Bombayite was far better. For three days, the mind drew on the memories of that woman. Then he felt that there was no depth in that relationship. It was at best a derivation of heady lust to be duly forgotten and to remain silent till the bodily desires showed up again. This woman glowers, disparages me, subdues me ethically; yet there is an odd attraction unfathomable to the intellect that herein is profound depth. Alongside would register the caution that this attraction was dangerous and lethal. Not just restrain this attraction, he tried to beget peace by repeatedly deciding to burn it to the roots. For two or three days, he would succeed in concentrating on his work, her memory not troubling him much. But in the following few days, she would fully occupy his mind causing his work to suffer. Yet to establish himself in this place, though he cautioned himself that at this rate he would perish at the formative phase itself, he could not resurrect himself. What sort of a charm is this? Why am I drawn towards her? He would ponder. Barring short temper and mostly holding me at fault for everything, it is indisputably true that her mind craves for me. Who else has strained their innards as much for my sake? He would ask of himself. In all my life, I haven't elsewhere got the solace that my mind gets when I put my head on her lap; no, when she pulls my head down on her lap and puts me to sleep. A comparison would show up that the solace derived by placing his head on her lap was similar to his experience early on, when, as a young boy, his mother used to put him on her lap, comfortingly caressing his locks and singing a lullaby. He would desire to just go and so recline. But he would dread too. Wasn't her tender feel akin to the solace that a frog would get under the shade of the spanned hood of a snake!

When he retired at nights, sleep would overcome soon. But in a few hours, he would be awake. Not necessary that memory or thoughts about her be alert in his conscious mind. Once awake, rolling this way or that, and try as he may, he would not get sleep again. At times, he would slumber by dawn and sleep soundly for a couple of hours. Many a day, not even that. Those days when sleep eluded him into the wee hours, he would feel drowsy all day, yawn, gasp, and be in a lethargic state, unable to cheerfully attend to his work. If one tranquilizer pill is taken at bedtime, sleep soundly till morning! Can put everything on the back-burner during the day at work, but the nights are hard nut. The remedy that it wasn't entirely improper to be on tranquilizers would show up through the night, but then he would be confronted by the poser that surrendering to drugs meant obliterating his willpower. He kept resolving that he would rather suffer than abuse drug. Have faced more grave situations in life. Of what significance is this after all? He perked himself up when a remedy emerged. I'm just forty. If I marry again, there will be no need for the mind to be swayed towards another woman and suffer in agony. He recalled that through four and a half years since his wife's death, another marriage held no appeal, and that he could never arrive at a decision. Now to start all over again! 'Moving here, have I not started a career afresh? So be marriage.' That thought would only provide temporary solace.

One night, writhing in bed without sleep unto the small hours, no sooner did he doze off than the neighbour turned on the radio and devotional songs beamed. In a short while, the dairyman was heard pacing up the stairs. He collected the milk sachet, paid a visit to the toilet, sealed the windows so that the radio from below would not be heard, and retired again. Can't one achieve the ability to invoke sleep as and when desired and wake up by design? Sleep meaning to control the inner mind, to reach the state where the distinction between inner and outer minds, between consciousness and unconsciousness ceases. He reflected that serious reading for a few hours before retiring at night not only begets sleep but also hones the intellect, divesting it of lethargy. He recalled with angst that he had lost touch of the habit he had cultivated over many years, due to lack of concentration, and the reason for being unable to concentrate was....His thoughts were disrupted by the sound of footsteps climbing the stairs. If it was the newspaper boy, he would have scaled hurriedly, flung the newspaper, and glided down as quickly. This is the pace of a sari-clad woman. Perchance she! The thought brought exhilaration to his mind. The sound of the opening of the main door was heard as he recalled that he had not shut it after the dairyman had left, and a voice came, 'Mr Somashekhar.' Hers! He did not respond. The sound of entry, door shut, and secured. She headed straight to his bedroom and, without speaking, not even caring to look around, she rolled the bottom of his blanket a bit and hugged his feet in a way rendering them unable to move or budge. Not just hold them, as she had added the weight of her head too by pressing her face firmly on them, he could not move his feet. He got angry. Despise too. This was a shameless one, he thought. But that did not convert to decibel. If he tried to bring it out, he sensed that it would course through some arcane cavern and dissipate. He could not resist or ask her to let go of his feet, or extend his arm and shove her head aside. Mindful that the feel of her face against his feet would pervade the depths of his mind if he shut his eyes, he lay still with eyes open. Her breath was warm and heavy. He could sense that her eyelashes brushed his feet. In two minutes, the eyelashes got moist and his skin felt as if caressed by a wet brush. Warm drops dripped and soaked his feet. But adamantly, she refrained from crying. He lay still. After a while she let go of his feet, sat beside him, and, eyeing him unaffectedly, said in a calm tone, 'Somu, for ten days I tried to call on you and plead pardon at your feet. But had I the fortitude, the ethical grit? First two days, I was ashamed. A misdeed committed within certain limits deserves pardon. But it forfeits such merit if committed beyond limits. Had I the face to approach you for seeking pardon? I felt utterly ashamed. Then I knew that it was not shame but ethical fear. Yesterday, I questioned myself: why should I be ashamed to face my Somu? Why should I fear to rest in relief at my haven? My Somu has the authority to get enraged. Even if he chooses not to excuse me, I can stay reassured in his company. He may shove me. He may even kick me. But if I hide in his chest and seek refuge, it is impossible for him to cart me out. When I so decided yesterday, know what solace I derived? After twenty-three days ... it is twenty-three days since you walked out on me in exasperation, remember? You don't. It is evident from your face. I haven't slept these twenty-three days. Sleepless, my head would reel if I got to my feet. One day I got giddy and fell by the front gate of my house. Nobody was there. When I regained consciousness fifteen minutes later, both the dogs were sniffing my shoulder, neck, and arms. Still, no sleep came. Just lay dreaming, Somu comes, comes and accepts my apologies, will at least call soon. If the phone rang during the day, the thought that it was probably yours would wring my heart causing it to miss a beat, and I would pick it up after a minute. Not one was yours. Finally, yesterday, when I resolved that you'll not be able to oust me if I buried myself in your chest pleading protection, know what sort of sleep came? Twenty-three days' pile-up all at once! Getting up at dawn and without even brushing my teeth, just rinsed my face and rushed here. You haven't once showed me this house of yours, but had referred to its location. Circling this street and that twice, I finally found it.' She then fixed her gaze in his and said, 'That was entirely my story. You too haven't slept; your face speaks so.' She placed her face firmly on his chest. 'Now I have nestled myself in your chest, you can't drive me out. You can abuse, punch, or kick me, but cannot expel me.' Laughing in splendorous triumph, she then burst into sobs.

All his anger, vexation, and disdain evaporated. Both his arms lifted on their own, embraced her head, and held to his chest more firmly. This depth of love, this intense sentiment, this warm bond, where else is? His mind concurred and became all the more firm. She started to say something. Abhorring any utterance, he placed a palm on her mouth and caressed her back with the other. For over a quarter of an hour, they were one with silence. Then she lifted her head and, eyeing his face solemnly, said, 'Have to take the children to the school. I'll leave now. Come at exactly 12:30 for lunch. I'll probably be home by noon. Call at noon. If I am home, start immediately.' His eyes reflected uncertainty. 'Hmm, if you don't come, it means you have not excused me, and that's it,' she admonished him. With a warning in her eyes, she added, 'Sleep for a while. Don't get up to see me off. Now sleep must come. I have thus ordained it.' She got up, turned around, and left hurriedly. He heard her close the door, descend the stairs, and drive off.

At that moment, vexation, revilement, self-contempt, and such belittling and self-deriding feelings evaporated, and enthusiasm, confidence, and acceptance, which he couldn't himself fully comprehend, teemed in. If he had retired, as ordained by her, sleep would have perhaps overcome him. But in the surge of enamouring moods, he couldn't sleep. He got up, went through his morning ablutions, drank milk for he was in no mood to prepare coffee, had breakfast at a restaurant, and went to office.

At noon he called her. On being invited to visit anon, he started immediately. By 12:10, when he arrived there, she was waiting with the gate held ajar. Having missed him for twenty-three days, the dogs started barking. As they sat in each other's arms in the lounge, it seemed they had decided not to speak either about the bygone period or about the unpleasant incident. Both felt that no potential words bestowed the tranquillity derived from silent physical contact. Now as he held her in embrace, he noticed that her body had gone scrawny and the bones of her chest and shoulders were prodding his arms. It was clear to him that the pain had stung her more than him. While he clearly saw the actuality and consequence of the pain that presently appealed to his touch, the inquisitive question as to who was to blame for it lost locus. He went about caressing her back, shoulders, neck, and face, as would a sculptor attempting to fill in the deficient contours of a figurine. She sat with her eyes closed as if such comforting perked her up. While at lunch, she broke the silence. 'Can't fast fully, but will you believe me if I say that in twenty-three days this is my first meal?'

While he nodded in assent, he was ashamed deep within. Like it or not, he would just force down his gullet whatever was served at the restaurant. He also noticed that his body had not gone scrawny like hers.

After lunch, he went to the lounge and sat on the sofa. Clearing the table and washing the dishes, she neared him and said, 'Get up. You and I shall not confine ourselves to this lounge anymore. I got a dhoti for you. Come on, take off your trousers ... ' She yanked at his arms and led him. When they reached the door of her bedroom, he hesitated. Scurrying, she looked back and asked, 'Why?'

Though the answer was obvious, words would not form and he felt that it would be abrasive if it did find expression in words. He said, 'Let's go to the lounge. Bring the dhoti.'

In a second, she was eyeing him fiercely. Though he did not face her stare, his resolve was firm. She said, 'Soft-spoken with a gentle bearing, but within, a butcher. Calls for magnanimity to be able to pardon.' He lifted his eyes and looked her in the face. 'Enough of sight fight. Now come inside.' She pulled him inside and seated him on the bed. Opening the wardrobe, she took one out from a pair of dhotis, and pulled him up by his arm. 'Come along,' she took him to the worship chamber, had him apply turmeric from the pentad case to the edge of the new dhoti, and said, 'Prostrate before God. Do it for my sake whether you believe or not.' After he complied, she applied a pinch of vermilion to his forehead, 'Now, wear the dhoti,' she led him to her bedroom again.

Reclined on the bed, hugging him, she cooed in his ears, 'We proceeded even before my mind was fully geared up. What befell me later was because of that. Now … ' she donned a false anger, 'You … you shouldn't be so mischievous as to get me speak out everything myself. Aren't you a good boy?'

He felt immensely peaceful. Conjugation came about with mutual swapping of confidence between two souls, sans any question, answer, thought, digging, or delving. The experience was so overwhelming that he was astonished if such peace and consolation, subsiding big and small agonies, were possible in the company of a woman. Though twenty-three days' fasting had depleted the flesh in her body, the tenderness of her body was the overt expression of the tenderness of her mind. In an experience where the low-and high-pitch phonetics of compassion, humility, submission, love, authority, and sacrament coalesced harmoniously, she thawed out and quelled him.

All that he remembered of that night was that he ate and slept. When he got up the next day, it was 9. The dairyman had delivered the milk sachet. Beside it lay the newspaper. He still had not got his full complement of sleep.

That day too, leaving his office at noon, the moment he arrived in her house, she said with a wily smile, 'I am as hungry as a wolf, but I will not serve lunch until you wear the dhoti and wash your feet.' He went to her bedroom by himself, wore the dhoti that he had worn yesterday, put his pants on a hanger, washed his feet and hands, and arrived. After lunch, when they retired to bed like yesterday, she said, 'I am really angry with you.'

'I know that you are not.'

'How say?'

'You are addressing me in intimate lingo.'

'Is it? Now Sir, I am angry with you. You don't seem to be inclined to know why.' She rolled over, turning her back to him.

Though he tried to draw her to his side, she did not turn even a wee bit. He applied more pressure, but did not overdo it for that would mean aggression, and he didn't want to dislocate the ambience of the situation. He cajoled her, 'Amrita, pardon me. Tell me why you are angry.'

'For you are unable to figure out the reason for my crossness and set matters right,' she said stiffly.

He could not understand a thing. 'I concede I am a dunce. Tell me.'

'I don't want friendship with a dull-wit.' She rolled over and hid her face in the bed. It was not before he caressed her back, patted her shoulders, placated her, and thrice admitted to his mistakes that she spoke in a low voice, 'Sir, you and I have got so close. This double bed is indeed ours. Will my husband not get wind of this someday? What if he does? Or have you once enquired about the status of my relationship with him?'

He felt uncomfortable. But his mind did not draw to a definite stance whether or not he was wrong in not enquiring.

She was observing him. In the focus of her sight, a sense of guilt gradually surfaced on his face. He, however, spoke his mind. 'It had occurred to me a few times to ask. But on second thoughts, I had checked myself.'

'Why did you think it better not to ask?'

'This is a personal matter. It is one thing if you volunteered.'

For a moment, her eyes blazed like white flame. But he noticed that she controlled it. She said calmly, 'So your conclusion is to keep me aloof. Relationship to the extent required only. For everything else, it is up to ourselves. Feelings, sorrows, happiness shouldn't be shared, right?'

'Not so,' he said, but felt guilty at a deeper plane. She asked, 'Said you had a friendly relationship in Bombay. Haven't you ever so enquired about her? Or has she educated you that such queries should never be made, that they are personal and mutually exclusive? Are you exercising caution here in keeping with those tuitions?'

The quiz caused in him pain that seemed to drip from his warped face. 'Amrita, I don't like to compare you with her. I don't like to speak ill of her either. Your standing is of a high order. Never ever speak of yourself in relation to her. I will be happy if you choose not to mention about her at all,' he said.

'Sorry,' she said and let her sight fall. Then again she lied down, her face to the bed. He sat his place, abstaining from touching, nudging, or turning her by her shoulders. Silence was prodding their ears. Instantaneously, she sat up, hugged him, and said in a coaxing tone, 'Somu, I feel like sharing with someone the agonies of my troubled mind. You are the only confidant, friend. I haven't any other. Whom shall I resort to if you stay aloof saying this is personal? You ask me not to compare myself with that Bombay woman. But your conduct depicts no differentiation between her and me.'

'Sorry, I have understood my lapse. Fill me in on all of it,' he said eagerly.

'There is a saying that one pleaded to be invited for a banquet. Know? Still, I will tell you. Will you prepare two cups of coffee? It will reduce the dullness.'

'Oh, yes.' He left for the kitchen. Excitement of sorts, like they getting closer, their relationship getting intense, an aspiration to make the coffee really good....Employing all his acumen, he arrived at the proper quantity and blend, prepared the coffee, poured it into two cups that he had already placed on saucers on a tray, and brought it carefully to her without tilting and spilling. She took one sip and said, 'It is really good. I should learn from you.' He felt blessed. After both finished their coffees, he put the empty cups and saucers on the tray and placed it on the teapoy by the sofa. She reclined, placing her head on his lap, and, not facing his sight, said, 'My younger son Vikas is now four years old. When I was carrying him, earlier to four years and nine months from now, was the last time I contacted Ranganath. Ever since, I have not had him even touch me.'

'Why?' he enquired in a deep voice.

'For that, I'll have to deliberate on the background of our relationship. I'll also have to explain my views about him. I'll tell you. That is why I asked for the coffee.

'From where shall I begin? My mother died when I was six. My dad did not marry again. Now if I look back, I feel differently. Our coffee plantations and paddy fields are all my mother's estate. She is the only daughter to her parents. My dad was well educated, a BA of yore. Was handsome. My mother was not unattractive, but wasn't as attractive as my dad either. After he gave his daughter in marriage, my grandfather weaned his son-in-law from his bureaucratic job and played host to him so that he could manage the farm. My perception is that he conducted him well and with utmost respect for, till he was alive, my dad shared with me highly regarded memories about his father-in-law. With all reverence, he performed his death rites annually. He had hung grandpa's photo in the living room. At twelve, my mother lost my grandmother, who was my grandfather's second wife. When his first wife died without an offspring, he married again. When the second wife died, grandpa was fifty-three. He was not foolish to think of marriage again. He decided that he would be duly discharged of his duties when, at an appropriate age, his daughter was given away in marriage to someone who would stay back here. He had plans to train his son-in-law and hand over all responsibilities of the farm to him. An appropriate groom, my dad was available. I was born two years after my mother entered wedlock. One year later, grandpa died. He complained of stomachache. They say he was operated on for tumour, cancer possibly. That name and its dreadful implications were not very well known then. Later, my mother twice conceived and aborted. Five years after grandfather died, mother died too. Dad did not marry again.'

'How old was he then?' Somashekhar, who was intently listening, asked.

'Eight years elder to mother. Mother was twenty-four, he was thirty-two.'

'Why didn't he?'

'I have contemplated enough. There was a certain detachedness to his disposition. He would have thought, "Have been through marriage once. Why go through it again?" I think that he loved mother. I have heard the maids say that though she inherited such a vast estate, she wasn't at all arrogant or haughty, and conducted herself with love and compassion towards her husband. There could be one significant reason for he choosing to remain widowed. "Entire estate belongs to my wife. There is a daughter born of her. My responsibility is to stay here, maintain it, and hand it over to her. She probably will be adversely affected if I marry again. Even if I bring in a bride from a poor family, she is likely to get ambitious and iniquitous eventually when she assumes the housewife status" – he would have pondered thus and thought the better of marrying again. Father's morality and sacrifice are exemplary. If I think of it, even now I get tears in my eyes.' He caressed her head as he saw her eyes well up as she said this. In a minute, she composed herself and, wiping her eyes, continued, 'Know why I spoke appreciatively of father's morality and sacrifice? Who would have questioned about the revenues and expenses of that vast estate? To grow up, blossom into a wise woman, and get inquisitive – call it foolish inquisitiveness if you want to – I should attain the age of twenty-three or twenty-four. Probably married by then, I should be accordingly goaded by my "greedy" husband. In those eighteen years, could he not have amassed ten, twenty, or thirty lakh and built estates for that wife and his progeny from her? Could he not have channelled my feelings towards them by rubbing it into me that they were my brothers and sisters? He did not do any such thing.' She wiped her eyes again. He sat still, watching her face as he imagined her father's conduct and personality. All of a sudden, she got up, collected the tray from the teapoy, and went to the kitchen. When she returned after washing them, he noticed that she had washed her face and eyes. By now he had understood that when her feelings pent up, it was in her nature to indulge in some work. Returning, she placed a pillow on the frame of the cot, reclined, and continued.

'I'll come to the main issue now. Who do you think is stronger – a man or a woman?'

'In many matters, woman.'

'Don't say what you don't approve of just to appease me. Alright, I'll tell. In physical strength, gaming, and bodily power, masculinity has the upper hand. But in family matters, do you know how weak the male is? My mother is dead. Though there was no dearth of maids, manservants, and cooks, father who was managing the entire farm came to his knees when he had to run the house, the one kitchen thereat. Many men are so. So are you. Why else would you live on that awful restaurant food? That aside, my dad has a brother – my uncle, still lives. Was a small-time grocer in Sakleshpur. He traded rice, pulses, beedi, cigarettes, pencil, paper, and sundry daily needs. Small outlet. Was a high-school dropout. Before his marriage, my dad himself had, with a view to his brother's livelihood, rented the premises, advised him, funded, and floated the store. Uncle was not mean. Neither had he the ethical grit to not commit felony, come what may. He was a commoner. But his wife, my aunt Jayalakshmi is a shrewd one. Under any circumstances, she cannot do anything irrelevant. Any amount of observation would be unsuccessful at warranting a finger to point objectionably at her. But within, she would have done the damage. Still lives. You must see her once. Where and how maybe difficult to arrange, but that can wait. Whenever this aunt visited, my mother played a good host to her. At this juncture, a small property belonging to my father's ancestors was shared. My mother told my father that God had given them enough; he is not to aspire for his share but give it to his brother. That lady overtly expressed her thanks, "Sister, your heart is big."

'When she got news of my mother's death, she volunteered to visit. The moment she arrived, she hugged me firmly. Do you know what mystifying powers such physical acts as hugging, caressing the head and back, warming the skull with heavy breath have? My mother lay dead. Father was in his own grief. He had to govern the rites, make arrangements, and give suggestions. He would not let go of me, his doting daughter, who was unaware of what death was, unaware of the full meaning and implication of her mother's death, and was suffering within silently. But once aunt arrived, she hugged me, grieving, "Sister, should you not have lived on at least for the sake of this child?" Caressing my back, she soothingly stroked me all over, invoked tears in my eyes, put my face to her chest, and successfully made me wail. How would father feel seeing this? How can a six-year-old girl manage without a mother? Who would tend her? Would he not have felt that at this moment, when she had lost her mother, that God had bestowed one in the form of aunt? My aunt never let go of me. "Can such a small child, more so a girl, be allowed to witness the rites to be performed before the corpse?"'

She covered my face with the pallu of her sari and took me inside. Even as a six year old, I was well-grown. My physique and facial features matched my dad's. Though I was unwieldy, she would not let me down. She would always carry me. Besides, she would advise dad on the handling of the rites of my mother in a way becoming of the lord of a big coffee estate, declaring with tears in her eyes that it was in her fate to partake in the funeral rites of this worthy sister, sending feelers to not only dad's but even to mother's distant relatives that without Jayalakshmi, this Ramaswamy would not be able to bring up this child. In fact, love for this aunt had not originated naturally in me. If love does not manifest innately, it'll never root even if reinforced by one hundred reasons later. But by virtue of the way she held me throughout, without allowing me to tread the ground, by virtue of the influence of the exclamations of the guests that henceforth she shall be my mother, my natural feeling did not clearly emerge. At the tender age of six, can a personal feeling override such influence and outdo the canvas of the deft handling by a woman of such calibre? Can you fathom the mental state of affairs?'

Figuring out the role of the aunt in his mind, Somashekhar nodded his head implying comprehension. As she had declared that she resembled her father in looks and physique, he was extrapolating the features of her straight nose and broad, alluring face to fancy a tall handsome man. 'What developments after the cremation rites?'

'I was about to come to that. My aunt suggested, "Brother-in-law, sister's heart is big. You are well aware of her dignity and esteem. Please send word to the labourers of neighbouring estates for dinner for *Vaikuṇṭha* day," and earned dad's appreciation. After the semi-auspicious rites of the next day, when the visiting relatives take leave, she carried me to the big living room where dad was resting and said, "One visiting on such occasions should not take leave formally. But belonging in this house, such canons do not apply to me. If I leave this child behind, what shall I answer to my sister in heaven if she appears in my dreams and asks, 'Jayalakshmi, how could you walk away on my child, a motherless one?' Whatever befalls me, I'll never leave this child. I'll take her with me. Will frequently bring her here. You too will be visiting Sakleshpur from time to time. Please visit your daughter then. Here you are alone. Have to eat the cook's insipid food! I'll visit regularly and supervise. But I have to run my household too. In my absence, your brother does not evince interest in business. Have to tend the kids back home." In one minute, dad replied, "Jayalakshmi, she'll not let go of you. Who is but close to me here? All of you move in here." Aunt too pretended to contemplate for as much time and then said, "I too do not like to leave you alone. But we should all understand the situation impartially. My sister has put only this child in my lap. But this property, this estate belongs to her. It belongs to this child. What you inherited from your ancestors, you were magnanimous enough to give it to your brother. You funded the business. We are making both ends meet by running that business. Now to close that business and move here would mean to wreck an established livelihood. Moreover, what will the relatives of my sister think of me if I eat into her ancestral estate? My obligation is to tend this small one whom she has put in my lap, educate her, and give her hand in marriage to a princely man. Not to move here and laze. A wise man, you speak up." What would dad say? He bowed his head in reverence to the righteous counsel of his sister-in-law. She was repeatedly mouthing that my mother had put me in her guardianship. But mother had not put me in anybody's care. Nearer her death, she was comatose and unable to speak. This aunt arrived five or six hours after her death. Now, on recollecting the sequence of events, I can understand. Back then, I was too young to realize. Even though in his prime age, dad did not understand. Instantly, he believed that his sister-in-law comes as a mother to a motherless child, and with unselfish affection gives mother's love to the child without expecting anything in return.

'They took me to Sakleshpur. I was enrolled in a school there. Dad visited within a week. One had to go to Sakleshpur for getting farm manure, pesticides, or for repairs and servicing of automobiles, lubricants, petrol, and for other household needs. Anyway, dad went there weekly even prior to that. Not necessarily he visited his brother every time. Later, he visited twice a week. He could not stay away from his daughter for long. Also, probably he would get vexed staying all through with cooks and labourers. How can one be friends with labourers? If shown such parity, they would shed apprehension and go slack on their work. Aunt was shrewd. When dad visited, she would prepare his favourite cuisine. She would affectedly say, "You are alone, no company, I feel very sorry for you." Dad would naturally feel reassured. She too was paying frequent visits to the barn. Taking stock of the pantry, she would prepare and stock enough of curry mix, pulse meal, and other ready-to-use spice meals and would give suggestions and instructions to the cooks. Six months passed by thus. One day, dad himself declared decisively, "Jayalakshmi, let people pass any remark. You are not moving there just for the heck of it. I am sponsoring your stay for the sake of my child. Back here, this business is not running profitably. All of you just move there." Not that there was no necessity for dad to invite them, but by her words and hints, aunt had the knack and resources to create such a psychological need in my father. Eventually, aunt established herself in the estate with her husband and two children. Jayarama was my age. Leela was two years younger to him. The last child Krishnamurthy was born two years after she moved here. In that vast estate, the big house provided subsistence to many. Plus five meant nothing.

'But aunt was not here to work and eat. Rather, she was here to take hold of the management of the farm gradually. In business, you have to rely on the rank and file of supervisors and clerks. And any supervisor or clerk would invariably indulge in petty embezzlement. Such things must be given a margin. Dad would have been aware of all this. Or not! Within six months of her coming, aunt uncovered a misappropriation by the clerk and laid it bare before dad. He resigned the job in shame. She did the same to two supervisors. They too quit. "Sister's property eventually belongs to Amrita. Would it be right for me to restrict myself to the kitchen and turn a blind eye to swindlers? I too will do rounds and keep a vigil on the estate. Instruct your brother also. Let him shed his lethargy and keep an eye", she told dad. She started checking the records maintained by the junior clerk. Besides this, she would get prepared dad's favourite cuisine and mine. Weekly, she would herself apply castor oil and bathe me. On every festival, she would order silk dress for me from Sakleshpur. Saying that his eyes had turned reddish due to excess heat, she would elaborately massage dad – though at first he was hesitant – with castor oil, drawing his attention as she massaged his skull, "Look at this froth. Excess body heat causes such foaming." At first, she asked her husband to bathe him. After three or four months, she took exception to her husband's competence. "If you were capable of handling this properly, the world would have been a better place." She yanked the big copper ewer from his hands and, in his presence, bathed dad. For the lazy uncle, it was good riddance from the slog and he excused himself. Eventually, the reins of the estate management fell in her hands. The reins of the household were already in her hands by then. But shrewd that she is, she did nothing without asking or informing dad. With proper action plan, budgeting, and analysis, she would bring to dad's notice diarized works one month ahead of due date. She would add, "Without you deciding, I should do nothing." She handled it deftly such that dad should always feel that he was the lord and authority in all matters, and that she was handling everything as his representative and lieutenant. The labourers feared her. Only roster, wages, and such regular matters were within the reach of the clerks. She exclusively handled purchases, sales, and maintenance of jeeps, cars, and trucks. Picture the rest.' Amrita looked at his face and paused.

'Well then, she started swindling and amassing,' Somashekhar noted the apparent.

'I haven't the precise estimation as to when she started it or how much she stashed away and during what periods. I was still young then. Eight years later, when I was fourteen, father breathed his last. Then onwards, the entire authority and guardianship was hers. Then too, she hugged and consoled me. After the rites were performed, she took me into confidence and said, "Look tottie, I am your mother and you my daughter. Yet, you should know about estate matters. I am apprising you so that tomorrow no one pours into your ears unfounded pronouncements. Before he breathed his last, your dad instructed me that I should stay here and manage all this till Amrita grows up, is well-educated, and is given away in marriage to a gentleman. I will discharge my obligations. You too are maturing. I am telling you all this at this juncture to caution you against people speaking ill and causing rift between mother and daughter." Who else could I resort to? What did I know of the economics of the estate? How could my imagination go beyond silk, lace gown, synthetic clothes that had hit the market thereabouts, tasty food, snacks, and the soothing words "my daughter", "my eldest daughter"? Presently, I was in high school. She would send all four of us – her eldest son Jayarama, twelve-year-old Leela, six-year-old Krishnamurthy, and me – in a jeep to school in Sakleshpur. Later, she got us enrolled in a college in Hassan and rented a house there. Her own acquaintance was appointed cook. Aunt would stay three days with us in Hassan and the other three days in the estate and manage both establishments. Sunday we would all go to the coffee estate. Any day, I was good at studies. Can't say if it was intellect, brilliance, or memory power. Memory was very sharp since childhood, enough to answer just by listening to the lessons in the class; didn't have to brush up. And was reading too. Aunt kept instructing me not to fall into bad company, but to confine to my studies. I would borrow books from the library and always indulge in reading. Given the voraciousness and gamut of my reading, my eidetic memory would readily recall what topic was on what page. Nevertheless, while I was in BA final year, aunt made arrangements for my wedding. "If your mother were alive, by now you would have been two years into marriage. Even your father would have given you away in marriage by now had he been alive. He breathed his last only after instructing me accordingly. No more delay," she caressed my head and my back, brought tears to her eyes, and convinced me. Do you know who the groom was? Guess?'

'Ranganath.'

'The name's right. But can you guess who he was?'

'A nephew of your aunt?'

'Own brother! One who bought an enrolment for his undergraduate engineering course. He would visit us infrequently. She would speak in his praise. "My girl is so beautiful. Her man should love her. Besides, I will not give her in marriage to one who has an eye on her estate. *Her assets are hers, I don't need a* pai *of it.* He should so give a damn to her riches. Else, what sort of a man is he?" For two years, she had been expressing so in my presence. Six months before the precise prelude to the marriage proposal, she started announcing, "I shudder in apprehension at the thought of giving away my daughter to an unfamiliar groom. These days, you never know the character of grooms. They appear decent without, but within they would be wayward." Never giving me a chance to think, she then said, "Ranganath however is a lad of this house. If he errs, we can rebuke and discipline him. We can stipulate beforehand that he tend our girl as if she were a jasmine in the palm. You too put forth your own stipulations beforehand." Did she ever allow me to mingle with the outside world and pave way for individual intellect and independent opinion to develop? She fixed the wedding date, and in summer vacation she organized the wedding.'

'So the entire estate fell into her lineage,' Somashekhar summarized.

'When I wed, I was twenty. By the time I got my BA results, I was carrying. Aunt was happy. Wasn't her lineage poised to grow! I had come first in the entire university. But as I had spent the vacations post wedding without reading any, my intellect had dimmed. Soon after the results were announced, I went to Hassan and met my teachers. They regarded me with pride for bringing fame to the college. "What a loss if someone like you discontinued studies! If necessary, we'll apprise your mother. You must go to Mysore and pursue post-graduation." That was the first time I fancied myself as a sitting duck sans studies, and felt that it was impossible to continue to do so. "Doesn't matter if I am pregnant, I'll still go to Mysore," I turned adamant. When she understood that I was unrelenting, she ceded. She planned to rent a house in Mysore and have Jayarama, Leela, and Krishnamurthy too move to Mysore. I preferred to stay in a hostel, but she opposed the proposal. I compromised. I applied for the PG course and had to start immediately. During Dussehra or Ramnavami, dad used to visit Mysore to attend the music concerts. He had acquired this house for such holidaying and appointed a sentry. After dad passed on, aunt had let out this premise. The tenants could not be vacated at a short notice. The others could not be successfully enrolled in their respective colleges by then. I took leave, saying that I would stay in a hostel till then.

'Presently, Ranganath had landed a posting as Junior Engineer at Hemavati Dam. By then I had understood that he was suffering from inferiority complex and sort of feared me. Two months into hostel life and I understood what freedom and independent thinking were. A classmate, Shveta, got intimate. She belonged in the same Sakleshpur taluk, the daughter of a coffee estate lord. The Gowri festival intervened. We travelled together till Sakleshpur. Thereafter, she went to her estate and I went to our Soogoor Estate. After the holidays, we met again at Sakleshpur and journeyed together to Mysore. I was into the fourth month then. Shveta too was a student of literature. When the bus moved, she asked, "Don't you know what 're-evaluating a role' is?" I asked, "Under what circumstances do you ask this?" She said, "Look, I'll relate what I know. I shared with my parents that I journeyed with a classmate, Amrita d/o Ramaswamy grd/o Kapaneepathaiah of Soogoor Estate. Pals we. After two days, my mother shared this with me. Your aunt has defrauded you much. Eight miles from our estate, she has acquired two coffee estates measuring sixty acres and forty-five acres. One in the name of a son Jayarama and another in the name of another son Krishnamurthy. Totally, they cost her twenty-six lakh. Wherefrom can a woman born into a poor family mobilize such funds? Who keeps the accounts of the Soogoor Estate? Who checks? Besides, she frequently orders gold from Hassan's Venkataramana Setty Jewellers. By now, she would have had about seven to eight kilograms of it. Swear on me, never reveal to anyone that my mother said so. Just know the truth. You are being cheated. Another matter. Your husband's education was sponsored by your aunt. She bought an enrolment for him for an engineering course in Tumkur and footed his hostel bills, that too out of the resources of your estate."

'Bus was still passing through woody regions. Part of my sight was on the racing greenery outside the window. The two estates' twenty-six lakh cost, seven to eight kilogram gold's worth in money, gratis paid for securing an enrolment to the academically average brother, his hostel bills – all these as if they had occurred to somebody else someplace else, not registering precisely in my imagination, appeared like a bubble outside of the mind against the background of the green acres outside the window. After that, Shveta and I nattered, among other matters, about the university, MA, lectures, and recent ideologies in literature. Her words sank into me gradually. Yet, after having reposed faith in a person these many years, the relationship having developed on mutual vibes, isn't it difficult to instantly imagine her in different light and grasp all details in a new-fangled way? I was into my fourth month then. As the foetus grew, how could I continue staying alone in the hostel? I would feel ashamed to carry my plump belly to the classroom. Besides, during the antenatal state of a woman, the want for and emotional dependence on her mother is more. One day, my shrewd aunt brought Ranganath to Mysore. This house was not yet vacated. She had rented a house in Yadavagiri as a stopgap arrangement. "I'll not leave a pregnant girl alone in a hostel. Till the labours and post-natals, I'll stay here. In between, a couple of days I'll visit there too and take stock. I'll summon the cook Puttamma from Hassan," she said. I too hadn't the mental stamina to turn her down, what with the unfounded anxieties and fears of the first labour! But I was against her children Jayarama, Leela, and Krishnamurthy moving here and staying with me permanently. I said, "Okay, but don't disturb the lads from Hassan. Let them continue their studies there." She readily agreed. "It would be convenient if we requested the minister to transfer Ranganath to Mysore or other nearby place. Let me do it," she said. As long as she stayed here, it was impossible to think antagonistically about her. I couldn't free myself from her nurturing, her adroitness, her warm sigh and think independently. Ranganath soon relocated to Mysore. In five months, Vijai was born. Post-natals were appropriately carried out.

'In spite of all these, I was good at my studies. I stood first in the first-year MA. By virtue of my studies, participation in symposia, and my critical essays, I gradually blossomed into a different person. By and by, I came to know that engineer Ranganath, who had bought his enrolment for the BE degree, was in fact a dunce. In the liberated environ of the university, I had understood the ways of an ideal marriage, the mutual intellectual responses between husband and wife, and that without intellectual development, the nuances of mental faculties didn't develop. Aunt was here till the child was eight months old. Then she got busy with making arrangements for Leela's wedding. I was finding it difficult to pursue my studies, and at the same time tending the kid. After I weaned him from breastfeeding, she took him to the coffee estate. I too welcomed it, for I could concentrate on my studies. There were the cooks. Ranganath would find time to attend to household chores. Aunt had deposited an amount of twenty-five thousand into my bank account. I confined myself to my study, participated in debates, workshops, and the like. Topped the university. Even before the results were out, I had resolved to pursue PhD and had tentatively decided on the topic for research. You know, Somu, I could submit my thesis within two years of enrolment and got my PhD three months later ! All the evaluators unanimously recommended that the university publish my thesis,' she looked him in the face.

'I knew that you were intelligent, that you excelled academically, but I didn't know of this,' he said in appreciation.

'That's okay. I had not forgotten the fact that aunt had amassed wealth. But I hadn't allowed it to perturb me either. I thought of enquiring about it thoroughly after Leela's wedding was consummated. The finer details of her wedding dawned on me by and by. Groom from Bangalore. They insisted that the wedding be held in Bangalore. Was complied. I made enquiries. A well-to-do family. A handsome groom. Three business houses doing agency business. She had arranged the wedding in a grand manner, as would be desired by them, and decked her daughter in gold. Even the daughter of a tycoon would not be ornate with as much jewellery. As desired by the in-laws, she had displayed in a separate room the entire kitchenware meant for her outgoing daughter. Ample to start a store ! Besides, fifty grand dowry to the groom. Breakfast, dinner, instrumental ensemble music, reception – all ultimate. My aunt would talk to me very cordially. Introduced me to her in-laws as her eldest daughter. I instantly recalled Shveta's words. Not just that. I understood her deceitful ways in the matter of my wedding too. I had true sisterly feelings towards Leela. I would surely feel happy if she wed a decent groom. But I ? I was more attractive than Leela and was superior to her in academics.. She gave me away in marriage to her brother who had no economic standing, was educated from my funds, and who stood nowhere near me in looks, and thereby saw to it that my entire estate fell into her lineage. Spending my own lakhs and lakhs of money, she gave her daughter in marriage to a well-to-do groom and entitled her to enjoy the riches there. Leela is just two years younger to me. Why, she could have as well given her in marriage to her brother ! In that case, her daughter would have been married to a poor man. Her brother could not have enjoyed my wealth. I understood that this deceitful woman had cleverly stabbed me with a dagger. Swallowing this, I put up with the anguish silently through the wedding.

'All through the wedding celebrations of his niece, Ranganath moved about with an air of gratitude. I recollected the manner in which my wedding was held. I never desired for silver, gold, or diamond; not even now. It would have been conspicuous and would have attracted everyone's attention if I wore no jewellery. To avoid that, I acquiesced to wear just ear studs, a necklace, and two bangles. I didn't ask for more jewellery. Neither did aunt give. But, all through the lord of that vast estate, has not my grandfather given gold to his only daughter ? In the absence of male progeny, should not the only daughter be adorned with those jewels at her wedding ? Not once had she showed me, rather mentioned about my mother's jewel cache.

What happened of them on the death of my mother? What would their worth be at today's bullion rates? My thoughts rolled on. The in-laws left a day after the wedding, and the venue was vacated the next day. I took leave on pretext of some work and returned to Mysore. Ranganath stayed back to assist his sister. I resolved to discover the truth of the coffee estates that she had acquired, as accounted by Shveta. I hired the customary taxi and visited the Jenkal estate of Shveta via Sakleshpur. She was not yet married. I knew she would be home. She was. In her room, I spilled out my heart. Later, she discussed with her mother and father. Her father, Veerappa Gowda, appeared in the room and said, "Look madam, Shveta keeps relating every detail about you. Those who are academically very astute are less adept in transactional dealings. When and at what price your aunt acquired those properties can be verified from the records of the sub-registrar. But usually, the true amount is not shown in the deeds. The sellers of these lands disclosed the facts to me. Fifteen for one and eleven for the other, twenty-six lakh totally. If you take me to Sakleshpur, I'll arrange verification of the records." We took Shveta along and went to Sakleshpur. Veerappa Gowda paid the clerk one hundred rupees and stated the year and the approximate month, and within half an hour he held open before us a fat register. The estate worth fifteen lakh was registered for ten. One year later, the other worth eleven lakh was registered for seven. Sri Gowda got all the details noted on a slip of paper and handed it to me.

'From there, all three of us went to Shveta's house. Evening, we were having snacks in the living area when Shveta's mother asked her husband, "This girl has been greatly duped. What can be done?" "What to do? The consideration amount can be evidenced in a court of law only to the extent registered. The photo album of her cousin's wedding can be procured and an assessment can be made as to the amount spent. The expenditures on manures, spray, pesticides, and such others for the coffee plantations, the quantities that were sold to the coffee board, the rates that ruled are all verifiable. The lawyers will handle all these. Nothing, though, can be proved about the gold and silver belonging to your mother. We can bring them to submit the accounts of the production of all these years, the source of funds for acquiring those lands, and can sue them for misuse of income from the estate of a minor. It is time-consuming, alright. But we can make them pay up, albeit a lesser amount. But first, give a thought as to whether your husband would stand by you in a plaint against his sister, and what its repercussions would be on your marriage."

'That night, Shveta and I slept in her room and talked about it. Aunt's arrival for the first time on my mother's death, hugging me, consoling me, and all her words and acts that followed began appearing differently. Within myself, I had never keenly evaluated if her love was unselfish by default. Not just the thirty or forty lakh fraud, for the first time I grasped the seriousness of the deceit that she inflicted on me for life when I related to Shveta my aunt's act of giving me away in marriage to her inept brother. Shveta was compassionate. She held my hands silently. Naïve and pointless under the circumstances, she said, "Buddy, the need for parents is all the more felt at such trying times." She cared to know if I was hopeful of my husband's endorsement of my moves, and in what way it would affect our relationship. Next morning, when I left in the waiting taxi, her mother gave me a sari and a blouse cloth, besides the customary vermilion and turmeric. I reached Mysore. Ranganath was home. That night, I spilled out to him all my ire and indignation. Surprisingly – I was surprised then – I noted that human nature was the same everywhere. Any neutral person would readily say that the aunt had back-stabbed and cheated me. What will you say? Be frank,' she watched his face.

He spoke in one breath, 'Not just deceit. Extraordinary manipulation, conniving.'

'But it never occurred to Ranganath that his sister had committed any fraud whatsoever. He said that she had rather saved the estate all these years from being alienated, and in the bargain had done small favours to her children. For the first time, I felt extreme disgust towards him. Wasn't he the one who had benefitted most from the schemes of his sister? I didn't speak to him any. My reticence continued through the next two days and nights. Later, he neared and consoled me. He said that we should ask about my mother's jewellery. I too discussed with him. After three days of inner tribulation, one morning I hired the same taxi and went to my estate. Aunt greeted me with the very same phoney enthusiasm, saying, "Even for a taxi ride, it's very hot." She neared me to wipe my forehead with the pallu of her sari. It was disgusting. I said, "Aunty, enough of this pretence. From where did you arrange funds for the two estates, one for fifteen and another for eleven lakh, which you have fraudulently acquired for each of your sons? I have copies of the registered deeds. Wherefrom did you get the money for arranging Leela's wedding and the jewellery you have given to her? You spent my money to buy an engineering degree for your brother, footed the hostel bills, and then schemed to channel my estate into your lineage by tying me to him. You gave your daughter in marriage to another prosperous family, and held a grand wedding with my money. I want the accounts of the estate right from the day my dad expired." She was astonished. Just two minutes. By such time, she had donned different expressions and airs. Then she brought tears to her eyes and said, "It is nothing great to love one's daughter. Pledging by the feet of the Lord that it is righteous to love a motherless child more than I would my own daughter, I cared for you. Nothing wrong in you enquiring about the accounts, for I have handled everything as your lieutenant. As a reward for my grind and as per the directions of your father, I, my husband, your brothers, and sister have had our subsistence in this house. I haven't touched one paisa more than what we would have earned had we continued with that store in Sakleshpur. I pressurized my brother into consenting to marry you so that the husband of a motherless child should heed to our advice in the event of a hassle. Else, better proposals – of the daughter of the very Deputy Commissioner of Tumkur – were in store for him. I averted all those and pressurized him to wed you." "Aunty, I know that you have the acumen to twist the implication of any word to suit your whims. Why didn't you give your daughter in marriage to your brother?" I asked. She threw a counter question, "When I tell the truth, why call it acumen? I can witness, though with distress, something go wrong with my daughter's family, but I cannot bear if such a thing should befall you. If it were our own man, we thought, he would look after you well so that you did not wilt even a wee bit. And so I paired you two. Now tell me, has he ever spoken so as to cause pain to you? Conducted himself as to cause anguish in you?" In fact, I did not have any answer then. But my innards were howling that every word of hers was pure lie. My mind was seething in anger. I immediately got up, spat at her without spittle, hurriedly left, boarded the taxi, and urged the driver to start immediately. She did not tail me or urge me to stay back. Reached Mysore at 2:30 pm. I did not report to Ranganath of my visit to the barn.

'Eight days later, aunt arrived in Mysore around 11 am. A small bag in hand. She carried no clothing. On arrival, she headed straight to the bathroom and washed her feet. "Come here," she took me by my arms and said, "Be it mother or daughter, once doubt shows up, there should be no more dealings; only love should be. After consulting the bank and the lawyer, I have given a letter of undertaking to the bank and the coffee board. Here's a copy of it. I have stated that acting on behalf of the daughter of my brother-in-law, I was managing the Soogoor Estate. Now that she has come of age, is married, and has acquired the ability to manage her own affairs, henceforth she shall entirely manage it herself. Yesterday evening, I removed my own kitchenware, the ones we had brought with us when we moved here on your mother's death – I had kept them in a gunny bag – and had them despatched to Sakleshpur. I urged the schoolteacher who had rented our house to vacate at a short notice and got the walls limewashed. All these took up one week. From today, the entire affairs of the estate is yours. I will never step in there, but my love towards you, my daughter, shall always be. I must leave now. If I leave empty-bellied, it does not augur well for this house. So just give me a glass of milk. I will have it and leave. Let God bless you and your family." Prostrating before the deity, she took a pinch of vermilion from the pentad case and applied it on my forehead and hers, then headed straight to the kitchen, poured milk into a cup, drank it, and left hurriedly. She had an autorickshaw waiting. The moment she sat in it, he started.

'In the combat of vibes of the moment, she had defeated me. But I didn't tail her and ask the auto driver to stop. When he returned from work that evening, I reported the entire event to Ranganath. He appeared fidgety, but that expression did not linger much. Calmness returned to his face soon. Two months later, I sensed that having left from here that day, she visited him in his office and then left for Sakleshpur. It had not occurred to me earlier. Two days after this, he went to Sakleshpur to visit his sister and came back after three days. On returning, he spoke in a philosophical tenor, "Now let's not ask her to run the estate again. It is, after all, our property. A bureaucrat that I am, I cannot regularly visit there to monitor. You go and make some arrangements. Employ a manager. You should keep visiting now and then. Let us get the car here from the estate. On holidays and Sundays, I too will pay a visit." But he did not raise a single objection like "you acted in haste" or "you forget the support she provided you". I felt a bit contented. Next day, I hired a taxi and went to Sakleshpur. The bank account had a credit of just rupees sixty thousand. There was a liability of about forty thousand with the board. Went to Shveta's estate and showed my aunt's letter. "Probably, she would be pained too. Or she could also be conveying that you *put a stop to these affairs; don't rake up old matters and take them to the judiciary*. Now you must appoint a manager forthwith. If required, I will recruit one for you. Please note, however honest we may think he be, he will not stay from eating dirt. In between, you should keep visiting and checking the accounts. You should monitor during the flowering season. During picking, you must be present here. Over a period of one year, I will train you about crop management. After this much attention, his embezzlement will be under control. However much he may swindle, your estate will yield three to four lakh per annum net of expenses," he said and added, "Why don't you move to the estate? Let the manager be and your watchful eyes prevail too. Then the theft by the manager will be about one morsel in a whole meal." I gave it a thought too. Three-fourths of my thesis was complete. Shall I finish it quickly, submit, and move to the estate? Buy enough books and spend time at the estate studying them? But after moving to Mysore, my intellect had developed. Besides thinking independently, I had also the strength to live alone independently. I would just not be a watch and ward of the estate. Let a manager be, I decided, and his siphoning a bit. I too will visit as frequently as possible and keep vigil. No matter how much he thieves, it would be impossible for him to swindle like aunt did. Eventually, I adhered to Veerappa Gowda's guidance. Know how much I netted in the first year?'

'Three to four lakh is what he estimated, right?'

'Three and a half lakh. But in the previous years, the rates were lesser. But then the value of the rupee was more. Still, how much could aunt have embezzled during all those years! More of that later. Meanwhile, another backstabbing! A malice that presently was caused by Ranganath and instigated by his sister. I told you, immediately after wedding I got pregnant. I did not take a liking to it one bit. It was hindering my postgraduate studies. "Then get it terminated," he suggested. But my mind did not consent to destroying the root that had already sprouted in my womb. I badly needed the relief, but my mind wouldn't concede. I decided that I would attend the MA classes just so. Nowadays, is it not embarrassing for women to attend classroom sessions when they are carrying? Yet, I salvaged the child and attended the classes. I subsequently apprised him that neither of us were experienced before, and that we should be cautious thenceforth. The pertinent devices were his responsibility. Until I desired so, he shall not sire a second time. I had to complete the thesis first. I had devolved onto him the responsibility of exercising caution and stayed unworried. I had just assumed management of the farm. Two months later, I skipped my periods. When I asked him about it, he acted as if he knew nothing. We consulted the family physician and he told us to wait for two more weeks. I waited. By then, I had started nauseating. "Your fault," I told him. "Whatever care we take, at times it happens so, can't help," he said. When the doctor was consulted, he advised, "Isn't the elder two and a half years old? By the time the second child is born, they will be three and a quarter years apart. Better conceive in your prime. Wide difference in their ages is not advisable." Somehow, I reconciled to the issue and continued to work on the concluding portion of my thesis.

'Third month was running. One day a doubt surfaced in my mind. By then, I had got to know of Ranganath's character. I decided to take him head-on and make him sing. On retiring one night, I made him swear on God and began quizzing him. Asking him to pledge *on God, on your sister, on the children of your sister's children*, I made him swear, citing them all by their names. "The doctor said that there can be no failure in caution, your husband has purposefully failed it. There is scientific proof for this. Tomorrow, I will take you to the doctor. Else, speak the truth." Colour drained from his face. I added, "Why did you do so? Tell me the truth. If you lie, I swear on God, you shall be responsible for whatever befalls your sister, her children, her husband, and others." He spilled everything. I told you he had visited his sister. She had told him then, "Your wife may abandon you. Let her get pregnant again and one more offspring arrive. After giving birth to two children, it will not be possible for a woman to leave her husband. And nobody will so much as sniff at a mother of two." Said he had made some modification in the device he was using, with an intent to "save the family", "save me", "out of love for me". He justified that there was nothing vicious about what he did, only honest intentions and love for me. That was it. I haven't had him touch me since. Not just that, didn't sleep in a common bed. I told him to move to another room. Two days he kept hovering about me, as would an errant pet dog that keeps tottering about his master's legs. "If you don't move to another room, I will yell so as to be audible to the maid," I said. "What will they reason if man and wife take to different bedrooms?" he asked. "You obstinate, don't you open your mouth again," I raised my voice. Frightened, he left, curling his tail. That was quits. It remained so for three and a half months.

'By that time, he was transferred to Channapatna. "Look, transfer order is served," he showed the letter on returning from work that day. "He that wants to keep his job must move on. Why ask me?" I said. He spoke no more. Though in the same house, I had not talked to him in that three and a half months. If he asked something, I used to answer him in satirical, scornful, and sharp questions. Would not respond directly. He left with his packed suitcase and holdall. He would write to me now and then, stating that marriage meant amity, harmony, and mutual cooperation, and would add lessons in ethics too. I never once replied. He was apprehensive of visiting on his own. Didn't. If he still came, I wouldn't talk to him. I myself attended to the post-natals. There were the cooks. Had brought the estate car here. When I went into labour pain, escorted by the cooks, I drove to the hospital and got myself admitted. I went into labour sans the pretentious love of any woman.' Having said this, she recalled something and looked at her watch, 'Oh, 4:45. Susheelamma had asked me to pick up the children early today because she wants to go shopping. If I dropped her at the marketplace, she would save time, poor thing. But now, I can't stop without sharing an important matter.

'I told you that the revenue from farm produce that year was three and a half lakh. I swelled in rejoice. The deceit that she committed against me, to hell, let her eat the fruit of her deeds. I was trying to forget it in munificence. After earning another year's revenue, I contemplated pulling down this structure and build it in a novel way. Not that I had pardoned her. I hadn't pardoned Ranganath even. I had decided to put them behind me, stay away from them, tend my children on my own, evince interest in studies, and live contentedly. After I gained experience in managing the farm, I even estimated that the revenue would touch four and a half or even five lakh. Three months passed by thus. One day, I received a registered envelope by post. It was redirected here through my estate. It was from the Sakleshpur bank. My heart splintered on reading it. "You have till date not repaid the principal amount of the loan you have availed. You have however been repaying the interest regularly. But this year, though by now it is three months since you harvested, sold, and realized the proceeds, you have not paid the interest. If you do not remit an amount of Rs. 3,22,350 within fifteen days of receipt of this notice, we will be constrained to take recovery measures against you and take possession of the estate." A caution notice! I couldn't get the head or tail of it. My heart seemed to split. It was 11:30 in the morning when I received the letter. What loan is this? Who borrowed? Can only be known by visiting the bank. In that advanced stage of pregnancy, at 2 pm, I drove to the estate along with Vijai. The new manager verified the accounts and said, "Interest has been paid in the previous years." But he could not get the details of the loan. Stayed there overnight, and went to Sakleshpur next morning along with the manager and enquired with the bank. For purpose of development of the estate, aunt had borrowed thrice. Before his death, father had himself signed the mortgage and borrowed three lakh. He had stated that the rains had failed and he needed funds to run the show. In all, a liability of nineteen lakh was outstanding. I got wild and yelled at the manager. He said, "Madam, bank is a public organization. Its duty is to recover the disbursed loans with interest. If you feel cheated, please take action against the offenders. I have been here for just four months now." I felt stymied, but then I told him that I was speaking to an institution, not to an individual.

'I headed to aunt's place. She had said that she had moved to Sakleshpur. When I arrived there, I saw that though she had occupied that house, she was presently living in the estate that she had acquired for her youngest son. I enquired its whereabouts and drove on. Didn't take the manager along. The moment she saw me, she said, "Ahoy, my doll! Did you drive by yourself in your advanced stage of pregnancy! If you had sent word, Krishnamurthy would have fetched you." She hugged me and then picked up Vijai. "Oh, the journey has withered this tot." It was she who had tended him during his childhood. The moment he saw grandmother, his face beamed. Holding his face firmly to her chest, she started fondling his head and back. "I was about to visit Mysore myself. How can you help yourself with the labour and post-natals?" she asked. "Aunty, enough of pretentious affection. Bankers have served notice that the interest remains unpaid. On enquiry, they say that nineteen lakh loan is outstanding. How did it all happen?" I asked. "First, come in and have lunch. Let me prepare some hot pudding for this kid. Let's talk later," she tugged at my arm. "I will not step into your house. First answer me," I said. Oozing patience and affection in her face, she said, "Dear daughter, just because you, a young thing, rebuke me, would it be proper for me to rebuke you in retaliation? Be seated on this bench. I will make two pancakes for you. Do you think that estate management means just amassing money and hoarding it in a bank? There will be seasons when the crops fail due to failure of rains, and also years when they fail due to excess rains. Yet, expenses like manure and pesticides must be incurred. The labourers must be paid wages. When these pile up, if we don't borrow, we will have to sell the estate. You will also experience it. Have patience." I immediately queried, "Where did you get the kind of money to buy this estate?" "Know from what sources I have borrowed for this? On attaining majority, you would rightly take the reins of Soogoor Estate. Your brothers! What about their livelihood? So I borrowed and established this. If it rains optimally, if crops are not infected by diseases, if yield is good, and if he gets a good price for the produce, he will run it. Else, he will dispose of it and wash dishes at a restaurant. Their lives shall run according to your blessings and good wishes. Now, come in and have the pancakes," she once again tugged at my arm. I felt revulsion. "You are a shameless one," I said, took hold of Vijai, dragged him along, plonked him in the car, gunned the engine, and returned to my estate. At least, the interest has to be paid to the bank first. I wrote out a cheque. Manager said, "Madam, if you write a cheque for this amount, nothing will be left in the account. What shall we do for wages, petrol, spray, and other expenses week after week?" "I'll make other arrangements for that. Now let this interest be paid." I sent the cheque and went to Shveta's father's estate. I felt that he was the only person who could assuage my anxiety, anger, and frustration and guide me. But he had left for the USA to visit his son. He, his wife, and daughter, all three. Away for three months, I was told. Helpless, I returned to Mysore. Know how spent I was? Advanced pregnancy, the excruciating drive, the mental agony, the disappointment, and the helplessness. In whom shall I unburden all this? Whose support shall I beg?'

'Didn't you inform Ranganath?'

'Forgetting that he was a sister-bred dog, I called him. He was still in Channapatna. He came scampering. "Your sister's deceit knows no bounds. She has silently embezzled nineteen lakh. What shall we do now?" I asked. He hung his head, as if in deep contemplation. "At least, now can you understand her deceit?" I said in a contesting tone. Unable to answer, he stayed silent. "Speak up," I urged him. "She would have usurped some, as one would lick one's fingers after extracting honey from a beehive. But it is possible that crops would have failed due to shortage or excess of rain. When he was alive, if your father had borrowed three lakh, does it mean that he has deceived you? These matters have to be discussed patiently." He spoke as if placating me. Now that he cited my dad as precedence, confusion surfaced in me that aunt's words could be true. But the inkling deep within that she was a liar, a fraud, could not be unseated. In a little while, I got the feeling that this husband was supporting the perpetrator and not me, the victim of the deceit. That night, he stayed back and ventured to enquire about the nursing home I had arranged for. "I will safely deliver and raise the seed of deceit that you and your sister have sowed in me. Don't worry," I said. He put down his head like a chastised dog. Let me come to the important matter. I enquired with the coffee board. They consented to lend one lakh for maintenance purposes. Incur the daily maintenance with that, pay the interest to the bank out of the produce, this is how I am running it till now. Here, the salary I earn in college is feeding the family – myself and my children. Without funds for even a limewash or colourwash, with just an asphalt and cement patch-up to this leaking house, I am toiling and just about grappling. Oh, it's 5:10!' Looking at her watch again, she hurriedly got up.

'Is Ranganath still at Channapatna?' Somashekhar asked.

'No. About a year back, he came here and said that he was transferred to Krishna Upper Bank Project, four hundred miles farther. "Transfers are typical of the bureaucracy. No necessity to report it to me," I said. He hung his face like a rebuked dog.'

Having said this, without changing, she just stood before the mirror, tidied her hair, took the keys and vanity bag, and started to leave. He hurriedly put on his trousers and shoes. 'Should come at 12:15 tomorrow,' saying so, she exited, opened the gate, and boarded the car. He gunned his scooter.

That day, he had to work in his office till 10 in the night. He felt that it was improper for him, from the perspective of advancement in his career, to absent from work four and a half hours every afternoon when the business would be in full swing. Memories of Bombay returned. Likewise, I would absent from work there twice weekly. But I would compensate it by working till 9 or 10 pm each day. He recalled that in his absence, Naveen was there to attend to it. Here, I am alone. As he contemplated on skipping those afternoon visits and … barring that, which other time is available? That her kids would be home proved a deterrent. The thought of changing the weekly holiday from Sunday to Monday provided a piece of a solace that, besides saving a full working day, the clients would be benefited too. At 10, he went to the restaurant and had his cold supper. When he reached home by 10:45, besides the feeling that he had endeared himself more to her, his mind was filled with compassion towards her. How sad she is! Being an architect and having supervised the construction of houses and apartments in a prosperous city like Bombay, and having heard and known about the deceit and backstabbing among brothers, sisters, and relatives for the sake of property, he was not much taken aback at the ways of Amrita's aunt. It couldn't hurt me, an outsider, one who listens to it as one would a story, but what an onslaught for her who has faced the deceit! Mulling over that, he reclined. Besides money matters, giving her away in marriage to her (aunt's) brother and hastening her second conception on sensing her disposition! On recalling these, he felt that this was not just mean, it was crime rather. Sleep eluded him. He closed his eyes and tried to sleep even as he pictured that on that large cot in her bedroom, she would be lying alone. A section of his mind began cogitating that she was in need of sincere friendship, and he shall give her that. He even quizzed himself if it was possible at all for him to insincerely associate himself with anyone. In a short while, he fell asleep.

Next afternoon, no sooner had he arrived there than she seized him by the arm and led him to her bedroom. Then untying his shoelace, she removed his shoes, seated him on the cot, held his hand, and said, 'Somu, I think my subconscious has the ability to detect truth. I discovered this morning that my surmise about a particular matter was true. Know how delighted I was?' She was gliding over a ripple of glee. Before he could ask what it was, she went on, 'But I won't tell you, for if I do, you will become headstrong. If, arrogantly, you then stiffen your neck and hold your face towards the sky, how shall I reach up to it?' She pulled his head towards her and planted a long kiss on his lips. 'See, how I tame you? However headstrong you get, I have the power to subdue you and make you play to my whims. Do you agree?' Through his sight, he conveyed approval. 'Swollen-headed even at that. If you mouthed that and said, "Yes, I agree", your pride would be discounted. Come, let's chat while we dine.' She rose, brought his dhoti, and held it before him.

Placing the chairs very close, as they dined sitting contiguous to each other, she said, 'A colleague of mine, a physics lecturer named Jalaja, aged forty-five, is the daughter of one B.K.N., your teacher in engineering college who was known as "structure teacher". Remember him?'

He said, 'Yes, yes, a very nice teacher. At least, he has helped me a lot. I was a weekly victuals guest at his place.'

'Is it? Share with me the incidents that occurred during your stint there.'

'Nothing much. He used to get me all the books I wanted. And during *Gokulāṣṭami* festival, they would give me loads of snacks.'

'Is that all? I will tell you one other matter, listen. Once, when the teacher was away for about a fortnight, you were asked to lodge in their house. You would retire to his study upstairs. I was told that you had the liberty of picking up any book from his collection arranged in a shelf; an open shelf, not even covered with glass. One night, when you pulled out an old book from the inner stack of the shelf, something heavy packed in an old piece of cloth dislodged. You opened it only to see a four-stringed gold chain. You replaced it, waited till dawn, brought it to the attention of your teacher's wife, and said, "Mother, see, this was here. When I retrieved the book, it fell." Is it true?'

He recalled it and confirmed.

'At that time, you still hadn't a victuals host for two days in a week. Even in those days, the chain would have fetched five or six thousand. If you had quietly taken it away, no one would have questioned. Nobody would know about it. The teacher was a charitable person. Keeping under wraps from her husband, the thrifty wife would get jewellery made for her marriageable daughters. A sister of the teacher, whenever she visited her brother's, would check all the containers in the house for things squirreled away by her sister-in-law. Hence, on the eve of one of her visits, she had stashed it away in some place where it would never draw attention, under that old book, which the teacher never read. Even if you had stolen it, she would not be able to declare it to anyone. If she did, her husband would have taken exception to it. "*How come you ordered it without my consent?*" She would have presumed that that sister of her husband stole it. "Such an honest boy," Jalajakshi's mother had told her. Wonder why this matter came up? They want to build a house, and recommending you, I said that I know you well and that you are an honest person. "Oh! That Somashekhar? Even as a student, his hands were clean," they said, related the story of the gold chain, and asked me, "Give me his office address and phone number.

I will have him design and also supervise the construction of the house." You have a new order. What percentage commission will you give me?' she eyed him teasingly and, after about half a minute, with an emotive gaze, she said, 'Somu, know how proud I feel that such a person, honest by birth, is my friend!' She held him with her left arm around his neck. He was still thinking about the teacher who had helped him, and the teacher's wife who had fed him.

After lunch, as they reclined together in bed in each other's arms, she said, 'Look, what I related to you yesterday, I hadn't confided all that in anyone. Hadn't found a confidant that shared my wavelength. Shveta is married and has moved to America. Besides sharing a common wavelength, if a confidant turns out to be an honest person, know how soothing it is? Relief, as if the other just voluntarily took the load off me and transferred it to his shoulders. Ever since Jalajakshi told me all that, I feel I should disclose everything to you.'

He was naturally pleased at the appreciation. But when anybody spoke appreciatively of him, to encourage it or to get interested in it was, in his opinion, disgraceful. Immediately, he deviated from the matter and asked, 'Look, this question has been nagging me since yesterday night. Towards Ranganath, you nurse despise. But you had once said that he was present at the christening of Vikas. Remember? Why did you invite him?'

Instantly, she turned contemplative. Feelings of regret, wrath, and dejection wrung her face. Though he felt poignant for spoiling her good mood by that question, justification surfaced too that he could not have been aware that such a query would dwindle her feelings. 'If you are not disposed, it's okay,' he said even as he enviously tidied a shock of tress that was fondly caressing her left cheek. But she replied patiently, 'That is the trouble with me. I simply can't stand Ranganath, brook not his very sight. Towards his sister, I nurse a smouldering hatred. Maybe I'll have avenged her if I shoot her with a revolver! All the same, my mind gets soft towards them too, probably owing to my traditional temper or beliefs. A child is born. Shouldn't the mother and father perform the christening in unison? I wrote to him immediately. I wrote to his sister too. Probably due to the enervation from post-natals, my mental stamina had diminished. How much more shall I bear their aloofness? Could also have been an inner desire to check people from presuming that I am abandoned by my husband or I have abandoned him. When the priest instructed that I consecrate the feet of elders, I complied by prostrating at her and uncle's feet, showering their feet with consecrated grain. I have no reservations whatsoever about prostrating at uncle's feet, for he is not of sly nature. After the rites were consummated and while I dined, I repented thinking why I assumed all these rituals. Without him, had I lighted a lamp before the deity and whispered the name into my child's right ear, would he not be christened? Coherence is not mine.

'Unstable brains mine. That is my weakness. For having invited them, I came to know about something else that would stab me from within. She had taken with her my elder child Vijai when he was eight months, for he would prove a hindrance to my studies. Whenever I visited there to see my son, Ranganath would also accompany me. Till the fraud about the second pregnancy was uncovered and he got transferred, father and son were in touch. Vijai was with his grandmother till I told her in the face about her fraud, took control of the estate soon after, and brought him here. Though four, he has not forgotten his father; intimacy with granny has not faded. During the christening ceremony, he stuck to his dad. Within half an hour of her arrival, he moved to his grandmother's lap. She nevertheless has the uncanny knack of conning anyone for that matter. During those two days, employing her skills, she has rubbed malice into his head. Shortly after his brother's christening ceremony, one day Vijai started wailing that he wanted to see granny. "Why, what bounty has she showered on you? What have I failed to do?" I wheedled, hugged, and asked him. What says he! "Granny loves me very much. She is the one who brought me up. You don't love me. You carted me out when I was still very young so that your studies wouldn't be hindered. Granny brought me up." Hitherto, he had not said any such thing. Who goaded it into him? During the christening ceremony, while I was busy with the guests and rituals, this aunt had sown it in him. Another day, he said, "I want to see dad. It seems that you have told him to stay away." Is it possible to pierce a sharper thorn in my heart? Is it possible, tell me?'

He nodded solemnly.

'It was then that I came to know of my foolishness. I decided that if I have to clear his mind of the notion that his mother didn't love him, that he was a hindrance to her studies, I must strive greatly, else I would lose my children. Since then, after bringing them home in the evenings, I would spend every minute with them, play with them on their terms, chide them in their slang, narrate tales, hug, kiss, provide different snacks each day, and get them new dresses. At times, I would feel ashamed that the persuasion for me to love my children is the contest with her! Also, I feel anxious that with this amount of pampering, the children, fearless and uncontrolled, may go wayward from lack of discipline and restraint. The younger one once asked – *why dad doesn't take us with him*! How did such words stem from his mouth?' She fell silent and looked downcast. Though her eyes were open, it seemed that she was meditating blind-sighted for more than ten minutes. After that, as if she spoke to herself, but also audible to him, she said, 'I am squandering all my time to earn the love of these children. Studies, research, development of intellect and knowledge have all come to a standstill.' He observed her face keenly and understood that these words, more than all others, had manifest deep within her. He hugged her and gently caressed her back, as if placating her. For some time more, she continued to be deeply introspecting.

A little later, she turned agile. Hugging and invading him, she said, 'I spent all yesterday relating my grief-stricken story. Even today, the same thing. Forget it. If you are with me, I get the strength to face anything. For the first time in my life, you have instilled confidence in me by bestowing love and sincere un-pretextual love. When we are in concert, no other matter than our love shall be discussed. Okay? If I broach something else, you should slap well on my cheek. And if you broach some other topic, your cheek … ' She started kissing him provocatively. He found it difficult to adapt and respond instantaneously, as if by throwing a switch. But neither inclined to excuse himself or to let her down, he oriented himself with effort and counteracted. Invasive feelings swept him too and he crushed her. She succumbed to him as if her only means of contentment was to be in a state of surrender and total relinquish. The turbulence and internal conflicts within her receded, and feelings of happiness and calmness surfaced in her body and face. He, too, felt a sense of triumph besides contentment. With compassion and gentleness, he held her in a supportive embrace as a mother would her child.

When both of them woke up, it was 4:30 pm. Glancing at his watch, he urged her, 'Oh! Get up, get up. You have to fetch the children.' She said, 'Today Susheelamma has nowhere to go. At least another hour I should sleep so. You too close your eyes. Shouldn't stir even so much as an inch. I will leave by 6 pm. Neelakanthappa would put to ease visiting clients and retain them till you turn up. You display on the board that henceforth your timings shall be 9 am to noon and 6 pm to 9 pm. Now close your eyes. Tell me what you see when you close your eyes? What picture?' she concealed his head in her bosom.

'Amrita appears. Barring her, no other form cometh,' he whispered.

'Now even if you lie, it is pleasant to hear. But because you are an honest man, I feel like casting off even the heavens.' She closed her eyes as if to relish her words. In this intensity, minutes froze. Sensing that she too was congealing time, not inclined to defrost it, he who had holed up in her bosom stayed still, taut and with bated breath. A little later, she spoke up. Now, not only was her voice overt, explicit were inquiry and analytics than feelings.

'Somu, your words *nothing other than Amrita is visible to closed eyes* in themselves are more sticky-sweet than honey. But I am your second woman, according to you, and I believe your words.'

He felt that this was brusque crosstalk. Even when intimate, such an enamouring state cannot be achieved by design. But when it dawns for once, she thus spills an acrid droplet. He chose not to answer. He attempted showing his disagreement by remaining silent. After a minute, she said, 'Displeased? In that case, let's not talk.' He said nah. 'I have no intent to displease you. You are an honest man. I will believe that you had no affair other than with that Bombay woman. Still, I am your second woman. Will not the feelings that you get in my company, the feelings that I impart you be comparatively evaluated in some corner of your mind? Will you surely not feel that in some aspect, the Bombay woman was more fulfilling than Amrita? Disagreeing with this would be to belie human nature. Speak out the truth.'

He just couldn't lie. It was impossible for him to lie. He said, 'The experience with you is deep and unique. It is despicable to compare this with anything. Please do not ask such questions henceforth.'

'My tottie,' she hugged him firmly, kissed, and said, 'Know how perked up I get when I hear your words? Unique depth! For even those who have done their post-graduation in literature and teach it, such expression is not easily possible. But even in that Bombay woman would an equal measure of unique depth be experienced. You yourself have declared that she would in between quote bits from ghazals and buoy you over ripples of romance and passion. The poems that I have read are pale in comparison to the ghazals. Besides, I do not bring up any verse or literary bit of someone else, their brilliance notwithstanding, during our intimate union. In that case, how can the depth and magnitude of that pleasure be present in me?'

'I said that you were unique, for you express everything in your own intense silence without quoting someone else,' he said in his justification.

'Meaning that comparison sets in in that mind of yours. It goes on. Why lie that it doesn't?' she caught him unawares.

He felt angered. This was a woman who, after preparing delicious pudding, stirs it with a broom. He weighed against the thought of feelings of goodwill being meagre in her. Didn't utter anything though. But being aware that silence would amount to accepting her accusation, he said, 'I remain speechless for I think that silence is more dignified. Silence does not mean that I concede what you said.'

'Yes, *I* lack dignity,' she shot back. Slackening her grip, she let go of him, turned her back, moved to the edge of the big cot, and lay apart, leaving an empty space of two feet in between. He contemplated why she conducted herself thus. He felt like getting up and leave. But rise or exit from there he just couldn't. Realizing that some unknown force bound him to her as to render departing impossible, he was incensed at that force. Yet, neither taking it out on her nor rolling over towards her, he just lay. Time once again got very dense, and motion seemed to cease. Mind began deliberating on time – the beginning, currency, and terminus of time. Will the terminus of time be thus? This question led to further musings. Does the terminus of time indicate the denseness of feelings? In which case, is time delineated by feelings? Mind grew fully introspective. Heartbeat had subsided so low that it were impossible to be heard even if his palms were surrogate ears. Even its pace seemed to have slowed. Is there any nexus between time and heartbeat? Another question surfaced and his brain was muddled by dense feelings, heartbeat, and time. All of a sudden, she sat up at the same spot where she lay – two feet away from him –and spoke in a manner of solemnity, 'Look sir, a man can indulge in whatever he desires, in whichever way he likes. Loss of purity for a woman is a damage that she can never set right. My relationship with you has rendered me weak and crippled me so as not to face up to Ranganath. Understand?'

For a moment, her words did not appeal to his intellect that was already muddled up in the melee of confusing feelings, but soon their undercurrent stung him acutely. Though he felt like replying, he checked himself and tried to retain calmness on his face. She stared at him with fierce eyes. He did not put down his gaze, neither did he stare back fiercely. Obdurately, he donned serene looks and continued facing her gaze. She got wild. More wild. 'Can understand what's going on in your mind, man. In your sight, I can notice the feeling of disdain, of belittling, belittling even inferior to a street dog. Disdain and belittling feelings within, why that exterior mask of serenity? Call a spade a spade,' she said aloud contentiously.

'Why accuse me falsely?' he asked gently without raising his voice.

'Yes, *I* lie. *I* am a liar. You alone speak the truth. You are an honest man. You declared it. It shows your arrogance, ethical arrogance,' she suddenly got up, went to the bathroom, and slammed close the door. Washing her face, she emerged in two minutes and combed her hair, tidied the pleats of her sari, took her vanity bag, and stepped into her slippers. Realizing that he still lay in bed, he hurriedly got up, put on his trousers, wore his socks and shoes, took his helmet, and left. She did not speak to him. He too didn't speak any. Just exited, opened the gate, and, amidst the barking of the dogs, he gunned his scooter. By then, she was opening the door of the car.

When the car arrived, Vijai and Vikas, who were playing with Susheelamma's children, were in no mood to abandon their play and get in the car. How can a game of squares be abandoned? The two played on as if they had not noticed the car. It pierced her heart. Yet, without calling out to them, she stayed glued to the steering.

In a short while, Susheelamma emerged. On seeing the car, she neared the children and said, 'Vijai, Vikas, look, mother is here.' They still did not turn their attention away from the game. Susheelamma approached the car and said, 'Come in till they finish their play.'

Locking the car, she entered the house and said cheerfully, 'While visiting your home, they have no other wants. Aren't even demure in their teacher's presence.'

Susheelamma said, 'Isn't it today's perception that there should be no unease between the teacher and students?' Announcing coffee, she headed to the kitchen.

'No, no. I just had it. If I have more, will not get sleep at night.' When she declined the coffee, Susheelamma returned to the chair opposite her.

'You may contest it, but surely children imbibe the qualities of their parents. It is not at all difficult to babysit your children. They are naughty, but not brattish. Besides, they are very bright!' Susheelamma started a chat.

She felt happy on hearing the teacher speak appreciatively of her children. 'However astute they are, isn't the development of the intellect dependent on able tutors? It is their good luck to have you as their tutor.' With a smile on her face, she sincerely repaid the appreciation.

'Look, if children are to be of composed nature, parents too, especially the mother, should be calm and collected. My sister-in-law's daughter studies in the college where you teach. She opines, "Pleasantness is synonymous with Amrita madam. She always wears a contagious smile and keeps us cheerful. However much din be in the classroom, and answers not be forthcoming to the questions, she never gets annoyed. No other lecturer has her patience. Only those who have happiness and serenity within them can impart it to others." She even quoted a few lines from a verse that were pertinent to you.' As Susheelamma related this, Amrita recalled her attendance and conduct at college. All other teachers would, at times, lose their patience. She, on the other hand, hasn't once lost her composure. She took pride at that capstone of her career.

A clapping sound was heard from outside. Having got wind that the game was over, Susheelamma went out and found the children getting ready for another round. 'Vijai, mother is waiting. You shall play tomorrow. Now leave.' The teacher's words propelled the children towards the car. On the way home, enquiring them both about the day's lessons, the new song that was sung at school, a new story told by a teacher, Vijai's friend Rajiv, Vikas' friend Bharat, she drove on, maintaining both their enthusiasm even keel. When they were home, she gave them both semolina laddus that Puttamma had prepared that morning and Bournvita to gulp it down, enquired and learnt the rules of the game of squares, drew the lines with chalk in the backyard of her house, as directed by them, and challenged them to play with her. 'Mom, it needs four players,' Vijai protested.

'I will play for two, come on,' she challenged him.

'It is okay for small boys. Adults don't know how to play,' he objected.

'Teach me once. I will learn. Else, I will learn it from your teacher tomorrow. Now come, teach me,' she urged him.

'It is boring for us to play with you,' he shot back.

Realizing that her children were resisting her, she felt stabbed within yet again. It was difficult to suppress that pain and exude serenity on her face. Still she coaxed, 'Vikas darling, you come over, teach mom.' In fact, Vikas was not fully conversant with the technique and rules of the squares game. Besides, Vijai and Chandru, the elder son of the teacher, were the ones that really played. Vikas and Shanta, the younger daughter of the teacher, played freestyle and were reckoned only as players, not as contestants. So the mother had to plead with Vijai alone. Instantly, she felt that the game could be modified to accommodate three players. But the children did not concur. When she invited them for a game of shuttle badminton, they turned her down.

After some time, Vijai said, 'Of all places, you have moved here where there is no company for play.' She could tolerate it no more. She went into the house apace and sat alone on the sofa in the lounge. Eyes got taut and tears flowed. Even though her sight blurred, she did not wipe the tears.

Having provided nibbling biscuits, milk, and cooked millet-flour balls warmed in boiling water to the dogs, and allowing them to loiter in the house for a while, she fed the children and munched on something herself. Though mind and feelings had sunk to the very depths and even blotted out, she broached this matter and that while dining with the children and kept the conversation going. Her mind had gone numb. Yet she led them to their cot, sat beside them, and told the story of the Moon and the Poseidon. Children need explanation, details, and narration. Abound in melancholy, her mind and intellect not in a state to embellish the narrative, it was becoming torturous to indulge them. This is not the first time this is happening to me. How many hundreds or thousands of times have I been thus assailed ! Yet, each time it seems that the torture was never before crueller than presently. Despite this affliction, without showing any signs of unhappiness, seated or lying beside them, she was to wheedle them and delineate the story till sleep pervaded them. And so that they vibe well with it, she had to create emotive aspects about it. *What an insipid chore this !*

Quite sometime after stretching the Poseidon tale, the children slipped into sleep. Quietly, she put off the light, turned on the dim red night lamp, went to the lounge, and sat. She felt that she would be relieved of her pain if she cried from within, so as to fragment the silence inside the house, outside, atop the hill, and in the skies.

But then she understood that tears were not benevolent enough to emanate when required and desired. They can be avoided when they issue forth, but it is impossible to educe them just so. When, for the first time, she learnt of this trait of tears, what a peculiar nature of this torture! She reflected that people – till now even she – had not understood that tears not just meant the heralding of woe but also a means of alleviating them. Thus engaged, the mind had a reprieve from the woe. But that was only transitory, and grief set in again. God, any amount of any sort of bodily pain can be endured. Don't you know that the torture of this pain and grief within is truly appalling? She got enraged and decreed that the persona called God, or rather the almighty called God should be summoned and asked to clarify. By questioning His motive of inflicting such agony, He should be burdened with the onus of explaining. Mind slipped elsewhere. As if recalling something, she got up and went to her bedroom, unlocked the chest by her cot, drew it, and extracted the revolver. Releasing the latch and priming it for discharge at the touch of the trigger, she pointed its nozzle to her right temple and held it pressed there. No need for tears or dependence on the notion called God or whatever. And as she sensed that herein lay all relief, self-confidence set in. She decided that she would not cry and not even wish for tears. The interlude between depressing the trigger and relief from all agony is just a millionth of a second. In fact, there isn't any time interval at all. Her confidence received a boost that the grand finale was in her hands. The nozzle of the revolver still pressed to her right temple, she moved over to the dressing table with firm strides, threw a switch with her left hand, and in the light that instantly flooded, she looked at her face in that fifty-year-old mirror. Not only was absent the self-confidence that she had presumed, she felt that her face was a carcass, void of essence. She stood her place, observing it for quite some time. She understood that when void overcame her, she was truly dead. Yet, why do I labour futilely to die, when there is hardly any interlude between the trigger and death? Her thoughts drifted. When life's meaning is fully wrecked, when the only relieving way out is death, though stationed at that very threshold, why do I vacillate without simply crossing over? As if in ratification of that question, the vent assumed the clear-cut outline of the nozzle of the revolver. When, at once, it occurred to her that instead of aiming the revolver at the temple, sublime would be the devouring of death by inserting the nozzle in the mouth, pointing it towards the palate, and then squeezing the trigger, she felt exulted as would a scientist who discovered something novel. Moving the revolver from the temple and putting it inside her mouth, she watched her face in the old mirror. Still the same void on the face, the lustre of a corpse. Felt weary. She removed it from the mouth, put off the dressing-table light, and sat on the cot. The revolver was still in her right hand. After quite some of sitting idle, as if reminiscing something, she pulled herself up, walked up to the window, slightly drew the curtain aside, and peered out.

Moonlight. Pallid, melancholic moonlight that has soused the universe in sorrow and anxiety. Should go out and see, should stride the world that is succulent with sorrow. What with the artificial comfort of indoors cosseted by secure doors? Instantly, she took the keys to the house and the garage, locked the main door, opened the garage, drove the car out, closed the garage and the gate, and steered in the direction of the hill. Neither did she put on the floodlights, nor stop anywhere in between. In the murkiness of the melancholic moonlight, the road was blur and she drove slowly with the trepidation of the second gear. With the expanse of the gorge of grief to the left, she scaled the gradient while surveying the incessant distressing terrain. Leaving Mysore to the northwest, as she drove in the direction of the sleepy southeast that, sans a single streetlight, was distorted by the grief of vapid moonlight, she had presently scaled three-fourths of the hill. Having parked the car, as she got out and watched the warped ravine, her mind drew a parallel with the shape of a two-day old corpse. With that metaphor in mind, as she kept watching at length the amorphousness before her, the pain within her instantly intensified. Pain that contorted and wrung the face. God! Where is reprieve? This place is ideal. Nobody will be in any doubt whatsoever. I have arrived in my car, it will stand parked here, and my own licensed revolver does away with the need for a note addressed to the police. If it were home, the children would hear the gunshot, wake up, witness the gory scene in that forlorn suburb, shriek, and all through their life, the stigmatic horror of their mother's death by shooting herself in the mouth! In comparison, here, to this side where the house is totally obscured by the hill, where nobody can hear the sound....While she surmised that this was an ideal place on all counts, she was disappointed when she realized that she had left behind the revolver on the cot. A resolve formed to get back into the car, put on the floodlights, and, in spite of the meandering descent, drive at fifty miles and return with the revolver. As she boarded the car and gunned the engine, a thought occurred to her that for stifling out life, a revolver wasn't the only resort. In every hill, there will be a suicide spot. A hundred-foot steep rock is enough. Where is such spot on this hill? She couldn't recall. The spot behind the temple where she would occasionally watch the sunset came to her mind. But there may be people there. The sound of a car at this hour! If anyone noticed a lone woman alight and head in that direction, they begin enquiring as to who, what, why! The very thought brought fear in her, making her shiver. She shut off the engine and simply sat, hands resting on the steering.

A little later, she got out of the car and started looking at the moon that seemed to embody grief. Slowly, her sight shifted upwards. The moon trudges, bearing all the grief of the likes of me. His grief is greater than mine. The tears I shed in a lifetime, he spills out the same as moonlight over the whole universe in about a minute and then wanes. His loneliness is precisely the same as mine. For quite some time, she stood observing that. When her neck started to ache, she lowered it. She could stay there no more. Should go some place. Where to? If she drove the car further on, she would end up by the temple and the eat-outs where many people would be milling about. As she loathed that idea, the revolver that she had left behind on her cot struck her mind. If one of the boys woke up, sought me out 'Amma, amma', and took it! It is loaded and ready, my! Anxious, she quivered and sweated. By now, what if they have already meddled with it! Her limbs started to tremble and she was nonplussed. Though her intellect decreed that she immediately rush home and verify, her feet would not heed the instruction. She strove and steadied herself, got in the car, put on the floodlights, and drove speedily at thirty or forty, not possible any faster along these curves, and descending the hill, my god, how far! Finally reaching home, having lent her voice to the barking dogs, she left the car by the kerb, ran to the door, unlocked it, and, heading straight to her bedroom, found it wide awake on the cot awaiting her arrival. Locking it first thing, she emptied the chamber, consigned everything to the closet by the cot, and locked it. Then she went out, parked the car in the garage, locked the gate, and came inside. The pounding in her heart was audible to her. She went to the sofa in the lounge and put up her feet.

Later, all of a sudden, she craved to see the kids. She got up and went to their bedroom. Their faces appeared hazy in the dim red light. She put on the fluorescent light. She knew that it would not disturb their sleep any. Perchance, one of them had woken up, entered my bedroom, and touched the revolver! That thought returned and sent a shudder through her. She kept watching them lovingly. One aspect severely stung her entrails, as if with a scythe. Their faces resembled their father's. And as they grow up, the resemblance only increases. Eventually, it will become one with it. I will be isolated. Even in the lineaments of my children, my fate is thrumming my suffering. The elder yearns for his grandmother and the younger adores his father. He dared say, 'You don't love me, you love your studies. So you left me at grandma's.' For their sake, abandoning my studies and writing, stooping to mere career academics! Antipathy surfaced in her mind and she could no more continue to look at her children. Turning off the light, she returned to the lounge.

Mind regressed in time. When I discovered the fraud, I was into the third month. If I had resolved, it wouldn't have been any difficult to do away with it. If I had expressed my dislike for it and insisted that it be removed, no doctor had the authority to talk me out of it. If I had done away with the foetus, it would have been a fitting reply not just to Langurnath, but to his sister too. Later, I could have visited her and given her a showdown. The burden of pregnancy, the sluggishness of post-natals, and the unending wheedle-deedle that followed! Had I spent that type of time and energy on studies, I wouldn't be languishing now. Yet, why did I retain it? Why did I keep the perpetrators at bay and retain the fallout of deception? Memory uncoils. A life has sprout within me. It is okay to exercise caution so that it doesn't sprout. Be it unjust or fraudulent, sprout it has. To pluck and cast it away! It is I who must bear the pain, the fraud, and the injustice. In my haste to shake free of it, should I sin and nip off the sinless being in the bud? Tweaking, destroying, eliminating – the very thought brought tears. To accede to it would tantamount to the alienation of womanhood from myself. Should retain it; retain and love it. With effort, she squeezed out affection, buttressed and caressed with her hands the cargo in her belly that seemed to weigh down from within, thereby streaming compassion through her palms. That was a feeling of generosity, of lofty ethics. She would consciously encourage the feeling that by disregarding such fraud and injustice, she was elevating herself more and more. If it had occurred to me that when this offspring grows up and asks why father does not visit and take us with him, would I have tweaked and eliminated it? Seated in the lounge, she looked out the window. The grieving moonlight was becoming murky. Had it occurred to me, would I have eliminated it? The question came up again. No answer takes shape. The moonlight is getting fainter. Or is a sheet of moisture developing in my eyes? For a while, she sat still. Sleep cometh not. So expending the nights without sleep, I am ruining my life. Besides, she thought, by merely holding the revolver in my hands, I am soiling its butt by soaking it in the sweat of my palms. Checking the doors once again, she went to her bedroom and lied down. It was customary for her to go to the children's room and glimpse them before retiring to her bedroom. Have seen them once, she thought lackadaisically. The bond that draws her towards them did not dribble in her heart. Whether or not I see them, they will be unto themselves in deep sleep. The awareness, memory, and feelings that their mother would often behold them while they would be asleep will not stay in them unto the future. Rolling on her right, as she put off the bedswitch and reclined, she felt that she should have drawn the curtains apart so as to allow the moonlight come in. Nah, enough of the grieving feelings of the gloomy moonlight! The moon's fate is his, and as she thought of him as an unfortunate fellow without a home or family, she felt like expressing that in verse. It stayed on for quite some time, feigning a certain rhyme. But even the first line did not take shape. Neither did sleep come. At once, a semblance of a relief was felt. She became aware of guilt too.

I should evince interest in studies. After putting the children to sleep, I should firmly stick to my study and read. In between if sleep takes over, good. Good even if it doesn't, for study will progress, she pondered. She recalled that she hadn't rearranged her study even after these many years of moving here. A big room adjacent to the lounge, shelves extending from floor to roof, shelves that can in all accommodate three to four thousand books. Down the line, when finance permits, should order glass shutters for them. Haven't even properly arranged the books that I have procured. What's debilitating me? Getting up at once, she put on the light and went out to the study, whose doors had not been opened in quite some time. Taking a big towel, she started dusting the books one by one, segregating and arranging them according to their subject. Better seek the assistance of the college librarian to arrange this. His arrangement will be more systematic. I will readily know where to insert the books that I buy in future. Should remunerate him, she thought. All of a sudden, Somashekhar surfaced in memory. Anger too. All night I suffer from sleeplessness and repeatedly visit the brink of death. He would be cozily asleep at home. That sybarite wants bodily pleasures from a beautiful woman younger to him! Love, affection – what do they mean? Very smart! Has he once said that he loves me? Naively, I fell for the guile of Langurnath and his sister. Despite knowing it all well, I fell for the deceit of this guy even. Abandoning the cleaning, she picked up a voluminous book, put off the light, went to her bedroom, and, lying down, started reading it. Though her intellect would not grasp, she impelled her mind to concentrate. But when the elusive sleep began bothering her, mind began roaming again.

Recalling that she had emptied the revolver, she reflected that if robbers attacked at night, if they really attacked, could she leisurely load and prime it with their permission? She got up, opened the draw of the closet, loaded the revolver, replaced it, and lied down again. Even if sleep came now … she resented it, recalling with anxiety the early arrival of Puttamma at dawn. At once, the letter she had received from the manager this morning surfaced in memory. She had glanced at the contents once on picking it up from the box at the gate as she returned from college. Absent was the equanimity to peruse it again. As she put on the night lamp and stretched herself a bit to pick up the envelope from the closet, she recalled that whenever she received a letter from the manager, not just lack of equanimity, she wished she could avoid reading it a second time, and if possible, discard it without reading it at all. The sight of the envelope from the estate would necessitate apprehending and coercing the mind to read it. Problems, borrowings, exigencies, the tension of arranging funds immediately ... recalling that it was the same story even today, she retrieved the letter from the unsealed envelope and read, 'As the board is in adverse funds position, they have stated that no loans will be disbursed for another three months. The present balance of Rs. 15,250/- on the bank current account is not at all sufficient to cover the expenses of the three months. The only way out is to obtain materials on credit from the society. Yesterday, I visited Sakleshpur and enquired with the society. They said that credits were discretion of the chairman, the owners should themselves negotiate, and that managers were not authorized. The president would not be available in station from this eighteenth. Therefore, your early visit is very much solicited.' Even as she read the letter, she reasoned that for one to-and-fro visit, Rs. 350/- would be required for just petrol. To travel by bus would necessitate engaging a taxi from Sakleshpur to the estate and back. If no evening bus is available to Mysore, stay in Sakleshpur, and in effect the same expense. Inconvenience! This bloody estate is not generating even conveyance expenses. Shall I just sell it and repay the bank loan? That solution surfaced. And another: shall I just toss a letter to the bank asking them to offset it against the liability? Anyway, it is mortgaged to the bank. But after a while, she recalled that this solution and modus had not taken shape in her mind for the first time. And once again, the doggedness not to dispose of the estate but to save it by somehow extracting good crop and repaying the loan got the better of her. Sleep eluded again. Go to Sakleshpur, meet the president of the society, and bare all thirty-two before him. A lady baring her teeth would bring to the fore all his mean inherent predisposition. She felt disgust as she saw that in her mind's eye. All the same, she donned confidence that notwithstanding the mean inherent predisposition dawning on his face, none has the guts to say but one erroneous word to her.

~

Previous night being thus, the next morning at college would witness not just yawn and drowsiness, but sluggishness would bring on sleep even. Yet, when she returned home and lied down, sleep would not come. While she lectured in the classroom, intellect would dim owing to the drowsiness. In order to banish it, she would have two or three cups of strong coffee. Initially, the coffee did drive out the sluggishness, but it failed to continue to do so.

That day, she was home exactly at noon. While she drove, she wished to just reach home, lunch, and sleep well. No sooner than she had arrived, she got eager to see Somu. He arrives anytime between 12:15 and 12:30 daily. At times, he gets late by about fifteen minutes. She hurriedly washed her hands, feet, and face. She fed the dogs and set them free inside the house, then placed the cuisine on the table. By then, it struck 12:30. Any moment now, the scooter will be heard. She went to her bedroom, took out his dhoti from the wardrobe, and placed it on the cot. It was five days since she washed it. Should have washed it. Should have ironed it. Has not given it to Mahadevamma for washing. She herself washes and dries it in the bathroom. Herself presses it. Not just from love that it is worn by her beloved Somu, also from the caution that the domestic help should not get ideas as to who is the man who comes here and wears it! Somu is not yet here. Sometimes, he gets delayed alright, but why should it be today? She went and stood by the gate. Vikrant follows her, lifts his forelegs, and invites her to play. Though she trained her sight as far-off as possible, no sign of any scooter. If he arrives, he will come inside. Why should I stand here? If he did arrive while I stand here and somebody witnesses it, they will understand that I was awaiting him. Let anybody understand it anyway. Why should I fear anyone? Yet, why give room for inferences? She got cautious, but thought who the hell would be engaged in scrutiny in a faraway place as this where bungalows are spaced one acre apart? She received the right handshake that Vikrant offered. 12:40. It occurred to her at once – no, he isn't coming. Yesterday, he left exasperated with me. She had forgotten about that. Aware that she had delightfully kept his dhoti ready and was waiting by the gate, she got infuriated with herself. Shoving Vikrant who was repeatedly proffering his right paw, she entered the house apace and sat on the sofa. Her core dominion plunged down an abyss. As if everything were ruined and there were no meaning in anything, she was filled with a sense of complete void, a lack of strength to move from her place, and of a paralytic attack to both her sides. Silence everywhere, a state where even the sway of the leaves and the murmur of the leaf-fall seemed to congeal, a feeling as though the air in that faded house had been sucked out by a vacuum pump. She sensed that movement had ceased, awareness of movement had ceased, rather time had ceased. And though she saw a fly hopping and flying at hand, she had a feeling that it was alien to her and was an event of a world some million light years away. Time having ceased, she wasn't aware how much ticked away. At last when Vikrant and Vishvas both barged in, coerced her into playing, lifted and placed both their forefeet on her lap, and with their protruding tongues started caressing her arms, she came to the present. She immediately got up and, holding them by their collars, dragged them out. Knowing that she would jail them, they adamantly tugged back. She scoffed at them and pulled them out, first consigned Vikrant to his kennel at the fore, then gave a beating to Vishvas who was still adamant, led him to the kennel at the back, and locked him there. Then, shutting the door, as she once again came and sat on the sofa, she felt spent and was gasping.

The clock on the wall that was urging the second hand to move apace displayed 2:15. Now her intellect went into action mode. Wears a mask of love. When the truth was out, when questioned about the truth, he distanced himself forthwith. He was on the lookout for an excuse to stay away. Such dramatist leaving is for good, she mouthed in a voice audible not just to her mind but also to the silently clicking clock. The blaring words resonated in her ears and seemed to rupture the coagulation of her mind. Much is the intensity of the state of thoughts that are about to go verbal, she felt. Why did I mouth those words like a mad one? She was ashamed of herself and, for some time more, went silent again. Resolvedly getting up, she went up to the sink, washed her hands, sat at the dining table, and appointed her plate. My meal is mine, no need for me to wait for anyone. She started to eat. After having four morsels, she became aware that she was eating faster than usual, gulping it as if with the sole intention of getting through with it. Then she could eat no more. The fifth morsel that she ingested milled about in her mouth, lost flavour, and became insipid. Unable to withstand it, as she tried to force it down, she retched, went to the sink, spat it out, rinsed her mouth, and returned to her plate.

Rascal, you knew this will befall me. That is why you stayed back. That you are aware of the nuances of women's response to assorted stimuli implies that you have fooled around not just with that Bombay femme but with many others and gained expertise. Be it known that I will not cede, she resolutely so recited within herself. You are arrogant about being honest, but in fact you are a cheat, she silently decreed. Even if the food in the plate were shoved into the mouth, it would not go any further, and mine would be the discomfiture of spitting it out again. That caution surfaced and she emptied the contents of the plate into the receptacle, put the plate in the sink, replaced the cookery in the fridge, cleaned the table, went to her bedroom, and lied down. She shut her eyes, determined to get at least half an hour's sleep. But from within the crimson glow that encapsulated as her eyelids drew up, his form emerged. Regret surfaced that she was quite well before she got acquainted to him. I myself furthered acquaintance into friendship, friendship into... When friendship itself was unfounded, furtherance to the next stage is unfounded too. Yet, it came in handy to him that *I* furthered it. And so he fools around. I will take it upon myself now to initiate the process of severance. Let the rascal understand. Having committed herself to that resolve, for some time, for quite some time, she steeled her mind. But in between, when she glanced at the clock, it was clear that it was just a couple of minutes since she made that resolve. She got wild that even the clock deceived her.

Sleep won't come. She thought at least she read the book that was kept on the pillow for reading at night, picked it up, and turned the pages. Her eyes had glided across two pages, but nothing sensible got into her head. She at once got up, reached for the phone that rested on the small stool, and started dialling his number, reflecting – *one who loses first shall eventually win*. But if he picks it up on the first ring and asks who the caller is, what shall I say? Contemplating that even if she said nothing, he would still understand that it was she, she disconnected the call by replacing the handset. I am not a bitch to go and surrender at his feet. Let him approach me on his own or call, I will reprimand and keep him at bay, she resolved. That resolve stayed stiff as steel for full five minutes. Then she got up at once. She opened the chest in the closet, extracted the revolver, and held it. When she lovingly caressed it, she noticed that it was a bit soiled. Realizing that she had never removed it during daytime – the dirt wouldn't be visible after dark – she wiped it clean with the pallu of her sari and held it properly again. This is the right time, she felt. Children not home, they wouldn't be aghast at the sound and the gory sight. She stretched her jaw, opened her mouth wide, inserted the nozzle, and, as if with much love, began relishing the taste of the galvanized metal.

While the nozzle stayed in her mouth, the self-inquisitive question popped up – why hasn't the resolve to pull the trigger materialized and the task accomplished, though I have taken hold of it many a time all these days? Fear of death? Love of life? Love for children? Hasn't my agony reached its culmination?

I'm neither afraid of death, nor do I love life. Let not even my enemies ail from such agony. Even if I die, the children won't suffer. She will not stay back. Will rear them, educate them. The brother earns from a servile bureaucratic chore. Will anyway not clear the liabilities and save the estate. Am I keeping myself alive to prevent that? She held herself in derision. What a foul creature am I! Even if I have to prove to myself that I am not a foul one but one with dignity, I have to end myself with a bullet. Finger moved to the trigger. It touched it, and stopped at that. Felt like recalling her last wish. She had none. Felt that when she stood before death, she hadn't any perception about segregating on priority first, last, and intermediaries among wishes. Finger stayed on the trigger, stayed on for quite some time. But it did not garner the small amount of energy to jerk. The nozzle got damp and soaked in her saliva, and pain surfaced in the dilated jaw. Disgusted, she removed the nozzle from her mouth, locked the firearm, and flung it on the bed. She felt revulsion. Each particle of her body seemed to heave and made her want to vomit. Judging that this body neither had the ability to kill itself nor is entitled to be reckoned for killing, she turned silent. Being unaffected for a while, she at once got off the cot, picked up her bag, put on slippers, left the house, ignored the barking dogs, got in the car, and speedily started scaling the hill.

In the broad daylight, not just the road but pebbles, boulders, plants, trees, pasture, all appeared clearly and in their true shapes. As she scaled higher and higher, she felt that vitality in the breath kept increasing. Sunlight pierced her eyes, and the chi that issued forth through her eyes and ears engulfed her. Increasing the speed, she drove about the hill, arrived, and stopped at the spot from where she could see her house. Marking her way down among the shrubs, thorns, and creepers, she walked up to the black granite ledge beneath the canopy of the intertwined jungli mango trees and sat. Felt tranquil within. Down there, hmm ... there, I see my house. While observing, she recalled that she had not visited there since that outing with him, that it was here that he had told me about the Bombay woman, and an incensed me ripped my sari as I left abruptly with scant regard for the thorny shrubs in my trail. Maybe it is good that he related all that! Had he not, it would probably have not been possible for him to further this relationship! Failing to grasp that, I ... she at once got furious thinking that the rascal did not deserve such tolerance and benevolence. The singe of the sun descending in the west seemed to assuage. Why should I get angry with him? Who the hell is he to trigger my anger? She asked herself as she kept watching the converging zone of the earth and the sky that seemed to thaw in the silence and sunshine. Mind got engrossed in that.

A little later, a letter took shape in her mind. Love, no, my, no, my love, no, my life. Any day, addressing is a difficult proposition. It is not at all important. During these many days, we haven't exchanged even one letter. Even as she reflected that the common domicile did not warrant exchange of courier material, the mind pictured a sheet of paper in the background of the juncture of the earth and the sky and prompted a draft. No sooner had a couple of lines formed than the heart disgorged, as would water released through the gates of a dam spill into sluice. Words that sting you come out without my cognizance. I will then set out to justify them too. It is euphemistic to dismiss as 'unwise' my inclination to get enraged not at those who merit derision, but at you, one who bestows unblemished, sincere love; it rather is 'unjust'. Nonetheless, between you and me, gratitude should not serve as the bond. To call it gratitude would send feelers of a debt repaid. Having received what can't be repaid even if I am born seven times over, how and with what amount of gratitude can it be repaid? I am the unfortunate one who has not known what love is since the death of my mother. But being in delusion of benefitting from motherly love, and later getting disillusioned, I arrived at the bitter notion that in this world, love is sham, a pretence. Till I met you, it was impossible for me to construe the constitution of love. In literature, when I read about the intricacies of love as delineated by bards and novelists, I would wonder why they, who would so effectively grasp and express the underlying truth in other matters, are afflicted by delusion when it came to affection, love, and romance! But now I understand that in their depiction, every word is nothing but an expression of pure truth. When it comes to delineating love, even the most gifted of litterateurs suffer defeat from deficit in one's linguistic capabilities. If you get five minutes late, how edgy my heart gets! How often I look towards the doorway! I post myself by the gate and excruciatingly crane my neck to look up to the farthest point in your path. If I notice the changes in the quality of my life after your advent, I will get to know what sort of *sap de vitae* you have been streaming into me. A barren terrain that my life was earlier, is transforming into a bounteous garden from the time I met you. But the foolishness of squashing it is mine as well....She thus kept writing on the canvas of the mind. As the day slipped into dusk and sunshine paled, routinely she looked at her watch. It was 5. Prompted that it was time to fetch the children, she got up. Once again, comprehensively perceiving the canvas of the mind that had manifested as a page of expression, pervading the entire stretch where the sky arched to get hold of the earth, she returned to her car, carefully marking her path among the shrubs and rubble, and ignited the engine.

Expression, that is to say, the consolidation of feelings – delving deep, discerning, retrieving the intricate of intricacies, and arranging them so as to assign a form: a method of delineating me to myself. It occurred to her that this was how relationships were appreciated, and she felt that she discovered, excogitated something novel. Mind assuaged some. She felt her spirits levitate akin to the white clouds that buoyed in the eastern horizon. He should have been by me now. By just watching my face, he would have averred that my mood was thus, and would have responded accordingly. Somu, come over, just come, come fast, take the form of a bird and fly here. Lift me with you and take me beyond those white clouds. I surely won't be unwieldy. Won't strain your wings. Will channel all my strength to you and serve as energy for the motion of your wings. And as she proposed, 'Let's both sit on those white clouds and drift', she had arrived at the foot of the hill and the view narrowed. An onward bus, a truck behind it, and two cars that followed the truck demanded all her attention, and she got cautious.

The moment she arrived, both the children boarded. Today, they were in no mood for play. She just exchanged smile with Susheelamma from within the car and returned home. Vijai alighted and opened the gate, took the keys from her, and headed to the main door. By the time she parked the car inside the garage and closed the gate, Vikas too had entered the house. As she stepped inside, Vijai queried, 'Amma, there is a dhoti on your cot. Had father visited? Why have you kept the revolver here? Vikas was about to take hold of it. I checked him.'

Her heart skipped a beat. Not that the children are unaware of the revolver. She clearly recalled that she had locked it. But the dhoti? In the haste of dispirited feelings, I left, forgetting to replace those things and without even locking my bedroom. What would the children make of it? How would they fancy me? But instantly, as if she were ignorant of it all, she asked him, 'What dhoti, man?'

'White dhoti, Amma, the one on your cot. Had father visited?' he repeated.

'Always thinking about dad. Though I strive so much for your sake, you nurse no love towards mom.' She displayed ire so that he would refer to dad no more. Then she went to her room and, appearing surprised, as if she were seeing it for the first time, said, 'This? It is an old one. Mahadevamma asked for a mop cloth. I had rummaged for it and chucked one here,' and in his witness, she tore it into four. 'Here, take this, put these two in the pail for her. The other two are for wiping hands in the kitchen.' She flung two pieces before him. As he picked them up, she decreed, 'No need for anyone's old dhotis in this house. None need visit here and enquire our well-being. I will tend you. I will provide whatever you want. Don't worry.' Vijai understood that he was to be obedient when mom was angry.

By the time she fed the children that night and sent them to bed, her mind began teetering whether Vijai's mind endorsed my act of splitting the dhoti into pieces and flinging them before him. Vijai is not an outspoken type. He will hoard it within. At this young age, grasping the import of the events is difficult; neither are they forgotten. A few years down the line when they surface in memory, they bring up new meanings. Recalling that it had happened with her too, her entire personality seemed to shrink. Contemplating the situation wherein she would have to bow her head before her son, she perspired. What a pathetic situation, what a pathetic life! He is seven now. Another seven or eight or, say, ten years from now, he will be able to grasp. He will then size up his mother and punish her with live death penalty. Why lead such a life? I will have to end it then, anyway. Why not now? She felt like taking hold of the revolver. Even though I take hold of it, I am a coward who sits tight in the crucial moment, with the nozzle in my mouth! She rebuked herself that she was a worm that neither has the desire to live nor the courage to die. Outside the window was moonlight that was void personified. She desired to drive out like she did yesterday, locking the big main door of the house, carrying the revolver, scything through the void moonlight, and scaling the winding road through the hill....The very thought brought about a stirring attraction. Getting up and entering her room, she picked up the keys to the car, garage, and the house. As she next took hold of the revolver, she pondered why one, who is set out to die, needs this defence equipment? Anon, she reflected that it was rather an exterminating device and felt confident that it would be facile to shoot herself in the pallid, void moonlight in that forlorn place.

Ignoring the barking dogs, she accelerated the car, exited the gate, and drove on without turning on the floodlights. She scaled the eastern section of the hill and parked by the ravine as she was wont to on her nocturnal visits there. Taking hold of the revolver, she alighted and, as she stood by the ravine, the plants, shrubs, rocks, and caverns that appeared hazy in the moonlight assumed various ghostly forms. She fondly aligned herself with those forms, reflecting that *this is death indeed, no need for a more congenial environment to die, to pull the trigger*. Silently beseeching them to admit her as one amongst them, she placed the nozzle of the revolver in her dilated mouth. The index finger hooked itself around the trigger. Eyes closed, she stood still. On her mind's canvas, the various forms of ghosts came together in choreography, as if on a stage. Eventually, their contours and constitutions dissolved, and they all vanished. When, finally, the misty moonlight got denser and darkness descended, pulling the trigger seemed simply easy. When motive power was about to be transmitted to the index finger, why not drive there to his house and deposit this same bullet in his chest even as he slept contentedly? It would be more worthwhile. For having defiled my dedicated sanctity, it would be a befitting punishment to the sinner, the raison d'être for my act of possessing the dhoti and the same being noticed by my son today. Had I not met that loafer, I would somehow have stayed contented, would have got the house repaired by some other architect. No need of any architect, would have got it done by an ordinary contractor, a mason. The anger that till now was seething within began spewing hundreds of thousands of bubbles. It swelled, spilled, and streamed till his Jayalakshmipuram house and paused. With utmost care, she uncoiled the index finger from the trigger, removed the nozzle from her mouth, latched the revolver, and got in her car. As there wasn't enough space to reverse direction there, she scaled a further mile, reversed at an even spot, and drove speedily in the floodlight past her house, the zoo, Hardinge Circle, town bus stop, and Sayyaji Rao Road. The light from the streetlamps coalesced with the moonlight and the amplitude of the void eased. When the market building, the shopping avenue, and the black tar roads with the white arrow signs that she had seen during daytime appeared in view, she winced as she turned left into Danvanthri Road. What a foolish job have I on hand! She put on the brakes instantly and stood still. Just then, she saw an armed police constable at that very spot. Beyond him materialized a police station, at the gates of which he stood sentinel. A lone woman driving up in a car in the stillness of midnight and stopping here would solicit his attention and query. Though some reply could be given, she cautioned herself that the innocuous fact of a lecturer called Amrita driving up alone in a car numbered so and so and parking here at midnight would be stashed away in the minds of the personnel of the station. Before the attention of the armed cop could turn towards her, she stepped on the gas and went farther. After passing through Danvanthri Road and nearing the petrol bunk, she swerved into Narayana Shastri Road and was homebound via Devaraj Urs Road.

She lent her voice to the barking dogs. As she opened the door and entered the house, she felt that it was erroneous to leave just the two kids in this forlorn place by the foothill and venture out at midnights. If ever they got up and looked for her, they would panic on discovering that she was missing, that she has locked the house and left someplace. And if something befell! She shuddered. She told herself that she should not so venture out at midnight henceforth. Behind came the awareness of the difficulty in adhering to such resolution. Closing the doors, sliding the crossbars, and locking them, she entered the children's room, observed the kids' faces for a while, then went to her room, changed, and retired. Henceforth, I never will leave the children alone and....As she again resolved, she reflected that she better take oath in the name of her children, for then her resolve would be fortified by the spikes of fear and caution. Realization dawned that she should not avow by the children what she knew was impossible to abide by. When depressive feelings abound, she would feel that life was a meaningless occurence. Shooting herself with the revolver appeals clearly undoubtedly as the only means of liberation. Should simply die. When this urge comes forth from within, should either die here or should go alone to the hilltop in search of death. I know what I am up to, but haven't the strength to check myself. The stress within me drives me unto the phase of attempting suicide in the void zone atop the hill in the void loci of the sky and the horizon. Yet, didn't once die. Didn't pull the trigger. Why didn't I? What attraction does the inner mind harbour towards life that I myself am unaware of? As she closed her eyes and combed her insides for the answer, anguish gushed forth. Mortal agony. A suffocating hot sauna that at once pervaded the body and the mind. The expelling of life appearing as the only means of liberation, torturous agony churned her stomach and she retched. She writhed and fidgeted in her bed. The seething blind agony that was looking for a way out presently found vent through her throat and billowed out as cry. Some of the magma erupted from her eyes too. Even in that agony, she got anxious that her wail would confound the children. She, therefore, thrust the tail of her pallu into her mouth and cried to her heart's content, arresting only the sound. Owing to the intensity of the sob, she felt that her heart would explode. She rolled over on her belly and banged her forehead to the edge of the cot quite a few times. More tears, some more, a little more flowed and then ceased. She slept with her forehead to the pillow. She felt drowsy. Consciousness faded. She slipped into sleep. The light kept glowing.

In a while, she was abruptly awaken. Confounded as to her present locus, she sat up. In a moment, she came to the present. I'm in my house. Sitting on my bed. The light is glowing. The clock on the wall reads 2:30. Scab in the eyes. A trail of half-dried saliva from the edge of her mouth. She got up, washed her eyes, rinsed her mouth, washed the cheeks that had got clammy on being soaked and veneered by tears, finally washed all of her face thoroughly, and retired. Mental tension abated. Sans the yank of agony and unhappiness, she felt she weighed nothing more than her corporeal mass. A good amount of cry is most welcome. But it never comes. Bloody tears! If ever I had the faculty to cry and get light when desired! Cherishing that wish, she put off the lights and closed her eyes. In a short while, sleep came. Such deep sleep that Vijai tugged at her and was hollering, 'Amma, Puttamma has arrived. Where have you kept the keys to the crossbar of the main door?' Having returned at the odd hour, she reflected, after locking the main door she would have absent-mindedly put the keys in her handbag. Her mind got heavy again as she rummaged the handbag, for all of this was brought to her cognizance the moment she woke up.

~

It was clear to him that unless he distanced himself from her completely, it was impossible for him to live in peace. Be it the matter of intimacy between us or other details of my life, she would elicit every fine detail from me, and applying her acumen she would extract from my words imports that I myself was not aware of or intended, parade them before me, court-martial me, and hold me in bad light. As is severe love, in her disposition is severe cruelty. A sort of sadist, he decreed. This being her nature, no point in empathizing with her and fretting, he tried to steel his mind. I modified my working hours so that I could be with her. While everyone worked, during the visiting hours of clients, between noon and 4:30–5:00, when my presence would be required at constructions spots where work was in progress, I would while away in her company. He chastised himself that this was not the way to build his career and establish it well. If I thus absented myself daily, what would Neelakanthappa think of me? The thought loomed large that Neelakanthappa would wield influence on the clients and begin dealing with them directly to my detriment. Not that these thoughts have not occurred to him earlier. But on such occasions, the desire to be with Amrita would supply sorts of justification for it. Money alone is not important; advancement in career alone is not the goal of life. Would the status of being the number one architect of Mysore or, for that matter, the entire state beget contentment, triumph, and accomplishment that I get in her company? Such justifications would spring up before him. Nonetheless, owing to the displaced empathy now, he decided to cry halt to the negligence of late towards his career.

Is it not for reason of feminine enamour that a man retards in his career? He repeated oft this oracle to himself. I have noticed in Bombay too. Those that have scaled certain heights in their vocation have caved in for reason of woman or wine. He recalled a few instances and fathomed that it wasn't just a waste of time; it was loss of zeal rather. I have even suffered thus at the hands of that Bombay woman. But that was not *in perpetuum*. Once, or at the most, twice a week, four or five hours, and though it would be during working hours, no harm would be caused, as Naveen was supplementing. Besides, he noticed a clear difference. In her company would be delight, not the encumbrance of gruelling feelings. Hence, when I distanced myself from her, I didn't buckle. Though, for a couple of days, I felt deceived, I eventually got rid of it on clearly grasping her character. But this woman is diametric vis-à-vis. Fervid she is, and has inducted such feelings in me too. Hence, it calls for an immense resolve to distance from her. With that Bombay woman, would have two or three intoxicating bouts of lust, and then with a culminating lusty cuddle, would part delightfully with the anticipation of meeting again at a specified time on a specified day the following week. No distress, no pangs of separation, no face that muddles in tears. Even as we eyed each other at the threshold of eventual leave-taking, we would step out only after mutually exuding provocative gleam in our eyes. And without any affliction would stay contented till the hour of our next conjugation. In fact, it was a sort of exhilarating and optimal alcoholism. This, rather, is a potent emotion that nags by permeating not just the heart, mind, and intellect, but also the nervous system, the circulatory system, and the vertebra. Once again, he clarified to himself that though it would be trying, there was no way other than disentangling.

Next morning on arriving in his office, he told Neelakanthappa, 'From today, I will alter my timings. I will stay in office till 7 pm, breaking for lunch in between just for about ten minutes. Keep this in mind while giving appointments. To go home in the afternoons would mean waste of time, that too during office hours.'

'True, sir,' Neelakanthappa said obediently.

At this juncture, another opportunity came by. The office premises that he had procured on Ramavilas Road was constricting. His table, the reception area, the big table on which Neelakanthappa would draw plans, the copier, and other desks had to be accommodated in one big room. Clients could not be counselled privately and confidentially. While one party would be engaged in consultation with him, others who were awaiting their turn would poke their nose and give more advice and suggestions than the architect himself. Though he was on the lookout for alternative premises, it was difficult to procure one. All of a sudden, he could get one, owing to the good offices of a client. Office space of

700 square feet on the first floor of a shopping complex on Devaraj Urs Road. The architect in him instantly fancied the segmentation of floor space. An exclusive cabin for himself with an attached washroom, reception area furnished with luxury sofas for clients, an enclosed work area for the draughtsmen....He resolved not to let go of this prospect. But two and a half lakh rupees to be paid up in fifteen days. If I liquidated all my sources, it would yield two. Besides arranging for the differential fifty, another fifty to appoint it well so that it would be readily appreciated as an architect's office the moment one steps in. Totally, one lakh. Naveen came to mind immediately. He will definitely chip in. If not one lakh, he will at least give fifty. Better defer the sprucing a bit. But he decided that it should not be occupied unless it was well appointed. Advancing fifty thousand, he signed an agreement to pay up the balance and get it registered within a month, and left by train for Bombay via Bangalore the next day. He instructed Neelakanthappa to give appointments on the sixth day since, deciding to return positively in five days.

All through the train ride to Bangalore, mind was ruminating about the new office premises. My own place. Can design it according to my liking. Had not reckoned the registration overheads. One is not enough; should ask of Naveen one and a quarter. 700 sq. ft meaning the Bombay one was 450. Typical of Bombay to transact sizeable business in small premises. Deck it appropriately and conduct the inaugural function in a grand way, invite the contractors, engineers, coffee planters, landlords, city municipality executives from Mysore, Mandya, Hassan, Kodagu, and South Canara districts by finding out their names and addresses, splurge ten grand. Should evince interest in my career henceforth, and within the year, operations should increase so as to call for recruitment of two graduate engineers and a full-time accountant. He was being consumed by such thoughts. Late evening, changing trains in Bangalore, he slept, and when he got up the next sunny morning, while the train was passing through rocky countryside, sorts of vainness engulfed him. Naveen will definitely give the money. If he strove, not in just the couple of districts, can even procure work in Bangalore, can acquire a car in about three months. What next? A life as busy as in Bombay. He recalled that he moved to Mysore for the sake of clean air and sunlight. Instantly he felt, why this new premises, this Mysore? Why not move to Bombay and resume working with Naveen? No need to slog like him; just work optimally and live contentedly. When I lost contact with her, I was downcast for a few days. But life wasn't soused in darkness. Came in contact with her perchance, got intimate over the next two years, and then abruptly broke up! That indifference had seasoned him. Or, is it due to the availability of my wife that its effect was not acute? One at home is required, à la shock absorber. He reflected that it would then be convenient to iron out the disappointments of the extramarital affairs. If I get married even now! When they visited, even Naveen and Induben – resolutely and with a flight of her eyebrows – opined that per the latest trends, forty was the age for a man to enter his first wedlock. Were I married, courtship with Amrita would not have received an impetus! Can't be sure though, he reflected, as to what stimulates and what deters the attraction between males and femmes. He headed to the toilet.

Seated by the window, as he witnessed the sunlight, the acres, and the rocks recede behind him, the Bombay sun glared. It was his usual practice to leave the footwear outside before entering. Had no intention to sneak silently or to test. If ever there were an indication that she was so, verification would be warranted. Very rarely, I would go to her house in between scheduled visits and enquire about her well-being. She had informed when we met the day before that her husband was away in Geneva on official work. It being school hours for the children, and perchance she were in, the possibility of relishing an unanticipated bout of conjugation! The door was ajar and I stepped in. Pacing silently, I turned right to her study. Behind the tabla and the tanpura, huddled in the percussionist's arms was she. And he! Soiled old pyjamas, betel-sodden mouth, stubby beard, and facial contours of an illiterate! She saw me. I saw her. The percussionist was drunk. Not she, at least not to an intoxicating extent. It was clear that they were engaged in foreplay. Feeling giddy, I just retraced my steps, donned my footwear, and climbed down the steps. Without returning, had I stayed back and rebuked her, *so much for your integrity, is that all your loyalty*? Didn't. Not even later. Never even met her. Ignored the upcoming Thursday's usual appointment at her friend's flat and distanced myself. She would have arrived there and awaited me. Or thinking that I would rebuke, would probably have stayed back. Why didn't I reprimand her? Detestation? Disappointment? Pain from backstabbing? May be all three. After all these years, a new explanation dawns, drawing a parallel with the forlorn ethos of a running train. Not once had she told me that in her life I was the only friend, devoted friend, or any such. Hadn't extensively used the words 'devotion' and 'undivided devotion'. Would just talk of the intensity of our bodily desires. Inciting me, tempering my coital propensities, and coaching me in the techniques of boosting my tenacity, she had turned my guru. Had also declared that to suffer defeat at the hands of the pupil was the sign of accomplishment for a guru. When she once queried, 'Shekhar, how many other lovers do you have?', I had taken serious exception to it, had gone wild at her. What did she think of me? 'Why get angry? I am not jealous even if you have ten other girlfriends. It is evident from your ways that you haven't another. That makes me happy. Worried as well,' she had said. Then I had thought of it as just her assessment of me. And when, for the first time, it occurred to him that he hadn't then grasped that she indicated about herself too by saying so, his jaw dropped and its reflection in the windowpane of the running train readily drew his attention against the background of the sunlit acres. A little later, he felt that she had deserted him, thinking of him as naïve. When not coupled with expectation of devotion – he reflected – feelings don't heave, everything is weightless.

As ordered the previous night, the caterer boy delivered the breakfast packet and the coffee flask. While he ate, memories of Amrita returned. Not only am I more experienced than her, she is one inexperienced, uninspired woman who, for the first time, was being triggered by me. As she insisted that our inner truths be mutually shared, I related my Bombay affair. But, he recalled, unable to digest it, she pricks him variously. Enough of this devotion, of this cruelty! In a short while, the caterer returned and collected the coffee flask. He felt that loneliness would set in if he kept looking out the window at the boulders, the sun, and the dome of the sky that emitted and held sunlight, wherefore he stretched on his berth and reclined. The fan kept spinning. He closed his eyes. He could feel the train gain distance and Bombay slowly zoom in. He felt eager, tomorrow I will be with him. Naveen, Induben, and Digant surfaced in memory. Slowly, he slipped into sleep.

When he awoke in the next ten or fifteen minutes, he felt that the train was slowly inching away from Mysore. And though he was comforted by his plans of returning via this same route the fourth day thence, or possibly the third, he found it difficult to come to terms with the fact that presently, he was moving away from Mysore. Something amiss. The feelings of a lad who, for the first time, was moving out of his native to a faraway town for higher studies. What is there in that town? Didn't I live in Bombay those many years? The crowd, commotion, and density notwithstanding, what is in Mysore that isn't in Bombay that should cause homesickness for missing it for just a couple of days? He inquisitively probed within himself. Is it the bund of the Kukkarahalli Tank? The Chamundi Hill? Lalitamahal Extension? The fountains? The Gangotri Campus? As he delved into them one by one, each one of them immersed in her memory and emerged restructured. He was surprised. Haven't visited Kukkarahalli or Gangotri with her. Still they stand, soused in memories of her. This – or something akin to this – might be what philosophers refer to as *illusion*, he marvelled and, listening to the rhythmic beats of the rolling wheels, he slept. Though mind was engaged in analysing this oddity, he could not find a plausible explanation. In some time, the train came to halt at a certain station. Outside the window, he could hear the announcement of the newspaper vendor, '*Pēpur, pepār*!' Getting up, he beckoned him from the window, bought the day's paper, and began reading. Time slid by as the train resumed and traversed another thirty or forty miles. Nearer lunch hour, another aspect flashed in his mind. When the picture of Bombay comes to mind, her memory doesn't flash. Whenever I would pass through the street where her friend's flat was, would just faintly recall it as if it were an occurrence of yore; never would it be drenched in memory. By and by, the faintness faded further. As he ruminated on this, the caterer delivered his lunch.

~

On his return journey, he took a morning flight to Bangalore, arrived in Mysore by bus, and, lugging his luggage, came directly to his office. He took report from Neelakanthappa about the works that were underway. Before affixing his signature to the two bills carefully drawn by Neelakanthappa, he was broadly verifying the same when the phone rang. He always got irritated when the ringing of the phone impeded his billing arithmetic and affected it. Still, he lifted the receiver and said hello. 'Somu, when did you return from Bombay?' The very voice brought cheer to him. Mind swelled. Even the simple reply 'just now' didn't occur to him. Though this was an unexpected call, having known her disposition all through, he felt that it was but natural that she would call, would visit. 'Hey dude,' she reeled off, 'there is Neelakanthappa before you. He has not yet left for lunch. You are angry. Feel like barking at me, "Who are you to ask, you donkey?" Also feel like withholding any response. Without replying, if you keep silent just holding the receiver, Neelakanthappa may still infer something from your distended face. So answer me directly. I had come over to your house to see you. Your landlord on the ground floor told me that you had left for Bombay and would be returning this morning. Why Bombay now, I enquired. Though I knew it was improper to poke my nose, I still queried out of anxiety. He told that you had gone to arrange finance for buying the premises that was on offer on Devaraj Urs Road. The same day, I visited your office and asked Neelakanthappa, "Mr Somashekhar informed me that you are acquiring new premises. He has left for Bombay in a hurry in that connection. Will you please show me the place?" I went along with them and visited the place. Beautiful place. Well, it is clear to Neelakanthappa that you share with me the significant aspects of your profession, and that we meet often. So be it. I acted so to convey that I was not any apprehensive. I was told that the sale price is two and a half lakh. Twenty-five for the registration. At least another fifty for partitioning and interiors. Totally, three and a quarter. How much do you have? How much have you brought from Bombay, tell me?' "What of this lordship of yours? You impertinent one!" 'If you want to scoff at me thus, you can't do it there in the presence of Neelakanthappa. Come home and rebuke me to your heart's content. Now tell me, how much did you borrow from your friend Naveen Shah?'

He had no other go than to answer. He couldn't abuse in the presence of Neelakanthappa. It is true that I am angered, but it is also true that I am joyous on hearing her voice. Wanting to tell it straight and be done with it, he just said, 'One and a quarter'. 'Did you carry that much cash on you and travelled alone by train? Just got anxious about security.'

'Didn't travel by train. Flew to Bangalore, from there to Mysore by bus, and headed straight to my office. Have brought a DD. No cash.'

'Is it? What is it, the DD?' surprise was explicit in her voice.

'Now don't pretend. You have been through enough banking transactions.'

'No, I am not joking. Other than cheque and transfer, I do not know anything about banking. Do tell me what a DD is.'

'On remitting a certain amount in one branch, the manager thereat will give us an authorized cheque on their branch in another place of our choice, directing that a certain amount of money be paid to the payee stated in the cheque. Besides this, they will courier a secret document to the manager here. The one, cheque-like, given to us is called DD, Demand Draft.'

'Somu, for the life of me, I was ignorant of this simple matter. Will you show me the DD that you have brought? Want to see how it actually is. Getting off the bus, you have headed straight to the office. Scooter is in the house. Hire an auto. Or else, I will pick you up in my car. Of course, I will drive you back to your office later. Now tell me, will you take an auto or shall I pick you up? What time shall I come to get you? You may be attending to the pressing works that were pending during your six days' absence. I will not come right away and disturb. Tell me when I should come. Deposit the DD in the bank after showing it to this dunce. Would they object if you deposited it tomorrow?'

'It has a validity of six months. I am coming at about 2 pm,' he said cheerfully. 'I will not have lunch till then,' she said before replacing the receiver.

He began totalling the bill again that he had been checking and, after he had authorized payment of the same, took up the calculations of the steel required immediately for a house under construction.

By the time Neelakanthappa returned from lunch, he had finished perusing that and also a floor plan. Announcing his lunch break, he left with his briefcase. While travelling in the auto, he felt happy that they were no more at loggerheads and that he was now visiting her. All the same, he recalled her smartness in ensuring his visit without giving him room for hedging. Rascal! This Hardinge Circle, zoo curve, Lalitamahal yonder, to the right the Chamundi Hill obstructing the sky, he felt that it was ages since he last saw them. In fact, it was just thirteen days, he counted up, since he last returned from her house, vexed.

As expected, she stood by the gate. The white stones of her ear studs shone. And her tender face shone brighter at his visit. It is false that cruelty exists in her disposition, he felt. Silencing the barking dogs, she escorted him in and, sealing the door, she pulled him by his arms, hugged him, and, hiding her face in his chest, whispered, 'Somu, thirteen years conclude today.' He too felt that it was right. He caressed her head and watched her face. It had blanched, as if from hunger, thirst, and forestial exile. However, he did not broach that matter. Neither did she. She took him to the kitchen, turned on the tap, cleansed his hands with soap, served his lunch, and ate from the same plate. Then she led him by his arm to her bedroom, seated him comfortably against the bolster, and, exuding childlike curiosity in her eyes, asked, 'Now, let me see the facade of a DD?' He opened his briefcase, took out the DD from the plastic envelope, and held it before her. Persisting with her curiosity and surprise, she took it and examined. 'Oh! Just like a cheque. The figures are machine-written. Two signatures, one by the manager and another by the accountant. This dull-wit was ignorant. Well, give me that plastic envelope.' She took it from him, inserted the DD in it, and took it to another room. When she returned, her hands were empty. She sat by him and said, 'If this DD is returned to whoever gave it, would the bankers refund him the money?' Tentatively, he said *yes*. She walked up to her study table in a corner of the room, retrieved a sheet of paper, cardboard, and pen, and, handing them to him, said, 'Write as I dictate. *Dear Naveen, you loaned me immediately on my request. But by the time I arrived here, an amount that was due to me awaited me. Therefore, I am returning the DD. Save the funds. You shall lend me if I need it later.* Or write whatever you feel goes well with your friendship with him and give it to me. I will send it to him by registered post.'

He could never have imagined that she would do this. It just couldn't have occurred to him. Besides, he had a misgiving. Her penury tearing her apart now, how could she arrange for such a huge amount? In whatever way she had arranged for the funds, in effect it was nothing but trapping him. For some reason, his mind vehemently opposed such arrangement. Even before clarifying the reason to himself, he said, 'Nothing of it. No.' Inadvertently, his words were brusque.

'Why not?' her voice was calm and confident like that of a lawyer who had the situation and oration well under control.

'After travelling that far, and he having given it the moment I asked for it, what will he make of it if I returned it immediately on coming here?'

'The reason I gave you the pen and paper is to write to him in such a way as to allay any such apprehension in him.'

'All that is not possible.'

'What is not possible? Returning the DD, or taking the money from me?' she set them apart distinctly. He felt it difficult to face the precision in her question.

He cited the reason that came to his mind instantly. 'I am aware of your financial situation. Sometime back, you had consulted me for whitewashing, distempering, repairs to the flooring, and fencing. I had quoted thirty thousand. You have not got those works done. That means you haven't the money. After I came to know of the mortgage on your estate and the interest thereon, I keep thinking what to do of it. This being the situation, how will you arrange funds for me?'

She plainly looked him in the eye and said, 'It is mutually agreed that there shall be no lies between us. Answer my question justly. Will you or won't you pay interest on the Bombay funds?'

'I will pay it even if he refuses. This is a deal.'

'The moment I came to know that you had gone to Bombay to arrange for funds, God knows, I felt unhappy. I thought that if I didn't support my Somu in such a situation, there would be no justification to my life. I enquired with my bankers. They agreed to finance me on the security of this house. I applied for it that very day. Yesterday, they informed that it is sanctioned. The interest that you would pay to Naveen, pay it to this bank. Avail of these funds. If you don't, it only means that you have set me aloof, that I don't mean anything to you. That is it. Think about it.'

He was wedged and could not even budge. Just kept looking at her face. She gazed at his face without batting an eyelid. Overcoming irritation and vacillation, he came to a conclusion and said, 'You are ill-mannered to be adamant about everything. Dealings vitiate love. I desire that my love should remain pure to the exclusion of dealings. You too cooperate. In future, if I need it, I will seek your help.'

She did not speak. Tautly, she kept looking at him. In two minutes, she left the room and went to the other. Returning with the plastic folder in hand, she placed it on the cardboard he was holding and, donning a tranquil expression, said, 'Love isn't that which dawns by imploring. It should spring from within. If one beseeches like a mongrel, not love but disdain onsets.' He stared at her. Not to be outdone, she too faced him more defiantly. This combat went on for one full minute. By then, a cry pitched from within her. Though she tried to stem it with all her poise, it breached and spilled from every nook of her face. 'Somu, if you do this to me, why should I stay from killing myself with the revolver?' Involuntarily, the words emerged, drenched in her tears, and tumbled down in shreds.

Not reacting, he set the paper properly on the writing pad, uncapped the pen, and started scrawling in English. And so as not to send feelers that it was written in haste, he preluded it with descriptions of his visit to Bombay, the four days' hospitality he relished thereat, recalled Induben, Digant, and other common friends that they had together met, and related the fact of realization of his dues here, and hence the DD returned with thanks. He then formally invited him *with family* to the inauguration ceremony, once the new premise was furnished and suitably appointed. Finally, he wrote Naveen's address at the bottom-left corner of the letter, placed the plastic folder on it, lifted his head, and looked at her.

He was not really cognizant of her presence beside him while he wrote the letter. In her hand was a big sheet of paper. A typical architect's drawing. She removed the DD and the letter he just wrote, placed them beside her, and spread the drawing on the cardboard. 'I have designed and drawn the plan of the office of an ingenious architect. Now *I* am the architect. Think it over and tell me what changes you want. I will effect them. The segmentation of the cabins, furniture, wall designs, alcoved shelves in your cabin and those of your assistants, all are to be left to my choice. I have already done the rounds to the marketplace and decided on the types of plywood, semi-transparent glass, and the sofa needed.' His face swelled. She has done so much groundwork already! His heart became one with hers. She reeled off, 'Look here, this is your chamber, soundproof and air-conditioned. This is your desk, telephone to the left. When the phone rings, you should pick it up first, not your assistant. Why should they get to know who the caller is? Whoever you talk to from the confines of your chamber should not be audible to anyone outside. Not even in the extension receivers of your assistants. They should receive the calls only when you are not in. Understand?' He grunted assent. 'What did you understand, you dunderhead!' she said with a melange of cheer and jeer.

Then, glancing at the clock on the wall, she said, 'It is 3:15. Let's go to my bank. I will get the money transferred. Let's also courier the letter and the DD to Naveen bhai. Meet the seller tomorrow and fix the date of registration. We should start the interiors the very next day after registration. I will visit twice a day and supervise. After all, I am the architect. Now, tell me what percentage you will pay me.' She got up.

She did not ask him to visit at the usual 12:30 the next day. But when he came at that hour, she was waiting with two plates and glasses laid on the dining table. They both smiled in unison. While they lunched, she asked, 'What did you bring me from Bombay?'

'For you? I visited a few bookstores. My interest centres mostly on drawings. Inherent in my architectural pursuits are the basic tenets of drawing. Besides that, philosophy, psychology, poetry collection, fiction, in all I selected thirty books. As it would exceed the luggage limits on a flight, I have asked Naveen to send it by lorry parcel. You shall open that parcel.'

'While selecting the books, did you really recall me?'

'How badly my mind lugged me towards Mysore even as I was Bombay-bound! Mysore means you. Otherwise, I would have stayed back in Bombay. *Stay back, there is more than enough work for you too,* Naveen urged me.'

'Should have stayed back.'

'Truly?' he looked at her with investigatory alertness.

Shifting her sight to his plate, she said, 'Knowing your liking for the lady's finger stew, I prepared it immediately on return from college, but you haven't touched it as yet!'

~

The layout and interiors of his new office premises were carried out fully as per her imagination and planning. Though she sought his technical advice selectively, she herself thoroughly contemplated and determined as to the colour designs, choice of fixtures, chairs, tables, sofas, light points, design of the display board, the exclusiveness of his chamber, and such. Every day, she was present there and supervised the works, giving instructions to the carpenters, the electricians, and the telecom crew. She assigned some small works to Neelakanthappa too without overburdening him. She designed the visiting cards and got it printed. She organized the inaugural ceremony of the new office. As on the occasion of Vikas' christening ceremony, she sought the services of the caterer Suryanarayanappa and the priest Sri Yajneshvara Jois. Housewarming rites at the hour determined by Sri Jois, luncheon for august guests at the same venue afternoon, and a grand dinner with the traditional valedictory hamper for the professional invitees late evening. She had carefully chosen the menu for breakfast and dinner.

She was present all morning at the *homa and* puja performed by Sri Jois. Appointing a large tray with oranges, apples, grapes, plantain cluster, coconuts, a clump of tender betel leaves, and areca for consecration, supplying coinage and raiment to Sri Jois, and artistically stringing up the jasmine strings so as to attune with the already laid mango-leaf festoons, she moved about, nimbly running the show, giving suggestions and advice, sending feelers to onlookers that *she* was the de facto mistress of the premises and of the occasion. Sri Jois had other appointments to keep, and hence was awarded immediately on consummation of the rites, and she offered to drop him in her car. Somashekhar was witnessing everything. As she handled everything in a befitting manner, which he could never have conceived to do by himself, he stayed from intervening in any manner whatsoever. He felt that not only would such interference irritate her, but also affect the finer details. Without the presence of a woman, a man could never bring such splendour to such occasions. He reflected that a male, though a professional event manager, could not impart such sparkle to it as would a woman.

Luncheon was at 12:30. But Amrita, who left at 11:30 to drop Sri Jois, was not back even by 12:15. Nearer to lunchtime, most all guests had arrived. He began speculating if she had gone to bring the children and got delayed by an extended classroom session. The caterer Suryanarayanappa is a very responsible man who does not sit on an indent. Without waiting for the host, he goes on to procure the requirements and see the occasion through. Somashekhar knew too that he would serve the food judiciously, and later properly dispose of the remaining pantry. But it was his – Somashekhar's – job to receive the guests with a smile and lead them to their seats in the pandal. He and Neelakanthappa had together catalogued the guests, professional contacts, all. Once he had received the guests and chatted some with them, further hospitalities devolved onto Neelakanthappa. But why isn't she here yet? Ten minutes past 12:30. By such time, he had glanced at his watch seven or eight times. There were more guests than one dining session could accommodate. Neelakanthappa came to him and asked, 'Sir, why hold up? Let us serve up those who have arrived. At least, that will vacate the reception area for others.'

At a loss, Somashekhar squirmed. As she had taken entirely on herself everything about this occasion, he not only felt it difficult but embarrassing to now decide on his own. He was also worried that if she should return in a couple of minutes and get angry – *one thing was left out. Why did you hurry?* Let us wait for another five minutes, he said and glanced at his watch again. But in those five minutes, another ten to fifteen guests arrived. The caterer Suryanarayanappa sought him out and stated that the first dining session better get underway. He grunted consent. He accosted each and every waiting group and prompted them, 'Lunch ready, please', 'Lunch, please'. Neelakanthappa led them all to the dining hall.

While they dined, Somashekhar's eyes awaited her old car to drive up and come to a halt by his gate. Four times he came out and looked up the full length of the road. He climbed down the stairs, requested the pharmacist below, and telephoned her house. It rang, but no one is home. Who else? If anyone were to be, it was she. Or would she be at her kids' school? He looked up in his diary and dialled the school number. On enquiry, he was told that Vijai and Vikas were there, but their mother was not. He called her residence again. No response whatsoever. Where would she have gone? Went to drop Sri Jois. Could have rather sent him by an auto. Should she have gone herself? He got irritated. While he climbed up the stairs, a doubt surfaced in his mind. Home, would she have abstained from taking the call? No, no, why would she do so? She has handled everything suitably, he convinced himself. Without her, I could never have arranged this so thoroughly and grandiosely. Did something befall while she drove? He got anxious. The truckers drive recklessly. Along came the certitude that she drives cautiously, doesn't hasten. First round of dining concluded, and no sooner were they bade farewell with the valedictory hamper than more people, enough for another round, were ready, even as the helpers cleaned up the dining tables. After they were seated, Neelakanthappa neared him and said, 'Sir, madam is not to be seen. It would have been ideal if she led the women to the dining hall.'

As Neelakanthappa had witnessed her supervision right from the moment of registration till now, and also carried out many of her instructions, his query was but natural. Baffled, Somashekhar just said, 'She was referring to a visiting relative, and that she had to fetch him.'

By that time, a guest accosted him, 'Nice place. Interiors very good. You are not just an architect, but also an interior decorator. Congratulations,' and proffered his hand. He felt a temporary relief from the disconcerting situation.

While the second round of dining was underway, he beckoned Neelakanthappa and said, 'More or less, everyone has turned up, right? If some more arrive, receive and humour them. I will be back in ten minutes,' and left with his scooter. Crossing the Hardinge Circle and the zoo, as he encountered the curve, her monition seized him as it invariably did. 'That spot is not safe. Even though you honk, oncoming motorists cannot hear it. Nobody adheres to the road rule of keeping to the left. Be very cautious.' Almost every day, she would suffix this to her ciao. Her caveat was ingrained so deep in his mind that he would get conscious even as the curve was about half a mile away. Past the curve, he drove speedily to her house only to find the gate locked. He was at best successful in eliciting a friendly yodelling from the dogs. While he repaid the greeting by lending his friendly voice, he began worrying as to where she was. For ten minutes, he stood there. College? He recalled that it wound up at 11:30 and would be occupied by another batch thence.

It was 2:30 now. Though he had had his breakfast, he felt woozy. He didn't know what to do. Neither was he keen on returning. Five more minutes, he stood holding the gate. Shall I cross over the gate and peek through the window? No, that is very demeaning. He banished that thought. She is not the type that hides inside, sealed. It later occurred to him that investigating wouldn't befit him either. Reminding himself that he should return, should bid the guests farewell with the gift hamper, he kick-started his scooter. Dogs started barking. While returning, he recollected the day's occurrences in chronology. Morning she dropped the children at school and came directly to the function. Had taken leave of college. Moved about very sprightly. She had worn the silk sari that I had given her for the occasion. But while Sri Jois conducted *homa* and other rituals, she looked solemn. I, too, was otherwise preoccupied. Did not notice as to what nuances her mood assumed and why. Yet, he recalled that while the rites were undertaken, her facial contours were grim. Why so? Though he gave enough thought to it, nothing struck him. Well before reaching the curve by the zoo, he got alert and drove carefully looking ahead. By the time he returned, dinner was over and many guests had left too. Neelakanthappa was bidding farewell to the rest. None else was due to arrive. The caterers had to get preparation underway for the evening's reception. The number of visitors would be greater in the evening. Neelakanthappa urged him, 'Sir, let us dine too.' But Somashekhar was in no mood to eat. She hasn't eaten. They both had concurred a week earlier that she would bring the children at lunch hour. Neither fetching the children, nor herself staying on, not even home, which only means she had not eaten. Not eaten even outside. Even if she had eaten, his heart ruled that in her absence, he could never set his hands on the plantain leaf served with all of the sumptuous bonbons that she had thought of and got prepared. He said, 'You go ahead. My tummy is not fine. I had been to the doctor's now. He has prescribed just buttermilk. Get me a glass of buttermilk, will you?'

'Today, at least for protocol sake, a morsel of sweets ... ' Neelakanthappa persisted.

'Sweets shall be there. If I defy the doctor's advice, I will have to face the after-effects. By evening, if I feel better, I will have some. But for now, he has strictly prescribed nothing but buttermilk. No choice.' When he would not relent, Neelakanthappa fetched him a glass of buttermilk. Neelakanthappa's family had dined with the second batch. Now Somashekhar himself served food to Neelakanthappa. Then feeling giddy, he reclined in a chair.

Visitors start arriving from 5 pm. The veena records that she had selected for the occasion would be played at low volume in the background. Donning the new suit that she had got tailored, I should pump the hands of the guests and receive them with a confident professional smile. Dressed in the new shirt, trousers, bush coat, and new shoes that I have gifted him, Neelakanthappa should steer them, hand them their buffet plate, and make them comfortable. Rest of the hospitality would be undertaken by the wards of the caterer, Suryanarayanappa. And while bidding farewell, a plastic bag containing a bouquet, coconut, and his visiting card to everyone. All this is her idea. For this purpose, she has designed and got printed two thousand visiting cards. From the professional viewpoint, this is the most important aspect of the function. Now she herself is absent. I alone wear the new dress and with a smile….Not only did his enthusiasm receive a setback, he even thought of entrusting the conduct of the function to Neelakanthappa and just leave. That resolve stayed for about half an hour. But thinking that his absence at this momentous occasion would severely affect his profession, he left for his house to get dressed. He told Neelakanthappa, 'You leave now and come dressed in the new ones. I too will go home, change, and see the doctor on the way back.' At home, he did not feel like wearing the new suit, matching shirt, and tie. When he began rummaging for a good white shirt, trousers, and tie from among the existing ones, he recalled that quite some were with the launderer. Rode his scooter, brought them, selected a good bush shirt and trousers, wore them, washed his face, combed his hair, and was back at the venue by 4:45. He was bodily spent. Mind revolted – who wants this office, this profession, this occasion! He went to the pharmacist's below and dialled her house again. Even now it rings. No takers. He did not call the school as it was well past the school hours.

He did not dine even after everything was over. Enough remained of the *kesaribhāt*, deep-fried delicacies, chips, *uppiṭṭu*, samosa, and fruit salad prepared for the buffet. He did not feel like eating any of them. He got some of it packed, asked Neelakanthappa to distribute the remaining among the workers, and left for home on his scooter, empty-bellied. It was 10 pm. To talk to so many people, greet them with folded hands, and/or shake hands with them was a draining chore even if the stomach was stuffed well. Now though, the stomach seems to have lined up along the backbone. Besides the feeling of loneliness, smarting him was the injury of being abandoned by her and left to fend for himself. He drank two glasses of water and sprawled on the bed. It became explicitly clear to him that she was the font of his vitality, and that all fanfare or ballyhoo he indulged in without her would be void of any life.

Why did she do so? He was really cross. Doesn't she know that without her company, I wouldn't dine, couldn't dine? Did she do so purposefully? For one and a half months, without break, besides chipping in the money, she wholeheartedly handled all work, pertaining to the beautification of this office and this occasion. Today, what the heck! He thought of calling again, but had no telephone connection at home. At this hour, no public phone would be available too. Why not visit her? Though exhausted, he exited, locked the door behind him, and took out his scooter. It was 11:15 then. There were streetlights, but above, darkness congealed and the shining stars increased the intensity of the darkness. As the cool breeze coursed about him, he felt his fatigue subside. Leaving the Kukkarahalli Lake to the right, passing by his new office premises that was inaugurated this morning, and crossing the Hardinge Circle, as he neared the curve by the zoo, even though it was desolate, his hand squeezed the clutch lever, his feet applied the brakes to decelerate the vehicle, and as he sped up after passing the curve, he reflected that her caution was ingrained into his nervous system. This place is really forlorn. Of all places, why has she chosen this for her residence? Though owned, it is in a really dangerous place! He accelerated, and when he was about a furlong and a half from her house, the rear red lights of a car, yes, it is reversing, which house is it, the streetlight pole indicates that it is hers. The car reversed. He slowed down. The car turned towards the hill. Floodlights are on full blast. He accelerated. Car lunged forward. He, too, increased the speed. Everything was fully visible in the scooter light. It was her old

Fiat car – cream colour, faded, the number plate behind, that same number ! Where is she going alone ? Where else ? The gradient on the hill. Along with the kids ? Or has she left them behind in the desolate house and is headed alone to the woods ! He jacked up the speed and, in the light of the scooter, clearly saw that she was alone. None else. At that moment, she looked back. She has noticed the headlight of the scooter. The light is seen. But the rider would not be visible. She jacked up the speed. His scooter lagged. Ahead where the road split towards Lalitamahal, he deliberately swerved left. After she had scaled the hill more than two miles, he returned and tailed her. Why is she driving up the hill at this hour ? Mysterious curiosity pervaded, dissolving his hunger and fatigue. He increased the speed of the scooter. The gradient of the meadow paved way for the gradient of the hill proper and the momentum regressed. As he shifted to lower gear and accelerated, the glow of the headlight increased. It is impossible for her to escape from this place. He jacked up the speed of the engine to its limits. By the time I catch up, she would have reached the temple. It is difficult to keep pace with a car, he thought as he scaled, but at that moment, he saw a parked car to his left by the curve that led to the big pond. Yes, it is her car number. Steering still in hand, she has shut off the engine, the headlight, and the taillight. Thrilled and feeling a sense of accomplishment for having caught up with her quickly, he drove up to the driver's window, stopped, and, without cutting the engine, asked anxiously, 'What on earth is this lonely drive at this unearthly hour ? When you left with the priest, didn't you promise to drop him and return ?'

The light of the scooter was aglow. She did not turn towards him. Didn't speak any. She sat her place as if she hadn't heard him, as if she had no nexus with not just his words but with her fond purlieu, and as if she were a preternatural image that belonged in a different world altogether. 'Don't you know how dangerous it is to be here ?' Even these words did not reach unto her. For two minutes, he sat on his scooter and waited. Then he cut the engine, pushed it forward to the kerb, parked right in front of her car, retraced his steps to her car, extended his arm inside, and threw the switch of the cabin light. In the light, the revolver that rested beside her came in view. 'Even though you possess a revolver, it is dangerous for a woman to go here at this hour,' he said. Her face was visible. The lustre of a corpse! A cadaver state that was oblivious of the environs and of its body. Taking hold of her right shoulder, he shook her, 'Amrita, Amrita, you hear me?' and tried to elicit response from her.

Slowly, she turned her ghostly eyes towards him and said, 'While a lonely woman drives at night, no gentleman follows her and pretends to deviate at the fork. Why did you come here, sir?'

'I came searching for you. Even as I was one and a half furlong away from your house, I saw you exit and turn in the direction of the hill.'

She did not reply any. She turned her face towards the bonnet, donning the same inanimate mien. He could not think of anything more to say. She is very angry with me. He knew that when void pervaded her, her lingo turned deferential. It occurred to him that since this morning, she was swathed in void. Deciding that he should dint that void and instil at least some amplitude, he asked, 'Why have you come here at this hour? You must answer.' No response. She lifted her left hand and switched off the light. Darkness pervaded the car too. Her locus and her form ceased to appear even hazily. Now darkness became a medium and served as a mysterious conduit for conversation. He said again, 'You must answer.'

'What authority have you to ask, sir?' she replied immediately, as if it were easy to converse in the darkness.

'What authority? Authority of I being your Somu. The authority of love.'

'Mr Somashekhar, enough of fancy-gadding. You wield no authority over me whatsoever. Neither have I any authority over you. Don't you turn out to be a deterrent to understanding the actuality of this relationship ! Now on, don't pull this bamboozling crap on me.'

'Does that mean that my love for you and your love for me is false ?' he asked helplessly.

'At least it is false that I love you. I was in delusion of being in love. Now, with the illusion banished, I got to know the truth. If *you* desire to hover in illusion, it is up to you. Well, move the scooter and make way. Or, let me reverse and move.' She gunned the engine and put on the floodlights. He felt unsettled. He felt the root of his life, of his soul yanked out, and got dizzy. He could not lay hands on anything else, so he held on to the window of the car and stood. He sat down when it became difficult for him to remain standing. The swish of the still night that engulfed the outside world streamed into his head and he lost all consciousness as to where he was and what was becoming of him. He leaned back against the car and spread his legs. In a state where the consciousness of time ceased, he knew not as to how long he stayed sprawled. At long last, when he regained consciousness, the car's engine was off and the floodlights too. He became aware that he lay crippled, completely drained. The mud, grime, and bits of tassel that stuck to his clothes pricked his skin and itched. No strength to stand up, neither the desire to. The feeling that he was a lone, vile creature in the entire hill that was darkness congealed and personified engulfed him. Leaning on the car, he still sat.

In a while, her voice poured into his ears. 'Somashekhar, I am not averse to coming to terms with reality. But this drama to extract sympathy detests me.'

He never imagined that cruelty could be as ruthless as this. He wanted to contest her words. He felt irate. In the sway of ire, strength pooled. He instantly got up, turned towards her, and said, 'Rascal, don't just spill your vocabulary. You don't deserve to know what throbs my heart.'

'What would be in a heart?' she asked in calm disdain.

'Love. Such degree of love, the understanding of which is beyond your merit.'

Indifferently, she said, 'Fine,' and turned silent. After some time, she said as calmly but in a challenging tone, 'Can you prove that?'

He felt as if he got something to latch on to. He reeled on, 'Prove? Tell me how I should go about it. Should I bare my heart and show? You may chide me if I cite the instance of Hanuman stripping his heart to show the form of Rama. But how shall I convey to you the depth of my love?'

She didn't speak. He stood in the darkness waiting for her reply. In another minute, she spoke calmly but in a firm tone, 'There is but a way of proving. It will at least establish how fancy-gadding your words are. Are you game?'

'Sure,' he committed without even a second's delay.

'Truly?'

'Swear on you. Haven't anything more endearing for me to swear on.' Vivaciously, he pledged all the more.

Now she put on the light inside. The light pierced his eyes. Her eyes though were opaque entities that were oblivious of the divide between dense darkness and glowering dazzle. Slowly turning to her left, she picked up the revolver and, offering it to him, said, 'Here, hold this.' He took it. 'Aim it so,' she took hold of the nozzle, aimed it at her temple, and, holding it firmly there, said, 'Nothing else. Just pull the trigger. That's all,' and closed her eyes. He perspired profusely. He knew very well the constitution of guns and revolvers. While in college, as part of the cadets training, he had got to know about the guns – LMG and MMG. He knew that the trigger was volatile and would blast off bullet at the hint of a touch. Eyes closed, she sat like a statuette, ready. His body began to shiver mildly. Wary that this quiver should perchance cause pressure on the trigger and dispatch the bullet, he retrieved his arm and held the revolver aimed toward the sky. After two minutes' silence, she turned towards him and said, 'Finished proving your love?'

'You may speak foolishly, but I can't comply,' he scoffed at her.

'It won't become foolishness if you so label it. Neither would it become sagacious if you so reward it. I'll ask my wish. If you haven't the ability and fondness to confer it, it is your airs. I will suggest an alternative. Will you abide?'

'Tell me.'

'I am not stating this in the spirit of one who tenders a plea and begs to be blessed. This is rather an opportunity to prove your love, and *I* am making it available to you.'

'Tell me.'

'Point the nozzle of the revolver at your temple and pull the trigger. It is okay even if you point it at your heart. Very many times, you have declared that you are ever-ready to shed your life for my sake. Come on, now prove it.'

At that moment, he felt that this was rather an easy way out. It was at once clear to him that it was easy to shoot himself than to shoot her. 'Can do this,' he said.

'Not *can*. *Should*,' her gaze rooted in the void, she exhorted without turning towards him.

By then, he had regained his senses. 'If I did that, what would you gain?'

'You will not do it. All your words are lines from a play. I just wanted to establish that they are the limericks that come forth naturally while merrymaking with a beautiful and educated girl who does not entail the onus of any maintenance.'

'Is it your understanding that if I shed my life, my love would then be genuine and not voluptuous? I will establish that my love is genuine by living and resuscitating you, not by the foolishness of killing or getting killed. If you so desire to kill, here, take this, shoot me yourself. I will stand still,' he placed the revolver on her lap and stood like a statue.

'But then, you have no desire to die,' she combed out a flaw in his words.

'Yes, I haven't at all. I rather desire to live; that you live too. But if you want to kill me, go ahead. Wait, I will put it in writing and insert the note in my trouser pocket that I alone am responsible for my death, that I have shot myself with a revolver.'

'I am not so cruel as to kill someone who wants to live. You are a cruel one that forbids one to die even if one wants to. People reward the likes of you, referring to their words as great and profound. Nobody understands the truth of my words. There is none as cruel as you. The sinner God too cannot understand your cruelty.' She turned right and struck her forehead to the sill of the car door twice. He saw a lump appear on her forehead, inflame, and the blood clot from the blunt strike. He extended a hand to check her and console her. But a primed revolver sat on her lap. Even a slight shuffle could set off the trigger. If not directly, the bullet may still enter some part of her body by rebounding on hitting the inside of the car. He moved his hand towards the revolver. 'Lay off your hands. Don't dare touch it!' she barked. He withdrew his hand. Instantly, she put off the light, gunned the engine, and abruptly reversed. Startled, he stepped back. She drove backwards speedily. Anxious that she may slide into the cliff, unable to see properly in the dark, he called out, 'Amrita! Amrita!' She heard nothing of it. She breezed backwards till the road was a bit even and manoeuvred thrice before gaining direction. She then drove speedily down the hill. In seven to eight minutes, she had drove far enough as not to be heard even in the stillness of midnight. He stood there, not knowing what to do next.

Not even was enough strength left in him to guess whether she would have gone home or elsewhere after leaving from here. He became flummoxed. The darkness was so intense that he wouldn't be able to see his hand, even if it were waved before his eyes. At midnight, she has gone to this forlorn hill alone, taking the revolver with her. Maybe it was in her purport that if she shot herself, it should be heard only by the sleeping birds, squirrels, rabbits, and foxes, and not by any human being. Why this instantaneous desire to die? His heart empathized with her. Even now if she went home and thereat … he got anxious. She has driven from her house to this hill. No, she wouldn't do that at home, for it would petrify the children. Maybe, she didn't want the children to be witness to the scene of their mother's gory death. So if she were back home, she wouldn't do any of that. Or has she gone elsewhere and … that apprehension increased his anxiety. He thought of riding his scooter and scour for her. But where to? Which road to take? The T-Narsipura Road, Bannur Road, this road to Nanjangud, or which of the other routes that branch out after exiting Mysore? He was indeterminate. In case I do get to her, what next? Can forcibly snatch the revolver from her. But even that is dangerous. In the skirmish of taking hold of the primed revolver, what if it went off! He surmised it was impossible for his scooter to catch up with her at her speed. By such time, his eyes got accustomed to the darkness and he sighted a boulder by the side of the road. As he sat on it after examining it, he felt a bit fortified. As if he had held his breath still all through, he took in deep breaths, one too many. The laboured breathing, like on an unremitting uphill trek, made him feel that he would then and there collapse and die in exhaustion. His chest continued to heave and, after many more deep breaths, his memory got clear. Even if I forcibly took hold of the revolver.…Well, she would not let me near her. Not just repelling words, severe repulsion exudes from her persona. Sans any verbalization, it will denigrate me, mock, scoff, and cast me off as something inferior to filth. It will create a taciturn situation wherein my tongue gets tied, wherein anything uttered by me will be labelled a lie. It will give a warped meaning to the words that emerge from within me and rub it in my face. It will doubt my honesty and thereby malign and disparage my personality. Thus rolled on the analysis of his feelings. The thought that he was rejected by her dwindled his credence.

In a while, fear overcame him. The shrill darkness. The valley at the waist of the hill. Though there wouldn't be any tigers and cheetahs, there is no dearth of foxes, iguana, snakes, lizards, and scorpions. And possibly owls and bats. He reflected that an owl which can see in darkness has more destructive capacity than a human who cannot. What of staying back here? He thought of just driving back home. But for her to come here at this frightening unearthly hour alone, what courage! He recalled that to live with two small children in that big house amidst forlorn surroundings on the outskirts of the city wouldn't be possible without guts. But to go to this hill alone in the dark! What fear has one who has set out to die? Isn't the love of life, the fear for life the basal tone of apprehension? What if she would have shot herself by now? That thought bothered him again. Shall I drive straight to her house, jump over the gate, and ring the doorbell? If she has really committed it, it would have all been over in a split second. That thought made him sob. His eyes got moist, throat wrung, and breath got stuck. God, Goddess Chamundi, bestow wisdom on her, pervade her mind, and contain her. None other than you can check her now. His jolted mind sought orientation. Even if he went now, he thought, she would not open the door; she would rebuff him and shove him out. He forfeited even the smallest amount of mental strength required to pull himself up, and stayed seated on the stone. Having nothing to lean on, pain surfaced in the waist and back. Searing agony churned in his stomach. Why this vacillation? What happened of my determination? Introspecting, he sat, supporting his drooping head with his hands. Quite some time passed. He began to doze.

By then, he heard the sound of an automobile. Could not say if it was a car or a jeep. There is the Rajendra Vilas hotel on the hilltop. Is anybody who has attended some party there descending? Atop is the police wireless relay centre. Could be a police van. Sitting here alone at this hour, what are you up to? Who are you? What brings you here? He got anxious as to what answer he should give if they interrogated thus. Could say that I just came so for a stroll, an lolling. But what time is it now? If he had to consult his watch, he had to start his scooter for light. Haven't the least idea to tell the time by looking up and noticing the position of the stars. And as he considered that he wasn't conversant enough to recognize even one in the melee of the countless stars, he heard the automobile proximate, scale up from below. Not a big one, a car, may be one from the hotel's fleet. As he reflected that it could be a taxi ferrying those who disembarked from a delayed flight from Bangalore, its light was in full view. As it drew nearer, its two floodlights devastated the mysterious darkness that abound hitherto, and he felt as if he were bared for scrutiny. He wanted to turn his face away as the lights blinded his eyes. But he became aware that his visit here alone at this hour would send wrong feelers if he shied away. Neither turning his neck nor eyeing the car, he fixed his gaze in the yonder peak and sat still. The car drove up speedily and pointedly came to a sudden halt right in front of him. The engine shut out and the light inside went up, revealing the identity of the lone occupant, Amrita. He did not even look at her directly. She opened the door and came out. Passing by the car front, she neared him, flung out her arms, and held him in a snug embrace even as he sat his place, thereby squashing his face against her bosom. Leaden, he sat like a cold stone statue. He did not utter a single word. She arched a bit more and further tightened her embrace. The heaving of her heart was audible even to the feel of his forehead, eyes, and cheek. As if to inundate him with her warm sentiments, she held her lips pressed to his head. The tears that flowed from her eyes penetrated the hair and dampened his head. 'Somu, asking to be excused or saying *forget it* hold no meaning now. I know that even if you choose to pardon my misdeeds, God will not. I too can never pardon myself. The festivities of the afternoon, the dinner of the evening, I know that you haven't eaten even one morsel all day. I also understand that you have rejected the new clothes and worn the old trousers and a bush shirt. Now don't speak any. Ride your scooter ahead. I will follow you in my car. I have realized that it is in God's edict that we both eat my cuisine, not Suryanarayanappa's. Drive to my house. Let's dine first and talk later. There is much to tell. In who else shall I disgorge myself?' He still didn't utter anything. Sat unaffectedly. 'It is but natural that you harbour disdain towards me. It is also apt that you resolve not to speak to me for life. Punish me in whatever way you wish. But I too am deadbeat from starving all day. If you don't come, I will continue my fasting. Any number of days. Unto death. But it is easy and facile to shoot with a revolver than to die by fasting. If you now say that you won't excuse me or if you don't escort me, pulling the trigger will become so much easy.' She stood still for half a minute. Then she tugged at his arms and, pulling him up, said, 'Get up. No matter how much your indignation is, I know that it never will be so much as to shove your Amrita to death.' Silently he got up, ambled up to his scooter, and kick-started it.

Reaching the house, after they had shut themselves inside, she looked at him and said, 'First you should change. Should take off these and wear the dhoti. Know why? You got giddy, leaned against the car, and collapsed. Yet, I callously remained still. The mud and grime of the road is all on your shirt and trousers. As you drove ahead, I could see it from behind and felt mortified. Not because you fell, but because I stayed unaffected despite. Wait, let me hand you the dhoti. Meanwhile, wash your face and feet.' She took him to the toilet in the guest room. By the time he washed, changed, and entered the kitchen, it was 3:15 am. She had lighted the stove and was frying semolina and ghee in a pan. Water was boiling in the kettle.

'Don't prepare anything now. Let's eat a bit of whatever is left over,' he neared her to check.

She said, 'There is curry in the fridge. Rice is almost done in the cooker. There is curd. But today is the inauguration of the office premises. We haven't eaten. We must have sweets today. I am preparing *kesaribhāt*. It will be done in five minutes. Your peel some cardamom and pound it. There is no raisin or cashew in the pantry.'

Thinking that it would wake up the children if they sat at the dining table outside, she laid the dishes on the breakfast table in the kitchen. She closed the kitchen door and, sitting on the chair next to him, said, 'Should eat *kesaribhāt* first. You have ground the cardamom, so it must be tasty,' and with a spoon, she fed it to him. Though his mind wasn't presently tempered for gaiety, he nevertheless ingested it, took a spoonful from his plate, and fed her. Both sensing that it would have turned out to be one helluva fiasco if this ritual were not observed, they fed each other no more. He began gobbling it up, reflecting that he never got to know the taste of Suryanarayanappa's *kesaribhāt*. This, though, is delicious. Hungry all day, she too silently munched. Both their hunger satiated, when they started on the chill curd-rice that she removed from the fridge, she said, 'The question why I abruptly left in the morning is on the tip of your tongue. Tell me, don't you feel like asking it?'

'When I know the answer very well, why should I prod you?' he put his left arm over her, squeezed her shoulder, and said in a consoling tone.

'What is the answer that you know?' she asked in a credulous tone.

Lovingly tightening his embrace and succulent with feelings, he said in cadence, 'Amrita, I know that not infrequently, you are plagued by feelings of void. You have shared it with me many times. Suddenly, you will turn tart, will bark. But to exit from the house in the dark and go to the other side of the hill alone, taking the revolver! Swear on me and give me your word now that you will henceforth never venture out of the house and never touch the revolver unless robbers attempt to break in. I will take serious exception to it if you don't. Come on, hold my hand and pledge in God's witness.'

She put her arm around his shoulders and said in a parched voice that had a typical logical tenor to it, 'Your account of the pervasion of the feelings of void are all okay. To cause to pledge in the witness of God only demonstrates your copious sentiment. But you are not inclined to think and gather why I so departed this morning.'

'Don't say I am not inclined. Many a time, you will suddenly be nagged by feelings of void … ' She cut short his contentions and said, 'Suddenly! Nothing befalls suddenly, just like that, and for no reason whatsoever. You are not inclined to figure out the reason. Even if you knew, you don't like to openly admit it.'

'Amrita, I am aware of your situation, of the injustice that has been perpetrated on you. I have even told you several times to just forget it, or just pardon them all and be rid of it. Now, what does it mean when you say that I don't understand?' he said, not meaning to counter her scorn but to make his point clear.

'Somashekhar, it is clear that you are not inclined to broach the subject. Enough of discussion now. Get up and wash your hands. It is 3:50 am now. Will you go home or will you retire to the guest room?' she collected their plates from the dining table.

The ingested food made him feel sluggish and his mind went blank. 'If I sleep here, would not the children ponder why uncle slept here through the night? Wouldn't the help and the cook, on arriving at daybreak, get ideas?'

'If you are so apprehensive, leave now. You indicated an answer to my question. Thanks.' As if she had finished conveying the final words, she headed to the sink. He washed his hands and mouth under the tap by the backdoor, returned to the lounge, and sat on the sofa. He felt so fatigued that he wanted to recline and slide into sleep. Knowing fully well that if he did sleep, it would only fuel her ire further, with effort he kept his eyes open and sat. Yawns that dilated his jaws so wide as to tear apart the mandible came a dozen. He heard her go to her bedroom. Vacillating whether to recline here on the sofa or just drive home, with effort he kept his eyelids open and stayed awake for ten minutes. By then, she arrived there and, posting herself before him, said, 'If we assemble here and talk, the children will wake up. So I will not talk. Isn't this the reason why you left the kitchen and came here?' she put the blame squarely on him.

'No such thoughts occurred to me then or now. I was tired. I came here to recline on the sofa,' he said.

'It is not just you who is tired, sir. I have walked more than three miles this afternoon. All day I fasted too. It may just be my imagination that you were fasting. The fact may be entirely different. And I am not interested to know about it.'

He had understood that it was in her faculty to craft a scalpel out of any issue and perforate anything with it. Aware that she would antagonistically twist each word, try as he might with utmost patience to bring to her cognizance the state of affairs, he beckoned her to the kitchen, escorted her there, and sat on the same chair by the breakfast table where they had been a little before. Following him, she closed the kitchen door, firmly hugged his face, planted an intense kiss on his lips, and said, 'Somu, I know that you are tired and sleepy. You know that barring you, there is none else with whom I can share the misery that is searing within me. Yet, did you care to ask why I abruptly left in the forenoon? Where I went? What I did?' And so that they could converse easily, she sat opposite him.

'Know how much I awaited you? At 1 pm, I called your house. And when the first batch of dinner was underway, I took leave of

Neelakanthappa and came here. Gate was locked. I waited for quarter of an hour, and leaving....' He related all his anxieties, reminiscences, and pains.

'I know that you harbour love towards me. Else, wouldn't you stay away without enduring all the excruciating battering that I inflict on you? Know what happened of me? I did visit there daily and supervise the wall designs, furniture, your chamber, and everything else by applying my mind day and night, even in my dreams. I thought out the details of the housewarming ceremony too and sent word for the same priest and caterer who handled Vikas's christening. What were the priest's feelers? He surmised that it was my office that was being inaugurated, my husband's, and hence the hustle and bustle. Morning I did not pick him up. He came by himself in an auto. You weren't there yet. I received him and took him upstairs. Inspecting all the effects that I had appointed for the occasion, he said, 'Everything is perfect. Let's start. Call your husband.' What would be my feelings! You are the lord and I am the lady of this office alright. But can I share that with him? Can we share the altar together, hold the spatula in unison, and consign ghee to *agni* that he invokes and raises? If we do, will *agni* accept it? Besides, due to my misplaced discretion, I had sent for Ranganath to partake in the occasion of Vikas's christening. This same priest then had us both consign ghee to *agni*. Now if he saw you, wouldn't he notice the difference? I said, 'This is my relative's office. He is single. You please handle all the rites and distribute the consecrations.' He started on it. A battery of questions began pricking, digging, and burrowing my mind as if with a crowbar, pickaxe, and hoe. This isn't a question involving either just the priest or partaking in the rites. The priest's oeuvre would all be over in one and a half to two hours. Not much guests would be present then. It is at lunch hour that the majority of guests assembles. In the evening, they arrive in lots. In their presence, what is my standing? Who is this woman – they would discuss among themselves – clad in a new sari moving about like the lady of the house, supervising? What is she to architect Somashekhar? What would the furtive glances of thousands of eyes make of me? You may think, "Why, shouldn't a friend handle all this?" But actually, we aren't just friends. People wouldn't believe of just plain friendship between a man and woman.

'As I kept noticing the flames invoked by the priest flare by the intermittent fuelling of ghee, the question of my position there began bothering me. By now, you would be aware that my memory is really good. The priest was uttering the very same mantras that he had pronounced during the *homa* of the christening ceremony. From there, my mind was drawn to the *homa* at hand. While I shared the altar during that ritual, I recalled that I had conceived and borne that child by deceit. That Ranganath who sat by me was never my husband. What sort of a *homa* was that as his consort? The thought that I should go some place and kill myself with the revolver occurred to me for the very first time there at the altar. But I am the lady of the occasion. I just couldn't leave the place. I had no refuge. Even here in the *homa* at your office, I am devoid of locus. Understand?' she stared at him.

He kept looking at her face. Her pupils were truly fossilized as of a rootless wraith. He was at a loss for words. She too silently kept staring. He found it difficult to counter her stare. He toned down the onslaught of the stare by a question that just flashed in his mind. 'The first one hour I was wondering as to why, instead of sending him in an auto, you should have gone yourself to drop the priest.'

'That pretext came my way to exit from there. I left to drop him. Even otherwise, I would just have slid out. Straight to where? Know? Guess.'

'Nothing strikes. Can't guess.'

'The Kannambadi Dam. Paid the entry fee, drove straight in, and parked by the restaurant. Then I scaled the stairs past the

Kaveri statue to the dam. The waters were furiously pummelling the barrier that had arrested them. By the dam, it would be hundred or hundred and twenty feet deep. I stood watching it intently. What would be the stamina of the dam that has arrested the surge of the water and caused it to pool into backwaters, stretching over a score mile? Sorts of amazement! In a while, I got an idea. I turned around and noticed. Nobody was nearby. A fatal attraction overcame me, of going over the waist-level fence into the water. If an irate wave would instantly engulf me, whirl me in a ten or twenty feet arc, and, within half a minute, smash me against the stone wall of the barrage! Even before the strike is executed, the water entering the stomach and lungs through the mouth and nose would have evicted the life. Life's agonies would be rid. Then, a state where there would be no suffering or agony. Every stoma of the flesh and marrow being waterlogged, the body morphing into water – water has no pain, no suffering. It will keep buoying sinuously, presently here at the dam, and then all along the river. Culminating in the ocean, it will keep wafting gracefully there too. Why shouldn't I become that, relieve myself of this agony? The desire was irresistible. Once again, I looked around. Nobody. Though there were one or two people at a distance, no certainty that they would notice me crossing over the fence and jump. Even if they did, by the time they would notice and dart, it would all be over, what with I partaking in the cyclic tides and my body serving as a mould for the water. What can a panicky man do? Nobody would jump into this deathtrap to save another. However accomplished a swimmer be, what with saving another, he can't remain alive himself. No possibility whatsoever of my effort going in vain. Why not cross over the fence? I kept thinking and stood my place. Did not execute what would be over in a jiffy. Even now I wonder what befalls my resolve at the crucial moment. I am filled with remorse at my cowardice too. Watching the cyclic tides of the reservoir for some time more, I walked further to the other end of the dam. There, a little above the Vishveshwaraya canal, is an opening from where you can trek down to the canal. Seen it?'

He nodded in assent.

'I trekked down there and stood by the canal. You would have seen that. Who hasn't! Which other spot is there as ideal and sure-fire for people attempting suicide? If once seen and the scene imprinted in the mind, enough, those who aspire to terminate their lives will go discerning it even from hundreds of miles afar. Today, no, isn't it dawn already, yesterday afternoon, I came to know what the enticement of the sluice of that canal was.' As she related it, the picture of that spot surfaced in his memory. He had first seen it with his classmates and teacher during his engineering course. The technical aspects of such and such cusecs of water gushing out at this amount of force per minute, the force itself depending on the pressure of stock to the other side of the dam, etc. received a backseat, and, yes, gushing out as white froth at a feverish pace, whirling inside out, water cramming within a hundredth-thousandth of a second the lung and stomach of whoever fell into it, twirling the body over and over again before releasing it for further journey, spinning it at least a thousand times....One watching it would get a feeling of the heart being thrust upwards and get stuck at the throat, of a temptation of static dread. One would be so rooted to the sight that to think of retreating would be most difficult. He explained it all to her. Quite naturally, the contentment she derived had fraternal overtones.

Extending her arm over the table, she squeezed his right hand and said, 'Somu, the fact that it engenders feelings in you similar to mine begets solace that I am not lonesome. Why hadn't you shared it with me even once before? Know how many times I have been there? To go there and stand by it in total submission to its gravitational force is in itself an intense experience. An experience cherished and hankered by my mind that is wont to be in a state of death. I will not go there just to get the feel of it. Will rather go there with a compulsion to really go down. Yesterday, I came to know that death and the locus of death could be so very beautiful, so artistically attractive. Felt that to exterminate life with a revolver was an ugly method. Yesterday afternoon, I stood there for more than an hour. Why I stood? You may ask as to why I didn't just jump and become one with that allure in a fraction of a second. The fact is that by then I had understood the situation. The reason I drove straight there was the ire against you, a compulsion to go away from you. By then, it was 2 pm. What would be happening there by now? The second batch of dining would be underway. You would be everywhere, bequeathing civility on the guests. Hungry, you would have helped yourself to some halva or *kesaribhāt*, sipping a glass of the thin of curry flavoured with fresh ghee. Or, I even thought that after showing everyone to their seats, you too would have sat before a plantain leaf and had your belly full. Know how angry I was? What a dejected feeling! Whether I am alive or dead or preparing to die, nothing ceases in his life. New office premises, inaugurals, dinner, evening reception, his victuals and nourishment, nothing ceases. Dejection! At that moment, it seemed so easy to just jump into the invitingly gushing hubbub of the waters; there were even a few moments when I came very close to take the plunge. Really. But to go over, the resolve has to concretize. It was indeed steeling fast. But presently, a man came from behind and yelled so as to be heard even in the midst of the roaring waters, "Who are you madam, standing alone? Is that your car parked on the other side?" I looked back. A burly man. From his trimmed hair and the style of the moustache, I surmised that he was a watchman or a works supervisor or a policeman in plain clothes. Anyone would get ideas as to the intentions of a lone person, a woman, who stood there at the ledge of the killer gush for a good length of time. I got irritated. I yelled so as to be heard above the din, "I have bought an entry ticket. I have the right and liberty to stand at any place and watch anything as long as I wish." "Yet, there is an order in force not to allow anyone near this spot. Okay, suit yourself, but I too will stand guard here," he said and posted himself a few yards from me, as if to watch the scenery below. If another person keeps observing us, stands in close proximity to us, will our feelings remain ours? I glared at him once and moved away from there. In the sun, I walked past Brindavan and drove out in my car. Where to go from there? It was 3:15. Then it struck me. I had told the children that I would take them to the housewarming ceremony of uncle's office premises. Hadn't even given them their lunch box. They would be waiting, hungry. If they informed Susheelamma that mother had promised to come but hasn't, she would feed them. Yet, promising them, I had failed to keep it. A sinner I am! Felt like smacking my head in regret. Drove speedily to the school. It was closing hour. I first comforted them – too much work at college, hence could not take them to the function. Susheelamma had indeed fed them. Vijai asked, "Mom, today Susheelamma madam taught us a lesson on gardens. She showed pictures. Brindavan gardens was among them. Mom, will you take us there?" I said okay. How could I leave out Susheelamma's children? Invited them too, and Susheelamma. Quickly attending to their toiletries, freshened up myself, and along with them drove to Kannambadi again. At 5 in the evening. The children's joy knew no bounds. Added to that, Susheelamma would become one with them at play and keep them happy. I gave chocolates and popcorn to all. I just had a cup of coffee, complaining of a queasy stomach. Just three hours before, I was in an intense state of mind, determined to end my life by going down the chute. Though the severity of that desire had reduced a bit presently, the feeling stayed. Yet, I had to mingle with the children – run, hop, and partake in their childlike enthusiasm and eagerness! What a torture! Besides, without exposing the agony within me, I had to chat naturally with Susheelamma about the animation and afflictions of the grown-ups. She is wont to talk to me about all and sundry whenever I meet her leisurely. Fasting since morning. No energy left in the legs to walk. Had to trek the length and breadth of Brindavan along with the children. At 7, when the gardens were illuminated, the children got very excited. It made me cheerful too. The children's happiness, I thought, what else do I need? Red water, green water, blue water, they would collect handfuls of them and scoop them up. I too would emulate, and in between playing hide-and-seek, the fatigue of fasting was forgotten. At 8, with the lighting going off, the excitement waning, and reality returning, getting them all into the car, I first dropped Susheelamma and her kids at their house, and when I returned home with Vijai and Vikas, the anchored dogs were in despair from hunger. The sight brought tears to my eyes. I let them out of their kennels, fondled them, showered my love, and fed them. Later, I fed my children who were spent from the romping and playing. After consigning them to their beds, feelings of void set in.

Exhilaration and agitation aside, life has no meaning at all. The onslaught of the shameful feeling as to why I was keeping myself alive, trudging through such a brazen life, began pounding me. The resolve surfaced to finish myself with the revolver, not wasting even one minute. But with the sound of bullet reverberating in the house, I reflected that the children would recoil in horror at the sight of the bleeding corpse of their mother in the wee hours. So I took hold of my revolver and drove out. By the time I left the gate, I noticed the headlight of your scooter. I instantly knew it was you. Know how irate I was with you? Augmenting this was the anger that had brewed on that plainclothes policeman who had approached me at the threshold of the spillway earlier and had proved a hindrance to my liberation. Both causes of my indignation were targeted at you. Yet, I habitually drove towards the hill....' Presently, the caw of a crow was heard outside. A peek out of the window revealed that it was dawning. She had finished relating her travails of the previous noon. He sat through it all in gloom. He could not think of any words. In a short while, light streamed in through the window. She said, 'The cook Puttamma may come early. I have to wake up the children and get them ready for school. You go to Jayalakshmipuram and get some sleep at least.'

~

Though he returned home and retired, sleep did not take over. Not only was it daylight and past the resting hours, the picture of her standing at the ledge in the dark, ready to kill herself, revolver in hand, would appear as soon as he closed his eyes. She could accomplish this any night. The hill is nearby. Car will be ready. The loaded revolver will be in the chest by the bed. And though he had heard it from the horse's mouth that the desire to die would surface now and then, it was clear to him that he never imagined that it would be this acute. He shuddered from the thought that she could any moment shoot herself. What if she did shoot herself! His mind clogged, rendering it impossible for him to even think or imagine what was in store after that. Lying down, he opened his eyes and looked at his watch. It was 7. By now, the cook Puttamma would have arrived. Mahadevamma, the domestic help, would have come too. She would have wakened the children and getting them ready for school. She would be tottering, drained from being denied overnight sleep. Let her totter – he prayed closing his eyes – but let her not die by shooting herself. Till about 10 am, the cook and the domestic help would both be in attendance. The housemaid would keep up with sweeping and mopping that big house, washing clothes, cleaning the dishes, putting the kitchen back in order, and sweeping and irrigating the garden thereafter. She leaves a little after noon, subsequent to Amrita returning from college. Would she go to college or take leave of absence today? Mahadevamma would be in – he felt encouraged – so she won't be lonely, wouldn't shoot herself. That reassurance brought some sleep.

He got up at 10:30, bathed, and left for office. Neelakanthappa was engaged in shifting the files, duplicator, the draughtsman's sloping desk, typewriter, manuals, etc. from the old premises to the new. The telecom people had assured that they would transfer the connection today. He went to a nearby restaurant, had breakfast, and participated in the shifting work till after noon. Everything being suitably arranged, work would systematically start tomorrow. Instructing Neelakanthappa to take care of everything, he excused himself for lunch.

As he drove, his heart prayed silently – God, let her be safe. After passing the curve by the zoo, he drove speedily and stopped by her house. Hearing the sound of the scooter, Vikrant at the front gate barked in greeting. Vishvas behind woofed in tandem. Gate was not locked. But the front door was shut. He stayed from ringing the doorbell for it would cause reverberation. If she were home, she would have opened the door on hearing the scooter and the barking dogs. Rather, she would be waiting outside, rendering redundant the need for such auditory alerts. Has not returned from college. Or, like yesterday, Kannambadi, the sluice of the Vishveshwaraya canal! His heart began pounding and he panicked. Gently, he tried the door. He could gather that it was not locked; was just latched. Even if in, perchance the revolver....He got panicky again. But a kind of faith arose within him that she would have inflicted no such thing on herself. Guessing that sleep having eluded her all night, she would be asleep, he just stood his place. After about two minutes, he circled the house from the right and peeped through her bedroom window. One window was open. She was asleep on the big cot under the dawdling fan. The left side of the tender lovely face appeared in view. Breathing is causing her chest to swell and fold. He was relieved. His heart's craving to call out '*Amrita*' turned into a want and furthered to a point of parting his lips and relocating his tongue. But he contained himself, reflecting that despite not having slept all night, she probably wouldn't have rested in the morning too and possibly attended college. Two minutes after taking in the panorama brimful into his eyes, he silently moved away thinking that such alien observation would possibly be sensed by the inner mind and disturb her sleep. He then exited the gate, closed it, and so that the sound of the scooter would not wake her up, he towed it for about two hundred feet, gunned it, drove to a restaurant, had puri and coffee, went to his new office, and began organizing his cabin. In a while, the telecom crew activated the telephone line. Everything as she designed. If closeted inside with the air conditioner on, not even an iota of sound from outside is heard. Shall I make the first call to her? She is also alone at home. She can pick up the phone by the bed and converse, reclined as she is. But he restrained himself, not wanting to disturb her sleep. Opening a file, he began drawing the facade of the proposed building of a tobacco planter from Hunsur.

When Neelakanthappa left for the day at 8 pm, he called her. She received it herself. Didn't speak much though. Gathering that the children would be present, he related his afternoon visit and asked, 'I wish to see you very much. Shall I come over now?'

'If you want to, help yourself,' she said in a tone parched of any feeling.

'But at this hour, the children would be there,' he explained.

'Don't if you are apprehensive.'

He felt slapped in the face. It was not new that she talked to him in such a tenor. But she derides me, one who only spoke without forfeiting judgement, who, since morning, has been anxious and thinking of her well-being. He just wanted to replace the handset. He did not speak any. Rather, no words came, even though he gave a thought to it. He just stayed so for a while. He got curious if she would speak any or just cut the call. She did neither. He conceded at last, 'No apprehension for me. I just referred to our agreement that I shall not visit during nights when the children are present.'

'The authority to invite anyone I wish for supper is mine,' she said.

'Be there in half an hour,' he replaced the receiver.

Locking his office, he went to the market, discerned the mildly aromatic royal-jasmine string and bought arms' length of it. Then he went to the best sweet stall and bought enough of *badam halva* and *jangiri*, got them packed in an ordinary package without the logo of the store, rolled it in a newspaper, consigned it to the dicky of the scooter, and started. While he got the house repaired, her children had seen him a few times. He had talked to them affectionately. Ever since their friendship turned intimate, they had exercised care so as not to bring his visit to the children's notice. But a couple of times in between, on holidays, he had visited them, as if unexpectedly, dined with them and talked to their mother. She had suggested that he do so. Today, at the hour of his visit, Vijai and Vikas stood waiting by the door. It was they who opened the door. She came out later to greet him. 'Madam, you did not attend the inauguration. Neither sent the children. I just kept waiting all day,' he assumed precedence in conversation. 'Even my Vijai and Vikas asked me. But know what happened at college yesterday? Students went on strike. Principal was on leave. What is this? Have you brought the sweets of the occasion? What had you ordered?' She took hold of the packets and, opening them at the edges, said, 'Ah, my Vijai sir's favourite *badam halva* and Vikas's love *jangiri*. You got exactly these prepared. And though we did not attend the dinner, you have brought enough for eight days. You love the children so much. Haven't brought anything for me. Lads, that is uncle for you! He doesn't even know that my favourite is *āmbodē*. Seems like he has not got it prepared! At least, he hasn't brought it. Am I cross?' She went inside, unpacked them, put them in two plates, stuck a spoon, and gave it to the children. Though they just had supper and their bellies were full, they started to eat with relish. 'Look, sir, yesterday we could not attend the dinner of the housewarming occasion. Now though, you must have supper here. Will prepare rice in a jiffy. Please be seated.' In the presence of the children, she insisted that he stay on.

In front of the children, her face smacked of smile and merriment. But when she returned after consigning them to their beds and putting them to sleep by telling a story, the smile had disappeared and great sorrow exuded. In fact, there was enough stock of cooked rice. Her verbose statement of the need for cooking rice was for buying time to put the children to sleep so that they both could sup exclusively. Now, like yesterday morning, she served two plates on the breakfast table in the kitchen and took him there. While she served the curry, he asked, 'You had told me earlier. But I never understood that the stress would be as much.'

After helping herself to the curry, she said, 'Only those who have the experience know of it. How can aliens understand?'

He felt as if struck in the face. Even as I go about consoling her, tell her that your pain is mine, that I'm here to share your sufferings, with her very first words she thus wards me off! He could say nothing. Silence prevailed. A void silence. She did not attempt to talk. Head hung, he finished his curry-rice.

'Finished?' she asked. Finished what? He could not understand. He lifted his head and saw her face. 'I can very well see that the curry-rice is finished. I asked if you are finished with your words of consolation,' she said, laying the logic threadbare.

He was pained more. 'Do you think I am just expending words?'

'Just that, or maybe those filled with feelings! What else is it other than words?'

He could understand nothing. Words were a vehicle of expression of feelings, expression of the mind, and of what was deep inside the heart. Without them, how can one convey love and affection? He was perplexed. Did not utter anything though. After anticipating his response for a while, she said, 'I am a fool for expecting you to reply. Thou hath already replied, no, alluded.'

He still could not gather what. He just understood that her lingo had turned from intimate to formal. What have I alluded? What have you understood? He wanted to ask. But he contained himself, afraid that she would rub him in the face again. For the very first time, he realized that at such times, he feared her. Without any exchange of words, the curd-rice was being ingested. Ignoring his apprehension and her spiky retorts, he uttered what took shape deep within him. 'Know why I came now? To forcefully take away the revolver from you.'

She straightened up and looked him in the face. He could gather that her face was saturate with disdain. But she relented on the disdain, brought calmness to her face, and said, 'I have obtained the firearm licence for self-protection, as I reside on the outskirts of the town with two small kids.'

'If it were just for self-protection I wouldn't be worried,' he added hastily.

'If so, you move in here, sir. I will have no fear during nights. I will surrender the firearm licence.'

'I will,' he said enthusiastically as if he derived happiness by just uttering it, though he knew very well that it would simply not happen.

'True?' she asked, staring at him, indicating that he cannot get away with untrue and slight words. He was silent. 'Why silent?' she debated. He still kept quiet. 'I am fed up with the *poor thing* crap. Speak out the truth,' she egged on.

'Let us consider suggestions that are practicable. I am speaking seriously,' he replied.

'I too am speaking seriously. I too aspire for worthwhile talk.'

'How about appointing a gurkha at night? Let the police register his name and ratify his appointment. Let's give him a monthly salary like the watchmen in workplaces are given.'

'How about you posting yourself at the gate and undertaking surveillance each night? Monthly, not five hundred, I will pay you six hundred. If you insist, let's register with the police even,' disdain returned to her voice.

'If it is your intent to deride me in your every word....' He got up to wash his hands. By then, both had finished their supper.

'Please understand that I too will be belittled if you just go on and on with your smart talk,' she too got up and retorted as sharply.

'It is you who is acting smart. Don't accuse me of your meanness,' he retorted.

She glared at him as if she would rip him apart. He too returned her glare as if he would slash and cast off her sight. She instantaneously lifted her right hand and struck him right on his left cheek. His cheek began smarting where the four fingers that had curd on them struck. His right arm stiffened. But he instantly contained himself. He got giddy for a couple of seconds and his eyes went blur. She kept looking at him with the same ire in her eyes. He shifted his sight sideward, went to the tap by the backdoor, and washed his hands. There, in the mirror, he could see that the impression of the curd-smeared fingers was turning red. And though he considerably steeled himself, a tear strained through his eyes. Not only did it sparkle, his vision blurred too. He felt that he better not clear the trace of curd on his cheek, but then he chastised himself as to why he should be exhibiting this shame again in her presence. Turning on the tap again, he splashed water on his face and washed it. He did not know what to do next. He chose not to take the towel that was perched on the peg at hand. He took out his hanky, wiped his hands and face, returned to the lounge, took his helmet and scooter keys, exited the door and the gate, kick-started his scooter, and without looking back, drove speedily past the curve by the zoo and Hardinge Circle. Passing by the Devaraj Urs Road, where his new office was, he drove by the district office straight to the bund of the Kukkarahalli tank, parked his scooter, locked it, trekked the gradient of the bund about a furlong, and sat on a bench.

Though the sky was dark, there was light from the lampposts erected along the bund, widely spaced. The water in the tank being indistinguishably one with darkness, the reflection in the water of Gangotri of the lampposts to the other side and those along the facing Hunsur Road evidenced its existence. Mind, though, was an expanse of darkness with no glimmering spots whatsoever. Without ire or requital, the burdening feelings of anguish sinking his heart to greater depths, as he reclined leaning upon the steel grilled backrest of the bench without so much as making an effort at recalling or weighing anything, he heard the sounds of trampling boots and whistle. The track of the bund illuminated with the light of a torch. He understood that it was the watchman of the lake. In a short while, the watchman in khaki neared him. He said pre-emptively, 'Look, the scooter you just saw is mine. Came here to lounge for a few minutes. I am an architect having my office in Devaraj Urs Road. Name is Somashekhar. Reside in Jayalakshmipuram. Haven't come here to jump into the lake and die. You get going.'

'*But ther' is an order naat to allo' yeni-one ut night, Saar.*'

'Look man, neither will I die here nor have I brought along any girl or woman. If you wish, keep watching. No femme comes here looking for me. Just leave. Here, have coffee at dawn,' he searched in the torchlight and handed him two rupees.

'*Saar, yu aar alon', theeves, and … tha' skootar ther,*' he cautioned. Somashekhar devolved that responsibility onto him, 'Keep a watch over that.' He left, blowing his whistle.

His mind that had paused with the watchman's arrival resumed its activity. It started hovering about the question that presently popped up: *What have I come to?* No synopsis formed. The question kept revolving about its locus like a grindstone. Renounced a mechanical Bombay where interpersonal relationships were sparse, where were absent such a Kukkarahalli Lake, Chamundi Hill, the plains of Lalitamahal, and where twinkling stars could not be seen. But what a mess have I got into here! The question popped up again. In any profession, one should conduct the clients with cordiality, not at all with conviviality. The infraction of this rule is the chief cause of my landing in this situation. It was she who came after me, not the other way round. He recalled that moment when their relationship had concretized. If she chose to entice me, why on my part did I drool in acquiescence? I am rightly punished. He owned up the ethical responsibility for the consequences. He ran the fingers of his left hand on his cheek. It was still smarting. It may have inflamed and turned red, if I look in the mirror I will get to know. What of looking in the mirror the shame and disgrace caused? It appeals well to the mind. His mind and feelings were all immersed in acute self-abasement.

Abound with such feelings for quite some time, a question arose. Which of her special traits lures me towards her? Attractive, educated, chats, and conducts herself affably, yes. Besides, the innate attraction towards the 'femme'! Though these justifications surfaced, what sort of a beauty? Superior to that Bombayite? Comparison set in, but behind came the deterrent that these two cannot be likened. But as opposed to that woman who lived and pursued her PhD in America, gained enough exposure by travelling in many countries, associated and dealt with the high society of Bombay, what allure does this one possess, one who is confined to a coffee estate amidst forests, has seen just Hassan and Mysore, and has a local PhD? Yet again, disregard surfaced. But that relationship severed, never to be unified again, a relationship that I myself stemmed and stayed away from. But he felt that it was incorrect and disreputable to liken the two women. Against his wishes, another aspect found its way to the scales. This is a supercilious woman. Though cheap desires were default in that woman, she wasn't at all snobbish. In a short while, self-deprecation swelled and engulfed him again. My! What a cheap trait this, engaging myself in comparing and contrasting the contours, qualities, and temperaments of two women? Thereafter, no thought occurred to him except that he deserved to be raked over the coals.

By then, he felt spent physically too. All yesterday night, he hadn't slept. He pulled himself up, recalling that he just had two hours sleep by dawn, half sleep at that. He limbered so as to expunge all the bodily aches, turned right, and trudged in the direction of his scooter. By the time he traversed about half a furlong, he felt as if the kinetics of his motor nerves went kaput, and he came to a halt. He felt it impossible to pace one more. Will I be able to tread any further or will I drop dead here? Are both my legs paralysed? Feeling a sense of misgiving, he checked by lifting an arm, then lifted and swayed his other arm too. Arms, eyes, ears don't seem to be affected. With his left hand, he stroked his left cheek where she had slapped. Still stings. The moment he got conscious of the smarting, the nerves of his legs seemed to be remedied. Pacing became possible. He paced briskly. The darkness above, the waters to the left, the docile Bogadi Road along the gradient to the right – none of these registered in his conscious. He arrived at the end of the bund, unlocked his scooter, gunned it, and, in its light, checked his watch. It was 12:45.

Would still have not slept, he thought. Whatever hour it be, okay, even if retired, phone is right by the bed, plead sorry for disturbing at this unearthly hour. He drove straight to Devaraj Urs Road, parked by his new office, climbed up the stairs, took out the keys, and opened the door of his office. Going inside, he put on the lights, went to his cabin, and lifted the phone. He had committed the number to memory. No need to consult the phone book. It was picked up on the second ring and, readily recognizing the voice at the other end, he enquired, 'Naveen bhai, were you asleep? Did I disturb you?'

'Was about to put off the lights. Did you receive my letter? Had on hand the construction of a textiles factory at Navasari. Was impossible to attend the inauguration of your new office premises. How was it?'

'All went fine. I have erred some. You alone have to set it right.'

'You would not have erred professionally; would have in some transaction. Tell me what.'

'I shouldn't have returned your DD. The person who had chipped in then is now in urgent need of the money. I want one lakh forty-two thousand immediately. Can it be arranged?'

'Just tell me the name of your banker and your account number. Tomorrow I will arrange for a telegraphic transfer. You get a phone connection at your house. I wanted to call you myself. Can you put whatever work you have on hand on the backburner and come over for about a fortnight? I have gone through the preliminaries of the factory. Together, we can finally go through the calculations. Since we have worked together before, it will be easy for me. Besides, our ideas match. To-and-fro flight ticket, lodging, food, and take back with you twenty grand in fee. Should strive day and night but. Just call tomorrow and inform Indu when you will be arriving. Now tell me the account number and the name of your bank. It is one lakh forty-two thousand, right?'

On replacing the handset into its cradle after providing all details sought by Naveen, he felt relieved, as if liberated of her influence, as if he were light as a feather. For a while, he continued to sit on his new revolving chair. Later, he got up, locked behind him, climbed down, and drove straight to his house in Jayalakshmipuram. He opened the windows, changed, and retired. He felt that he was right in not repaying her assault. It occurred to him that reciprocating an assault in letter and spirit would mean attaining parity with that person. He limbered even as he lay in bed. Then he closed his eyes. In a couple of minutes, deep sleep overcame him.

He awoke at 7 in the morning. Though not enough, he had got quite some sleep. Even after waking up, he was in no mood to get up and, as he continued to lie down, memories of her came. He got curious as to what she would have done after he exited from there last night. To strike me as one would a slave….Even hitting a slave would be an uncivilized conduct. These days, no slave would put up with it either. Would she be grieving? He couldn't think of a precise answer to that.

After a while, he chastised himself for wishing that she grieve, wherefore he had indulged in such incontinent supposition. Whether or not she grieves is nothing to me. Let her suit herself. He assumed indifference and rolled over. Behind the thought '*let her suit herself*' came another that if she would visit the ravine like yesterday, revolver in hand! He got anxious. Not the inflicted but the perpetrator will suffer greater pain and grief if one is of sensitive disposition. Is she really sensitive? She is sharp of intellect, memory is stupendous, and is very proactive in certain matters. Once, when I was working with a screwdriver, I hurt a finger and when all of four drops of blood oozed, she got tears in her eyes, washed that finger, bandaged it, and, holding that finger, kept puffing out cool air for fifteen minutes, though I myself felt no pain! But at other times, all day long, for no reason at all, she pricks and tortures me by contesting everything I say. Alas, what a vindictive callousness against me! Blow hot, blow cold! Her modus operandi seems to be to annexe me by her love soused in compassion, and then torture me by holding me captive in a trap. Should free myself of this entrapment. What of *should*, I already *have*. Thank God I could understand this this soon! He congratulated himself, got up, threw the boiler switch, rinsed his face, and shaved.

While he bathed, a doubt surfaced. Yesterday night, would she have gone to that ravine to the east of the hill and pulled the trigger? He recalled that she had once said that at times when the desire to commit suicide gets acute, she would then go wild not just with him, but with one and all. Engulfed in such rage, if she had shot herself yesterday! He shuddered slightly even as he bathed. Filled with pity, his heart thawed. But greater in momentousness was the smarting of his cheek, especially when he applied soap or shaved. Pity was promptly replaced by anger. In case she had shot herself, the investigating police would find out that I had visited there yesterday, that I had stayed even after the children retired – the children themselves would vouch for that – and will establish a nexus between me and her suicide. The police is capable of coining any narrative out of any incident. What a fate, mine! The thought made him shudder more. Now it is 8:45. If any such thing had occurred, they should have been here by now. Or – he got anxious – they may arrive any moment. He made a hasty toilette, put on the first trouser and shirt that he could lay hands on, and left for office on his scooter. Neelakanthappa had just arrived. Making a beeline to his chamber, when he took the receiver in hand, he did not know where to call. On duty would be the cook Puttamma and the help Mahadevamma. My anxiety will be put to rest if I hear one sentence in reply – '*Madam has gone to college*'. Just in case she happens to be home and takes the call, she gets to know it is I! He got inhibitive. He felt determined to bar any association and relationship with her. Or, he got an idea, how about calling the college and enquiring if Amrita Madam was present? If queried about my identity, will just say that I was from the car garage. He looked up in the phone book and called the college. He was told that she was there and in the middle of a class. No queries whatsoever as to who the caller was. He hurriedly replaced the receiver and let out a long breath as if he had earned back his life. Then, as he left for the restaurant, taking leave of Neelakanthappa, he felt extremely ashamed. He chided himself that he went about the enquiry, worried as he was about what would befall *him* if she committed suicide, rather than getting anxious about *her* life and *her* family. He felt that he was not just a coward, he was a mean one.

Finishing his breakfast, as he discussed with Neelakanthappa about the details of a certain estimate, the phone rang. It was the bank manager. 'You have received a TT from Bombay for one lakh and forty-two thousand. I chose to call you, presuming that it would be an urgent matter.'

'Will I get the money if I come over now?' he asked eagerly.

'Sure, sure,' the manager said.

He took leave of Neelakanthappa, informing him that he would be back soon. He knew her bank account number. He wrote it on a piece of paper, instructed his bank to transfer to her account in the other bank, and got it done immediately. He was well acquainted with the manager of that bank too. The manager knew that he had borrowed from her. When he returned to his office, he recalled Naveen's proposal.

'I have to go to Bombay urgently for professional counselling. Tell me what tasks I have to personally attend to before leaving. We shall see them through today. After getting done with them, I will go to Bangalore tonight. Can you arrange for a flight for tomorrow morning?' he asked Neelakanthappa. Even as he strained himself to finish the jobs that he had to go through before leaving station, his heart felt cheery. Have cleared her dues. I am leaving Mysore. It was also clear that both were Naveen's generosity.

~

The moment she struck him, she too was confounded. Couldn't even guess what he would do. When she heard the main door being opened, it was clear that he was leaving. The gunning of the scooter confirmed it. She was aware of the movement of the scooter passing through the gate, turning left, accelerating, and heading downtown. If she had acted the moment he opened the main door, she could have checked him. On holding him back, God knows what exchange of dialogue, debate, and pleading would have ensued! But her mind could not gear itself up to dash and stop him. She just stood still for quite some time after the scooter had cleared out, not moving even so much as an inch. Then she slowly ambled up to the gate, closed it, talked to the dogs, returned inside, bolted from within, and secured the crossbar. When she lied down on the bed and put off the light, though she felt empty, there were no feelings of void that drove her to suicide. The emptiness in her heart now was of a different type, and so were the reasons for it. It is the awareness that he has left, that he won't return, won't return even if I souse his feet with my tears. I too will not go to his place, won't bow and touch his feet, won't shed tears before him. She is very much conscious of the analysis that goes on within her, but unable to graduate to any further thought, the mind stops at that. However, there was a sort of lightness. In a while, sleep overtakes.

She woke up quite early at 4 am. Mind was vacuous, despondent, of having lost something, everything. She felt bereaved. He is lost to me forever. He will visit here no more. Why did I slap him? That too with such cruel force and with a defile palm? It would be false to own up innocence. But – she consoled herself – keeping him at bay is for good. He is honest, will not lie. But even in matters of interpersonal relationship, he is calculative and aims at equilibrium tactfully, without letting it overweigh this way or that even one bit. She told herself that she had no need for such relationship. Still, the feeling of emptiness did not mitigate. What was more astonishing was the fact that the previous night, she fell into a deep sleep the moment she put her head to the pillow. Normally, it is at night that feelings of void engulf, when light has cleared off the earth and the sky, when all living beings are quiescent. On the afternoon, evening, and night of the day before yesterday reigned the acute hankering to end life. Had some sleep yesterday afternoon. The temptation continued through the evening, though the children were home. After having struck him, and he leaving, it should have intensified. But intense sleep came over. It continued unabated without me waking even once overnight, sending feelers that this was what I aspired – to beget this much sleep each day. Did friendship with him aggravate my desire to die? She raked her brains. It was there even before his advent. It was as grave. It had mitigated when I befriended him. Of late, it had gone awry as never before. But since yesterday, when I rejected and packed him off, it seems to have suddenly cured. I can somehow bear the loss and grief of having lost him, but she weighed, I rather be rid of the tormenting feelings of void and of the desire to end myself. She got up, quickly bathed, collected flowers from the courtyard, lit the lamp in the altar, performed puja, and prostrated before God. Her resolve got firm. She seemed fortified. I need none, I will just nurture these two kids, in the spare time I will study, research, acquire knowledge.... What else do I need? She walked up to Vikas's bed, leaned on him, hugged and kissed him, and prodded him, 'It is time for school, wake up kiddo!'

Content with her concentration, she handled her lectures very well that day. Returning home, she went over her library and made a list of the books she had not yet read. Later, she retrieved one book, read it till evening, and went to pick up the children. After she played with them, fed them, and put them to sleep, another thought invaded her. Yesterday night, he left on getting hit by my sullied palm. As she recalled that he hasn't called once the entire day today, a question popped up whether he, the aggrieved, should call, or I, the perpetrator? The distancing is right, but it should have occurred without ill will, without me causing it. She fretted again. Though my act was justified, I should have said that I was wrong in hitting him in fury and to please forget it. Tomorrow I will call myself and convey it. I have the ethical grit, she reflected. If there were a phone at his home, I would have expressed it right now. Ten times I have told him to get a phone installed. Never acceded. Just warded me off. 'Till 8 pm, I will be in office. Why one for home? Double expenses!' She got piqued. If it is okay with him, well! Why should I get annoyed? She donned indifference and lied down, book in hand. In between, when she lifted her eyes and looked at the clock, it was 10:45. She recalled that it was exactly twenty-four hours since she slapped him. She felt that to assault someone wasn't just physical atrocity, it was much inferior to that. Not just him, she told herself that she shouldn't ever strike any being, not even an attacking dog or a ramming cow. She lifted her right hand and looked at her palm. Four fingers at once! Then with her left hand, she felt her right palm and checked whether it was rough or smooth. The difference between the roughness and the smoothness is inconsequential, and as she told herself again that she would henceforth not stoop to the misconduct of assaulting anyone, she recalled that she hadn't hitherto. She lay with the book in hand. The lamp by the bed still burned. Maybe, I smacked him in fury. But why didn't he care to patiently enquire, 'You never did any such thing hitherto. Why now?' If love were to be, patience would be too. She reflected that his love was just superficial. If ever – she told herself – a situation warrants that I speak to him or telephone him, I will surely exhort him to answer this question. Call he should, I never will, she resolved too. As she lay, she fancied him calling on her and expressing atonement, '*Sorry, I could not grasp the insinuation in your words.*' She thought the light to be a hindrance to the thinking and shut it out. The thought of his surrender was heartening. In a while, sleep overcame.

When she got up next morning, she thought that she should somehow contact him today. Should visit myself and talk to him. Drive speedily now, wake him up, speak to him, then return and get the children ready. But by then, it would be late for the children. After dropping them at their school, I would then have to go to college. By the time I return from college, he would be in office. So what? The room is soundproof enough that nobody without can hear a thing spoken inside. Have so planned and designed it myself. She decided that she would go there straight after college. But after college at noon, as she sat in the car and started it, she felt petrified to face him in his chamber. She felt anxious that his very sight would send shivers down her spine. Why do I so fear? After all, what may he do? Will he reproach? Will he say, '*Who are you? Why did you come here? Get out.*' Or, getting up from his chair, would he slap me harder than I hit him, causing my head to reel? At once, she felt relieved. If he so punches me, all my agony would be rid and peace and happiness would be mine. The cheek may smart for a second, for ten minutes, half an hour, a day or two. Let it, but the solace that it would bring is beyond imagination. A resolve surfaced to enter his chamber, close the door behind her, walk up to him, stand by his chair, extend her cheek towards him, and say, 'Don't speak any. Lift your right hand and strike once forcefully on my cheek. *Once* means not just one. However much you desire. To your, no, to my mind's content, one hit after another, on the same spot, or wherever else you wish to. You too don't speak. I won't utter even one syllable.' While she reversed the car and set in the direction, no, he won't hit me, I know him. He has no sympathy. A butcher. Hence, exercising restraint, he has chosen not to repay the infliction. He who did not retort to all my scoffing and taunting, will he avenge even if I went there, stood before him, and beseeched him to? Intrinsically, he is cruel. What if I post myself before him and he chose not to punish me! If he chose to plainly ignore me by not even speaking to me! She felt scared again. Without heading to his office, she turned her car in the direction of her house.

She set the dogs free, fondled them, fed them, and then resigned to the sofa in the lounge in a torpid state where she could think of nothing. Though hungry, she wasn't sentient enough nor inclined to get up, appoint a plate, and eat. *What with eating, what with starving* – she wasn't left with enough energy even to consider that indifference consciously. She leaned back on the sofa and closed her eyes. She felt drowsy. A little later, when she woke up, she resolved – today, I will certainly make him come running here, however irate he be. I am familiar with the timbre of his heartstrings, and I will strum it. I will just handle it over phone. If I can't, I am not Amrita. She got up and glanced at her watch – 1:45. By now, he would have had his lunch. She dialled him from her bedroom. His voice would come flowing, '*Hello*,' and I will just say '*It's me*' and go silent. He should take it up thence. As she reflected that she would wedge him as with a visor upon isolating the tenor of what he says and how he puts it across, 'Hello, Shekhar Architects,' Neelakanthappa's voice.

She asked, 'May I speak to Mr Somashekhar?' Her confidence waned in half.

'He left for Bombay, Madam.'

Neelakanthappa can readily recognize my voice over phone. Recalling that during the recent setting up of the office premises, he had talked to her over phone many a time, she said, 'When did he leave? All of a sudden?'

'His partner had called. A certain big project had come up and consultation was sought urgently. Yesterday night, he left for Bangalore by train and would have reached Bombay by flight this morning. He will be away for two weeks. Madam, that day you neither turned up for the lunch nor for the evening reception?'

She felt enraged at this last account. Though she took exception to his extraneous enquiry, without expressing it, she said, 'An ailing relative dropped in. I had to get him medical care. I later got to know from Mr Somashekhar that the occasion was a grand success. With you at the helm, it had to be. Will it be two weeks before he returns?'

'Yes, Madam.'

'Okay, thanks.' She replaced the receiver. She felt as if her mind was engulfed with smoke. Partner called! When did he call? Angry with me, he has gone on his own to consult his friend for his future course of action on being slapped by a certain woman whom he had befriended. This is the urgent work, consultation. What advice would the friend give? 'Why do you need the convoluted company of such a woman? Stay away from her.' She was sure that this advice would be dispensed. He will also share with him my desire and urge to shoot myself. 'Then, this is a good opportunity,' he would surely counsel. 'Utilize this to sever the relationship with her immediately.' Naveen Shah, a very successful administrator that he is! Very many times, he has sung praises of this friend. When he returns after two weeks, he will not have remained 'Somu'. She told herself to be rest assured that he would have morphed into 'Mr Somashekhar'. She felt curdling in her belly. She got up, went into the kitchen, appointed a plate with some rice, two ladles of curry to one side – she cared not to see what vegetables Puttamma had sunk in it – two ladles of curd to another side, some vegetable stew at one corner, stuck a spoon, went to her bedroom, sat on the sofa, and started eating. When I am hungry and disconcerted, my belly burns. My head reels. My eyes go blank. No such thing happens to anyone else. Everyone looks to one's own well-being and happiness. As the final realization dawned that everyone looks for one's own happiness, all of a sudden, the Bombay woman surfaced in mind. She began thinking if he was visiting there to wallow in her company for two full weeks? Only whatever she had hastily gulped down till then, she could eat no more. She placed the plate on the teapoy and simply sat. She felt churning in her stomach, like the silent blaze of petrol fire. Now I know his integrity. I am a fool who aspired for his association and bestowed my everything on him. I rightly deserve to be punished. Tears filled her eyes. She got up, dispensed the plate with all the leftovers, rinsed her mouth, returned to the bed, and reclined.

That night, she could not get sleep. Anger and introspection took to each sides of a scale. Where did I slip? What was the threshold event? Against the background of these doubts, the Bombay woman emerged in comparison. What was her name? She recalled that he never uttered her name once, never once fondly recalled her. What would be his musings about her? He never got in touch with her since turning his back on her. Neither did she. He said that it just came to a conclusive end naturally. Would meet each other with the purpose of pillaging pleasure, and all through their four to five hours' concert, they would not waste even one single minute. She would never squander even one single minute's pleasure by getting irritated or going wild. She was a guru who taught him the methodologies of exploiting the depth and gamut of coition, as one would suck out every iota of nectar from the folds of a beehive. She would take his coital propensity to its zenith, herself benefit from it, and immerse him in it too. If I speak any about her, however weary he be, a fleeting flash of delight can be detected in his eyes. He is unable to conceal it. Whenever I prod him, he has spilled all these details. These reminisces rendered herself in stark contrast.

In fact, in these matters, my knowledge was limited – limited to the poets' intended figurative allusion devoid of direct delineation. Notwithstanding the fact that desire would, at times, arise in me, it has been incident upon him to temper me by peeling apart my mask of inhibition, for I haven't the faculty either to accede or to invade with gay abandon. In between, I would suddenly go cold and his joy would be dampened, as with water. Past the phase of a pleasurable orgasm, many a time I would be abound with feelings of void, would desire to die and turn dead silent, which would promptly carry to his senses, and he, who by then would have reached a sensitive phase, would get readily cognizant of it and admonish, 'Amrita, why have you turned dull all of a sudden? I see boredom and rejection in your eyes,' thus inciting my ire beyond limits. 'Not yet done with your bestial crave yet?' I have thus retorted many a time, making him disappointed and pained, only to find myself lamenting that I am not adequate enough for him, and eventually pleading clemency of him who would have recoiled in a penultimate state. A question comes to mind now. What will a male aspire from a female? What should a woman confer on her man to ensure his adherence to her forever? Pleasure? Happiness? Peace? Vivifying his self-confidence? I never gave him what the Bombay woman gave, and in that measure. Maybe, that is why he has left me to accost that Bombay femme, to revive the severed bond. She turned gloomy, but made attempts at resigning to reality: hasn't he the right to discern his happiness? Having reclined in the same posture for quite some time, pain surfaced on that side. As she rolled over, she reflected if discerning pleasure was the only purport of a relationship. That annoyed her. The likes of him would have pioneered the inclusion of the word *libertine* into the lexicon. No need of a relationship with such a person. Good that he exited, she consoled herself. Even as she told herself that it was depravity to even think of him, agony swept through her and curdled her stomach. Wail boiled up and erupted. She didn't know why. No amount of effort could contain it. The sound of the wail that erupted, dilating the gullet and the jaws, pounded her ears and was exceptionally audible. Worried that the children sleeping in the other room should hear and wake up, she gathered some of the pallu of her sari and thrust it into her mouth. Yet, it keeps gushing from within. Not just the gullet and jaws, a mighty wail that is set to batter my ribs rather. Then she heard footsteps. She turned to find Vijai awake and in her bedroom. Nearing her and placing his hand on her shoulder, he asks, 'What's the matter, Mom?' The cause of her tears re-entered her consciousness, but she would not share it with him.

'Kiddo, my stomach aches,' she extends her left arm and hugs him.

'Call the doctor, Mom,' he suggests.

'At this hour, no. Found a tablet. I've taken it. Seems like it is subsiding. You get back to bed.' But he doesn't leave. After a minute, she got up and, putting on a smile, said, 'Seems okay now. Samosa was served in the college party. Could be that. Will keep off it now on. You get back to bed. Let me. Vikas is alone there.' She hugged him, took him to his bedroom, put him in bed, sat by him, patted him gently, and when he slid into sleep, she exited.

The cause of the tears is clear now. I am the depraved one who fell for such a libertine and lost my chastity. No such issue that fidelity towards Ranganath is eroded. Chastity should be reserved even after staying away or abandoning the man who has tied the hallowed connubial string. Once forfeited, it can never be earned back. Such libertines will keep hacking it. I fell into his trap. I made myself available. He did not defile it. Being attracted, I proceeded on my own, sent clear indications, and succumbed. God, I have no right to live. God, I have no right to face you, light a lamp before you, and shower you with flowers. Why should a vile worm like me live? It brought the revolver to her mind. She pulled the drawer beside and took it out. There is no more false pretext for staying alive. Should end myself today, now. Else, God will not pardon me. But not here, inside the house. Hearing the sound, the children would wake up and, seeing their mother, would collapse unconscious and be subjected to mental shock all their lives. The hill is just right, the silence of the darkness of the hill is just right. She took the keys to the house, the car, and the garage, got into her slippers, and started to leave. This is the final day, truly the final day. She took out her suicide notepad, wrote the all too familiar sentence that she alone was responsible for her death, inscribed the date and time, signed it, placed it on the bed, and, as she paced softly towards the door, a fear, rather a hindrance, showed up. Is Vijai deeply asleep? What if he woke up when I open the door or when I gun the car or when the dogs bark! She stood her place for more than half an hour and then returned to her bedroom. Drawing the curtains apart, she sat on the sofa and began observing the darkness outside and the hills that were darkness congealed. After quite some time, she slipped into sleep, reclined, as she was on the sofa.

When she got up in the morning, she recalled her thoughts of the eve and felt ashamed. If he is angry with me, he will distance himself from me. But he is not one to go in search of her whom he had himself ditched. He has disassociated himself so much from her that he even abhors talking about her. If I chose to broach or recall any matter about her, he gets irritated. After these many years of completely dissociating from her, after she saw him witness an uneducated, lowly man in her arms, she would not welcome it even if he went after her on his own. Rather, he will not accost her. Maybe, the friend really needed professional assistance and, on being summoned at a short notice, he has left. Though this thought eased her mind, she felt dejected. She reflected that all night, she had been espousing cheap, mundane thoughts. She dropped the children at their school and went to college. That day, she had three consecutive classes. She went through them with cultivated enthusiasm. Between 11 and noon, she attended a meeting called by the principal, and as she was homebound, something flashed in her mind. How about getting the Bombay number from Neelakanthappa, call him, and utter just one sentence that I called to seek his pardon, nothing else. And if a dialogue ensues, he can always speak in Kannada in case someone is at hand. Here, though I am alone, can speak whatever. Third day today, by now his ire would have subsided too, would have assuaged enough to grant pardon. It is impossible for him to stay stiff after my clemency petition falls on his ears. I know what he feels about me. She boosted her confidence.

On reaching home, as usual, she opened the letterbox on the gate, collected the two letters that were delivered, locked it again, parked the car in shade, and went in. One bore the logo of the estate and the other was from her banker. She tossed the latter and started reading the one from the estate. Monsoon forecasts, price of fertilizers, other such details, and '… better you visit here once at your earliest, as it would facilitate taking some decisions in your presence. I can come myself. But it is better you get a first-hand account of the situation here. The society guys are pestering us to clear the dues.'

Yes, should visit this Saturday and stay there till Sunday evening. While she contemplated this, she opened the other envelope and was taken aback. It was dated the day before yesterday and conveyed that a local clearing amount of one lakh forty-two thousand was credited to her account. In the statement, the 'Credits' column displayed the amount, and in the 'Details' column were scribbled the letters LC. Local collection! Though she was surprised as to what transaction it was, she had a misgiving. By any chance, would he have remitted the money? Considering the amount, it is probably his, but no, the amount he has availed of me is one lakh forty thousand. The additional two thousand means one month's interest. Two thousand interest for one month works out to more than fifteen percent! Her heart sank. She went to her room, called the bank, and enquired with the manager. 'Mr Somashekhar, your architect, he got it remitted from his bank, Madam. His manager personally arranged the transfer, at about noon.'

'I was not in station. I just got your advice slip. Hence, I enquired. Thanks.' Cutting the line, she dialled Somashekhar's bank. Not just from the transactions during the past one month, she knew him well, for he had requested her at least twice to invest in the term deposits of the bank. He doesn't know of my penury. Thinks that I am a rich landlady!

'Sir, Mr Somashekhar is not in town. He has gone to Bombay. You have remitted this amount of money from his account to mine. You may be aware that in his absence, I am the one who supervises the finance matters of his office. Will you please tell me wherefrom is this money? I need it for the records,' she said in a tone that gave no room for suspicion.

'We received a telex from our Bombay branch at about 10:45. He was in station then. I called him and informed accordingly. He came over and instructed us to immediately remit such amount to your bank. Since I did not want to inconvenience you, I remitted it immediately. What if I remitted it, just draw a cheque, and send it back to us? We have now introduced attractive interest rates for term deposits.' He permitted himself a long laugh, a laugh seasoned by his profession.

'Thanks. But Mr Somashekhar arranged that remittance for some pressing requirement of mine. I was not in station. Thanks again.' As she replaced the receiver, all the phases of his lightning actions became clear. He just left on being struck on his cheek, went straight to his house or to his office, decided to settle up and rid himself of my loan, and called Naveen and asked him to send the money by telex. It has been dealt with promptly there as soon as the bank opened for the day and has reached here by 10:45. Immediately, he has arranged to clear the dues. The purpose of his visit to Bombay is to execute the loan papers or to make other arrangements. She got very angry. She thought of handing him four more slaps with a similar sullied palm. Silly, she thought, he has conducted himself like an adolescent.

Changing, she washed her face and feet, went to the kitchen, prepared meal for the dogs, fed them, and freed them to loiter around. Later, she appointed a plate for herself, sat at the table in the kitchen, and, as she began mixing the rice in the curry, she noticed her fingers soaked in the gruel and her mind coasted back to that night. To get the money over telex and to immediately clear the dues with interest indicates that he has dumped me. She understood that he had deserted her completely, starkly, barring any possibility of her getting back to him. She quivered as if from electric shock. Darkness filled her mind and all thoughts and feelings congealed. Though the somatic tremble ceased in a short while, the darkness of the mind did not clear. The body lost its consciousness and turned inert. After some time, when she got conscious of her locus, the gravy of the curry and rice that stuck to her fingers had dried and become starchy. Getting up, she consigned the plate to the sink, held her hand under running water till the veneer got moist, scrubbed it clean, went to her bedroom, and retired. She was sure that this relationship had ended, that he had ended it. Enduring this, she should either suffer or die. No other alternative. She clearly envisaged the fork, with the hand-post, and rooted her gaze on it. Was he the one who presided all through ever since I was born, this Augustus IV ! Will live without him. Won't die. He has distanced himself with divine disregard for me. Will show him that I will not succumb, that I can withstand. Will live to be a hundred, she resolved. Instantaneously, she got up and dashed to the kitchen. She took another plate, put in it more than the usual quantity of cooked rice, enough curry and curd, gobbled up all of it, standing as she did, washed her hands and the plate, and returned to her room. Deciding that she better not sit or recline there, she exited, opened the garage door, picked up the hoe and pickaxe from the shelf there, firmly strapped the pallu of her sari around her waist, tucked its end into the waistband, and began working on the plant beds in the garden. There was energy in the arms, and thereabouts was work that would never end however much one slogged. Should ask Mahadevamma to tell her husband to get four cartloads of farmyard manure. Should order manure from the zoo. Should myself dump bucketfuls of the manure to each plant bed, cover it with earth, and irrigate with the hose. After working non-stop till 4:30, she went in, bathed to cleanse the sticking sweat, wore a laundered sari, consigned the dogs to their respective kennels, drove her car, fetched her children, gave them snacks, and began a game of shuttle-cock with them in the backyard. No sooner did she retire that night than sleep came. Sound sleep.

She awoke well past midnight – at 2:30 am precisely – not abruptly but naturally. Shoulders and arms ached. They wouldn't ache if I so care for the plants regularly. It will also be a good exercise for the body. While she was deep in memories of the rigorous gardening work she had engaged in the previous afternoon, she recalled the way she had arranged funds for him. When I offered to get hard cash, he declined vehemently, instructing me to give a cheque. The amount in the cheque was one lakh only. I had cumulatively expended thirty thousand on different occasions. No records are available for that amount. Even for the lakh, no other document of proof barring the cheque. In court, it could have been argued out that I had earlier on borrowed from him. I would have had no stand against that. He has returned even the overheads of mortgaging my house to my bank. For my misconduct of slapping, he could have offset the entire amount as penalty and still severed the relationship. But he has chosen to cut off by immediately returning the money. She was suddenly afraid of him. Jalaja's words surfaced in memory. Even as a student, without enough victuals arrangements, he chose to forfeit the opportunity of usurping the pricey golden necklace and had brought it to the notice of the host. Would he acquit himself differently now! She appreciated him. But also got angry. She thought, *Somu, you are not a benign one, you are scary*. Fear surfaced. It was impossible for love and gentleness to be typical of him. Along came memories of Ranganath and his sister. What lies! Deceit to what extent! Forty to fifty lakh. The engineer Ranganath is known to accept bribe. It seems there is a system whereby, though he won't demand it, a certain percentage accrues to him and the contractors simply pass it on. Memories of Ranganath soon made her despondent. Consequently, emptiness pervaded. Thereafter, it got dense and she aspired to take out the revolver.

Somashekhar, who was incessantly engrossed in work from morning till 8 or 9 in the evening, hadn't even enough time to look out through the window of the air-conditioned offices of 'Shah and Shekhar' on the thirteenth floor. When he recalled that he had so worked in this city for twelve years, he would think, why not I get back here? 'Som bhai, in the first place it was erroneous that you checked out of here. Just return. Let's do business together.' Naveen had so proposed more than once. In him too, the allure of Mysore abruptly slumps and the mind strays. To one who just slogs it out, what distinction do Mysore or Bombay hold out? Natural socializing was impossible in one deprived of the unimpeded view of the skies and of the placid countryside tread – such dated musings that had caused him to quit Bombay now seemed inadequate truths. Alongside would register the judgement that it was the infirmity of mind to abandon the just established business in Mysore and go back to Bombay, that too owing to the relationship with her and the same turning acrid eventually. His resolve to get over with this work on the Navasari factory as soon as possible and return to Mysore had not slackened. Every day at 8 pm, he would call his office, take report from Neelakanthappa, and give instructions. He would inform him of his tentative date of return, instruct him to apprise and appease the clients accordingly, and handle the situation effectively. Memories of Amrita would be interspersed throughout. Landing here, visiting Navasari, inspecting the site of the proposed factory, comprehending the initial draft by Naveen, and, after four days, his anger and disdain towards her subdued and his mind was set to calmly understand her conduct. This was not the very first time that she went wild without reason, or launched a tirade of searing words. To slap with her sullied palm is just a verging graduation from that. Why does she behave so? She has been deceived in life. She has been duped. Not just the thirty or forty or fifty lakh, she is on the brink of losing her entire ancestral estate. She is deceived in the choice of her spouse too, being coerced to suffer an incompatible marriage all her life. It was evident that her lack of strength to cope was the genesis of predilection to redemptive suicide. It also occurred to him that this predilection is the cause of anger. But to always get angry with me and strike me with soiled palm! What sort of rectitude is this? Let her scoff at those who have meted out injustice to her, let her punch them, let her shoot them with revolver or sue her aunt for embezzling colossal amounts of money from Soogoor's revenues for acquiring land for her children. Just that bit of report about them once, no mention of them since, and no venting anger at them. All her ire, swearing, and persecution are directed at me. A reward for unblemished love, eh! These thoughts occurring repeatedly, a resolve would concretize that to distance from her was the only wise act. Why unnecessarily get chastised like a schoolboy? Though he would ward off her memories, they would be saturate in his mind.

One night, he went to Naveen's house for supper. Naveen was not home. Induben said, 'Somu bhai, last year when we visited Nilgiris and Kodagu, I had asked you to marry again. Why haven't you given a thought to it?' He said nothing, just smiled. 'You are a fine architect. Business is good too. Nowadays, men tend to enter their first wedlock at your age. Advertise in the classifieds of newspapers. Or just respond to the ads by the brides. Or else, let me handle the correspondence for you. If you can't return home to a family of your own in the evenings, why earn?'

Later, when Naveen was home, and while everybody, including Digant, supped, she brought up the matter again. 'I was asking Somu bhai why he isn't contemplating remarriage. Why should you not discern a bride for him? Courier me Bangalore's newspapers of Sundays. I will select and correspond with the box numbers.'

Naveen added, 'Wed a woman who has either an architecture degree or a mechanical engineering degree. You can work together.' Somashekhar just heard it and did not respond any.

But Induben was quick to add, 'Know what your friend's words mean? Nowadays, the brides don't bring in enough dowry. Let them instead work in your office as a partner without salary or profit share. Be it known what a business acumen Naveen Shah is. Nowadays, he has started grumbling that the two hundred grand cash and three-fourths kilogram of gold that I brought in dowry is below par. The piping hot breakfast, tea, and lunch that I fix for him by confining myself within these four walls doesn't satisfy him, so he asks me to report at his office daily and do duplicating, typing, and such other work. I tell him that I have enough of a homemaker's job on hand, that I can't slog at his office too.'

Somashekhar knows that she was not saying anything anew, and that since a year of his losing his wife, Induben wishes that he wed again and restart a family. He also knew that she was against career-minded wives. He munched on without uttering anything. When he retired to his nearby hotel room, her words began doing rounds in his mind. One of the points she raised readily appealed to his mind. *If, at evenings, you can't return home to a family of your own, why earn?* True. Naveen's loan shall be repaid within a year and a half or two. Why should I slog thereafter? Eating out at some restaurant in late evenings, and the weariness of opening the door to a house with no occupants! These thoughts are not occurring for the first time though. The mind, yet, is not inclined towards marriage. Marriage is synonymous with manacle, a bogging duty irrespective of whether feelings are fount or desiccated – surfaced the unremitting oracle. Having worked in his office continuously from 8:30 in the morning till 9 in the evening, he was exhausted and sleep overcame. Besides, he had to get up early tomorrow morning and leave for Navasari.

Second day since, at 8:30 pm, he was at his desk, working. Dighe, the draftsman, who worked in this office since long, stood before the sloping table and was drawing the lines as instructed by him when the phone rang. Dighe picked it up and buzzed him in his cabin, 'Sir, seems like it is for you, long distance.'

Presuming that it was Neelakanthappa, as he picked up the extension in his cabin and said, 'Hello, Somashekhar speaking,' he was shocked to hear the voice at the other end. At the root of the amazement that pervaded his mind was a feeling of serenity that very well appealed to his conscious. 'Somu, I got your number from Neelakanthappa. He informed me that you would still be at work and shall be available till 9 pm. Hope there is nobody beside you. Even if anyone be, no problem, you just talk in Kannada. I have locked myself in my room. Can you hear me? If you keep mum, how shall I speak? If you don't utter anything, it means that your anger has not yet subsided. Even the dolour of bereavement stands quelled by the eleventh day. If your anger outdoes that, how can I hold on to life? Somu, Somu kiddo, mumble something, my boy. Just once, say *hmm, I am hearing*. There is just one thing I am dying to tell you. And I am unable to say it until you grunt something. You are a good boy, mutter something, smart boy.' '*Hmm*,' mumble he did. She continued, 'It has been months since I lost my propriety to ask pardon of you. It is not the first time that I am committing such offence. Yet, I know that by now, you have pardoned me. Not that you are one great saint. It is your love. It is great, great enough to quickly douse and put out ire of any magnitude. That is why, I behave so childish. Tell me when you will return. I will wait for you at the Bangalore airport.' Not just a reply, he could not think of any utterance whatsoever. She offered, 'I know that you are tied up. Can't decide on the spur too. When you decide, call yourself. If you can't, tell me at what hour you will be alone. Don't get anxious that your friend Naveen will get ideas if a woman called daily. Just say, a customer, I am getting her house built. Ok, then? Bid me goodbye. I will not replace the receiver till you say that,' she waited silently. He said bye.

After that, he worked for about half an hour and went to a restaurant to sup. Even as he started on his meal, he was perplexed as he became aware of the changes that occurred in him. All his ire and ill feelings towards her ebbed, and his mind and heart were filled with compassion. If she has to behave thus, there must be a reason as severe. Else, how come she hit me, especially me, with soiled palm, she who would not cause pain to even a puny ant? Not just her contours, muscles, arm, face, or cheek, her mind too is gentle, tender like jasmine, no, like royal jasmine. A fount of sympathy to understand the cause of her random bouts of callousness issued forth in him. Mind became light pronto. The outer walls and windows of the buildings of Bombay that weren't limewashed or coloured, the air charged with soot and dust, and the crowd akin to the myriad flies at a litter bin were erased from his mind, and he experienced a journey through the lofty peaks of a mountain range, getting the feel of the sky. He reflected that anger and pig-headedness weighed down and bogged a person. A feeling to let go of them and float in the sky pervaded him. He called her the next day.

Before embarking on his return journey upon concluding his work in Bombay, when he called her to inform that he would arrive in Bangalore at 7:30 am, head straight to the bus station, and arrive in Mysore at about 11:30 or 11:45 am, she offered to drive her car straight to the Bangalore airport. Don't. That would mean leaving the children elsewhere overnight and making arrangements for guarding the house for the night. When he so protested, she insisted that she would wait at the Mysore bus station. He grunted consent. Nevertheless, he was swayed by the imagination that to journey from Bangalore to Mysore in her company would be comforting and cheerful. But such expense in the light of her financial constraints! He ratified his wisdom of checking her.

As the bus pulled into the stand, he recognized the car. She readily spotted him, seated that he was at a window seat. The royal-jasmine string that he had bought at Bangalore bus station was in a handbag. Without broaching any topic reminiscent of bitter memories, they drove straight to her house, suggesting just their eagerness to look into each other's eyes. The suitcase stayed back in the boot. Immediately after unlocking the door, they fell into each other's arms and sighed. When the words '*I can't live without you*' were uttered in unison, their gazes were locked and their faces beamed. He noticed that her face had blanched. He said, 'If you don't eat properly now on, I will kick you.' Her eyes brimmed with delight. She had prepared sugar-rice, black-gram doughnuts in curd, curry, and fruit salad. They fed each other from a single salver. They enjoyed a sumptuous meal. In between, he kept relating his errands while in Bombay and the difference in the jobs there and here in Mysore.

After lunch, she fed the dogs, freed them, and sealed the door. When they both converged in bed, gradually he noticed a change in her. She has shed inhibition and turned more creative. In between, she crooned lyrics from romantic odes and buoyed up intimate tête-à-tête to the stratum of poetry. Proactive, she is in consonance with his rhythm. Though thrilled, he felt that this wasn't the default constitution of his Amrita. Inly, gentle temperament, intense feelings, half-closed eyes soused in bashfulness, the disposition of masking me – the cynosure of her eyes – within her gaze were all absent, and surrogate were aggressive overt acts. To his sensitive perception, this appealed as brusque. 'Gawd! What has become of you?' he asked, his lips on her ears. 'What? I don't know!' she mimed astonishment on her face. 'If I put everything in words, it will be plebeian. Not that these are erroneous. They are just not innate to you. Tell me why.' She did not answer.

All her creativeness suddenly turned static and she turned inly. When he insisted that she speak out, her face was suffused with shyness. When he whispered to her, 'Speak up man, I insist,' she said, 'You've just returned from Bombay. Mysore should not seem insipid.'

He could not understand. For a minute, he just blinked. Then he asked, 'What does that mean?'

'If I put everything in words, it will be plebeian,' she rebounded his metaphor.

After a long minute, he could comprehend her words. Displaying false anger, he smacked her on the cheek, 'Lunkhead.' She was silent. He continued, 'I am sure Neelakanthappa would have told you the context of my visit to Bombay. At 8:30 or 9 pm, you called me at Naveen's office. Are you still in doubt?'

'Pardon me, Somu,' she said in a low voice without facing his sight. 'That your friend had bagged a big commission and sought your help for it, I got to know only six days later. Prior to that ... let go. Why rake up all that and spoil this beautiful moment,' she checked herself.

'I want to know. Speak up,' he insisted. 'Second day I called your office. Neelakanthappa said that the previous night you went to Bangalore, and at the juncture of my call, you would have landed in Bombay. Till then, I was in the dark about your telex funds and remittance of the same to the bank. My anger at you had not yet subsided. Why else would you have gone to Bombay? You would have felt that with respect to this Mysorean, a fiend, one who always inflicted just pain and torture, your old flame, who, during the four or five hours' rendezvous, gives nothing but unadulterated bliss was far far better. I surmised that you have gone there to meet with her and rekindle that old friendship. You deserved that association to alleviate yourself of the torment meted out by me. I have observed your eyes gleam involuntarily whenever I mention her. If I say that I am not invidious of it, it would be false. Since the day you replied to my call of four or five days ago, I am feeling envious too for her giving you the happiness that I cannot. Incensed that I was, the first two days I weighed her critically. But for the past few days, I have been a bit, if not fully, appreciative of her. Why does a man befriend a woman? To be happy for as long as it is possible. She had triumphed on this count. I have balked. It may nigh be impossible to contain my anger, scorn, and the torment that I inflict on you! When in bed at least, why shouldn't I consider her my guru like Ekalavya did? Why not invoke the fount of happiness? Tell me,' she insisted and awaited his reply.

He began pondering. It isn't wrong to delve deep into the fount of happiness, make it more intense, and to see that it exudes profusely; it is desirable rather. He recalled his union with that Bombay woman. The moment they shut themselves in and held each other's hands, excitement would instantly attain the speed and altitude of a jet aircraft. Her very disposition was so. No room for any aliquots there. Apparent would be the intent of the male in meeting his companion. Similar would be the intent of that femme in meeting him. That was her default disposition. 'Amu, you are aware that I am not inclined to discuss about her. It is ages since I severed contact with her. Though I have taken her off my mind, you haven't. Why? To liken yourself to her is unwarranted. I don't like to espouse even an iota of ill will towards her. It is just that I had misunderstood her. Barring that, I don't see any belittling trait in her.'

'I too am not likening her to me in a belittling way. I just said that she is a superior friend to you than I. Hence, my wish to fancy her as my guru.'

'Contradiction may be mine. I don't like to speak light of her. Neither do I take well to you comparing yourself to her. Not that you are superior or she is inferior. Rather, I feel that you are not amenable for comparison, that you are unique. You should always remain so.' He fondled her.

'Wasn't there any reason other than pleasure in seeking her out? Friendship? To help each other in need? To spill out your hearts to each other?'

'There was no need for any such. There arose no occasion to warrant anything other than just strumming pleasure. One day, after spending six hours together, we freshened up, tidied, dressed up, and were about to leave when she recalled that she forgot to go to her bank. She hadn't enough on her for taxi fare. She demurely asked of me. I took out a hundred and offered it to her. "Not that much, twenty-five is enough," she said. "It's okay," I said. But she took only twenty-five. When we met the next time, the first thing she did was take out the money and hold it out to me. I was pained. I said, "Why so scrupulous?" Was I nothing to her? She said, "If you were nothing, I would not have come at all. On the contrary, if I took money from you, what would become of my standing? If you don't take it, I won't allow you to touch my hand even." In her disposition was a refrain from obtaining any other benefit from our relationship. That day, I was anguished. But later, I appreciated that trait.'

Having said this much, he fell silent. No other matter came to his mind to take the conversation further. Though she had her eyes open, as if she were contemplating something, her sight wasn't focussed on anything. His mind was deep in introspection – what do I expect from a female? As long as I was in the companionship of that Bombay woman, such doubts had not occurred at all. But ever since I befriended this one, this question keeps popping up, especially of late excessively. A corollary popped up as to whether a man could stay contented without the camaraderie of a woman. His thoughts were interrupted by her response. 'It is true that you have said a hundred times that you have forgotten her and that you are not to be reminded about her. But it is also true that inside you, I am not the reality that she is.'

He took it that it was a point-blank accusation. 'What are you driving at?' he asked. Evident in his voice and on his face were pain, disgust, and suppressed anger.

'On the immediate next visit, she held out twenty-five rupees, declaring that the relationship between you two would be slighted if you didn't take it back, and that she wouldn't allow you to touch her hand even. You have now done nothing different. You called Bombay, got the funds by telex, and cleared my account. You too were bothered by similar thoughts as to what this relationship would tantamount to if you didn't do so. You have never visited Amrita's mind as Amrita's. The root of your perception, the locus of your feelings is therein, in that Bombayite. If I draw a comparison, you get angry.'

By then, not just the fervour of passion, but even the minimum enthusiasm had ebbed and wilted. Both became aware that the intimacy had petered out, and felt that their bodies mutually weighed down on each other. Inevitably, they mutually detached themselves and rolled over so as not to be a burden on each other but still able to eye one another. He couldn't mask the discontent within. And he knew too that if he did attempt it, it would readily appeal to her razor-sharp eyes.

After lying silent for five minutes, she herself neared him, held him close with her left arm, and said, 'What you said is right. I am one specimen, she is another. Day before yesterday, right from the moment you called and informed me that you would be arriving today, I had thought of merrymaking today as one of unflagging sublime exaltation and had planned accordingly. Wishing to give you much satisfaction, I executed the very many fine points that I had conceived. But I am I. She is she. I haven't the faculties to bestow happiness that isn't barbed. One who is not capable of giving doesn't merit receiving too. Pardon me.' She moved closer and warmly kissed both his eyes. What with responding to that stimulus, there wasn't even a pretence of gentility left in him. He was recollecting that he could never comprehend when and how she would turn any talk to rhubarb and educe mordant overtones and mordant diktats.

'My kiddo, I know that you are angry. I also know that at such times I should not egg on. Yet, it is simpler to get over with it when situation permits. Right now ... ' He cut her short saying, 'It is simpler for you to spill acridity even when situation does not permit.'

She stared at him with fierce eyes. Realizing that sight combat was promulgated, he refrained from countering her sight and slightly closed his eyes as if half asleep. For one minute, she lay staring at him and said, 'If you are indifferent so as to even speak to me, it is up to you.' She rolled over and lay with her back to him. He was unto himself. Didn't even console her. Neither did he attempt to extend an arm and turn her towards him. He lay silent, unable to anticipate in what unforeseen way she would pounce upon him in this intense, quiescent cold war. After a short while, she suddenly turned towards him and sat up. The sudden awareness of her nudity as she transpired from under the double blanket they shared caused shame, shyness, and anger in her. Turning away as briskly, she collected her blouse and petticoat that lay on the floor, wore them and the sari, sat at the edge of the bed at an arm's distance from him, and with a resolve not to go under, not to exhibit anger, for it would tantamount to buckling, she said in a tone that was meticulous in the selection of each syllable, 'You shall nonetheless maintain that the twain are quite apart. What you have on mind is that she repaid what she had borrowed for taxi fare, as she had no time to go to the bank. But the reason you arranged funds by telex is different, for you never inflicted upon her anything so mean as striking with a defile palm, right? Speak the truth.' Though he thought that it was not in his disposition to mouth what was obvious, he contained it so as not to let it arrive even at the threshold of the vocal chords. On seeing that she had fully draped herself, he felt abashed that though under the covers, he was naked. Besides the discomfiture, a feeling of abject disgrace engulfed him. Nudity is delightful and alluring when the duo gets intimate, sinking mutual egos. The moment ego is on the alert and the minds distance themselves, how embarrassing nudity becomes! He too contemplated seizing his undergarments that lay at the edge of his side of the bed, donning them under the blanket, emerge from under the covers, and sit up. But then deciding against aping her, he remained as if he were oblivious of it.

'You would say you repaid the money, abhorring against any sort of relationship with me for I struck you with soiled palm ...' He cut her short and said, 'I didn't say anything, it is you who is telling everything. *You* are imagining things.'

'So-ma-she-khar, enough of smart talk. Abstaining from uttering something doesn't prove that in your mind, you haven't mulled it over. Why else would you arrange for funds suddenly, that too through telex? And within ten minutes of its arrival, why did you get it credited to my account? If I court-martial you, you haven't the strength to stand up to it. The truth is on my side. That aside, you took serious exception to my act of slapping you. Did you but give a thought to it that if I, a well-educated and cultured one, who never so conducted myself, should behave so, there's got to be an overpowering reason? Did you make any effort at understanding it? Enquire with the college that I work for or elsewhere. If ever you dig out one instance of me losing temper and one loose word blurted out by me, I will get this nose scythed. Such a one, if I go wild on you now and then, and for once the anger getting out of control, if I slapped you with soiled palm, it is not that you don't know the reason. Though you know, you are cleverly dodging me and playing the puppeteer.' While she uttered the last sentence, her voice got heavy. Afraid that if it should morph to cry, it would mean shame, she checked herself from any further talk.

Craning her neck, for a minute she kept observing the slowly spinning fan and then continued, 'I told you that in Vikas's christening ceremony, engulfed with feelings of baselessness, I kept cogitating as to my relationship with Ranganath, as to why I summoned him and what my status was concerning the rites. Even as the guests dined, I drove to the hilltop to kill myself with the revolver. I also told you about the question of my relevance in the opening ceremony of your office premises popping up even as the priest went about the *homa*, wherefore I went to the Kannambadi

Dam to drown myself in the reservoir. You were also witness to my visit to the hilltop that night, revolver with me. Despite these, all you did was just offer your kerchief. Did you once say, "Amrita, your place is here. Just forget that Ranganath. Come, let's seek a priest this very day and I will wed you at a temple. What do you mean you haven't locus and status?" Did you at least get that thought? Leaving, you came later that night and declared intelligently that you had come to take away the revolver. *Poor thing*. I better appoint a gurkha registered with the police for guarding my house. This is the cogent solution you could think of in all of fourteen hours. It means you have concluded and alluded that all you need is the sort of relationship you had with that Bombay woman – none of responsibility, bond, intimacy, obligation, and the like. It was then clear to me that you were a cold, calculative sybarite, void of warm feelings. It is impossible for me to go through everything coldly, weigh them like you do. I got incensed naturally. Hand was soiled. I told you, it is not in my disposition to be so calculative as to go and cleanse it before delivering the blow. At best, I can ask your pardon for slapping. Pardon, please.'

He was dumbstruck. Even a hint that she could have espoused such a desire had never occurred to him. He also recalled that the thought of marriage hadn't strayed into his mind even once. He said, 'The thought of marriage truly didn't occur in my mind. If it did ... ' She cut him short, 'Mister Somashekhar, enough of it. I am not a beggar to concede to something that does not sprout and surge naturally within you. And now, even if you choose to plead at my feet, I won't marry you. All you want is my body, free conjugation with a forthcoming woman, beautiful and educated. I won't concede to be your girlfriend, a whore per se. I too have self-esteem.' She stood up and said, 'I know that it is embarrassing for you to put on clothes in my presence. I will go out. Get ready. Your suitcase is in the car. I will drop you at a place where you can hire an autorickshaw. I want to be left alone. In another five minutes, you should leave from this house. If you are abashed, you will not speak any.' She picked up her vanity bag, the keys to the car and the house, and exited the room. For two minutes, he lay dumbfounded. He lacked the energy to either speak or even pull himself up. But the moment he heard her start the car outside, he shot up, hurriedly dressed, ran a comb twice through his hair, put on his shoes, and left. By that time, she had the car outside the gate on the road. At the same time, an autorickshaw came by on the main road ahead. Very rare for autos to be spotted on that road. She signalled. He got hint of the suggestion. She unlocked the boot and opened it. He retrieved his suitcase, walked up to the auto, and boarded. The auto driver, who seemed to be in a hurry, hadn't killed the engine. The moment he was seated, he started downtown, not even enquiring as to the destination. He did not look in her direction. Neither did she.

He was mulling as to why it never occurred to him that she nurtured such a thought. If something didn't occur, it should be understood that the premise for the emergence of such understanding is absent in the mind and intellect. Which tendencies of my mind are causative of my failure to get wind of her intent? He introspected. After cogitating over it for a couple of days, a few aspects clearly emerged. I really love her. I love her despite being aware that I don't beget unvarying peace, contentment, and happiness from her. Not just deriving, bestowal rather is characteristic of love. I will do anything to keep her happy. But marriage? If need be, even that. He was clear to that extent. Marriage held no fascination for him. When his wife was alive, she cooked his delights, washed his clothes, and pressed them. Without displeasing him in any matter whatsoever, she fine-tuned herself for him, not even objecting as to why he did not give her enough company. She was presentable too. I grieved on her death. But never felt the need to marry again. There are no such emotional reasons however, like the impossibility to let go of the memories of first wife or the inhibition to instate another in her sacrosanct place. Was to go through marriage. Done once. No urge for another. Some friends egged him on to go for another. Went no farther than lending his ears. Have just felt the need to appoint a cook. Carrying on thus since! Had I ever given a thought to marriage, I would certainly have pondered marrying her. But when that never occurred at all ... that explanation emerged. Through an entire day, he fully believed that this was the truth. Later, he felt that it was not the whole truth. He recalled that he had never loved any woman so much as to be unable to live without her. But then, Amrita's attraction is of a different order. She strikes me with soiled palm, scoffs at me randomly, and always makes an errant schoolboy of me. If anyone else had done so, I would have distanced myself so as not to see him or her for life. Putting up with all these tantrums, why am I attracted towards her again and again? Is this love, this debility of subjugating one's self-respect? He ruminated over, but was unable to figure out. She is pained that I arranged for the funds through telex and remitted it to her account. But I did not rush through it with an intent to irk her. As long as that borrowing was outstanding, it was impossible for me to put up with her anger, derision, and tirade. Now, bereft of monetary or other obligations, I feel that I can calmly tolerate whatever she calls me. Is it mandatory in love to retain self-respect? That analysis made him reflect that maybe theirs was no love at all! It rather was the attraction and repulsion of two egos! At times, he would also reflect that this attraction might not endure even. Any moment, during our happy union, she turns derisive and disdainful, makes a culprit out of me, and goes to the extent of asking me not to stay on if ever I am abashed. Forfeiting self-respect, where is the need to keep on cajoling and accosting her? Such disregard would show up now and then.

Eighth day after his return from Bombay, and the consequent exit from her house along with his suitcase in an auto, when he returned home from office after having supper, an envelope lay by the door. By the handwriting, he could make out that it was hers. It was also superscribed and underlined 'personal' in red ink. The very sight of the envelope made him eager. No contact with her these eight days. She too hasn't called. Though his intellect decreed that this was a clear indication of annulment of association, his livid mind insisted that she volunteer to call, for erred *she* has. Without changing, he sat on the bed and opened the envelope. Two letters inside. Both in her letterhead printed with her name, address, and phone number. He read the first one hastily. It bore yesterday's date. It had begun with no address whatsoever:

> *There remains nothing that needs to be conveyed to you. Yet, I write this to discharge a duty of mine. You will get to know the nature of that obligation when you read the other letter enclosed herewith. Instead of beating around the bush, let me come to the point straight away. I have given much thought to the matter of our relationship. Even before the advent of it, feelings of void would invade me often. The desire to die would beleaguer me acutely and densely. The cause of genesis of those feelings is definitely not you. During the early stages of our relationship, it had considerably reduced even. But as the relationship progressed, the feelings of void began pervading more intensely and viciously. As of now, there's no feeling in me except that. In me, there is nothing of affection, love, complaisance, enthusiasm, glee, or gentleness. The faculty to exude them is fully corroded in me. I am not writing this letter to devolve the blame onto you. Neither do I opine that you are responsible for this. But it is true that consequent to my relationship with you, the feelings of void and desire*

to die have become insurmountable in me. Wherefore it is necessary to stem this relationship.

I have caused ill will very many times. I vividly remember every act, every utterance, and every word of mine in all minutiae. I never will be in a state of forgetfulness, a state of non-consciousness so as to be unable to recollect. Eventually, you may forget the wrongs that I have committed. But even an iota of it would not have erased from my memory. Also, I shall always remember your reservedness and demeanour. It is true that the other day I said, 'Since your suitcase is in the car, I will drop you at a place where you can hire an autorickshaw. I want to be left alone. In another five minutes, you should leave this house. If you are abashed, you will not speak.' Then I left ahead of you and started the car. It is also true that you got up, dressed, scurried out, and left in the auto that presently came by. 'To hell with your blurting. Just because you speak nonsense, I will not get going. This house is mine. You haven't the authority to order me out,' thus admonishing me, did you choose to stay back?

I am not hell-bent on dying. But I am not also able to withhold the desire to commit suicide when feelings of void surge. I do not also know when I will eventually jerk the trigger. Maybe, God doesn't know too. But before pulling the trigger, I will address a suicide note to the police without fail. It is possible that I may die without leaving such note. Even if I write, it may escape the attention of the police. If they do get it, they may still destroy it with the intent to cause trouble to others. Many people know that you frequent my house and that I personally attended to the interiors of your office. Naturally, the police will suspect you first. So please preserve the enclosed letter. It will come in handy in times of need.

That's all. No closing lines or signature. He unfolded the second letter. That she had clearly addressed to him and had also written his name. Printed at the top left-hand corner was Dr C.R. Amrita, MA, PhD. To the top right corner was her residential address and phone number. Below, she had written the date and clearly addressed to him in her own handwriting.

Faithful respects to Sri Somashekhar,

I am aware that to express my gratefulness to you for your amiable words on your previous visit to my house would be nothing more than etiquette. But without expressing any such, I am unable to acknowledge your help. I am inhibitive of relating all this in your presence and may get tongue-tied. Even over phone, words may not form properly. Hence this letter. I haven't shared with anyone other than you the fact that feelings of void often pervade and irrepressibly impel me to commit suicide. I am confident that you would not have shared this with your acquaintances, however intimate they be (pardon me for writing this despite absence of premise for the same). Having lent a patient ear to my tale of woe, you much consoled me. You insisted that I swear by God not to attempt suicide in future. You even suggested that I dispose of my revolver with the intervention of the police. Angry, you even said you would take it away. I am considering your vehement suggestion to surrender the revolver and appoint a gurkha registered with the police. But before that, one aspect needs to be considered. For one who aspires to commit suicide, revolver is not the only resort. A length of rope, some kerosene, a gram of pesticide, few tranquilliser pills – aren't there quite some means? Yet, I acknowledge the feelings at the base of your concern.

On your visit the other day, with this matter demanding all our attention, I failed to recall another important matter. Three weeks back, my bank informed me that you have fully repaid my monies. I tried to contact you immediately to convey that there was really no need for the urgency. You were not in station. Your assistant Neelakanthappa informed me that you were away in Bombay for two weeks. Now I am once again expressing sincerely that there was really no need for urgency in repaying the bank loan.

Regards,
Yours truly,
C.R. Amrita

He marvelled at the embellishment, measure, and the natural ways of this letter. He also noticed the dexterity with which the fact of remittance of money was cited, being well-evidenced in the records of the bank, leaving nothing to doubt. It was duly acquitted to convince any judge. He folded the letters, inserted them into the envelope, left it on the bed, so as to peruse again later, and got up to change.

Didn't read again. Put off the light and retired. He felt that she had written all that to prick him, to reduce his esteem. Her intent was clear. 'All you have is fear of what the police might do to you. Keep this letter, I bless you.' He felt that she had drafted the other letter with a lot of magnanimity. It is in her comportment to etch a slip-up in me, even though she is the one at fault, and then squarely devolve the entire onus of the situation onto me. What she actually said the other day was this: 'If you are abashed, you shall exit this house in five minutes.' Now she imports a novel meaning to those words: 'Why didn't you stay back saying that *this house is mine? You haven't the authority to order me out.*' Very smart! Student of literature, eh! Does literature mean to twist words? Twisting the meaning conveniently? He decreed that she is faulting and inflicting injustice on the literature that she pursues and teaches. In a short while, sleep came.

But he was awake at 3 am. He put on the light, glanced at his watch, and immediately put off the light. He recalled that if he didn't sleep properly till about 6:30 or 7, the deftness and grade of his professional work would suffer. He always believed that a lugubrious face, yawning or dozing off while at work, were signs of misfortune. Deciding to get sleep whatsoever, he persistently closed his eyes and strove to attain the state of shutting-out-the-business-of-the-mind recommended in yoga treatises. But the more he tried, the more time dilated and propelled the thought process. After some time, when he put on the light to check the time, it was still 3:15. He got up, emptied his bladder, and retired again, putting off the light. He got curious what she would be doing now. She wouldn't be asleep. He felt that if there were a telephone connection at home, he could have called right away and verified. Not asleep. She is seated on the sofa, revolver in hand. Or, she is parked by the ledge on the eastern side of the Chamundi Hill, preparing to die. No telephone, at least shall I drive there and check? On the way to the hill, if I stop by her house, the dogs will bark and she will open the door. Else, head straight to the hill only to discover that the car stands parked by the ledge.

But he couldn't pull himself up, dress, retrieve the scooter, and start. He just lay, unable to think, to act. When he had left for the washroom, a mosquito gained entry into the net. It is buzzing around and irritating. If he didn't track and eliminate it, it would keep sleep in abeyance. He felt for the switch and put on the light. After a minute's search, he zeroed in on the mosquito. Silently, he aligned both palms and instantaneously brought them together in a thud. The fly was exterminated. Great valour! Great deed! He told himself sarcastically. The light is on. Sleep simply won't come. He took out her letter from beneath the pillow and started reading again ... *Even before the advent of it, feelings of void would invade me often. The desire to die would beleaguer me acutely and densely. The genesis of those feelings is definitely not you. During the early stages of our relationship, it had considerably reduced even. But as the relationship progressed, the feelings of void began pervading more intensely and viciously. As of now, there's no other feeling in me except that. In me, there is nothing of affection, love, complaisance, enthusiasm, glee, or gentleness. The faculty to exude them is fully corroded in me. I am not writing this letter to devolve the blame onto you. Neither do I opine that you are responsible for this. But it is true that consequent to my relationship with you, the feelings of void and desire to die have become insurmountable in me. Wherefore it is necessary to stem this relationship ...*

He recalled their relationship that began one and a half years previously. In fact, it was she who took it each step further. Not that I was against it. He recalled that greater was her impetus. In the fluorescent light, his eyes were fixated on the mosquito net. The soft shadow of the net on the wall conveyed a peculiar meaning. The entire world seemed to him as the shadow of some such net. There was a hint of some obscure but mysterious meaning. But nothing concretized despite much cogitation. Then another question emerged. Why was she keen on encouraging this camaraderie with me? Because of this cordiality, she would possibly have overcome a bit of void. Or, possibly, an illusion of conquest! Hence, she has furthered it. But when eventually she realized that she hadn't the faculty to really conquer it or stem it, she is let down. She has felt that this relationship was meaningless and useless. Hence – he could gather – this relationship is increasing feelings of emptiness in her. Eyes were still glued to the shadow cast by the net. What am I to her? What is she to me? What nexus? Those questions formed. The contours of the questions assumed attractive dimensions, and he felt that they had some nexus with the shadow of the net. After a while, reflecting that such postulates could be extrapolated to apply to two boulders and be similarly subjected to inquisition, he smiled and continued reading the letter ... *It is true that after having said that, I exited and gunned the car. It is also true that you got up, dressed, scurried out, and left in the auto that presently came by. 'To hell with your blurting. Just because you speak nonsense, I will not get going. This house is mine. You haven't the authority to order me out,' thus admonishing me, did you stay back* ... His mind got pegged thereat. Is she just finding fault with me or is she speaking out the truth? And why didn't I say so? Declaring so, why didn't I just lie there and slip into sleep? He raked his brains. Nothing flashed. The explanation emerged that if nothing struck, it only meant that the premise for such a thought is absent. Eventually, he reflected that if one went on with such ginning, anything could be expounded at any rate. There can be an explanation – a sensible one at that – for 'why a thought came by', but an attempt at explaining the antithesis 'why didn't it' leaves us with nothing, as with ginned cotton consigned to the winds. Just yawns came. Sleep eluded.

By 6:30 am, he felt drowsy and was awake half an hour later. Light was still on. His hand lay on his chest with the letter. Opening his eyes, he glanced over the second letter. Besides the embellishment, measure, and the natural ways of this letter, he reflected that she probably had written this with the honest intent of insulating him against inconveniences in case she did kill herself.

~

That morning when he arrived in office at about 9:30, a medical professional awaited him. Aged about forty, he was a practicing surgeon in the USA. Wife too had an OB and GY practice there. They have planned to return to India and set up their nursing home in Mysore. He owns a big site in Lakshmipuram. The big old building in it has to be demolished and a nursing home and residential quarters are to be built. The couple have thought it over thoroughly and devised a plan, keeping in mind the amenities required in both the premises. He is here on a four-week holiday. Wife hasn't accompanied him. During his short stint here, if detailed plans were made available, he intends to return to the USA after procuring sanction from civic authorities. Two OTs, two consulting rooms, two labour wards, a total of thirty wards, two waiting rooms, parking, elevators for patients, reception desk, that is to say, well-appointed. He has brought with him quite some photographs from the USA on the unique designs of different rooms, and also model pictures of the facade and the side view. He is also well-informed about electrification system and desires to have the facilities here as in the USA. He has thorough knowledge of the terminologies of architecture too. He said, 'The lines that I have drawn are just to thumb rule, imaginary ones owing to lack of technical knowledge. We haven't any idea as to the merits of the construction materials available here. See the site first thing. I haven't any other work. I can sit all day in your office's waiting room. Or I will leave my residence contact number with you. I will make myself available whenever you choose to call. If you can get the rough plan ready in eight days, we can apply for permission with the civic authorities. You can get the proper working plan ready by the time I leave and we can keep improving upon it.' He went with the doctor in his car and inspected the site. It was two hundred feet by two hundred feet. Along the fence were neem, mango, and other full-grown trees. Ramamurthy was pleased when he suggested that the structure should come up by retaining the trees. The doctor conveyed the same.

On returning to the architect's office and comfortably seated in his air-conditioned cabin, the doctor said, 'Let me tell you what brought me directly to you. You got Jalaja's house built for her. She is a distant cousin. My wife is her mother's brother's daughter, but we meet up quite regularly. She said, "Just assign everything to Mr Somashekhar. He is a very honest person. Your single *pai* won't go waste." I am her guest now. She would have accompanied me, but the daytime college, you know. She may join us by noon. Will you appoint a builder for me? It is your responsibility to have supervise him and make or arrange payments to him. Now, tell me your percentage to the total cost.'

'Madam Jalaja would have told you. Four.'

'This is a job with a great deal of responsibility. Quality of work should be ultimate. Finances will also be under your control. I will authorize Jalaja to just sign and handover cheques to the builder as per your instructions. She, too, is familiar with these matters, as she has gone through the construction of a house. But she will simply heed your words. I have fixed your fee at six percent, for the quality of workmanship I expect is high. Besides, I will be personally visiting for inspection during three stages of the work in progress. In between, I will write to you detailed letters. You should send equally exhaustive replies. I will call you often. You too can call collect me whenever necessary.'

The job verily captured his imagination. Even the streaks with which the good doctor had illustrated the designs were ones induced by superb imagination. The photographs were suggestive of novel concepts. Sacrificing quality for the sake of economy was not this man's cuppa. All the same, I have never caused extra burden to any client in the name of quality and superfluities. He reflected that this job was one that would fetch him remuneration as well as fame. Even as of now, there is the need for extra staff. If this project has to get underway, should appoint one soon, and an accountant too, he instantly resolved.

It was three weeks since he had taken up this work. Every hour of Dr Ramamurthy's stay here was precious and not to be squandered. In addition to supervising the other works on hand, this had to be painstakingly dealt with. He had asked Ramamurthy to visit him in his office twice daily, at 8 in the morning and 8 in the evening. Somashekhar himself suggested that Jalajakshi, who had shouldered financial responsibilities and would sign all cheques, escort Ramamurthy on most all visits and be a party to their discussions for getting familiar with every detail. So it was impossible for him and his two assistants to call it a day till 10 in the night. They had to start the day at 9. They knew not when weekends came and went. One more week of such hectic slogging in the company of Ramamurthy to finalize the plan and costs, and work could be streamlined to normal pace once he left for the USA.

At this stage, one afternoon at 1, there was a call from Amrita. Ramamurthy had just left, promising to see him at 8 pm with Jalaja on tow. With Neelakanthappa and the newly appointed Nanjundegowda working in the outer office, there was none else in the cabin. 'You would be taken aback, hearing this voice. Can you recognize?' she asked.

'What do you mean?' he said, surprised, delighted, and confused all at once. Though her memories troubled him often, the pressure of the work on hand had caused his mind to digress, especially with the ever-vigilant Ramamurthy in audience. Since writing those letters, she had not contacted him. The statement – *the need to stem this relationship* – would often surface in his mind. She had taken pains to write. I didn't write back, didn't even call. That awareness rendered it impossible for him to think of any further response. What would her musings be about our relationship? Did it exist at all? If it didn't, why would she call now! He continued to stay mum, unable to think of any further response. For a minute, the telephone cable just conducted silence.

She broke it, 'If you are not inclined to talk, I will replace the receiver.'

'Ma'am, ma'am, don't, don't,' he said.

'There you go! If you don't want to talk, disconnect the call. That would be better than indicating aloofness by employing a deferential address,' she shot back. 'In the midst of work ... ' he trailed off. 'Anybody in audience now?' her voice had mellowed down.

'No.'

'Then, will you please come over for a moment please? We can chat while we lunch.'

'Right now?'

'Yes, right now.'

'I am very busy. A big commission. I have appointed the contractor to see me at 3 pm. I will be free at 10 pm. For one more week, it shall be thus.'

'I know. You have to finish working on all details before Dr Ramamurthy leaves for the USA. If I had the endurance to wait for a week, I would not have troubled your goodselves making this call, sorry. It is up to you.'

'Deference and informality should be on an even keel,' he said at once.

But she chose not to reply and disconnected the phone. He clearly understood that she cut the call after he said that. He continued to hold the receiver for two full minutes, the fact of the pointlessness of the act not at all registering in him. This is her nature, at once flaring up in anger and, in the tone of language and message, derisively casting me off and holding me at fault. After replacing the receiver, he glanced at his watch. It was 1:12. Why not visit her? Putting off the AC and the lights in the cabin, he left, instructing Neelakanthappa, 'Contractor Nagaraj is appointed for 3 pm. Give him the rate list that we have checked and ask him to go through it. I may be delayed by ten or fifteen minutes.' Then he climbed down the stairs and gunned his scooter. He recalled that this was his first time in twenty-two days that he was leaving his office premises for afternoon lunch. His mind traced the route to her house – Hardinge Road, the zoo curve, and the straight road to the hill thence – he felt that it was ages since he last tread that path, and it seemed somewhat unfamiliar. Calculating, he recalled that it was exactly thirty days since he had left her house and returned by the auto. He wondered, why do I rush to her the moment I get a telephone call from her, even though she verily detests me and I verily resolve to stay off her ! Having arrived at the curve by the zoo by then, his reflexes automatically applying themselves, he slowed down, swerved to the extreme left of the road, looked ahead, turned, and moved on. Sighting the Chamundi Hill, he felt that he got back what he had missed in this one month.

She wasn't by the gate. The main door was not open. Though she opened the door a full minute after he rang the doorbell, her face explicitly displayed her attempt at concealing the anticipation of his arrival. Stepping inside, he looked at her. He then turned to the corner and removed his pump shoes. She shut the door. From the veranda, he went to the lounge and sat on the sofa. She too arrived there in a minute and sat on the opposite sofa. As he looked her in the face, she just glanced at him and withdrew her sight. Two minutes rolled by. Nobody could think of anything to say.

She got up and went in. He continued to sit his place. After five minutes, she came to the lounge and said, 'It is 1:50. If you have to be there at 3 pm, you have to leave at 2:45.' He chose to remain silent. 'If it is pressing, you may leave right now. I will have your pardon for causing a reluctant one to drive that much in the sun,' she said.

'*If I had the endurance to wait for one week, I would not have troubled you by making this call, sorry …* ' he recalled her words. There's got to be something important. Should ask her about it, he told himself. But not knowing what to say, he just gazed at her mutely. She had rooted her gaze in his. After a minute, she said, 'A commission worth three lakh in fee. Your entire mind is therein. You may leave now,' and went to her bedroom.

He was taken aback. How would she have unearthed all these details? Jalajakshi has given it to her. It was because of her recommendation that I got Jalajakshi's commission. While they met in college, she told her all this. She has quizzed her and extracted all information – the total estimate of the building was fifty lakh, and my fee six percent of that. After two minutes, decidedly shrugging off wretchedness, he went to her bedroom. Though the door was shut, it ceded to the touch. She lay on the bed. Nearing her, he flung himself beside her and hugged her firmly. She lay still like a log of dry wood, without any reaction to his embrace, indicating that she was not game. He sheathed her in a total embrace and said, 'Why not speak, you mute?'

'Was your love on exile when you stepped inside?' she took exception.

'By delaying, why did you warrant me to bell?' he rejoined.

'How would I know that the lord cometh?' she too added smartly.

'Now face me and say that you didn't know that I would definitely come. Tell me.' When he held her head and turned her face towards him, he noticed that she gritted her jaw and held her lips pursed. 'Look in my face and tell the truth.' When he insisted, she burst out laughing and sprayed some on his face. That caused a smile to break in her face. But he noticed that at the base of that smile was intense pain and sorrow.

Even before he could speak any further, she sat up and said, 'Come, let's lunch first. I am intolerably hungry.' As he neared the dining table, he noticed that she had already placed two plates and two glasses. 'I was busying myself with arranging cusine for the lord, whose arrival was due in fifteen minutes. You, on the other hand, take objection that I did not wait at the door and open it the moment the scooter was heard. Shall I engage a rival wife for attending to the cooking?' She served the stew. He chose to be silent. 'Silence is consent. You desire that I instate one, a better one than me. One who is obedient and never hostile. Not a dunce who has seen just Sakleshpur and Mysore. A smart one who has been in Madras and Bombay. Yes? Say the truth.' She gazed at him. Though she was humouring him, he noticed that her voice strummed pain and that her eyes were shorn of lustre.

He pushed his chair closer, held her with his left arm about her shoulder, and said in a coaxing tone, 'Something within waits to be spilled. First, speak out that. Lunch can wait.' She lifted her neck and eyed him. He caressed her head and kissed her warmly. She did not respond. Just continued to eye him. The eyes that were arid and had lost the reflective sheen gradually welled up. When they became succulent so as to trickle, her sight got hazy and she leant over, hid her face in his chest, and sobbed. All his efforts at consoling her by caressing her head went in vain. She cried so as to cause her body to tremble fiercely, and all her bones rattled as if they would come apart. 'Amu, speak up. Whatever, speak up. I am here. Tell me.' Even that consolation could not contain her. He simply held her in a cuddle.

In a short while, he sensed that she had repressed herself. She withdrew her face from his chest and said, 'Let's quickly finish lunch now. If I start relating, lunch may get aborted midway. Yes, quick. Start.' She dissolved some rice in the curry in her salver. He was habituated to gobble up his breakfast and lunch ever since he embarked on the nursing home project, and finished his lunch faster than she did.

After both had finished, she brought him to the lounge, sat on the sofa, and said, 'You haven't the faculty to understand unless told. Hence, I will tell you myself.' Grief overcame again. While he held her in a smug embrace and caressed her back, she said, 'Know why I forced myself to eat? I may fast, but it is sinful to starve the foetus within.'

Silence seemed to hiss forth from his ears. He received a jolt – he had got himself into a new predicament. She craned her neck and inquisitively looked at his face. Then she spoke slowly, as if she understood his mind, 'It is twenty-five or twenty-six days since I suspected this. I wrote to you. Did you get it? While I wrote it, this was confirmed. I knew that you aren't someone who would wed me. The moment I asked you to get out, you left in an auto. I am not blaming you. You are not inclined to wed, and I am pregnant. What is my future? I wrote those letters to you, deciding that I would surely resort to the revolver, and in case I did shoot myself, you should not be put to any trouble. Have you carefully preserved them? Tell me, have you?'

He realized that by that query, she was denigrating him, bearing down the ethical grit of his personality to great depths. He said, 'Not with any care. Should be there somewhere at home if the domestic help has not cleared it along with other waste stationery.'

'Is that all the respect my letter commands?' she asked, turning towards him sharply.

'You are not content unless you speak with both edges jagged. That aside, tell me what happened later. Why didn't you inform me immediately? Why didn't you call?'

'On receiving that letter, why didn't *you* call? Didn't rush to me?' she shot back.

'If we keep debating, nothing can be conveyed. First fill me in on the matter.'

'Listen to me entirely. As I speak, I may lay the blame on you, for I won't be able to otherwise convey my feelings of that moment. I am just recounting now. There's no scorn or accusation. Who else shall I spill my mind unto? Would it not be pretentious if I share only pleasant feelings to the exclusion of irate ones?'

He affirmed.

'You said that my words are jagged at both ends. Not just that, I am also aware that when I start a conversation with you, it will necessarily lead to a debate, and the words will eventually turn tart. It is not your fault. That is my default state. You, however, have restraint over your words, a moderation to speak as much as required, and in the desired temper. Yours is a personality delineated by intellect. Hence, I get wild that you act smart.'

'If I conduct myself in the same way as you, will the situation be under control?' his question perplexed her.

'*My way* meaning *in anger*, is it? You mean I am short-tempered and you are a composed one? Your barbed words pierce within. It will be very spiky. Mine is overt, blunt. Right?'

'That's okay. What was your state of mind, tell me?' he tried to steer the conversation towards the issue at hand.

'I am pregnant. You have no inclination to wed. In such a situation, what does an average Indian woman do? Kerosene, rope, a waterbody! There isn't a more apt reason for suicide. Resolving to end myself with the revolver, I wrote that letter to you. I waited for a one-line reply, a call from you. I would eagerly check the mailbox. Whenever the phone rang, I would contend with myself that it was your call before rushing to receive it. If the dog barked for any reason, I would rush to the window hoping to see you. You didn't call or write or visit. Not your fault. I had ordered you *to get out of this house in five minutes, if you were any abashed, without speaking a second word*. I had written in my letter that there was the absolute necessity to stem this relationship. You did not proclaim, "This house is mine. You have no right to expel me." You didn't write back, "If you talk of severing this relationship, I will sever your tongue." Didn't even say the same over phone. Well, I wrote that letter with the untarnished intent that the police should not trouble you. Thus passed one week. By then, a new feeling surfaced in me. A life has sprout. I am no greenhorn. Neither are you. Though we had exercised enough care, the life has sprout, albeit accidentally. I have the right to end my life. But have I the authority to destroy the life that isn't mine, this life that has rooted and sprouted inside me? If I destroy myself, is it not as good as destroying it? The onus is on me to save and tend it. Otherwise, God would not pardon me. Though the revolver was in hand, I was not induced to aim it to the head or inside the mouth. I was certain that till this embryo stayed inside me, it was impossible for me to commit suicide. Once, I even reflected that this has turned out to be a pretext or instrument of keeping me away from death. But I held myself in derision that I am employing this foetus as a pretext for staying alive. Later, all of a sudden, know what sorts of love I begot towards this? Oh! I had never before experienced such deep love in any matter whatsoever, even when I conceived Vijai and Vikas. Know why? Tell me why? I want to hear it from you. Tell, man,' she held both his arms.

'For this is our child, a fruit of our love,' he replied.

'Somu, Somu, my Somu, this is indication enough that you love me, that you understand me. You were angry then. I thought of appealing to you, "I am pregnant. Shed your anger and come over. It is not righteous for the doting man to stay away in anger when the woman is pregnant." But self-respect and pride alert in me, I checked myself from the helplessness that normally ails a pregnant woman. I shall not fall at his feet. The onus of my pregnancy is mine. This is my problem. I decided that I would work it out myself. Isn't my decision right?'

'I didn't know a thing.'

'You couldn't know. All these were happening to *me*, and *I* experienced those feelings. I am now relating what befell *me*.'

'The nursing home commission coincided and I was busy slogging from 8 to 10.'

'Meaning that memories of Amu faded.'

'Nah. Wasn't in a state of mind where fine feelings would register. Now,' he said, checking his watch, 'it is 3:15. The contractor is appointed for 3 pm. I will be here at 10. Let's sup together. And talk till dawn.' He leaned over, cupped her face in both his palms, planted a kiss on her lips, and got up.

'Must you leave ? The three lakh commission takes precedence,' she expressed discontent.

'Not just the income. My work ethics command that once I take up a commission, I have to honour their time and see to it that every rupee is spent optimally. I am here tonight,' there was restlessness in his voice.

'I shall not place trust in you unless you relent on your egotism that you alone are the virtuous one,' she said. Though he felt that this was tickle for a brawl, without speaking any he kissed her again. Without waiting for her to escort him out and see him off, he just asked her to close the gate and sped away on his scooter.

After he left, she got fiery. Staying from closing the gate, she stuck to the sofa, seething. After a while, she glanced at her watch. It was 3:40. But now, he would have arrived in his air-conditioned office, the contractor and Jalajakshi's brother would be in audience, and he would be computing concrete cubic rupees and paisa. She felt like getting up, calling him, and telling him that there was no need for him to visit that night, or any night for that matter. But in the quiet cabin, her voice might carry to the others there. And, if Jalajakshi was there and should recognize my voice ! Cautious, she checked herself. He said that he would arrive at 10, and that they could talk till dawn ! What is there to talk about with that undeserving man ? She gritted her teeth and went and reclined on the bed.

While he presided in his cabin, discussing pricing and other details with the contractor and with Dr Ramamurthy – and Jalajakshi who arrived later – and in between, as he made calls to four different suppliers of steel, glass, plywood, and other construction materials, his concentration went off course. As his aide Neelakanthappa, conversant with all details, was in total concentration, he felt relieved.

He at once felt that he had got very intimate with her, that despite the extent of her anger and tirade, their relationship was rock solid as never to give away in future. All the same, he was troubled by the nascence of a disconcerting worry. It is not unusual for a woman to get pregnant when lovers come together. Though he tried consoling himself that it couldn't be disconcerting to them in the manner that it would be to inexperienced, impecunious adolescents who had no liberty to private absoluteness, an uncontainable agitation reigned in him. Though he was well-versed with estimation and pricing, he entrusted the day's work to Neelakanthappa and resigned to the role of a witness, as if it did not deserve the attention of his rank. And as they stuck to the work, ordering snacks and tea twice in between, they arrived at a consensus with the builder by about 8:30. It was also decided that some fittings were to be procured from Bangalore and billed at local rates.

After the others left, he instructed Neelakanthappa and Nanjundegowda that they are to arrive early next day, get the agreement and estimates typed, and keep everything else ready in two days. He then left on his scooter for the market. Even after searching thoroughly, he couldn't get royal jasmine. Instead of that moderately aromatic flower, he bought the intensely aromatic jasmine. When he visited her house, he noticed that the children were still awake. 'Uncle,' Vikas neared him. Vijai greeted him from a distance. On his face was a shade of discontent. 'Oh, the plans of the labour quarters of the estate! It had slipped from my mind. Please be seated.' After greeting him, she said, 'Jalajakshi told me that you would be exhausted, what with slogging out the commission of her cousin till 9 or 10 in the night. Now you have turned up for my job. Sorry.' He understood that those words were intended to be heard by Vijai. He was aware that the eight-and-a-half-year-old lad exhibited aloofness when they met in this house. It was she who had brought it to his notice.

'Just a minute. The lads have to be up early in the morning. I will put them to sleep and be back.' She led the boys to their bedroom. Returning after fifteen minutes, she said, 'Well sir, we better discuss the plan as we sup,' and led him to the kitchen. He retracted to the sink by the backdoor and washed his face and hands. When he returned to the kitchen, she said, 'Vijai said, *Uncle has brought jasmine. I smelled it the moment he entered*,' as if reporting his lack of prudence. He felt whether it was erroneous to bring it. After laying two platters and sitting across each other, she said, 'I am suspicious of Vijai. I feel that he is being goaded by someone. Else, a kid that he is, why should he be prejudiced towards you who has behaved with him affably?'

'Why, did he express something?'

'Nothing pointedly. But I still get that feeling. A mother readily gets to know the mind of her child. That's okay. What about you?'

'About what?'

She did not speak. He gathered that anger was surfacing in her. Instantly, he became cognizant of his lapse. 'That was just in reflex to your query, an unconsidered one. I fully endorse whatever you decide in the matter,' he said, consoling her.

She did not respond immediately. Head hung, she just munched. Then she said, 'When you left in the afternoon, you said that you would be arriving tonight so that we can talk till dawn. Didn't you mean a discussion when you said *talk*?'

'We have to together take a decision, right?' he replied calmly.

She turned silent. After two minutes, she said, 'Have to decide together? When I gave you the news this afternoon, if you had jumped three feet into the air with joy and said, "Amu, this is my child. We have to care well for this. You now have to adhere to your diet without remission. If I catch you negligent in tending it, I will slap you," it was enough for me. What is there in this to consider, score points, and discuss from 10 in the night till dawn? To discuss would mean to consider the pros and cons and to weigh the for and against, right? If love were to be, it would surge instantly. It would readily induce the heart to spill affection and douse the progeny in it. Owing to lack of it, you proposed a debate. And now you were careless enough to even let that proposal slip from your mind. Then a blanket endorsement of whatever I choose to decide. In effect, you devolved the entire onus onto me and excused yourself.'

His intellect could not fault the singe of her logic. Yes, why didn't I pronounce – *this is my child, should nurture it, I command thee?* Is it that the affinity that a woman develops towards the foetus is obscure to the man? Maybe, there are men who develop kinship. Maybe, my disposition is different. How is it possible to express a feeling, which, not being innate, does not surge from within? And leap three feet into the air like a Pidikhtos dancer? She is watching him, her sight studious. Since it was now imperative on him to offer some reply, he said, 'It is very simple to announce that this is my child, that it should be saved and nurtured, that its nourishment being via your diet, you are to choose a nutritious diet and adhere to it without an iota of laxity. Literature that you have studied! To weave a tête-à-tête is in your faculty. How much ever beautifully imagination may soar, it shall not be venerable to me unless reinforced by steel, gravel, brick, sand, and cement. Besides, I cannot build exclusively to my satisfaction. It should be built to the complete satisfaction of all concerned – the man, the wife, the children of the house, the callers, friends, et al. If we retain this, what will be the consequence? You have now distanced yourself from Ranganath. If he gets to know of your present state, will he continue to stay mum? How would your aunt react? You just referred to Vijai's misgivings. How will you acclimatize him to this new development? What will you tell Vikas? All your professional colleagues, how will they look up to this? Should these not be considered? That this is my child, look … ' he washed his hands in the salver, got up, placed his right hand on her belly, and said, 'I swear on this, on God, that I am ready to announce to the whole world that this is my child. And prior to that, I am also ready to wed you. Nevertheless, we should consider every issue beforehand, as to how to cope with the possible reactions of everyone concerned. As far as I am concerned, there is no issue at all. All issues are concerning you. Hence, I said that I fully endorse whatever you decide. It is you who must decide about all these issues. Hence, intending to partake in all your pleasures and displeasures alike, I offered to talk, discuss, and resolve with consensus. What's wrong with that?'

Her face turned red with anger as if her movements were restrained by applying holds and pinning her to the floor. His hand still rested on her stomach as he stood slightly bent beside her. She lifted her right arm so as to strike him across his cheek. But recollecting, she instantly withdrew it. The fact that he had washed his hand before placing it on her stomach, and that her hand was yet soiled, registered in her conscious only later. He very well understood the motion of her right arm and the anger in her face. Yet, without distancing himself, he held his face close to her and continued to hold his palm on her stomach. 'You should have been a lawyer. In brief, you have stated that I have no alternative but to get this aborted. You can never understand my feelings. No man can understand the feelings of a woman. Your feelings will never cross the transactional threshold and enter deeper domains,' she stuttered in an emotional voice.

By then, footsteps were heard approaching. By the time they both trained their sights in that direction, Vijai was entering the kitchen doorway. Though he was very sleepy, his eyes were open. Somashekhar swiftly withdrew his hand that rested on her stomach. She was dumbstruck, but in the very next moment, said, 'Yes, kiddie? Sleep doesn't come?' She got up, neared him, hugged him, and, patting his back, humoured him. He complained of thirst.

'It is that *masurpāk* I ate, kiddie. Nobody should eat *masurpāk* henceforth. It gave me such an intense stomach ache that I felt I was dying. Uncle massaged the aching spot. Come, let me get you water. Huh! It still aches, look, here,' she took hold of his right hand and, placing it on her stomach, said, 'Can you feel? The churning pain! Bloody chickpea flour,' she mimed pain and then, washing her hands, handed him a big glass of water. After he swigged it down, she put her arms on his shoulder and led him to his room, 'Let me put you to sleep.' Though this scrape bewildered Somashekhar, he marvelled at her resourcefulness in bringing up a pretext. He returned to his dining chair. Returning ten minutes later, she said in cadence, 'When he retired, you were here. Even in sleep, his mind would be resisting that fact. Hence, he woke up and came here. You leave now. Be here for lunch tomorrow afternoon without fail. Make yourself available for at least two hours. I have much to talk about. If he so much as hears the scooter exit, he will sleep fine.'

He had forgotten to give her the jasmine that he had brought. When she came to the door to see him off, he extracted it from within the helmet, adorned her plait at the nape with it, softly kissed her on the lips, left, gunned his scooter, and drove away. He felt that his scooter was disturbing the tranquillity that had pervaded the environs. As he drove, he reflected that it would have sent out wrong feelers to observing strollers if he had towed his scooter some distance in that unearthly hour. At home, as he opened the windows and stretched himself on his bed inside the mosquito net, his mind was filled with her words that no man shall understand a woman's feelings. His wife was three months pregnant when the foetus aborted. How much she wept! For days on end, she kept recalling it and weeping! Vexed, when he enquired why she lamented so much, she had said, 'How can you understand the woes of a woman?' The foetus that grows in her belly will, in effect, be an organ of her body and a part of her mind, and hence, he now understood such intense affection and the feeling of oneness. Besides, another reason appealed to him that Amrita's feeling of oneness with this progeny was copious as it was the fruit of their love. Cogitating on it, he felt that the oneness a man begets in the earlier phase of love, rather in the intense moments of coition, do not remain as compelling later when the woman heralds pregnancy. Within him, he conceded that her words might be true.

For quite some time, sleep eluded him. He couldn't fancy how the present situation would be resolved. One matter surfaced in memory, the words of the Bombay femme. I had once said, 'We are coming together often. What if you get pregnant?' She had asked, chiding, 'Will you marry me?' I had said, 'If we wed, the university will be lost to you, and my career to me. Then on, no sustenance for us both.' She had decreed, 'Understand that if we were married, this intensity will not remain twenty-four hours, thirty days, and twelve months. This intensity is possible only when we come together occasionally as lovers.' Then it didn't occur to me as true. When in concert, I had felt that we would be so even at a ripe old age. 'I got myself a contraceptive surgery after my third daughter was born. No fear of getting pregnant,' she had said. When he had queried as to why she went for such a surgery, she had cooed and incited him, 'Prospectively, I would meet an infatuated lover called Somashekhar. So, I thought, let there be gay abandon for him.' She then related an earlier episode. They were one year into their marriage. Husband was very passionate. *She* was one sizzling covet. They had resorted to a provisional contraceptive. Presently, the husband left for Canada on a year-long training programme. She enrolled herself for an MSc degree in Bombay. There she befriended a classmate. Got pregnant. 'What next?' she looked on my face. I put away my sight, puzzled, as if the onus of the situation were on me. Smiling, she said, 'The classmate got anxious, wretched. A bachelor. Greenhorn. I consoled him, "Don't worry, it is the woman's responsibility, mine." I saw a doctor myself, tossed two hundred, and got it relieved. Third day I called him, "Come on, dear. All clear," and took him to my apartment.'

She had looked at my face inquisitively. 'See, the easing of anxiety is obvious in your face now. These concerns are the woman's. She alone should get rid of them. Should not devolve the onus onto the man. It is incorrect to cause anguish in him. I have never conducted myself callously. Once, this slip occurred with my husband even. I didn't then blame him of carelessness. This has happened, but don't worry, dear. I will see a gynaecologist. I had humoured him and seen him off to his office. I later called him at his office and said, "Dear, I saw the doctor. All's done. But it is abstinence for you for a week."' Much to his chagrin, not to liken these two women, comparison did set in. In her association weren't anxiety, pain, and sorrow. Neither were intensity, allegiance, and devotion. Sleep overcame.

At morning, he went to his office early. He deputed Ramamurthy to the city municipal offices in the company of Neelakanthappa. The preliminaries of Ramamurthy's commission were almost over by now, so to say. Only the works that were to be carried out in his absence remained. He was to leave for Bangalore tomorrow on a four-day visit. He was invited by Ramamurthy for dinner that night. He worked in the company of Nanjundegowda till noon and, informing him that he would be back by 3 pm, he started on his scooter and headed to the bazaar. He discerned and bought the royal jasmine, and as he headed to her house, his mind was troubled more by the anxiety regarding the kind of her reaction than the attention that the situation at hand demanded. An unexpected situation has popped up. I haven't the full freedom to resolve it. What with the whole of it, I haven't even my rightful share of the freedom. She acts adamantly, as if her own musings and her own reflections are thetruth. Exasperated, he reached her house and, without killing the engine, he leaned over, threw open the gate, towed the scooter inside, parked in shade, and by the time he returned to the gate and shut it, she appeared in the doorway and permitted a smile to her face. In the drawing room, he adorned her plait with the royal jasmine, gently cupped her face, and kissed her lips. He then went to her bedroom, changed, washed his face, hands, and feet, wore the dhoti, and, by the time he turned up at the dining table, she had appointed both their plates. Taking his seat, he fed on a spoonful of spiced raw sprouts in curd and enquired as if in gambit, 'Did Vijai retire and sleep well later?'

She did not speak. Steely silence had concretized on her face. After a minute, she said in a sheer matter-of-fact tone, 'Shall I serve the plain curry or vegetal curry first?'

'Either,' he said.

She lifted her face, looked at him in reproach, and said, 'Enough of smart talk. Tell me precisely.'

'What smart talk? The order of menu that is customary to you is fine with me as well.' Though he said this calmly, there was pain in his voice.

'To say that you accept whatever I decide and that you wouldn't own up any responsibility on your own. Right?'

Getting wind of her inner note, he reflected that any utterance whatsoever would put them at loggerheads. He just said, 'First let me have rice with the vegetal curry. Then a cup of plain curry to sip. If I have rice with both, it will be excessive. Got to return to my desk by 3 pm.'

'True sir, you are a workaholic. Not a lethargic one like me,' she served the vegetal curry. He chose to remain silent. She too. Face was as concretized as before. When they were polishing off their curry-rice, she said, 'You ask if Vijai slept well. If he didn't, can you put him back on track?' He did not answer. Didn't even lift his head. Just kept masticating the morsel in his mouth. 'Why, is it difficult to gulp it down?' she asked. Though he got wind of the double entendre, he remained silent. 'Why did you enquire about Vijai, sir?' she queried again.

'Just like that. To know the fact. If I shouldn't have, I'll have your pardon. I am sorry.'

The words *pardon* and *sorry* instigated her. She said, 'Look sir, you cause provocation. If I react, you will hold it out against me lifelong that I struck you with soiled palm. If you shed this legerdemain, I may get some solace.'

He pleaded sorry.

'You repeat those very words. Instigative words,' she said.

'In the language we are conversant with, what other term is there to convey that I am at fault? In what way should it be expressed? You have wallowed in linguistics and literature. Teach me.' Though he said this in a calm tone, he was aware that there was an edge to his words at the very base where they issued forth.

'The legerdemains know no expressions other than words,' she said.

She was to his right. At once he pushed back his chair, bent over, and as his right palm was soiled, he touched her feet with his left hand. Though she instantaneously withdrew her feet, his hand rested firmly on them both. Irate, she shoved his elbow with her left hand. The force of the shove caused the elbow to smash against the table with a thud. The pain contorted his face. She accused him, 'You seem to have come here today with a resolve to pick up a brawl.'

'If I pleaded sorry or pardon, you opined that verbiage was the resort to legerdemains. The only other way to express regret, without words, which appealed to me, was to beg at your feet,' he explained helplessly.

She did not utter anything, just sought to put some more rice in his plate. 'Enough,' he intercepted her with his hands. 'Why enough?' she asked in an objectionable tone. The ladle in her left hand that held a dollop of rice appeared as if she were brandishing a pedagogic baton at an errant pupil.

'I told you. I got to return to my desk. Ramamurthy has to go to Bangalore tomorrow,' he said in an obedient tone.

'I too told you. You are one workaholic. Not a lethargic one like me,' she said, piling one accusation on another. Unable to think of an answer, he remained mute. Still balancing the dollop of rice on the ladle, she awaited his response. He sat silent. Putting back the rice into the container, she said, 'I have understood your intention. If you don't eat, I won't too. It would only mean that if a pregnant woman doesn't eat well, the lack of nutrition would cause the foetus to die in situ. You would then be happily relieved.'

His resolve to remain composed cracked to the core. He said fiercely, 'Endowed with verbal skills that you are, how much lies you fancy!'

'The saying goes – *self a felon, trusts none*. Falsehood is within you. You just devolve it on to me.'

'What lie is it that is within me?' he asked anon.

'Don't you wish that this foetus be born still? Are you not praying to God that it be uprooted? Speak the truth.'

'I haven't utmost faith in the existence of God. You know too that I have no faith in the cause-and-effect nexus of such submissions to God, and God sanctioning them.'

'If you held such faith, you would surely have made such a submission. Even in the absence of that faith, you still have appealed now,' she reiterated.

'Look, I am not inclined to answer that. But if I choose to remain silent, you will readily construe it as my assent. Hence this reply for the record: your words are unfounded.'

'Not just the abortion, in your mind you have also secretly submitted to your native deity Maramma that she recall me too along with the still foetus. That would be good riddance! Ask your conscience. You'll know the truth.' He pressed his palms to his ears, as if it were blasphemous to hear it.

She turned towards him and eyed him fiercely. For quite some time, her eyelids didn't flap. Face steeled. In between, lips quivered as if they embarked on some tirade. His palms remained pressed to his ears. 'Hands off,' she ordered. He continued to stay still. 'Hands off,' she said aloud. His hands, face, neck, nothing moved at all. 'I repeat. Your hands off,' she raised her voice as if in final warning.

He was motionless. She waited half a minute. Then she snatched his arms and flung them to each side. Muddled, even as he contemplated whether to submit or resist, and if he should resist, in what way, she struck his left cheek hard with her soiled right palm. Heeding an inkling of his inner mind, he continued to sit calmly, expressing no defiance in his face, eyes, tongue, hands, or else how.

Fierce-eyed, she anticipated his reaction for ten seconds and then said, 'I can understand it if you mime the ethical ways of Jesus Christ.' He replied not. 'Bray the answer. You displaying the dramatics of lending another cheek if struck on one?' she scoffed at him.

He felt enlightened; the genesis and intensification of a hitherto unknown feeling too. Awaiting his reply, she kept fanning the fire in her eyes. He addressed her coolly, 'I don't merit the distinction of Christ's message. What he said was, if an enemy struck your left cheek, turn over the right one to him. You are not my enemy. Between us there is no hatred. There is only love. Therefore, there would be no greatness in my act even if I proffered the other cheek.'

For another couple of seconds, she kept staring at him and then said, 'An expert at twisting words.' Then she slapped him on the right cheek with the same soiled palm. He remained still. Her anger swelled. Raising her hand, she slapped his left cheek, right cheek, this again, that next, back and forth again, delivering seven to eight blows on each. He did not budge. Did not react. Her anger went haywire. She pulled herself up, lifted the curry container, and poured it over his head. She did the same with the curd. She emptied the rice over him. He sat still. She then turned away and, with thumping paces, went to her children's room. Though he impelled himself to sit his place without any movement whatsoever, and thereby hold even his mind in a still state, the curry that was poured on his head trickled into his eyes and they burned. He got up and went to the bathroom. Removing his watch, he came under the tap, washed his head, face, and eyes in the cold water. The tingling in the eyes persisted. His hair already drenched in cold water got tacky from the oil in the curry, the ghee used for seasoning, and the oleaginous curd. Through the corner of an eye, he rummaged for the soap-nut powder, shut the door, and bathed, applying the soap-nut thoroughly first on his head and then on his face, torso, and limbs. He could open his eyes a bit now. The vest and dhoti that he had removed were stained from the spillage of curry and curd. He rinsed them twice in a concentrated solution of detergent. The launderer would fully remove the stains. It's okay for now. He squeezed dry the dhoti, placed it in the bucket, dried himself with a towel, wrapped himself in the same towel, and came out with the vest and the brief in hand. She was nowhere to be heard. She wasn't in her bedroom where he had kept his clothes. Entering, he put on his clothes without any inner garments, combed his half-damp hair, left, and glanced at his watch. 2 pm. If he chose to, he could stay another three-fourth of an hour. But his mind would not acquiesce. The door to the children's room was ajar. He peeped. She was reclined on Vikas' bed, facing the window. He could just see her back. In a calm tone, he said, 'Amu, it is about time for me to leave. Secure the door.' Departing, he started the scooter and left speedily.

When he was about two furlongs away from her house, his mental stability slackened and his eyes got moist. When his sight blurred and he felt it impossible to drive, he pulled to the kerb and came to a halt under a tree. Presently, not only tears trickled, sobs and tears gushed forth. He felt that the entire environ, road, trees, the Chamundi Hill yonder, and the sky above were all immersed in a sea of grief. The sound of cry escaped his throat. For two full minutes, he cried unhindered, shedding any inhibition that though a forlorn locale, a passing automobile or a stray stroller might witness and enquire. He then took out a hanky from his trouser pocket and wiped his eyes. His eyes cleared and the road appeared distinctly. Starting his scooter again, as he drove on, he felt like resting on the bank of Karanji Lake. He swerved right. He chose a bench in the shade. Parking his scooter nearby, as he sat on the bench, his mind became docile and awarded no latitude for thought, motion, or anything whatsoever. Without ripples even as much as half an inch high, the lake before him was planar. Sopping up all sorts of turbulence, the vegetation and the sunshine appeared to be in static equilibrium. After a while, he glanced at his watch. It was 2:45.

Presently, he became aware that both his cheeks stung. Getting up, he looked in the rear-view mirror of his scooter. Red wales had appeared on both his cheeks. It would not be proper to go to his office in such a state. He also considered if he should think of a pretext to resign tonight's dinner – which, he was told, would be in some restaurant – for the swelling would not abate even by then. How about applying ample cream and topping it with a coat of cosmetic dusting! What will Ramamurthy make of it if I apply make-up exceptionally? It is just between the two of us. Why not call now and excuse myself, conveying that I need to urgently go to Mandya or someplace else, and that I might be detained late into the night? But howsoever earnest and satisfying professional dealings be, it is during dinners and socializing that friendship advances. Recalling that they had not discussed anything but professional matters, he set aside the thought of backing out. But after a minute, he reflected that being a specialist doctor, would he not see through the coats of dusting and cream? Mulling over that impediment, he remained before the mirror for two more minutes.

Later, deciding to somehow resolve this and stick to the appointment, he started on his scooter, went to the store opposite the zoo, and called his office. 'Neelakanthappa, I am down with flu and headache. I am not coming now. Will be there at 7:30. Dr Ramamurthy may arrive ahead of me. Retain him for a while.' Then he recalled that Ramamurthy was appointed for 8 pm. Accustomed to American lifestyle all these years, it was nigh impossible that he be late; would not also arrive ahead of appointed time. I have been noticing these twenty-four days.

He went home straight from there. He applied some old cream that was available and lied down on the bed, face up. He was conscious that if he rolled sideways, the cheek would come in contact with the pillow and hurt more. He closed his eyes. At once, his wife surfaced in memory. Seeing no point in recalling the dead and rehearsing the bereavement, with effort he would divert his mind to other things whenever her memories came. Six years have elapsed since she passed away. Such disturbing memories never came. But now, her face appeared clearly before his mind's eye. She would lose temper only very rarely. If on occasions she did slip, the anger would not be ferocious, never fiendish. It wasn't in her nature. Not a very brainy one, but always very composed and patient. He recalled that he had kept their framed photograph in the almirah, face down above the row of books, so that her memories would not bother. Getting up, he retrieved it and kept looking at her face intently. He reflected that it would have been impossible for her to raise her hand and slap anyone whosoever.

He recalled that one day, while in Bombay, witnessing a brawl between two coolies on the street below from their flat, she had drawn his attention to it and started crying. After looking at her face for five minutes, he replaced the photo in its place, returned, set the fan to the first speed, changed, and returned to his bed. As he closed his eyes, he began contemplating if such unspeakable conduct was in her very nature or … or …

He became aware of another thing. Though I have remained calm and exhibited patience, it is true that I am pained mentally. If I deny this, it will be false. But after slapping me like a demon, having poured the curry and curd over me, is she not pained? At that moment, he peered at his wristwatch. 4 pm. What would her state of mind be? Only uncivilized brutes will not feel soreness on beating others. True, Amu is not a composed one, but she is subtle, her perceptiveness is subtle. Besides, she is intelligent and very analytical. He felt that she would presently be suffering in greater pain than he was. He reflected that if he had a telephone at home, it would have augured well. He recalled the justification for refraining from having one. Not only would his clients keep it ringing and trouble him with scant regard for time, double expenses had to be avoided until he was well established in his profession.

Shall I go out and call her from some store? The thought stayed on for two minutes. Yes, he resolved and got up. But if I call her in next to no time, her mood still down, she might get all the more infuriated. My very call might throw her into a rage. Deciding against it, he retired again. She errs and then repents. The real indicator of repentance is not to err again. But she commits the misdeed again to a terribly greater degree. Can't she realize this? The more I hold myself back, the more her misdeeds advance. How about I retaliating in the same tenor? His mind was pegged at that possibility. When she goes wild senselessly, I respond calmly and expound sagacious words. She gets annoyed. On the contrary, what if I too permitted myself to go livid? He kept thinking. To get livid means to scoff, scare, prick, and holler with bloated ego. He reflected that he can at best enact fury, cannot really get furious. And to enact fury would mean to still stay within the limits of reason. It will not be scorching enough to singe her. Ultimately, when no other way of reaction occurred to him, he reflected that such a situation may not arise again. If I stopped visiting her! Well, that's it. He resolved that henceforth, he shall not visit her. But pat came the thought that until the issue of her pregnancy was resolved in some way, his staying back would tantamount to shirking responsibility. So what can be done? The question came up for the umpteenth time.

He continued to lie down. A little later, he snoozed. Only for fifteen minutes. Though awake, he continued to lie down, face up. He got up at 6:45, rinsed his cheeks in plain cold water, and washed his forehead, eyes, and nose with soap. He applied coconut oil to his hair, which he had cleaned with soap-nut powder in her house, and combed. He applied cream to his face, topped it up with talcum powder, and looked in the mirror. The transformation in the cheek still appealed. He got another idea. He wore his muffler around his neck, thereby obscuring the cheeks. Affected by flu that he was, he could maintain that even the smallest amount of moisture in the atmosphere would cause sinusitis. Fine! From the clothes that were delivered by the launderer, he selected a good shirt and trousers, wore them, left behind the scooter, hired an auto, and arrived in office at 7:45. Dr Ramamurthy did not suspect the explanation that he offered even before queried. He understood that, thanks to his Western experience, he had shaken free of the typical Indian temperament of unwarranted expounding on some trivial aspect of a conversation. With the muffler still around his neck, he climbed down the stairs and, boarding the car, seated himself next to Ramamurthy, who proposed, 'I have reserved a table at the restaurant atop the hill. Shall we go?' That was Ramamurthy's prerogative. 'Fine,' he said. When the car went past Amrita's house, he flinched. It coursed variously even as they scaled the hill. Apart from this, their conversation was cheerful. His profession, American lifestyle, the couple's feeling of loneliness despite their very comfortable economic status, the social conditioning of their two children thereat … Ramamurthy spoke affably at length on various matters. Ramamurthy was not habituated to drinks before food. To Somashekhar, who was no connoisseur in alcoholic matters, drinks were nothing more than unobjectionable. Nevertheless, for two hours they sipped their choice beverages as they chatted on the lawns of the restaurant, seated on rattan chairs. Then they went in and had dinner. Swayed by their new-found friendship, they dined quite sumptuously. Post dinner, their chat resumed. When they eventually looked at the time, it was 11:30.

They continued their conversation as they drove down the hill. After about two miles' drive, when they swerved left on the eastern side, he first noticed a car parked at a distant gradient. Though he could just see the top of the car, he readily understood that it was hers. She is here, and with the revolver. His heart began pounding. Presently, the car came in full view. In the floodlights of their car, though the faded colour of that other car did not readily appeal, he was all the more certain that it was hers. At once, the headlights of that car came on and flummoxed Ramamurthy seated behind the steering. To avoid the bombarding of the two deluges of illumination, he put off the headlight of his car and proceeded slowly, groping his way in the light of the parked vehicle. Past that car, he put on the headlights of his and, stepping on the gas, said, 'The inconvenience that is caused to others is totally lost on us Indians.' Somashekhar understood that she had done so in order to escape the attention of the oncoming motorist. He thought of excusing himself, alighting, and talking to her. In suicidal mind, she may pull the trigger any moment! He was terrified. If requested to stop, he will not just pull up. He will reverse and drive up to that car. He would be introduced to her. Enter Jalaja! His wisdom checked him. When they passed by her house, he noticed that the gate was shut.

Pulling up by Somashekhar's house, the doctor said, 'It is quite late into the night. I will have your pardon. But I enjoyed your company. I cherish it and look forward to more of it.' Having dropped him, the doctor headed to Jalaja's. Immediately after the good doctor left, he dashed into his house, picked up the keys to his scooter and his portion of the garage, wore the helmet, departed, retrieved the scooter, and sped in the direction of the hill. Hitting Hunsur Road, Devaraj Urs Road, Hardinge Circle, the zoo road, and at the curve thereat, he saw the glaring floodlights of an oncoming vehicle, and as he slowed down to let it pass, that vehicle came to a sudden halt. When the scream '*Somu*' reached his ears, he was overjoyed to note that it was she who had set out in search of him. Reversing, she neared him in a moment and said, 'Now head straight to the Jayalakshmipuram house. I will too.' He drove his scooter a little further and reversed. She waited for him to get past and then followed slowly. He parked his scooter in the garage, and she pulled up the car by the kerb and locked it. After climbing the stairs, entering the house, and sealing the door, she said breathlessly, 'Know what? I saw the lights of a descending car. To obscure the fact of a lone woman lounging about at that hour, I put on the floodlights of mine. How would I know whose car it was! Taken aback, you put off the lights of yours. I could see you and your American client. Somu,' she neared him and held him by the shoulders, 'the moment I saw you, I felt that I should not die, should live. Eager to see you, I drove further till I could find enough space to reverse and headed straight to your house. I made a beeline in order to catch you before you left your house. Somu, Somu,' while she hugged his shoulders firmly, a smile bloomed in her face and her eyes welled up.

As he looked at her face out of the corner of his eyes, his sight fell on the arms that held his shoulders. Absent were bangles and watch. All over the forearm were wounds that bared flesh and slopped blood. And encircling ridges of wales! 'What is this?' he asked, drawing her attention to it with his sight.

'What?'

'The injuries on both your forearms!'

'These?' smiling, she replied as if it were some mundane matter. 'Injury caused by your mistakes.'

'What do you mean?'

'I am ashamed of telling you. But I can't shake it off either. Had you avenged my misdeeds of this afternoon by delivering four blows on me or by kicking me till my waist gave away, I would be relieved. But you never did it, never would. Who should punish the hands that whacked you? I did it myself, one hour after you left, at 4, to be precise.'

He recalled that at that very hour, he had been contemplating about her mental state. 'What did you batter yourself with?'

'With the dog chain. I vividly remember. I had delivered seven blows to each of your cheeks. My retention faculties will not fade even when my brain is possessed by the devil. It will in fact be sharper. Therefore, I allotted fourteen beltings to each arm.' There was childlike triumph in her face.

He glanced at his watch. It was 12:45. He instantly enquired, 'Iron chain? That too the one used to put dogs on leash? There has been bleeding and the gashes – thirty to forty of them – have bared flesh. Have you got yourself anti-tetanus injection? Buck up. I know a physician. I will wake him up and get you treated.'

'Shh, your Amu won't die. She hasn't the gumption to die. Nor has the tetanus the strength to bring about her demise. I am here to talk, not to see a doctor,' she resisted.

'There is a doctor nearby known to me. Come on, start the car. Let's resume our dialogue later.' Pressing a palm against her back, he urged her to move out and secured the door. The doctor stayed and practised in Ontikoppal. He knew him well. Without demur, the doctor purchased his explanation that the injury was caused by improper handling of a coil of barbed wire meant for fencing, and administered the anti-tetanus injection. Another injection for fast healing, and some pill and ointment were also given. Pre-empting the doctor's demand for fee, he tendered fifty rupees, pleaded sorry for disturbing his sleep at that odd hour, and led her out.

While driving the car, she said, 'Not content with the pain caused to me by the injury, you took me to the doctor to add to it the pain of the prick.' On returning to his house and having seated themselves on his bed, she noticed the muffler that still masked most of his head and all of his neck and said, 'When I saw you both in the car, I noticed this muffler. Instantly I understood why you had worn it. I felt ashamed that compared to my barbarity, the bullet of the revolver was grossly impotent.' She took off the muffler. Though the marks were diminishing, they were still visible. Observing it, she said, 'You said that the dog leash posed the hazard of tetanus. But these fingers that struck you,' she proffered the four fingers of her right hand, 'are stuffed with neurotoxic venom. If these four are severed … ' She raised her arm and struck her fingers hard on the edge of the bed.

'Shh, now don't act stupid.' Angry, he slapped her on the cheek and held her hands that had just hurt themselves.

For a minute, she kept staring at his face and then said snappishly, 'You are now angry. But your hands lack the strength to slap. Though it pounces with all might, by the time the slap is delivered, it will have morphed into a pseudo blow, akin to the beating a suckling receives from its mother's hands. It will not even hand a warm pat. It will just be a tender touch.' She then hid her face in his chest.

He kept caressing her back. In a short while, she was stroking his back. She soon switched to his chest. She clumsily yanked out the shirt buttons that posed a hindrance to her feel and started caressing. He got wind of the suggestion. Presently, he was not game for it. Given the amount of turmoil within, and with no issue getting straight, he felt that that indulgence was nigh impossible. Checking her hand, he said, 'Not now. I am not inclined.'

Burying her face in his bare chest, she said, 'If you have really pardoned me, it will be possible for you. If you think of me as a demon, assumption gets arduous. If you think of me not as a demon but as *my dear Amu*, enthusiasm will font on its own.' He felt that her talk was always so – cornering, trapping, and tethering. But soon, enthusiasm overcame and caused a surge of assumption and submission, getting mellowed and imparting mellowness, and to meld in unison by sinking all disparity. They were both engulfed in passion devoid of memories of pain, not visited even by a fleeting nuance of distress and dejection, and were even oblivious of the pain in the cheek and forearm.

When she left, it was 4:30. Before leaving, she said, 'Come this afternoon. There is much to talk about. Just talk. Nothing else.' She displayed a false anger and started climbing down the stairs.

~

On returning after dropping the children at their school, she called the college, conveyed that she would be on leave for a day, asked Puttamma and Mahadevamma not to disturb her, retired to her room, and slept till half past noon. She had asked to pull the interlock of the main door shut as they left. Waking up, she unlocked it, attended to her toiletries, and by the time she was finished with the cookery, he arrived. The moment they started on their lunch, she said, 'Know what happened last night? Vijai was roused at midnight. Just like the day before. He has checked my bedroom. I am absent. Kitchen, lounge, guest room, another room, library, he has checked every place. The main door is secured from outside. Frightened, he just lay awake, restive. When I returned, it was 4:45. The moment he heard the sound of the car, he came running and stood by the window. He asked where I had been for so long. *Why cry, aren't you a man?* I admonished him and then explained. The injury to the arm ached more. I feared that if I didn't get immediate medical treatment, I would die from tetanus. Went in search of a doctor, found one, woke him up, went with him to his clinic, and got myself treated with injections. Hence I was long. I showed him the pill and ointment that were dispensed. I led him to his bedroom and put him to sleep.'

'Had he seen the wounds on the arm yesterday evening?'

'*Why, Mom?* he had asked. I had told him that the fencing wire at the backyard had given away at some places. I went about setting it right, and when I yanked it, it scraped against my arms. He fully believed it. He is getting accustomed to go in search of his mother at midnight. Should check him from that.'

After lunch, they went to her bedroom and converged in bed together. When he slept sideways, he had to exercise care so that his cheek did not come into contact with the pillow. She could only sleep supine. If the elbow came in contact with the bed or linen at any angle whatsoever, it would pain like hell. She did not accede to get it dressed by the doctor. She just applied the ointment. 'Look,' she began, 'till yesterday I was calling you Somu. When I would so address you, it is an expression of love, friendship, and feelings of intimacy. But know what I feel since this morning? I should call you *kiddie*. Only then would my heart find fuller expression. You are my kiddie, my baby kiddie, my giddy kiddie.' Despite the pain, she rolled on her side, caressed his face with her palm, sat up, drew aside the pallu from her chest, pulled him by holding his head so that his face pressed against her breast, swathed him in the pallu as would a mother her suckling, and, rocking her thighs, began singing a lullaby tunefully:

Laalee, laalee, laalee-laali
Sleep won't you darling bambino?
Colourful feather of the pea-co'
Whence found ye path unto this home
Like Eden descending on globe ...

He went through an experience which he could just not have imagined, wherein his heart surged and his childhood roots seemed irrigated. He closed his eyes. Crooning the song fully and polishing it off with '*laalee laalee laalee*' in decrescendo, she continued to rock her thigh and said, as if to herself, 'Yesterday, while you submitted yourself to the blows I delivered, your face was like that of a child's, incapable of fancying existence without maternal dependence. Did you protest? Did you question my authority to assault you? Did you ward me off with your hands? Your face was like that of a child who returns to embrace the inflicting mother. *Thou art my mother though thou beateth, thou art my mother though thou striketh*. Even when, like a demon, I poured the curry, curd, and rice on your head ... kiddie, yesterday I inflicted demonic cruelty on you. True, yesterday you went through hell, true, but as a result I was rewarded with this kiddie.' She lowered her head and planted three kisses on his head, covered with her pallu as it was. 'Else it would have remained Somu. Somu means remoteness, as distant as the moon, attractive to look at but elusive to the reach, deluding us to just tag along like a play in dreams. But this kiddie is not so. It can be laid on the thighs and be thus held as not to allow it to move this way or that. Even if freed of the hold, it will not move away. Will stay glued to the pallu. Right? Tell me. Tell me the truth.' Fully doused in the drift of her words, he just groaned assent.

Her eyes closed as if in trance. She sat cherishing a definite feeling of the incarnation of a new import to their relationship. One palm was on his back. Another held his head. A gush of enthusiasm permeated her mind so as to forever ward off and leave no room for feelings of void. She sat so for some time. He too lay motionless. Then she asked, 'At what hour should you be leaving?'

'He has left for Bangalore. Will return on Monday. Then we need to discuss for about an hour. That's it. That same night, he will return and fly back via Bombay on Tuesday morning.'

'Look, don't let your work be affected. If your career is affected, I will be terribly pained. Did you sleep well in the morning? And how long?'

'I fell asleep when you left. I was unconscious till 10.'

'Hey!' she teasingly slapped his back. He could get wind of her tone.

'Look dude, I have to share much with you. Who else shall I confide in? Who else can it be? I have given enough thought to the issue at hand. Did I think of it myself, or did it bring about the deliberation? That pervading my mind, what other thoughts can prevail? Abortion would mean expelling the life that grows in me. It is rather easy to die. All the same, it is not possible to retain this either, as it would mean leaving a disparaging tool in the hands of Ranganath's sister. Ranganath, however, is innocuous. He may at best seek divorce on grounds of infidelity. I will happily consent. But my greatest concern is how these two kids will take it. Not very young ones these. One is eight and a half, and the other five. They can grasp well. Deep inside, the younger one loves his dad. This being the situation, what if they alienate this child! That would add another thorn to my mind, as if those already there weren't enough. I have decided to get this aborted.'

'When did you decide?' he asked, getting up and placing his hands on her shoulders.

'Yesterday, when I regained my composure after flogging myself with the chain.'

'When everything was under control, why did you need to go to the hilltop?'

'You cannot understand the vagaries of my mind. I could not commit suicide as long as there was a foetus within me, for that would mean killing it. But when I decided to do away with it, I felt that if it would nevertheless be wiped out, there's nothing wrong if I got myself killed. But this was not why I was seized by feelings of void yesterday. I felt that I could not put up with the sin of inflicting such cruelty on you yesterday afternoon. It is very easy to just take hold of the revolver and let off. But is it very easy for the mind to fully gear up to that act? Herein is the genesis of agony, writhing, and helplessness. Absent yesterday were any such agony and writhing. The sin of having inflicted torture on you was motivation enough. In all these years, my mind had not culminated so congenially to just submit to the impulse of jerking the trigger. I had just arrived there and parked, when, somewhere from within the tranquillity of the hill, the sound of an automobile was heard. Could not gather if it was scaling up or down. It had necessarily to go past me. I had put myself on hold till it did. In a short while, your car appeared from above. To escape being noticed, I turned on the headlights of my car. The dazzle caused that driver to slow down and cut off his car's headlights. Your mufflered face came in view. If you had sped away without slowing or turning off the headlights, I would have failed to notice. Thanks to all these coincidences, I sighted your face, and at that very moment, my desire to die was uprooted. Know what I felt instantly? If I depart, not from ill health or mishap but by committing suicide, what would be its effect on you? Not fear of the police. I had left a note in my purse. I will unfailingly do it. I had mailed one to you too, just in case. I reflected that if I commit suicide, could he stay in peace? Who will care for him? Barring me, who else will look after him? Immediately, I gunned my car and drove further till I found enough space to reverse.' She fell silent. Then she said as if she switched moods, 'Let it be known that I have no liberty to commit suicide till I find a good bride for you. This is the boon that you have conferred on me.' She extended her hand and painfully wrung his nose.

Recalling something else, she said in a solemn tone, 'This pregnancy is not your fault. A mother of two and in my prime, I am not an innocent one. Neither are you a simpleton. We, in fact, exercised caution. Nonetheless, our moods would reach intense levels that were beyond the threshold of such caution. Will the profundity and gamut of life appeal to those who observe the bounds of caution? Yet, know how irate was I at you? I thought you were responsible for the present state of affairs, that the transgression was yours. But fact and perception are mutually exclusive. Many a time, there will be no harmony between these. If there is harmony between them, our feelings will rather stray than be in tandem with such harmony. We will let ourselves fall in love with the undeserving. And perchance we get to meet a worthy one, love doesn't blossom and we ignore such a person. Alas, this is default human disposition. Accordingly, though my intellect would decree "poor guy, it is none of his fault," my anger on you would not relent. Not just that. In my mind, I was convinced that it was henceforth impossible that we come together again. Ever since you got to know that I am thus, you haven't once looked at me desirably. How could you? I was all through conducting myself devilishly. Yesterday when you took me to the doctor and got me treated for tetanus, I immediately felt that I would surely get this aborted. But the persistence of anger in me or the furtherance of guilt in you should not receive impetus. Rescinding them both now and here, we should revert to being Somu and Amu as before. Though your cheeks and my arms continued to ache, I decided that we should win and not let our ill feelings triumph over us. This lad seems to be in a pleasant anticipation.' Teasing him in an intoned voice, she lifted her hand and handed him a pseudo smack on the right cheek. Instantly, his injury came to her mind and pain surfaced in her face. 'Sorry, sorry, kiddie. For a moment, I forgot that your cheek is still swollen,' she leaned over, planted a soft kiss on his cheek where she had just smacked, and said, 'Did the pain vanish? Say yes. Else, I will hit again.' For a moment, she pondered on something and then said, 'I think Hidimba used to smack Bheema, as much in anger as in love. Would also bite, claw, and variously persecute. Despite being Bheema, unable to put up with her, he deserted her and fled within a year. The loving ways of a demonette are saddled with pain and suffering alright, but the vigour, gravity, and depth therein are lacking in the loving ways of an ordinary equanimous woman. I harbour the thought that Bheema could never forget Hidimba, and I have even thought of putting it in prose or verse. These are my musings. You being adept at comparative analytics should lay bare the facts.' She winked in mischief and continued, 'But I have just hit you. Not once have I bitten, clawed, or tore your ear or nose, haven't broken a finger. Shouldn't my love get more profound? More potent? Tell me ... ' While she said this, her face propped up to see his. She noticed that he was lost in thought. 'Hey, where is your mind wandering, you Bombayite? Are you thinking that you don't need this demonic love, and that you are rather content with the Draupadi type shared with four others?'

Her last few comments did not register in him at all. Extending his right hand, he held her right hand and said, 'Amu, let me tell you something. I am saying this solemnly. Without retorting, lend an ear and think about it.' At once, the gravity of his words struck her. Matching the firmness of the grip of her hand to that of his, she asked him to go on.

Rooting his sight in hers, he said, 'Just forget Ranganath and his sister. It is but natural that some disturbance will be caused in the minds of Vijai and Vikas. We shall both patiently rectify and set it right. They both are my children. I will not discriminate. Let this child be. This is my resolve. You just stick to it.'

She turned grave and tightened her grip a little more. Silent, she gazed at his face. She then came closer and pressed her face against his chest. In a short while, her eyes got moist, but she didn't cry. She lifted her face, looked at him, and said, 'Kiddie, I can understand your feelings. But I can better perceive the children's mind than you. I have given it enough thought. Only one thing needs to be done now. This Mysore is a small town. Seeing any doctor whosoever would only mean to run the risk of being traced to the end. You consult some surgeon in Bangalore and get an appointment. For a couple of days, I will make arrangements for the children's stay and will apply for leave. Let's go together and terminate it. There's another thing I want to say, provided you don't scoff at me for being sentimental.'

'Tell me.'

'Let one more week pass. It will anyway depart. I desire to hold it as long as possible. By then, you should get me a new silk sari. Draped in it, I should tread the sands of Talakadu, the river bank at Srirangapatna, Tirumakudalu Sangama, and so on in your company. And take about twenty to thirty snaps of me. My pictures with your child in me, wearing the sari given by you, should be in my archives through my entire life, even when I am a ripe old woman.'

He got angry, 'Instead of the photograph, let us retain the child.'

'Just listen to me, man. You cannot comprehend better than me,' there was a ring of agitation in her voice.

~

On a certain day, they went through the medical procedure at Bangalore, and the next day they were seated in a first-class compartment of an afternoon train headed to Mysore. She had scorned his suggestion that on discharge from the nursing home, they stay in a hotel for two days so that they could consult the doctor in case she developed complications.

From their talk and their suitcases and holdall, it was clear that the co-passengers who sat opposite them were tourists from north India. There was therefore no restriction for Amrita and Somashekhar to converse in their native Kannada. Yet, she didn't speak even one sentence. The children were quartered with Susheelamma on the pretext that she would be leaving on examination duty and be away for three days. The maid Mahadevamma and her husband had taken the responsibility of guarding the house day and night. The train moved slowly.

He said, 'You rather not continue to sit. Lie down. I will move to the edge of the seat.'

'I don't need anybody's sympathy,' she replied scathingly.

What if the co-passengers understood Kannada ! He got anxious that even if they did not understand the language, the expression on her face would send them feelers that this was a warring couple. As the train moved on, she kept looking out of the window. At a loss, he just peered into a periodical that he had purchased at the station. He just glanced through the first page of an article for five minutes.

Turning towards him, she asked brusquely, 'Shall I look for a vacant seat in another compartment and shift there ?' He stopped reading, closed the book, placed it beside him, and sat still. She resumed looking out of the window. The train stopped at Bidadi. The other man made his wife's bed by spreading a sheet over the lower berth and placing a pillow. He then placed a pillow on the upper berth and climbed up. By the time the train resumed, they were asleep.

'You too sleep,' he said again.

'Why should you cringe if I continue to sit ?' though she said softly, it held temperature enough to melt iron.

'Nah. I said so considering your condition,' he spoke softly like a chastised pupil.

She did not respond. She continued to gaze out of the window. After four minutes, she turned towards him and said, 'My condition, my condition ! Watching it, you feel like jeering. I can verily notice reproach in you. And that is why you keep remarking so. Right ?'

He knew very well that when she was this cross, retorting, explaining, or corroborating were not only useless, it would also enrage her more and more. It was also apparent that if he remained silent, it would be tantamount to accepting her accusation. He felt helpless. At such times, no thought would take shape in his mind other than hanging his head and remaining silent. He sat watching the floor. She noticed that, but turned back to the window telling herself that she didn't give a damn. Craning his neck and looking in her direction seemed arduous, so he continued to gaze at the floor.

When, ten minutes later, she turned to look at him, he was still in the same position. She shot up. Crossing over his feet, she opened the door to the cabin, exited, and shut it. He heard her strides. Presuming that she has gone to the toilet, he continued to be silently seated. Two minutes passed thus. Then something flashed in his mind. Fed up of my company, she would have gone searching for a seat in another cabin. No cabins reserved for women. If she sought to occupy a vacant seat in a cabin whose occupants are alien men, what belittling, rather vain portend? He felt that it was his duty to at least go and look where she was. He got up silently, left, and then what he sees! She had the door of the speeding car fully open and stood at the verge. Owing to the blustering wind, her hair, pallu, and the pleats of her sari fluttered wildly. Even though she held on to the supporting bar, if the car swerved at a sharp curve, she would slip and surely be dead and minced in a moment. His heart skipped a beat.

Walking up to her briskly, he said, 'Why stand here? Perchance your grip slips!' She did not answer. He repeated, this time loudly, thinking that his words would not have carried to her against the sound of the train and the gushing wind.

Without turning, she said, 'I came here to be all by myself. Why did you come here?'

'If you want to be by yourself, go to the cabin. I will stay here. Or if you want to stand here, close the door. I will return to the cabin.'

'I have the liberty to stand in any manner I choose. Nobody has the right to object. If you are any decent, get away.' He did not say anything, but continued to stand close. 'If you are any decent, you should move away from here,' she repeated.

'I will not leave unless you safely retreat from the doorway and shut the door.' He was adamant. She snappishly turned towards him and eyed him fiercely. He kept mum. Moving a bit, she slammed the door shut and, with her footwear striking against the floor, went to her cabin. He continued to stay his place. She closed the door of the cabin. She wants to be unto herself. Let her. He remained standing in silence. The train came to a halt at Channapatna. Later, it moved on. When it gained speed, she opened the cabin door and went to him. He kept watching her face as she approached, encouraging himself to cordially respond to whatever proposal she had on mind. When she neared him, he noticed that she held a wad of hundred-rupee notes in her hand.

Extending her arm, she held it up to him, 'Take this.'

'What is this?' he was astonished.

'The expenses since we started the day before yesterday. There is one thousand here. If it is short, let me know, I will pay up.' He was hurt.

Experience told him that when angry, her brain worked adeptly at devising novel methods of ripping him apart. He now said calmly, 'I need not take this money from you. I have that kind of money on me. I have more.'

She retorted, 'I know that you are a thriving architect. This treatment is my personal matter. I don't take a liking to someone else footing the bill.'

'I am bearing this expense as I am a part of this. I am not *someone else*,' he said in a tone of finality.

She looked at him as if she would burn him down. Lips fluttered imperceptibly. Then she said, 'Look sir, will you just take this or shall I fling it out the window?'

'You have enough money to throw away. This is a paltry amount. If you feel like throwing it away, do it. Anyway, it is your money.'

'*Anyway, my money?*' her voice trembled. She hadn't turned her fierce sight away from his face. She asked, 'One final time, will you take it or not?'

'No.' The moment he said that, she leaned over, put her hand out the window, and cast away the notes. She could see them scatter and fly in the direction of the fierce wind. He that stood farther from the window could only see them being cast away. The scattering and flying registered in his imagination. Withdrawing her hand, she went to her cabin and shut herself in without even looking at him. The wind blowed wildly through the opening in the door.

Neither had broached the subject of who should foot the overheads of this journey and the treatment. What of discussing it, he reflected that both had thought it despicable to even think of it. There had been no hint of that notion in his mind whatsoever. Now the fact that she brought up the subject, though provoked by anger, pained him as if a kick was targeted at his stomach. Her threat to fling the money and then throwing it/away for real made him feel as if his gut was diced into a hundred shreds. Despair begets anger, causes a tirade to be unleashed alright, but – a question popped up – can it dig out something that is not within? First, the poser that if I didn't take it, she would fling it out the window, and then executing it – trampling, smashing, and crushing my ethical strength. This was not just callousness, he reflected, it was an act of devastation that outstripped plain callousness. The train was manoeuvring a curve. He opened the door, stuck his head out, and looked ahead. Ahead of five or six cars, he noticed the engine blinding along the rails. He felt that it was a sort of blind destructive power. But there was a certain attraction to it. He kept looking at it. In a short while, the rails straightened and the engine and the cars went out of sight. Closing the door, he stood as before.

Some time later, she opened the cabin door and came to him. He noticed another wad of currency notes in her right hand. Reaching up to him, she extended her hand and said curtly, 'There is two thousand here. Just tell me whether or not you will take it. If you don't, this time I will not cast away the notes. I will jump out the door myself. Tell me.' She opened the door and stood at the edge. Wind gusted with fatal force. Recalling her earlier poser and her act of actually flinging the notes, he shuddered. Outside, the black rocks flew past at a speed that muddled their form. If one jumped on them, the impact would be like bumping against a speeding train, causing the body to be mashed into a ball of flesh in half a second. While the fright constricted his eyes, she asked, 'Will you or won't you take it?'

'Haven't spent that much for sure,' he found a way of countering.

'I precisely know the expenses that have been incurred to the last *pai*. But a professional that you are, I am compensating for your two days' absence from work. Should take it. Should extend your hand. I will give you two seconds' time.'

Having just considered the impact on someone who leapt out of a moving train, he instantly extended his hand. She stuck the bundle of notes in his hand, receded from the brink of the door, closed the door with a bang, latched it, went to her cabin, and closed the door.

He felt like immediately throwing away the notes out the window. He even lifted his arm. But by then, he felt restrained from within. If I throw it, he reasoned calmly, I should do it in her witness, thereat in the cabin, not here in her absence. Those two may be asleep. Why not do it? The poser took shape. He took two steps towards the cabin. 'Look, I have received two thousand from you. You stand acquitted. It is now my money. Look ...' And then fling it. Rehearsing it in mind, as he paced a few more, he reflected why he should emulate it if her ego bloated intermittently? He returned and stood by the door.

The train slowed down. He leaned over and looked. A station called Maddur approached. He alighted and ambled on the platform.

She was seated by the window. Nearing her, he asked, 'Tender coconut is available. Shall I get you one?' She did not answer. He didn't stay by her for long. He kept pacing the platform till an opposite train passed and theirs resumed. Mandya, Pandavapura, and Srirangapatna passed by in succession. All through, he stood by the door of the car. In a short while, Chamundi Hill appeared outside the window, as if it professed to hold the gravitational balance of the whole of Mysore. By then, the other two occupants of the cabin lugged their suitcase and holdalls and arrived at the door. She is alone there. Seven or eight more minutes for the train to roll into Mysore station. He thought, let me stay put till the train stops, let me not incite her by thwarting her desire to stay alone. What if she attempts to take out the suitcase on the upper berth by the time the trains pulls up at the station! The doctor has instructed that she shall not lift anything heavy till the surgical incisions had healed. He went to the cabin and took out both their suitcases. Observing the hill that now came into sight, now obscured and now reappeared, she said as if to herself, 'It was not possible to pull the trigger as long as this was in my belly. Now, none has the strength to check me.' He looked at her. Her sight was fixed in the void beyond the hill.

~

Hiring an auto and seeing her off, he went straight to his office in another auto, taking the suitcase along. He was there till 9 in the night and returned home after finishing supper nearby. When he reclined, no sleep came. Only yawns. A feeling of defeat pervaded his mind. Nothing new in her getting vexed with him for no reason whatsoever, and he being tolerant of it. Her anger will have no cause or basis. But, at times, an afterthought reveals a cause, which would either be some limitation of mine or my failure to comprehend. At other times, he reflected, her ire just sought a vent, a target. Unfailingly, I shall be the target and – he recalled – only in my presence will the vent open up. But each time, why should I be the target of her ire? Though he had read and understood such psychological aspects as ire and love operating in tandem, love and hatred being two aspects of a single evocation just appealed to him as meaningless suppositions vis-à-vis the intensity of the pain he suffered. By humiliatingly flinging away one thousand into the blasting wind, she coerced me into extending my hand to receive a dole double that. As far as she is concerned, consigning to the wind and tossing at me were two streams that emanated from a single font of condemnation. Both trampled and crushed me. She did so in order to crush me. That realization brought to his comprehension the insuperable gap between him and her. Not just was my sharing the medical expenses unsolicited, she made it very clear that she had also to compensate for my two days' absence from station. That thought cast a doubt if there was love in this relationship at all! The unanswered question lingered and wrung his neckline for quite some time. Then there was a hint of an explanation that it could be the weakness of his mind. Very many times, intellect has decreed that he stay away. But without any pretext whatsoever, the mind readily flows towards her and into her. And it inducts poetic and temperamental corroborations for that very weakness. It was she who decided that getting rid of the foetus was the only wise decision. As long as it inhabited her womb, she was in festive mood, wearing silk and the like. When they started on their Bangalore journey, she was reticent – an obstinate reticence – bottling up all the pain within her. On being rid of it, feelings of void began shrinking her. The moment she stepped out of the nursing home, her smouldering anger was vented at me in a searing surge. What was my fault? If the bereavement was the cause of her agony, hadn't I offered to save it? He decreed that she hadn't even an iota of rationality. In a while, sleep overcame.

But he was awaken in half an hour. He glanced at his watch – it was 12. A suffocating quietness everywhere. What would she be doing now? In answer to that thought was a suggestion that she wouldn't be asleep; sleep wouldn't have overcome her. '*It was not possible to pull the trigger as long as it was in my belly. Now, none has the strength to check me,*' he recalled not only her words but also the void in her eyes that evidenced the introversion induced by them. The casting away of one grand in one stroke was in this same reproach. And recalling that if he hadn't taken the second instalment, she would surely have jumped, he felt that this was a very dangerous night. A definite suggestion that she would inflict something on herself tonight now caused despair in his mind. A resolve formed to start on his scooter immediately. He sat up and put on the light. Emerging from within the mosquito net, even as he dressed, he thought of going to his office and calling her. He felt that was better. Locking, he climbed down the stairs, opened the garage, and retrieved his scooter. As he gunned it, he felt hesitant that if he caused such noise at this unearthly hour, not only would the neighbours be disturbed, would it not send out wrong feelers to them? Helplessly letting his automobile disturb the silence of the night, he drove to Devaraj Urs Road and parked there. Introducing himself to the gurkha who was doing the rounds there, he climbed up the stairs, opened the door to his office, went in, closed the door, put on the light, and dialled. It is ringing at the other end. He waited in eager anticipation that she would answer it any moment. He imagined her posture of holding the receiver and speaking. The phone keeps ringing. Call not received. Has she left in her car for the hilltop? Or has she created eternal silence by pulling the trigger? Has she gone home alone without taking her children from Susheelamma's? His hand that held the receiver began quivering. From deep within – deeper than his mind – he cried out, 'God!' The phone keeps ringing. Or is she fast asleep from the painkiller and one of the SOS doses of tranquilizer prescribed? 'Let it be so,' he prayed. But how can I be sure? As he decided to go her place, the call was received at the other end and the ebbing chi streamed back into his body. 'Hello,' her voice, rather the anatomical remains of her voice, the life in it having burned and evaporated. 'I,' he said. He could not think of anything else to say. She too asked nothing else. Silence suffused. He collected his senses and asked, 'Were you fast asleep?' She did not reply. 'Heard me, dear? Amu, I am calling. At least say *yes*,' he said aloud. 'Hmm ... ' she murmured softly, as one drowning would.

'Couldn't get sleep. I felt like seeing you. I started to head there straight. Then deciding against it, for it may wake up the children, I went to my office and am calling from there. Hear me?' She didn't respond. Silence again.

After a minute, he said, 'My girlie, do you hear me?' Slowly, she stuttered, 'How can it stay from filling my ears when you have obstinately decided to pour it in?' He was reassured.

'Why didn't you readily lift the phone? Did sleep overcome you?' Lack of response again. 'Amu, were you asleep? Normally, the medicines prescribed for such treatments will have tranquilizers in them.'

'That is why I didn't take the medicines.'

He got angry. 'Why didn't you? What if something aggravated from lack of medication?'

'Look sir, you seem to nurse a desire to prompt me into saying what you already know, and then watch the drama unfold. Enough of this cruelty. I prostrate before you and place my forehead on your feet,' she remonstrated.

He was at a loss for words. At the other end, she too turned silent. Should say something now, but nothing flashes. Struggling for words, he eventually said, 'If you were awake, why didn't you pick up the phone? What were you doing?'

'None has the authority to ask that of me,' there was annoyance in her voice.

'Maybe none else has. I have it.'

'I am not responsible for your illusion. I know nobody has it,' she said scathingly.

'You are the one in illusion. I know the truth. You too know it. But you are lying,' leaving no room for any other ruse, he said in an admonishing voice, wielding authority.

She did not react; remained silent. But sensing that his words had reached unto her and registered firmly as not to be expunged by her, he put his anxiety aside and remained silent even though she chose not to reply. In a short while, some incomprehensible sound was heard on the phone. Focussing all his concentration and pressing the handset closer to his ear, he listened. Yet, he couldn't gather. Indistinct sound, as of undulating waves set in motion in quite some distance. Gradually, it became clear. She is crying. Not struggling sobs, but billowing cry. At first she tried to control, to hide it from me. But she now cries unreservedly. The receiver in her hand is also quivering. She cries, not bothering to withhold it or even cover the mouthpiece with her palm. From her throat emerges the sound akin to a whirlwind emerging from the crevices of a deep cave and struggling to escape. 'Amu, Amu,' he called out. She attempted monosyllabic replies. 'Do you hear me, Amu?' he called out again. When she attempted to get a syllable out, the whirl of sorrow that was stuck at the throat found vent in a wail. The loud unfettered wail went on incessant for quite some time, unvarying, and flowed so as to apprehend breath. Breath did get stuck. 'Amu, Amu, here,' when he came through again, the constricted breath eased. Soon, there was nothing more but silence. He still but held on.

A little later, she volunteered, 'Kiddie, you have now saved me. Having finally decided, I had almost stepped out, revolver in hand. Final resolve, in total finality. Such formidable resolve had never formed before. I had also written a note and kept on the bed. I was about to leave when the phone rang. Know how furious I was?

Who was this senseless one calling at this hour? I reflected it could be you. Hence, I did not take it. Even in that state, I knew that if I received the call, my resolve would collapse. So I didn't pick it up. But even when no one received it, did you give up by cutting the call? Maybe my ire measures the entire length of me, but you hold obstinacy unto your towering heights. You would not relent till I took it. You held through.'

Not only his mind eased, he felt a sense of blest. Abruptly waking up from sleep, this flashing in my mind and I leaving in two minutes! If I had driven to her house, she would have preceded me towards the hill speedily in her car. Driven by a formidable resolve, if she had pulled the trigger without much ado? Good that I called. This was the first time that the thought of calling flashed in my mind. Even as he was soused in the feelings of surprise and deliverance, she asked, 'Kiddie, I will ask you a question. No one has treated even an enemy as cruelly as I have behaved with you. Yet, why do you love me? Tell me. Tell me the truth.'

'I really do not know. Seems like I cannot live without your love,' he said, rummaging in his mind.

'Kiddie, your words will perk up my desire to live. You are not lying. You are not wont to lie for the sake of earning my appreciation. But then, there may be justification for lying if such a lie can save a life. The purpose behind your words is loaded with magnanimity. I surely appreciate it, kiddie.' The hint of encumbrance that made short work of his love pained him as if his essence were wrung. He was so disconsolate that he couldn't even protest. He turned mum. After a while, she said, 'My kiddie, you are angry now. If one's love is suspected, one would surely get angry. But if you say that you are unable to live without my love, it will be difficult for me to believe it to be true. Know why you love me? Shall I tell?'

'Tell.'

'Somehow, attraction has set in. Got intimate even bodily.

You are a man of commitment. In your nature are compassion and sympathy. With all that, and in the light of the recent medical procedure, you would perforce express sympathy for me. Isn't it? Speak the truth.'

He got angry, 'Just because you are endowed with a sharp intellect, don't bray whatever comes to your mind.'

'Kiddie,' she replied, 'the more you are irate at me, the more I am glad. At best, it evidences your authority of getting angry with me. My words cannot be proved wrong though. Whoever it be, he will naturally be incensed when he discovers that another has uncovered the lie within him.'

'In which case, will you admit that your love towards me is false too?' he affronted her.

'I will for sure. I don't love you. Nobody who is in love will attempt suicide. If one lives, at least love stays, err … a semblance of love stays. If dead, nothing does. Void. A void where there is nothing, where no word can be said of it. Why shall I, who is strongly attracted to it, lie that I love you? You too tell the truth. Not that you purposefully lie. Tell me by sifting out the truth inside you. Do you know what love is? If you know, are your feelings towards me those of love? If it is love, why do you love me? Meditate on these lines.'

By now, he was well aware that when she resorted to logic, her intellect was wont to intricately dissect the circulatory, muscular, and neurological systems and, through a magnifying lens, look for the locus of the core vitals. Hence, he didn't react immediately. After a while, he said, 'If cause cannot be dug out, it doesn't prove that love is false. Reserve your debate for another day.'

She relented. After a minute, she said, 'Look, your dhoti, shirt, and a pair of trousers are in my suitcase. A petticoat, blouse, and two saris of mine should have found way into yours. You are the one who packed them all. You are at fault. Bring those with you this afternoon.'

'I am not coming this afternoon,' he said.

'Well, you are angry. Stay at your office. I will drive up myself, be there in ten minutes, fall at your feet, seek mercy, and take back the two thousand that is in your shirt pocket.'

He got anxious that she might come over. The gurkha was witness to his visit here at this hour and to his scooter parked downstairs. He reflected that if she too arrived, parked her car thereat, and joined him upstairs, he would get ideas. 'Stay your place. I am coming myself.'

'Kiddie, no need for you to come. I am alright now. You set me right. I am ashamed for throwing away the money. But that misdeed cannot be undone. Bring that money when you come here tomorrow. Don't hand it to me. Keep it before God. I will take it after seeking pardon from God. Who else other than my kiddie has to give me pin money? Who else should I get to spend for me? Now go get some rest.'

'Now you take those medicines,' he said.

'Orders of the Lord,' her voice was saturate with obedience.

Gunning his scooter, when he returned home in the stillness of midnight, a thought struck him. If I pay up ten thousand, the department will provide instant telephone connection. Should get one for home, so that I can talk to her every night before retiring. It will help her in breaching the feelings of void, and I can stay contented. He thought of telling her that he too would have a phone by the bed, just like she did. Call at any hour you wish. Don't worry about disturbing my sleep. He patted himself for coming up with a good idea. He decided to enquire this very day and pay up the deposit amount, somehow arranging for the money. Returning home, he rolled up the garage shutter, parked the scooter inside, and while he rolled the shutter back, he felt deeply guilty that he was disturbing the sleep of the neighbours. Climbing up, when he changed and retired, sleep eluded him. He was sort of relieved as normalcy was restored without much complication. All the same, he was all the more anxious, as this relief was in tandem with a never-before intensity of void in her. What if she pulled the trigger any moment? The thought rattled his ribs. Tonight though, feelings of void are on the backburner. By now, she would have taken the medicines and be fast asleep. But tomorrow, the day after that, the night after that, who can check her each and every night thus? And though the solution of staying there every night crossed his mind, he almost immediately dismissed it as inappropriate owing to the children's presence. Perchance she did kill herself, will I live on? He asked himself. Won't commit suicide though. All the same, it was clear that there would be no meaning or charm to his life. What in this world is holding my fancy? To design a score buildings per year would, at best, cater to the basic necessities of life. It holds no delight. Reading during leisure time, food, and all else can be savoured only in her company. He felt that without her, all these held no meaning. How did I get entangled so deep in love? He rummaged his insides for an explanation. He recalled each and every phase, each and every incident that brought them closer. As delineated by her, is my love nothing more than customary moral commitment? Is it just humane compassion resulting from the thought of what would befall her if I abandoned her, abandoned her at this stage? Or is it just instinctive compassion towards her helplessness? He began analysing intricately. None of these are false. But, he felt, that a force that surpassed the aggregate of all these bound him to her. What is that force? Maybe its alternative name is 'love'. He felt that by just uttering the name, the meaning is not fully conveyed. More than the meaning, important now are the ways of saving her, and he began worrying about them. Gradually, dawn crept in. Though he knew that sleep would not come now, he shut the doors and windows, pulled down the mosquito net, put on the fan, and compelled himself to get at least some of it, for it would otherwise be impossible to attend to any work in office. He recalled that today he would have to visit the telephone department.

~

My dearie kiddie, I have lost my authority to call you so. Yet, I write. I do not know where you are now, how you are, and what anamnesis you are. How can one, who hasn't the authority, know about it? Where shall I dispatch this to? I still write it, though I am aware that it is foolishness to write a letter when I am ignorant of the means of transmitting it, rather the message in it, for if I don't express it, I cannot stay alive. After I am through with it, I will personally come over and hand it to you. You may question the need to write it when I can verbally say it to you. It is rather easy to convey in writing what would be inhibitive in speech. When in attendance, inhibition and humiliation choke the gullet and repress the words. I just know that you are my kiddie. I haven't any idea of your contours. Didn't I kill you even before your form clearly emerged! You were in a state where it wasn't clear whether you were a son or a daughter. Will you ever read this letter written by such a mother? After killing you, I returned from Bangalore. Driving up the car to Susheelamma's, as I picked up your brothers, I was enveloped in an awareness of sin, especially when I saw the face of the younger of your brothers, Vikas. He was born of scheming. Having understood that the conspired marriage was slackening, the sister educated her brother and caused it to be implanted. I had thought strongly of ruining her and her brother's intents by warding it off. Yet, I chose to retain it telling myself that if I had to punish anyone, it was those two, not the innocent being. But you were not born of any scheming. You came into being at a moment of elation that transcended caution. Your father too insisted that we save you. Yet, I was apprehensive about the way your brothers would look upon you, the perpetual ill-treatment that would be inflicted by the kin of their father, the denigration that would be inflicted by the teachers and classmates at your school, and the maids and servants at home. I pitied you. Kiddie, my mind lied to me. I was apprehensive that you would be hurt, that you would be denigrated. In fact, that hurting and denigration would accrue to me. I now understand that I was apprehensive about my pain and my dishonour. Whenever you would suffer pain and dishonour, was it not in my authority as a mother to provide protection to you? Baby, I am a murderer. I am a perverted murderer who has killed a baby, a foetus, tweaked a life. Will you pardon me? Pardon can be sought for any other sin, but after committing murder, how to ask pardon of the victim? I have to do it only by arriving at your present place. Please summon me. Give me the strength to come over. Two hours back, having tempered my resolve, I was all set to start. By then, your father intervened. A husband needs a wife; progeny is unimportant. The wife wants the progeny, the husband is a means to it. I am burning with rage to do away with that man who impeded my journey to join my child. Child, will you pardon me? Will you pardon this contemptible, unworthy mother? Before killing you, the doctor gave me anaesthesia. Had I died of it, this sorrow would not be. We both could have stayed together …

The drug took over and she slipped into sleep without even putting back the cap on the pen.

When she got up the next morning, the recollection of throwing away the sum of one thousand from the moving train caused her mind to shrink. She recalled that she had sold a gold bangle for three and a half thousand for incurring the charges of the medical procedure. To throw away one thousand out of it! She felt like striking her head against the wall in repentance. But it was time to see the children off to school. After dropping them at the school, she thought that she better attend college. In fact, she had applied for leave till today. Better go and cancel a day's leave. What of staying back at home? Returning home, she changed and started almost immediately. The cook Puttamma and help Mahadevamma were attending to their work. She arrived a bit late at college. She could not recall which classes were scheduled for the day. She quickly glanced at her timetable. She felt she needed some preparation. Before doing that, she wrote a letter to the principal, requesting annulment of a day's sanctioned leave, sent it over, and began preparing for the classes. In a short while, the principal's attendant came and conveyed the principal's instruction that she see her right away. Closing the book, as she scaled the stairs to the principal's office, Chamundi Hill rose right at her feet and appeared as if it neared her. Watching it, she reached the lobby of the upper floor and entered the principal's cabin by pushing open the flap door. The principal, aged fifty, hair dyed lustrous jet-black, wearing a silk sari, and peering through gold-rimmed glasses, was not smiling. She herself greeted her and, from among the sixteen chairs that were laid around the table, she selected one that was closest to the principal and sat. The principal rang the bell. The attendant appeared. She ordered him to stay outside and check anyone from entering. Amrita understood that something serious and unpleasant was on cards. The principal turned towards her and said, 'Dr Amrita, you had applied leave for four days?'

'CL.'

'Before applying for it, should you not check the balance on your CL account? There's twelve CLs in a year and you have already used up thirteen. The administration had failed to notice. Now you just chucked a slip for four more days and left. Is this responsible behaviour?'

She felt as if struck in the face. She recalled that she had applied for many CLs this year. At times, she had called at the eleventh hour requesting leave of absence, being unable to handle classes as a result of sleepless nights. Had applied for three days' leave for going to Bangalore in connection with the interiors of Somu's office. One on the day of the inauguration. Twice to visit the estate. Yes, it readily occurred to her that she would have exceeded the twelve days' limit. 'Sorry Madam, instead of these four days, I will apply for three days' medical leave. In fact, I was ill.'

'Look, Dr Amrita, it is improper to switch between CL and medical leave, or if neither was available, to seek leave without pay at your whim. To apply for medical leave, you should in fact be ill. It should be supported by a doctor's certificate, stating therein that you were down with such and such ailment, that he treated you for the same, that you were indisposed to attend to your work, and were therefore advised rest. And a real certificate at that.'

The word 'real' pricked her. She asked, 'Madam, am I wont to lie?'

'I didn't say you lie. Just enumerated the expectations from a medical endorsement. That's okay. What ailed you?' the principal looked at her and asked in a tone that suggested that her intellect, experience, and authority had the ability to detect lies.

She felt that her face would melt. Yet, without ceding, she said, 'Madam, it is personal.'

'I am not interested in learning anybody's personal matters,' the principal was angry. 'But I must tell you one thing. Availing leave is never your prerogative. The right vests in the principal to sanction the leave applied for, before which I have to take note of the present status of your assignments and ensure that you are on schedule so as to duly and appropriately conclude the curriculum by the close of the academic year. Maybe, you don't need this job. But the college that pays you expects a proportionate amount of work. Do you know that hundreds of unemployed candidates are around who also merit the very same credentials as you do – MA and PhD ? Give it a thought whether you can put your soul into it and work sincerely. Else, tender your resignation. That is a dignified way. Know why I say this ? One should not compromise on self-respect – lord or lackey. And self-respect is reflected in commitment to work.'

Amrita was abashed for being reprimanded by a superior for the first time in her professional tenure. If it were any other time, she would probably have replied fittingly. But now, not a single word formed in her mind. She found herself squelched, wherein even anger would not brew. She kept looking at the principal's face with unfocussed sight. The latter though, as if she had concluded her task, pulled the topmost one from a pile of files to her left, reset her glasses, and began examining it. By then, the bell rang. She lifted her head and said, 'Okay, leave now. Send in a medical application, alright.' As if liberated, she got up and exited without offering any parting farewell. Immediately heading to the classroom, she began the lecture right away, continuing to be on her feet. But she soon felt weak and sat on a chair. She recalled that she was not well prepared for this class. Even with her meagre preparedness, it was not difficult to expend one hour boisterously. But she weighed against the fact that it would not be an earnest lecture. Have I of late presented myself in classrooms with little or no preparation ? Has anybody reported to the principal of a possible slackening in the grade of my lectures ? Her mind got stuck at these misgivings and she sensed that her lecture today lacked content. Still, she went through the hour and then left. And during the intervening leisure hour, she prepared herself for the next class.

While driving back home, she began deliberating why that woman prattled on so much. She gathered that her reply, 'Madam, that is personal' to the query regarding her ailment would have irritated her. Well, I shouldn't have said so, but how dare she pry? Recalling that the principal's face resembled that of an investigating police officer during the conversation, she reflected if the woman knew something after all! And how would she have got to know about it? Who would report it to her? Or were my very looks eloquent about my pregnancy to another femme? She surmised that it was possible. Many people knew that I and Somu are close. Some would have even noticed his scooter parked inside my compound in afternoons. With all these reaching her ears, did my declaration of discretion prompt her to get ideas and deliver that lengthy sermon about ethical conduct? She reached her house presently. While she fed the dogs, she thought that she was the only one who owned a car among her colleagues. The principal commuted in the city bus. That jealousy might be. Though she could think of such superficial explanations, being unable to refute the core accusation in her words caused distress in her. Though I conduct my classes promptly, research has been given the go-by. My gearing up for upcoming lectures is akin to learning warfare at wartime. Doesn't commitment entail voracious reading? If I failed in it, would it not be negligence of duty? She cringed. I will be awake through midnight unto dawn. But will never read a single page. Afternoons, I am free till 5. I will await Somu's arrival. And when he comes, I will quarrel with him. Instead, if I used half of the squandered time for studies! She felt depressed. Entering, she appointed the table and glanced at the clock – 1:30. He is not here yet. Though she reflected that there would be three days' backlog of work, she got angry. He is committed to his work. It is more important to him than I am. I am a negligent one. I think of him as more important than my work. Her mind thus went on weighing this way and that. Leaden with anger, she sat at the table for quite some time, head hung, without even lunching. The phone rang. She continued to sit her place, thinking that it was him calling to inform that he wasn't coming over for lunch. It rang in dyad some twenty-five times and ceased. When it ceased, she was despaired. At least, I could have heard the voice. I forfeited that too. She was disheartened again. Anger billowed. Why should he choose to call instead of personally coming over? By then, the phone rang again. She sprang up instantly and scurried. She didn't even notice the chair she sat on tumble and fall. Holding her breath, when she reached for the phone and lifted it, he spoke first, 'What were you doing not receiving the call?'

'Instead of coming over, you make me wait. Why call now?' she affronted him.

'I got phone connection sanctioned for my home. They agreed to give it almost instantly. Office formalities are over. Now I am taking the department people home. I have to stay with them till they draw the line and set up the phone. You lunch.'

Instantly realizing what a phone connection at home would mean, she swelled with joy. 'If you know the number already, tell me. Or else call at 10 pm. What did you have for lunch?'

'Nothing yet.'

'Then I too won't lunch.'

'I'll have to give gratis treat to the telephone department people. I will have snacks and tea then. You should lunch immediately and take the medicines.' He replaced the receiver.

She munched some, took the medicines, and retired. Till sleep overcame, mind was shrivelled. She rebuked herself that for one who has arrived at a point where one is unmindful of the amount of leave utilized and the amount of leave available, what sort of commitment to duty could she boast of? The intensity of self-rebuke increased when she became aware that she was not getting any better as a teacher with the passing of time, and that her preparation for the upcoming classes was perfunctory. She reflected that she was a hopeless soul that lived on mulishly despite efforts at extermination. Defeat loomed from each and every nook of life. Nothing I can boast of as having achieved or will achieve.

After feeding the children that night and putting them to sleep, she glanced at the clock. It was 9:30. She thought that he would call at 10:30. All work would have been executed today and the connection would have been put through. Or, she had a misgiving that the department would have deferred it for want of a nail or a length of cable, a government department that it was ! She nevertheless assured herself that in such a situation, my kiddie will surely go to his office and call. He will surely not keep me guessing. She pulled a book that was needed for getting equipped for tomorrow's lectures and began reading it, reclining on the bed. Every five minutes, mind coursed towards the telephone. She would turn towards it in the illusion of hearing it ring. Anxious that if her phone should be out of order and he should be futilely trying from the other end, she lifted the receiver and replaced it carefully in its cradle after ensuring the dial tone. 10:30, 10:45, 10:50 ... it didn't ring. No, the phone was not set up as yet. The jackass did not have the sense to at least inform accordingly. No, not a jackass. Just plain disregard. She reflected that her life or death meant nothing to him, and anger overcame her. While awaiting his call, if I fall asleep without taking the medicines ! Whether I take them or not means nothing to him. Her ire discerned a score causes. Now I will take the medicines. In fifteen minutes, I will fall asleep. I would then not be able to hear the ring. Then the jackass will know ! She got up. Or, she thought, let me take the handset off its cradle. It will then not ring even if he called and will make him disappointed. That would be the right punishment for him. She took the receiver off the cradle and placed it aside. But she could not bear it for more than two minutes.

At once, she replaced it. She had a misgiving that if he had tried during those two minutes and resigned, deciding that the phone is dead ! She waited for another fifteen minutes, cursing herself for having shut her eyes against her own good fortune. Then she suddenly lifted it and dialled his office. If he were there ! It rang at the other end. No, it is not being received. He won't be there at this hour. If he were present but ignoring ? He is not childish like me who gets peeved every other minute. Deciding that he was surely not in his office, she replaced the handset. Then reassuring herself that he would definitely call from some place to update her of whatever development, she drank a glass of water and resumed her reading, reclined on the bed as she was.

After quite some time, the phone really rang. At first, she glanced at the watch. Five minutes past midnight. She thought of ignoring it. But anxious that he would cut it presuming she was asleep, she lifted it and instantly said hello. His voice, 'Dearie, I am calling from my house. Take down the number.' After jotting it down with a pencil that she had kept ready at hand, she asked, 'Why so late ? People are wont to think that I shall wait like a dog !' Anger flared up, but she was oblivious of it.

'Know what happened today ?' he explained calmly. 'By the time they set up the telephone connection, it was 5:15. From there, I went to office. The design of the pillars and beams of a residential structure was due to be provided earlier this week. I had told them that I would surely keep it ready by Monday. I couldn't even keep that commitment. I convinced them that I would give it on Wednesday. The contractor took serious exception that he had to retain the workers by paying free wages, else if they sought work elsewhere, he would find it difficult to find workers when needed. But we left for Bangalore on Tuesday for three days. He awaited me in my office all afternoon. Busy with getting the phone connection, I was elusive. When I went to my office at 5:30, he took me to task. The fault was mine. I persuaded him and took to his job. In between, we had to visit the site for inspection. Took him there and looked around with the help of a torch, returned, resumed the work, and it was 11:10 when I left after finishing it.'

'The summary of what you said seems to be this. *Because of you, I am unable to give due attention to my profession. I wasted three full working days by escorting you to Bangalore. I lost most of today for getting a phone connection and, as a result of this, I had to work till 11 pm.*' Hers was the tone of a bouncy seasoned lawyer.

In a voice worn out from patience and pain, he said, 'Did I say that? I just laid bare the facts, for you apprehensively enquired about the reason for delay.'

His words did not register in her. 'Look sir, you cannot simply shake off by giving smart replies like you meant this and not that. I am not a dunce who cannot get wind of the connotation of your words. Connotation, after all, is part and parcel of meaning, and is more veritable than denotation. Don't give me lessons in literature,' she retorted.

'That's okay. How are you? Did you take the medicines?' he donned more of patience.

'Look sir, I get irate. You rather enact patience and don the facade of a superior one. This is a subtle way of denigrating me. Don't for once presume that I am lost to your scheming. You are doing it purposefully. What does it mean to enquire whether I took the medicines? *It has tranquilizer in it. Just take it and drift off. Enough of talk.* Right? I would have been happier if you had scoffed at me directly. The art of circumvention and the finesse of mincing words typical of my aunt is not any lacking in you. Please shed these traits. I beg at your feet.' He could not think of anything to say. He just held the receiver pressed to his ears. She awaited his response and felt denigrated by the lack of it. 'If you are not inclined to talk, state it flatly, or else replace the receiver. Not content at toying with me afore, are you resorting to it over phone too? Is it not for this reason that you got a phone connection urgently?' She banged the handset into its cradle.

His entire body was sweaty. The previous night, he had gone sleepless except for the little snooze at dawn. Today, he had slogged daylong at arranging ten thousand and making rounds to the telephone departmental office, and had worked restlessly in the company of the contractor from evening till now. Returning home, he had thought of bathing and just retiring. But wanting to inaugurate the phone, he had called her even before he took off his shoes. Recalling his resolve not to lose patience whatever the degree of her anger, he kept his cool. Readily noticeable was the fatigue caused to his body and mind by efforts at such patience. Can call her again. But reflecting that it would only ignite her anger further, he took off his shoes and socks, changed, went to the bathroom, and though the water was nippy, he drained two buckets of it over him. When he dried himself and emerged from the bath, though exhausted, he felt light as the body was rid of the stickiness. He reflected that all he needed was a good sleep, nothing else. But he realized that he was hungry. He hadn't had supper. By the time he saw off the contractor at night, all eateries were closed. He recalled that there were cornflakes and milk powder at home. Aware that he would not get sleep if he didn't prepare milk to gulp down the flakes, he went into the kitchen.

By then, the phone rang. Hers. It is installed today. None else knows the number. Recalling his resolve not to divulge this number to anyone else, he came out and received the call. She asked, 'Somu, did you get angry when I banged the phone?'

'No,' he replied calmly.

'Look, if you are angry, why not say so?'

At once, he did not know what to say without getting incensed. Though it occurred to him that he should expose her presumption of his lying, he suppressed it and said, 'When in fact anger has not overcome, how to declare that it had or has?'

'Noticing your patience, I get both angry and appreciative at once. You seem to think that you are able to contain my anger by your perseverance. It, in fact, increases and incites it more. If the rage is countered in letter and spirit, it will be doused. Else, it will blaze some more from disappointment. Will you please understand at least this much?'

'Okay.'

'What *okay*? Much is your egotism to make it big, to conquer anger. This egotism is causative of my anger. You nurture a resolve to get the better of me. It only conveys your latent intent to cry foul of my inferiority. Isn't it so? Think and tell.' He did not get the import of all these words. He just wanted to shove some soaked cornflakes down his gullet and drop dead. 'Tell me what you feel,' she picked up a quarrel.

'I will consider your suggestion. This is a question of the "self" and of the methodology of the sanctity of the soul. It is difficult to answer on the spur.' Presently, a yawn dilated his mouth. Fearing that she would go wild, construing it as disregard towards her if she heard him yawn, he covered the mouthpiece and later enquired, 'Did you go to college?'

'Why enquire about that now?'

'To know if you rested or not.'

'I should have already shared it with you. I attended college this morning … ' she reported her encounter with the principal in full detail. She then asked, 'Tell me what you think of it.'

'Not just in bureaucracy, even in professional practice, there shall be instances where one has to hear such words from clients. Don't take it seriously. See your family doctor, tell him that you had to go to your native place on some pressing work, that you had no balance on any of your other leave accounts, and hence you need a medical certificate to apply for leave on medical grounds.'

'Can you understand my predicament at all? You dispense words of wisdom offhandedly that there are instances of being at the receiving end of such situations. I feel like quitting the college and flinging a resignation letter on her face,' there was an edge to her voice.

'Don't act recklessly. And don't ever quit your job without discussing with me. You aren't in that job just for bread's sake. Rather to teach and to build up on your knowledge.'

'I am not teaching well. Studying nothing.'

'You are teaching well. True, you are not reading enough. There may be a few reasons for that. All will be well soon. Take the medicines and sleep.'

'Why? You got bored? You want to excuse yourself from this tediousness. Tell me the truth.'

'Truly not. Thrice a day, and within half an hour of supper, you should have taken the medicines. It is now 1:55. If you delay a dose by four and a half hours, how will you get well? Take it immediately. Now. We shall talk tomorrow. Tomorrow, get that certificate from your family doctor.'

'That is to say, a false certificate! Do you ask me to lie?'

'The difference between and the critique of truth and falsity shall be undertaken later. Now take the medicine first.' But he did not assume precedence in replacing the phone. This was the usual time when she would hold the revolver and sit up or drive up to the ledge on the hill. He reflected that if he cut the call, she would think of it as disregard and would take out the revolver.

But she did not stop talking. She asked, 'Where is the need for me to lie?' Thus dilly-dallying, it was 2:45 when she concluded her talk. Ultimately, it was she who replaced the receiver first. After that, he hurriedly gulped some cornflakes, spread the mosquito net, and slept. Tomorrow morning, the contractor will be in my office at 9. By then, I should complete the work. I should sleep at least for two hours. If I reach office by 7, I can finish the work by the time he arrives. Shouldn't make him wait for more than fifteen minutes. Despite these anxieties, sleep overcame.

When he awoke next morning, it was 10:30! He could not believe his own eyes. Leaping out of bed, he just brushed his teeth, skipped shave and bath, dressed, and it was 11 by the time he arrived in his office on the scooter. Not just the contractor Boralingegowda, the landlord Dr Rajashekhar Shetty too awaited him. Somashekhar grinned sheepishly. 'I worked till 11 pm yesterday. Only a little remains to be done.'

The contractor said, 'I came at 8:45. After waiting till 10, I called him and asked him to come over. Whatever you got to say further, say it to him.' Somashekhar knew that the dealing had gone beyond just seeking pardon. The contractor had vented heated words yesterday night, and Somashekhar had categorically conciliated with him that the designs would be made available by 9 this morning. Now he felt ashamed of doing an encore.

The landlord spoke, 'The contractor has explained the amount of loss that would be caused by each day's delay. Even today's work is lost. Who has to bear this loss – he, I, or you? Not all those who build houses will retain the services of an architect. I chose to give it a try. You are a privileged tribe. Bombay denizens! Please, let's settle our dealing. Goodbye to you.'

He felt inhibited to placate the landlord. Such a situation had not arisen in his profession till date. It is true that the landlord had suffered loss, so losing his temper is only natural. He reflected that they both have already discussed and arrived at a conclusion. He turned to the landlord and said, 'I have done a fourth of my share of the work. You should have paid the first instalment of three thousand rupees. I have caused loss of fifteen days' wages, that is to say some two thousand five hundred rupees. You don't pay me anything. I too won't compensate you any. Fault is mine. Please condone. Let not any bitter feelings reign in our hearts. Inform me about the day of housewarming. I will visit without fail and dine.' He got up and brought his palms together, signalling farewell.

They both were taken aback. Pulling himself up, he said, 'Excuse me. I have an appointment.' Exiting from his chamber, he climbed down the stairs and went to the usual restaurant. As he munched, he reflected that he had just given a facade of grace to the dealing, but the fact that he was at fault kept pricking his mind. On finishing his breakfast, when he returned to his office, they both had left. Though he sat in his cabin, he could not apply himself to any work whatsoever. He felt that he was facing defeat in life. Not just the fact of losing twelve thousand in fee owing to abortion of a commission, he reflected that he had gone one step lower in the aggregate of his entire life. He could not just continue sitting there in his office. He felt like going to the countryside and sitting under a tree. I have much absented from work by now. For the past one week, I was hardly at my desk. If I conducted myself negligently thus, what sort of commitment can be expected of my subordinates ? Though he was mindful, he still left, unable to contain the tension within, and drove three miles past Bogadi on his scooter. There was a big peepul tree off the highway. He sat under its shade. He wanted to spill out all his pain and dejection in the company of a friend. But he hadn't one in this town. The only friend available was Naveen. But he is unable to appreciate such intricate feelings. He would not believe it either. At best, he can give apt and sincere counsel in commercial dealings. He decided that he shall not share with Amrita today's abortive deal and the consequent loss of three grand. The reason behind it occurred to him only later that if he shared it with her, she would get more depressed by assuming the onus upon herself. Another thought came. She has consented to take back the two thousand that she had given him in the train. Should return it to her. He recalled that out of the ten thousand he deposited with the telephone department, he had utilized this money as also eight thousand borrowed from another contractor Nanjappa. Now he decided that he should somehow arrange for two thousand and return her money. It should be new hundred-rupee notes. Else, she will notice the difference. He got up and gunned his scooter.

~

Ever since he got a telephone connection at home, she developed such a dependency on it to the extent that once she was done with supper and had put the children to sleep, her eyes and ears began focussing in that direction only, akin to the needle of the compass that points northward whichever way it be turned. She could not be absent from the bedroom even for a minute. What if the phone rang when I am elsewhere ! The door shut, I can speak for long and nobody can clearly make out what I am talking about. Wherefore she would depute herself to the bedroom as soon as possible. The call would usually come through at 11:30. That was the time when, on returning home and changing, he would be able to talk leisurely. Can't he call a bit earlier, at 10, for about ten or fifteen minutes and later leisurely at the usual 11:30 ? She would get peeved. But 10 is the hour at which he would be at a restaurant, supping. Why can't he come here for supper instead ? What if he came daily ? Why fear the children ? Why be apprehensive as to what they would make of it ? Though she got irritated, she could not garner the courage to categorically invite him. Why, on his part, should he be apprehensive ? Why should he not volunteer, 'Amu, after winding up for the day, I will come here straight. We can sup and chat together. The children are aware that we are close friends. Let them eventually get the larger picture too. Whom and why should we fear ?' He has decided to stay aloof. Hence, his reservedness. I know his propriety. She would thus get incensed. Some nights, the telephonic conversation would be very cordial and intimate as between lovers. The conversation would build up on mutual intimacy, tête-à-tête, mischief, jeer, and romance. But as luck would have it, such moods would come by very sparingly. At other times, her ire, derision, and accusations would heat up, and all her words would become sharp, piercing, and rending weapons. While she vented all that, she would be out of control, but when she analysed it the next day, she would repent for her conduct. But she had deduced that her moods were never under her control, and everything was directed by an internal impetus that was beyond her control. But he is not so. When I am in enamouring mood, he will involve himself in letter and spirit. On the contrary, if I resort to combat, he will calmly submit himself to all my outbursts and, without getting agitated, will play Shiva who swallowed the poison that resulted from the churning of the sea and leave behind the ambrosia for the others. Though this delineation would occasionally flash in her mind, it would not stay for long. She would go all the more wild, reflecting that he detested her anger wherefore he would not similarly counter it.

Despite all this, she is conscious of a definite transformation brought about by the arrival of the telephone. After supper, I will await his call. Am bound to it. Many a night, say seven out of ten, I will suffer from feelings of void and hold the revolver in hand. I am vehemently impelled from within to drive to the hilltop. I will take the keys and get ready. But in my absence, if I miss his call! I will anxiously await his call. This phone has obstructed my freedom to death. Akin to a sot's servitude to liquor, mine is to this contraption. What if there is a call! It rings for a while and then he will resign. No, he won't. He will understand that I have gone to the ledge and will drive up there on his scooter. Besides, if the phone rings continuously, it will wake up the children and when they go to my room to check, they would be shocked to find me missing! What if I take the handset and keep it aside? No question of the ringer then! That idea too was short-lived, for he would still understand that there was no possibility of my phone being engaged at that hour, that I have done so on purpose and he would nevertheless go to find me on the hill. He has got that phone installed not to converse intimately with me, but to spy on me, rascal. She would reflect that the telephone cable was meant to serve as a noose to lynch her freedom.

One day, when such feelings were intense, she herself called him at 11:15. 'Amu, you chose to call? Know how delighted I am that you called? I am just home,' he said.

'Delight aside, I will ask you one straight question. Will you answer straight, sincerely?'

'I have never talked to anyone insincerely. With you, never! Tell me what.'

'You mean you are a sincere one, an honest one, and I lack sincerity. Don't you?'

'I know that you too are equally sincere. No other explanation can form in my mind.'

'You are adept at deploying the vocabulary to build heavens. That apart, why did you get a phone connection at your home?'

'To talk to my Amu. Also to facilitate her to talk to me whenever she wishes to.'

'Do you need any more proof to establish that you are an insincere one, a liar, rascal, and loafer?' She banged the handset into its cradle.

She felt cornered and wanted to cry. A feeling of helplessness engulfed her that she was inescapably trapped in a net laid by a man in whose exclusive nature it was to mesmerize women and, having put that trait to generous practice, was adroit at it. She at once developed a desire to take the revolver and drive out in her car. She took the receiver off the cradle and kept it aside. Then she took off her gown, wore whatever sari that she could lay hands on, stepped into her slippers, took the revolver, and strode till the door of the room. Before she opened the door, she recalled that ever since he got himself a phone at home, she had not once visited the hilltop. I have deceived myself of the silence of the surrounding darkness. Why should I be let down? Today, I surely will go. Not just go. Will insert the nozzle into my mouth and pull the trigger. Who will check me? Who has the ability to? The authority to? I am inferior to none. I'm none's slave. Thus resolving, she came out of her bedroom. When she neared the main door, she reflected that he would have tried calling her several times after she banged down the receiver, and hearing the continuous engaged tone, he would decipher that I have placed the handset aside. What if he chose to arrive on his scooter! By now, if he has already started, and by the time my car hit the road, what if he intercepted me and asked where I was headed to? That possibility stymied her. I have done nothing shameful. I need fear none. I will put the phone in order. I will talk to him some and I will start after checking him from driving up. Deciding so, she returned to her bedroom, closed the door, replaced the handset, and stood staring at it. One, two, three, four seconds ticked away. It still didn't ring. He has not tried. Has he decided not to call me, furious with me for banging down the receiver? The thought made her feel that she had lost something, lost everything rather. Despondent, she told herself to contain her ire and also to refrain from talking rot henceforth. Nevertheless, she rationalized her acts too. With whom will I speak so? Only with him. If he gets angry at that, what distinction is there between him and the rest? And as she got wild wondering if his love was not ostentatious, the phone rang and exhilarated her so as to send a torrent of pulsation through her heart. She reached for it and picked up the receiver in a split second.

'Why take the phone off the hook for so long?' he asked calmly but authoritatively.

'My privilege,' she said.

'And why did you replace it now?' he asked.

'Even that is my privilege,' she said.

'Hope your conflicting privileges have valid reasons.'

'That too is my privilege.' No sooner than she said so, the meaninglessness of her words triggered a laugh in her.

Warmed by the tingling chuckle that flowed through the cord, he said, 'This, is my privilege.' They then chatted in excess of an hour. When their conversation began, there never was dearth of topics. They would spawn by themselves and would continue to accrue as would the horizon of earth to a voyager. Interspersed in between were mischief and enamour.

Next morning, she right away had a feeling of guilt. It was one and a half months since the Bangalore visit. He had had lunch at her place many a time, sat in her company, and reclined on the bed with her. He had suffered in agony from the one-sided fights with an irate me. Sweet-nothings were far less in comparison. But there wasn't even a single episode of corporeal union. Since the foetus was cleared, penitent pangs would stab me and I would go wild at him even if he just placed his hand on my shoulder in sheer amity with no trace of enamour in that act whatsoever. Calling him a lewd beast, I have many a day caused him to hang his head. During telephonic conversation, on several days, the memory of terminating the foetus would morph into ire, and I would devolve the onus onto him and call him names. Last week when, for once, I was in cheerful mood and got puckish, he was naturally swayed into an enamouring mood, and all he got for living up to the stimulus was a diatribe that brought blood to his face and tears to his eyes. Yet, he chose not to contest, but submissively took upon himself the full share of the responsibility of my every accusation! Damn it! She felt there wasn't another vile, wretched, and undeserving woman like her. Instead of me, if he had supported a maid, at least his bodily needs would be satiated regularly. She viciously struck herself twice on the cheek, reflecting that she was a heinous one who didn't provide even that little. She still went to the college. The contrition engulfed her while she lectured, and she felt that the lecture was perfunctory. For once, she sensed that she could not carry on with her present career.

While returning home from college, she was conscious that she was cheerful. She ardently desired to drive to his office and take him to her house. She even turned the car in that direction, but on second thoughts, she reverted. Let me not go there. Let me rather call him from home. She was bound homeward. If I don't so pre-empt, he will call at the eleventh hour to inform me of a certain appointment and of his inability to make it at lunch hour. She called him and said, 'There's something interesting to be shared. Come on soon. Now.'

'Gimme thirty minutes,' he said.

'Why shouldn't you make it in fifteen?' she pretended irritation.

'Will try.'

She got up and quickly fed the dogs. She changed and washed her hands, feet, and face. She applied cream on her face and topped it with a coat of dusting. She wore a pastel rose sari, then went to the front yard, plucked a bloomed rose, and tucked it in her plait. Scurrying inside, she laid the dining table and, posting herself at the front door, began observing the progress of the second hand of the clock. The moment he arrived, she said, 'Five minutes late. Know what the penalty is?'

He noticed the bearing on her face, the glint in her eyes, the hue of her sari, and the rose that she wore. But unable to gather the significance of it all, he said, 'Gawd, what a scorching sun!' Entering, he left the helmet in the lounge and took off his shoes.

Holding him by his hand, she led him inside, gave him the dhoti, saw to it that he changed, and in the bathroom, she rinsed his feet with water. He felt elated. She said, 'His Highness may get outraged if his feet were not rinsed and prostrated at.'

When he reacted by quoting the adage that a poor man's wrath was but perilous to his own jaws, she was disappointed that he hadn't yet attuned with her mood. Suspecting that he could be pricking her in retaliation for her slapping him on the cheek, she got incensed. But she became aware that if she ceded to anger, her mood would be ruined. Today, I will cajole him into this mood. If I don't, I am not Amrita. She owned up a challenge.

She dried his feet with a towel. Taking his hand again, she led him to the dining table, served for both into a single salver, fed him a morsel with her hand, and said, 'Kiddie, today I developed a desire to feed you.' Chuckling, she added, 'Now, don't get ideas.' He got wind of it. She understood that he grasped it. Devolving the next move onto him, she put her eyes down demurely.

He found it difficult to take cue from where she let off and further the ballet. During the few days preceding the elimination of the foetus, with effort she had kept her melancholy at bay. Later on, in Bangalore and on return from there, she had repeatedly treated communion with censure as if it were a base conduct. She would have called me a 'lewd beast' at least a hundred times. Ignoring all that, he had developed patience and tolerance towards her. To an extent, those traits were characteristic of him too. But … restraining the turbulence from surfacing, he picked up a morsel and fed her. The lunch went through gaily. He took precedence in reclining on the bed. His mind was revolting till she returned after clearing the table. Apprehending it, he kept up his attempt at containing it in a pod of patience and peace. Attuning to anything else could be achieved through patience, but to get set for coition, what a makeover had to transpire in the mind! If I failed to, she would today certainly fall prey to void. She will acutely suffer from the intense stress and sting of death. Eventually, she will direct all that ire at me. He was not apprehensive of facing her anger. He was acclimatized enough to it. She will not be any less pained either. Who would invite pain! Besides, when she is abound in feelings of void, just witnessing it causes unbearable agony in me. If I don't respond in letter and spirit now, she will understand it that I have parried her, rejected her. Therefore, I should summon all my willpower, supplement it with all of my love and patience, and stream enamour. This is an examination. Even as he reflected that it was easy to don patience but to respond proactively was sublime, she entered. Approaching him, she sat at the edge of the bed. Getting up, he extended an arm and embraced her. She now sat repressed, her head bent. Tightening his embrace, he lifted her face by the chin.

'If you don't want, it is okay with me,' she said.

'Why say so?' he asked, pained.

'I can understand your patience. But I am aware of the amount of pain and disgust I have caused you in this matter. Speak the truth. Have you really turned your back on that?' she asked, lifting her eyes and rooting them in his to probe.

'Don't debate now,' he tapped her cheek, and as if to dodge her sight, he hid his face in her bosom.

'My tot,' she hugged him as she would a child. He became aware that her tears drenched his head. He lifted his head to check. She was crying. All the tart pent up in his inner mind was washed out. He was filled with enthusiasm. Uttering nothing, they explored each other in sheer silence, mutually inciting and sating each other's craving, and synced so as to concurrently appeal to both that this was a unique conjugation attained like never before. The whelm caused in them obliviousness to the outer world.

When tranquillity of contentment pervaded, he said, 'Seems like someone's at the gate. Haven't the dogs been barking for a while?'

'That means your attention was elsewhere!' she rebuked him, thereby flaunting the superior manner of her engrossment. By then, the dog in the front barked again. 'Hear?' he strained his ear in that direction.

'They are very sensitive animals. They will bark even if a dry leaf stirs. Sleep quietly. Come nearer. I will thrash you even if you move a bit,' hitting him on the back, she pulled him close up, suffocating him. 'Now close your eyes,' she said, declining to exit from that inner world. Presently, the dog barked loudly. The one at the front, Vikrant's voice. Vishvas at the hind echoed more loudly. She heard it too. Who would it be at this hour? Mahadevamma's husband? To borrow money? 'You just lie here,' she told him, pulled a blanket over him, got up, briskly donned the night gown, stepped into the chappals, went out of the room closing the door, strode through the living room and the veranda, and opened the door only to come face-to-face with her aunt. It seemed like she had been there for quite some time. A suitcase and a bag on the floor and an expression on her face that she knew everything and that she was not really taken aback. Amrita felt the blood drain from her face. Her voice sunk and no words came for a full minute. Then she gathered some courage and said, 'Aunty, you! Shouldn't you have rung the doorbell?'

'I was in doubt if you would be home or away in college. I stood contemplating what I should do. But I didn't really have an option. Suburban house. No alternative but to await your arrival.' Amrita picked up the suitcase and the bag.

'Come in. I was asleep for a while. Come,' leading her in, she showed her to a bench in the veranda. Taking leave of her aunt on the pretext of changing, Amrita went to her bedroom, shut the door, and, nearing him even as he lay, said, 'My aunt. She has arrived quite some time back. She has noticed your scooter in the compound. Wily woman. Tight-lipped. You dress up and be ready. I will bring your shoes here. I will send her to the bathroom and signal you. Sneak out silently, tow your scooter for a little distance, and then ride away. Don't call tonight. If situation permits, I will call myself.' She hurriedly put on the petticoat and the sari. Entering the bathroom, she washed her face, rolled a comb over her hair, exited, shut the door to her room, went to the veranda, and took her aunt in, 'Come in, Aunty. Travelled by bus? Isn't it very hot! Your face is perspiring and clammy. Go to the bathroom. I will get you a towel.' She led her.

In fact, the aunt's face did not seem worn-out from the journey. Yet, she took the towel that Amrita gave her, went to the bathroom, and shut herself in. Amrita hurried to her bedroom and handed him his helmet and shoes. The aunt stayed inside for quite some time. Amrita speculated that the aunt knew everything and that she purposefully remained inside long enough so as to let Amrita buy time. She opened the door to her bedroom, signalled him to exit, and returning, posted herself at the door of the bathroom. Though the dogs barked and the sound of the scooter was heard, the aunt did not exit. She scurried to her bedroom, shut herself in, removed the creased bedspread, laid a fresh one delivered from the laundry, properly tucked it, and, by the time she was done, the aunt made an occasion of opening the bathroom door by noisily unbolting it, lingered for a lengthy minute at the bathroom door by drying her feet thoroughly on the foot rug, and announced, 'Too hot! The Sakleshpur bus was brimming with passengers! I was able to breathe only because I got a seat by the window,' so as to be heard by me wherever I was in the house.

While surmising whether a smart, veteran woman of the stature of this aunt would fail to notice the coital colouration on her face, Amrita called out to her as she headed to the kitchen, 'Let me serve you lunch.'

Amrita had no lead as to the purpose of her aunt's visit. Ever since she handed over the title deeds of the estate, what of meeting, they had not even written to each other casually. Thinking that she was here probably on a mission to set right her brother's marriage, Amrita observed her aunt's face, seated that she was before her salver, having just a cup of dilute curry and a morsel of rice in curd, pleading that she was not at all hungry. Owing probably to Amrita's prejudice, the aunt seemed like shrewdness moulded to perfection.

She had expertly dyed her hair so as not to reveal any grey even at the base. Clad in a silk sari with a broad aural borderline, she was adorned with a necklace of big beads of gold, diamond ear studs, nose stud, and six thick gold bangles on each wrist.

While munching, the aunt said, 'I want to rid my responsibility by seeing your brother off in marriage. He chided me that I was a dunce, that I was incapable of discerning a bride, and that he would only wed a girl approved by Amrita, else he would prefer to remain a bachelor. Some eight proposals are doing the rounds.'

Though Amrita gathered that it was aunt's default tenor of speech, she showed no expression on her face. After lunch, she led the aunt to the guest room and, placing her suitcase there, said, 'You are tired from the journey. Get some rest.' She then discreetly retired to her bedroom, so as to deprive the aunt of any intimacy or reverence. While I stationed her in the veranda and went to my bedroom, would she not have noticed the shoes? And the helmet on the sofa? She has certainly grasped everything. Tight-lipped but. She got anxious that the aunt would have archived the incident for use at an appropriate moment later. For a while, she tried to get sleep, though she knew she would not succeed at it. At 5 pm, she changed, stepped into her slippers, and exited. Aunt was inspecting the plants in the front yard. Vikrant had already considered her eligible for being enrolled in this house. He slept quietly, even as he eyed her askance.

'I will fetch the children,' she said.

'The school winds up this time?'

'It gets over at 2 pm. My classes are at different hours on different days. They will spend their time at their teacher's nearby.' She gunned the car and brought it out of the garage. As the car headed to Susheelamma's, she reflected that it was improper to let the children mix with the lady. She will souse them in pretentious love and win over their hearts. She will gather information about my family from them. She will cause the children to crave for their dad. None of her acts will be redolent of any transgression. But, Amrita was sure that before leaving, the aunt would have pitted everything to her – Amrita's – detriment. But what can be done of it? Can I quiz her as to her visit? Or tell her in the face to get going first thing tomorrow morning? She found it difficult to say so. Or send the children some place? Where to send pronto? If I offered the pretext of examination duty at Bangalore, she will ask me to leave the children in her custody. While her musings led her nowhere, she arrived at Susheelamma's house.

On their journey home, Vikas asked, 'Mom, is grandma home yet?'

'Whose grandma, man?'

'Mine. Who else's?' he said as if he had just one grandmother.

She was surprised. Mysterious! 'Come on. What do you know of it?' she asked.

'Raji informed that our grandmother had visited them and asked if she has not visited us yet.'

Raji was the daughter of Rajaram, who resided five doors from Susheelamma's. She was of Vikas's age and studied in the same school. Many a day, he and Vijai would go there to play. Raji's mother Chandrakala was from Alur near Sakleshpur. She was a buddy and a close friend of Leela, this aunt's daughter. The entire backdrop became clear in Amrita's mind. 'When was this, man?' she asked.

'Today. During lunch break when I went to Raji's house to meet grandma, her (Raji's) mother said, "No grandma or grindma is here. Why will your grandma come here instead of going to your house? Raji has lied." She disciplined Raji. When Raji insisted that she was not lying, she beat her again.'

'What did Raji say as to when grandma came?' she asked, driving at low speed. Vikas pleaded ignorance.

Start from her estate, go to Sakleshpur first, then by bus via Hassan to Chandrakala's and then here – Amrita surmised that the aunt would not have journeyed that much at once. There was no trace of sweat, grime, or exhaustion in her, which an extensive bus journey entailed. She reasoned that she was there by yesterday evening. Vijai kept mum. He was not a chatterbox like Vikas. She observed his face keenly. She recalled that he was an introvert who kept to himself. While she resolved that she would surely unravel this, Vikas said, 'Raji said that grandma had brought with her semolina laddus and a variety of other snacks. She said they were all very yummy.' Another evidence appealed to Amrita's mind. Aunt has surely brought quite some snacks, but has not yet handed it over. If she did, and if they were relayed to the children through me, the fact that it was she who gifted it to them would only register in the kids' brains. She, then, would not have won them over in their hearts. Therefore, she recalled, that it was her modus operandi to pull the kids onto her lap, kiss them, open the baggage, take out the snacks, and feed them directly herself. Back home, it happened exactly so.

She was by the gate, awaiting their arrival. The moment the car pulled up to the gate, she neared the door, grabbed the alighting kids, and praised them, 'How tall you have grown ! How intelligent you have become !' She attended to their toiletries and, seated on the sofa, held them on each lap, opened the luggage, and, taking out the snacks, fed them directly, amusing them, 'Will you bite my finger too !' Many more snacks than Raji had reported.

Amrita kept watching. The aunt seemed to put on the attitude that these were her brother's children, and that there was no need for her to establish rapport with them through their mother. The aunt didn't let go of the kids even for a moment. After supper, she exercised discretion to go to their bedroom herself, drew the two beds together, and with one grandson on each side, she stretched herself in between. When Amrita noticed it, she said, 'Aunty, they will be asleep by 9:30. It will be inconvenient for you have to shuttle to the toilet. Sleep in the guest room and suit yourself.' Vijai objected, 'Mmm, I will sleep with grandma.' Vikas chafed his legs, 'I too want gramma.'

Aunt said, 'I also need their company. For one, they are my brother's children. Also, they are my daughter's children. Both ways, it is blood relation.' Amrita noticed once again that she was suggesting, 'Even without you, I wield authority over them.'

When she slept alone in her room, Amrita got restive as she contemplated whether she was deficient in tending the children. I will play with them every evening irrespective of the fact that my mood is agreeable or otherwise, will feed them supper, help them with their lessons, sleep in their company, tell stories, put them to sleep, and then retire myself. Often, I will take them in the car to Kannambadi, Chamundi Hill, Ranganathittu, the estate, or some other place, get them clothes to their liking, which they would outgrow within the year. Yet, why do they so tend to lug towards that side? Will the blood exert a pull, overriding my deeds whatsoever? She mulled that over. My life is one grand defeat, she decried, and I will never merit victory and contentedness even into the future. When they grow up, they will reject me. They will identify with that faction. They will never understand the fraud inflicted by that lobby. The future was clear to her. Anyhow, they are sleeping in her company. Let her rear them. My living or dying is immaterial to them. She pulled the cabinet drawer and took out the revolver. No need to go anywhere. Will end myself here. If the police suspect her, let her suffer. She turned and looked at the door. It is not bolted. Better leave it open, else there will be no ground to suspect the aunt. For quite some time, she sat with the finger on the trigger. Perchance, her sight sailed to the wall. The clock that paced silently showed 11:30. The appointed hour of Somu's call. She recalled that she had asked him not to call. Shall I call myself? But she got cautious that the aunt would be awake and lurking in the stillness, all ears. Doing nothing, unable to drive out taking the revolver, unable to make a phone call, unable to attain the absolute state to facilitate jerking of the trigger, she just lay awake till dawn. By then, her eyes were strained. She locked the revolver and, replacing it securely, slept.

It was 8 when she woke up. The cook Puttamma and domestic help Mahadevamma had already reported for the day's duty. The aunt has established camaraderie even with them. She has bathed the two kids and dressed them in new clothes. Vijai stood in style, wearing shorts and shirts that were perfectly his size. Vikas came capering to her, 'Mom, look how nice this shirt and shorts are. Dad has sent them. He has sent three more sets. The shoes are slightly loose. But grandma said, they will be okay in two months.'

Amrita understood that the aunt had not just sown memories of their dad in them, she has seen to it that they rooted well. While she glanced at the watch, Vijai said, 'Let me absent from school for just one day, today. Please call the school and inform them. You go to college. We will stay home with grandma.'

'Should not absent from school, kiddie.' She later realized that it hadn't occurred to her that her voice was brash when she said that. Though he didn't react, she noticed that Vijai's face smacked of rebuff and hostility.

Vikas too started leaping, 'Mom, let me stay from school today, just one day.' When the children were being soused in the sap of love by their grandmother, her putting them on leash with discipline would irretrievably alienate them and cause their minds to polarize to that side. She acquiesced. When she went to her bedroom to call the school, she reflected that besides the children, this aunt would earn the goodwill of even the cook and the domestic help and gather information, wherefore it would be improper for her to go to college, leaving behind this woman. But I haven't even a single day's leave to my credit. She recalled the episode of the medical certificate and the unpleasant debate with the principal one and a half months previously. If I offered some other bait to the children, took them to the college, and made them stay in the car while I went through the classes? They surely will not accede. And even if they did, it would be improper to leave the aunt with the two domiciliary women. She felt that the only way out was to bark at her, 'Why did you come here? Get out.' But she could not pull herself up to it. Anger simmered within her. It boiled up, prompting her to take out the revolver and shoot her at point blank range. At that very moment, her fingers instinctively dialled the numbers on the telephone. The voice from the other side was that of the principal. 'This is Amrita calling. I have some pressing personal work. Please permit me a day's leave without pay.'

'Dr Amrita, someone like you does not need a job. Those who cannot survive without a job will not ask for leave as frequently as you do. Why don't you gracefully resign?'

'Alright, I will keep my letter of resignation ready. Send a messenger to my house.'

'The college has not employed a messenger to pick up your resignation letter from your house. Write it and post it in a postbox. It will reach on its own.'

'Alright, I will lob it. Thanks.' She plonked the receiver into its cradle. Immediately, she took out her letterhead, scribbled a few lines, inserted it into an envelope, wrote the address on it, and called out to Mahadevamma, 'Here, take this and drop it in the postbox at the end of the street. Now,' she tossed it at her. Later, all day, she didn't distance herself from the children and the aunt for even a moment. She stuck to them while they had breakfast, while they played, while they related the leaping and the barking of the dogs Vikrant and Vishvas, and even when they retired for their afternoon siesta after lunch. The aunt asked, 'Don't you need to go to college today? I will look after the house. You go to your work.' Amrita effectively countered it, 'You have given a sparing visit here. You may, at the most, stay for a day or two. I know it is difficult for you to stay away from your place and household for long. And you would not venture out if there weren't some important work. Hence, I have availed a day's leave today.'

The aunt understood well. She said, 'You are right. Your sister-in-law, Jayarama's wife, can't handle one single job on her own. For everything, I have to be present. I have told her that at any rate, I would be back by tomorrow evening.'

'If I could apply for more leaves, I would have personally taken you back in my car. But I am helpless. There is a direct bus to Sakleshpur at 8 am. It is convenient. Else, you would have to go to Hassan, wait in the sun there, and the moment the bus arrives, there will be such a stampede! If you got caught in it, you can't save your bones. Come, let's go to the kitchen. Isn't brinjal stew your favourite? I will prepare it. I wish to hold a banquet for you, but being in a hurry, you have left me with no time.' She led her in and, taking out the brinjal from the fridge, began cutting lengthy slices of it.

The children came in and pestered their grandma to stay on.

'My darling, I haven't the time now. I will ask Jayarama uncle to fetch you when vacations come up next,' she kissed them on both their cheeks. 'Hmm ... my tasty honey!' she added the nectar of loveable words.

Though Amrita anticipated that the aunt would discuss a point with her after the children retired that night, she abhorred curiosity and stayed with the children till they were asleep. She then said to the aunt, 'Get to bed soon, Aunty. You should bathe and have your breakfast early tomorrow morning. I will pack some semolina and *uppiṭṭu* for your journey,' and went to her bedroom.

Her anticipation was not to be foiled. In ten minutes, the aunt knocked on her door. Opening it, Amrita stood across from her so as not to admit her in and asked, 'Why Aunty, didn't you get sleep? Let me tuck the mosquito net properly. If one slept with the children, they will kick the net apart and mosquitoes will invade.' The thwart in her words was palpable enough for the snooper.

'All the while, I wasn't able to talk to you. I kept mum as I couldn't do it in the presence of the children,' the aunt set out tentatively.

'Tell me. Why hesitate? Let's sit there.' Without admitting her into the bedroom, she came out, closed the door, led her to the lounge, and seated her on the sofa. Then she walked up to the children's bedroom, closed the door, returned, and sat on the sofa facing her aunt. 'Yes ...'

The aunt was hesitating in broaching a subject. As if something flashed in her mind, she said, 'Such a big house on the outskirts of the city. An even bigger site. Estate is a different matter. How can you stay alone here!'

'There are the two dogs. They will signal even if a lizard or an anole slid inside the compound. There is always the loaded revolver by my bed. I have been trained at aiming it. Why fear? I am against hosting a stranger or employing a sentry that tends to advance beyond the portico,' she said categorically, indicating there was nothing left to be discussed in the matter.

The aunt was embarrassed again. But she was not the one to accept defeat. After two minutes, she walked up to Amrita and sat beside her. Caressing her back and streaming affection, she said, 'Look child, let me tell you directly. I know that you will get angry on hearing it. But who else than this mother should tell you? If your father were to be alive, I would be rid of this responsibility. You may be angry thinking that I gave you away in marriage to my brother with the intent to usurp your wealth. Only God knows what I had on mind. Unfortunately, my apprehensions came true. Know what has become of Leela? Her husband does the rounds to a club. He is an alcoholic. He is going soft on a female subordinate at his office. Leela related and began lamenting. How can we help? If a husband disregards his wife, will he be resurrected by the words of his in-laws? How can we ever broach that subject with him? We sent her back, advising her to inevitably put up with her fate. "That is your home. Stick to it. A couple of years from now, when the children grow up, he may reform on his own." Your uncle hollered that he would go, tell off his son-in-law, and punch him well. I contained him, asking him to do nothing of it for it may only prompt her husband to abandon her forever. Have I done injustice to you in the matter of your marriage? Now you tell me.' Finishing her discourse, the aunt looked Amrita in the face. Amrita's heart went out to Leela. Nothing flashed in Amrita's mind as to what the aunt was targeting at. The aunt wiped her tears. She was, in fact, weeping. Amrita sat without offering any word of consolation. The aunt continued, 'Know what Jayarama said? He said that I had blundered. "If she were given away in marriage to Ranganath, 'that lad of the house' could have been reined in if he went wayward. Amrita is a daring one. She would cut any man to size." I said that no amount of courage would stand up against an errant husband. At best, the wife may alienate herself from such a husband. But our girls are not of the ilk who abandon their husband. If they did so, what would people make of it? Besides, let this be known. When my sister breathed her last, she put Amrita on my lap. There is no greatness in tending one's daughter. Every mother will do that. But I gave her in marriage to Ranganath so that no such thing would befall her. If, as a son, you don't understand the magnanimity of your mother, can you call yourself a righteous one? He then relented. Not that he doesn't love you. He said so for you were more valorous than Leela.'

Now she got to know the intent of the aunt's words. Her right palm returned to Amrita's back. The eyes that had shed tears and were wiped clear of them were red. After a while, the aunt resumed, 'You think that I gave you in marriage to my brother for the sake of your wealth? Why does he need your wealth? Let that pass down to your children. He is now posted at the new canal work. His salary apart, in the last one year, he has amassed five lakh. He had visited us and said, "Sister, look, I have earned this much. Ask your daughter what she wants. Diamond necklace? Pearl and ruby-studded gold bracelet? Arm bracelet? Not just this year. I will continue in my present posting for another two years at least. In future, if I am transferred elsewhere, even if not this much, I have the capacity to amass at least half as much. But your daughter spews venom at me. For what fault of mine did you inflict on me the punishment of marriage to her? Having earned this much, why should I so suffer lonely? Do I smoke? Am I an alcoholic? Have I any vices? She has even alienated my children from me!" A boy that lost his mother early during his childhood, he virtually cried. I am a mother both to him and to you. What prevents you two from being in accord? It is in my fate to even lament at Leela's fate.' She started crying again.

Though Amrita was embarrassed, she remained quiet. The aunt wiped the tears herself. For ten minutes, she awaited Amrita's response. Then, turning in her direction and rooting her gaze in Amrita's, she said, 'Husband there. You here. You are not inclined to resign the college job. Don't. He is well acquainted with higher-ups in his department. He can get transferred to Mysore. If not Mysore, posting can be obtained to a nearby place that can be covered in an hour by car, say Nanjangud, Srirangapatna, K.R. Sagara, or Mandya. Would it augur well for you to stay alone here? People gossip much. An architect, I hear, got your house repaired. It seems they discuss the need for him to visit your house daily on the pretext of repairs, compound erection, plumbing, and this and that when your husband is an engineer himself. Well, it is in the disposition of the people to cry foul on paltry matters. A lecturer will surely have examination duties, and when you visited Bangalore for evaluation work, it was rumoured that you went there for some other purpose. I will never believe what people say. Your husband will all the more disbelieve it. He says that he would sever the tongue of the bastard who made false allegations against his wife. Such is his faith in the fidelity of his wife. He will swear on God that being his sister's daughter, it is impossible that she would ever do any such thing. You need not have any apprehensions in this matter. But people will never say anything in the face. Isn't it typical of them to speak ill of others behind their backs? If it falls on the ears of the growing children, will it augur well for the mother? Why all this? Just because he is afar. If he got a transfer and came here! You just tell what alterations you want for this house. He will personally attend to it. He will make this shimmer like a new one. Where is the need for an alien architect? Family reunion will be a reassurance for the kids too. Can the mother be surrogate father as well? The father and the mother should together tend them if the children have to develop well. Else, if their minds are allowed to gather trash, is it not we who will be witnessing it and suffer eventually?'

Having said this much, the aunt got up. Amrita still sat. By then, her face had drooped. Mind had withdrawn so much as not to notice the aunt get up. Having stood silently for a minute, the aunt stepped up to Amrita and, hugging her with both hands, she held her head pressed to her belly. Though Amrita tried to wriggle out, she did not let go. 'You are well read. A wise one. Intelligent. Though you get wild at me, you still are my daughter. I will not ditch you. I will slit the tongue of anyone that speaks ill of you,' she placed her right palm on her head as if in promise and bestowal of protection. 'Now you go and get some sleep. You are dead beat, having toiled all day,' she caressed and squeezed both her cheeks, went to the children's bedroom, and slept.

Left alone in the lounge, silence seemed to swarm her brain cells even as Amrita remained slumped on the sofa. It seemed like her conscious had dulled and she could not even contemplate getting up and retiring. Eventually, when her brain cells resumed activity, she felt there couldn't be a more congenial moment for death. Just dash to the bedroom, shut the door, take out the revolver, and pull the trigger. That is all! She felt that there was no need for any other thought, for a comparative analysis of the right and the wrong, or for scripting the death note. She got up.

But habit led her to the front and the back doors to check the latch and the crossbar. When she finally locked herself in the bedroom, it occurred to her that this was the most catastrophic moment of her life. I have failed, have hung my head, being unable to think of an explanation; rather lacked an explanation. Recalling that the aunt held to her belly her hung head, she took out the revolver and sat on the sofa. If the aunt tiptoed silently and peeped through the door! She craned her neck and observed the door. All bolts have been properly secured. But lacking the resolve to bring herself to point the revolver at the temple or the palate, she just sat holding it on her lap. She felt it was taxing to keep her eyelids open, and therefore allowed them to close. She got up after quite some time and slumped on her bed with her feet on the pillow and her head at the opposite end, the swapping a result of her disoriented mind. Eyes pulled up on their own.

At dawn, she was to be woken up only when the aunt tapped on her door. Hurriedly, she got up, sautéed some *uppittu*, gave it to the aunt, and, by the time she fed the same to the children, the domestic helps arrived. Taking the children and the aunt in her car, she first dropped the children at their school, drove on to the bus stand, and looked for a bus for the aunt. Inside the bus, she didn't talk to her much. The aunt kept uttering soothing words. Tend the children well, get one more domestic help, if you want I will arrange for a resident help....Excusing herself, saying that she would get late for college, Amrita alighted the bus and bade bye when the aunt summoned her close to the window and said as if into her ears, 'You just drop a letter. Ranganath will come running. He said that he would not go until you wrote to him.' Not expressing any reaction, Amrita went to her car and drove straight home.

For quite some days thereafter, she stuck to her bedroom. Her outing was restricted to dropping and picking up the children from school. Else, she would simply recline. Nothing held any enthusiasm.

She was not even impelled to commit suicide. She never touched the latched revolver that was in the cabinet. A state of vacuum. If there was a distinction between life and death, then would be the allure of death. Hence, the desire to die did not surface. Life, though, held no allure. Entire life was one clutter of defeat. In everything, in every facet, only defeat remained. But she didn't attempt suicide. She would contemplate whether the required resolve was absent, or if any other impetus was operating inside her. Many a time, it occurred to her that it was the anxiety regarding the ill fate of the children consequent to her death, but then, love for the children was fallacious. Howsoever I love them, whatever I do for them, their consanguineous allegiance is to that side, none towards me. Every jot of blood that their heart disgorges is channelled into that estuary. No point in keeping myself alive for their sake. Neither can I save the estate if I lived on.

For eight days, she was not aware of the effect of resigning the job. It just vaguely appealed to her as the shedding of an onerous chore. She had lost interest in lecturing. And she hadn't kept up with reading and writing. Sluggish on these, she was relieved that she resigned rather than hang on to the teaching profession. But when it occurred to her that no salary was coming up on the first date of each month, she felt that the only way left was to clasp the children and jump into the Vishveshwaraya canal. All day long, while she kept deeply worrying about her next step for livelihood, she wondered if the aunt came here just to see to it that I resigned my job! Would I then, like a dog, go and fling myself at the feet of her brother? The fact of her recklessness did not register though.

That night, at 10:30, the phone rang. She knew that it was his call. The children were asleep. It was him. 'Amu, I feel like seeing you. Got to discuss two important points with you. Aunt's there?' She didn't immediately reply.

'Heard me, you?' he asked again. She then said, 'Nobody need see me. But what will happen if you don't see me?'

He said that he would then go mad. When he said that he would be on his way anon, she got anxious. She got worried that if he came at this hour, Vijai might wake up and notice. If he informed his grandmother! 'Please don't, Sir,' she said.

'Aunt's there?' he asked again.

'Don't ask for all details. You want to talk to me, right? I will come over there. You calling from your house?' The moment he said yes, she said, 'I will start in two minutes,' and replaced the handset.

By the time the car arrived there, the whole of Jayalakshmipuram was asleep. Light was on in his house only. Climbing the stairs, she arrived at his door and was about to tap when he opened it. Entering, she pulled a chair, sat, and asked, 'Yes?' in a businesslike manner. He observed her face. He could not make out if there were feelings of void or those of having distanced from him. Shutting the door, he neared her and, pressing her face to his belly, he held her head in embrace. Staying still for half a second, she wriggled free and said, 'Let pretension be. You said you had two points to discuss.'

Pain wrung his face. 'If you don't express cordial feelings, how can I talk?' he asked.

'Those who espouse real love can talk without pretentiousness. Those who expect dramatics are a different cup of tea.'

He went silent. For two minutes, he stood looking at her while she gazed at the wall. He sat opposite her on the floor and said, 'I called the college. They said you had submitted your resignation. You didn't inform me why you did so, didn't even discuss with me before doing so. I am worried about your ... ' She interrupted him, saying that she would not ask him to be supportive. Ignoring her, he continued, 'I didn't mean just livelihood. There is the need for the mind to be engaged. Give a thought to the possible ways of withdrawing the resignation. If you insist that you don't want to, I want to give this piece of advice. If you sell this old suburban house, you will get some seven or eight lakh. Deposit it in a bank and rent a moderate house.

You can lead a peaceful life. Even if you bought a small house for two or three lakh, you can lead your life with the interest income on the balance. Or, if you clear the estate loan, you can save the interest being paid on that and utilize it for your livelihood.' He noticed her expression. Not just disinclination, her face smacked of rejection. Yet, he continued, 'The day when your aunt sneaked up and you silently dispatched me, I got an idea that night. There are many aspects, like the year you attained majority, them obtaining loan after you attained majority, how on its part the bank sanctioned it, etc. If you consult a lawyer with all the relevant documents, he could possibly sue your aunt, her estate, and the bank – all three parties. Possibly, you may not have to pay the interest. Maybe, you don't have to repay the principal even. This is my guess. The lawyer will be able to give definite counsel. Think about it.' He fell silent.

Embarrassing silence pervaded. Two minutes passed. Five. Ten. Her gaze was fixated on the wall. 'Got it?' When he eventually tried to pull her to conversation, her face snapped up like the hood of a snake and she shot a glance at him. 'That is a house bought by my father for his sojourn on his occasional visits here. The treasure of memories that I cherish towards it can never be fancied by architects who expend their lives in the economics of cement, brick, and steel. And then, suing in the matter of the mortgage on my estate is nothing but to drag my aunt to the court chambers. Whatever she inflicts on me, she is the one who held me in a cuddle when my mother died. She had held my face pressed to her belly to stream reassurance. I still remember the odour of her sweat, she arriving just then from a taxing journey. Even when she visited here the day before yesterday, she hugged me likewise. The very same sweat, redolent of deep-rooted memories! You too held my face to your belly now. The sweat reeks of hypocrisy. You don't transude at all. How could you be so audacious as to suggest suing such an aunt and dragging her to the court? You are, after all, alien. You would have understood it all if you were kinfolk.' She continued to watch his face as a snake would. Not just his sight, even his fortitude slumped. After two minutes, she got up. He still sat, his sight down. He heard her leave, gun the car, and move. Yet he sat, his head hung.

The remedy of withdrawing her resignation appealed to her when she was home. But by now, the principal would have forwarded it further and also have rushed through the processes and seen to it that it was accepted. She still thought of giving it a try, but decided against it when, in her mind's eye, she visualized her act of standing before the principal and pleading pardon. She even visualized the virtuousness of death by terminal destitution as opposed to the sin called suicide.

~

It was one week since. One afternoon, at about quarter past noon, the phone rang. She just lifted it, lacking any enthusiasm or curiosity to know the identity of the caller. Of late, she received less and less phone calls. The greeting from the other side evidenced that it was him. She did not reply. After a minute, he asked, 'Is your aunt still your guest?' She still did not reply. After a while, he said, 'Amu, even that day you did not inform me whether your aunt had left. You didn't even call. Why?'

'Whether or not she has left, you are in no way concerned with it.'

'I am coming over. Hence I asked.' She could not immediately think of an answer. 'Got me?' he repeated.

'Suit yourself.'

'You mean that I am welcome even if your aunt were there?' he sought clarification.

'I have no time for augury in every matter. Those who want to may come over.'

Saying that he would be there in fifteen minutes, he replaced the phone. She did not go up to the gate to receive him. Till he rang the doorbell, she didn't even open the main door. She was in a state of apathy rather than contempt. Entering, he shut the door and hugged her. 'Aren't you well? Why didn't you call me?' Not responding any, she held her head hung. 'When did the aunt leave?' he asked.

'I packed her off the very second day.'

'Why then did you dodge me till today, without even calling me? Every night, I would ward off sleep in anticipation of your call.' She looked at his face. He had paled. The bones of his face and chest were prominently visible. Even that did not invoke any feeling of pain, compassion, or compunction in her. Hugging her, he led her to her bedroom, seated her on the bed, and sat beside her. She continued to remain silent. Holding her face, he turned it towards him and planted an intense kiss on her lips. She neither refused nor resisted. She wasn't incited either. He felt as if he had kissed some smooth, lifeless rubber. He felt dishonoured that he was being despicably rejected. He felt that she was shoving him out by his neck. He thought of getting up and leaving. Just a thought. The faculty of executing it was lacking, or deficient. Shouldn't be unwary – he told himself – should understand her state of mind. She has called me an alien. He resolved that he should understand her as kin. He felt it strenuous to continue to sit. So he removed his shoes and reclined with his socks still on. She continued to sit, staring in the direction of the window. She too has waned. Has paled from deficiency in nutrition and haem.

Some time passed during which no one spoke. She abruptly turned towards him as if startled at something. Anxiety and tension evidenced in her face. 'What?' he asked.

'Didn't you hear the dogs bark?' she asked, straining her ears.

He focused his attention and said, 'No.'

'Where have you parked the scooter?'

'Under the shade, in the portico.'

She got up, left the room, shut it from outside, and peered through the window by the main door. She then opened the main door, strode up to the gate, surveyed around, returned, sealed the main door, and went in. On her face were writ pain and doom and gloom. She said as if with utmost patience, 'I think you won't rest until you have dragged me through the streets! Couldn't you have parked the scooter elsewhere, unseen? You could have opened the garage door, rolled it in, and shut the door.'

Recalling the predicament of that day when her aunt was here, he got up and, tying his shoes, said, 'Sorry. Give me the keys to the garage. I will park it inside.'

'For how long? Let it be there,' she said.

He understood it that she was suggesting that he leave soon. 'Amu, why do you say so? Whom should we fear? Why fear? You didn't even tell me why your aunt was here. I have mulled it over all these days. Vijai and Vikas are my children. Let's simply tie the knot. Enough of this anxiety and sentience of stealth.'

She turned her head sharply towards him as a snake would. From her eyes that seemed like a snake's, distrust stemmed. 'Marriage, you say?' Groping behind her pallu for the hallowed pendants of the connubial string that she wore around her neck, she held it out for him to see. 'I am blemished. Having committed adultery, I have fallen to disgrace. I have destroyed the sanctity of this. Will you marry such a woman?'

He could bear it no more. 'You mean I have caused your decline? I have incited you to commit adultery? I have caused destruction to the sanctity of that hallowed string?'

'I didn't say so. I just related my state of affairs. You are one experienced man. This is no first experience of yours. You are wont to think of me as another of your girlfriends. Therefore, there is no reason, neither possibility for the genesis of guilt in you.'

'You are giving it a start now.'

'So you admit that there was nothing of it till now,' she shot back, as if she had won a point of debate. He could not understand his fault herein. 'Shouldn't you have exercised discretion that you should not touch a married woman, a mother of two, and that you shouldn't play upon her impulses? I am not repudiating my role in all this. I own up my share of the guilt. A part of it should be yours too, albeit small. If you own up nothing of it, then you are bestial, for they are indifferent in these matters.'

She was wont to infuse such a sin or censure unto herself and suffer. She desires that he too suffer in tandem. He felt that he must answer her now. He said, 'Where love is, sentience of guilt isn't.'

'You mean that I have no love towards you! True, I have no feelings of love towards you. There was lust. Now that too is rid. I am telling the truth. But you are lying. You too have no feelings of love,' she said, as if propounding an ultimate truth.

He got wild. 'Don't talk nonsense. If you don't nurse any love towards me, that's okay. But I do.'

She laughed mockingly, 'How do you prove that?'

'Proof? Look, just as Hanuman pulled open his chest to evidence Rama residing there, you can see yourself in my chest too. Wherever I sit, stand, keep rolling this way and that, sleepless ... I shouldn't declare my present condition. You should attempt at understanding it. I swear on you that I love you. Who else is mine, as lovable and worthy? Hence, I swear on you,' he placed his right palm on her head as he said this.

She could not bring herself to believe it. 'The premise for oath on love for me is myself! Your acumen is laudable. Isn't this oracle devised so as to cause the covenants of the oath to boomerang on me if the pledge were false?' she giggled in mockery.

'Okay, not on you, I swear on God,' confounded, he blabbered in despair what he thought was his last available defence.

She cut him out curtly, 'You have earlier declared your lack of belief in the existence of God. To pledge in the name of something that you don't believe is nothing but to lie consciously. Look, a man's obstinacy at love gets denser with the woman resisting it. Yours is nothing but that obstinacy. Shed it and own up the truth, not before me, but unto yourself. Discern a suitable girl, wed, and live happily. Look up the matrimonial column of Sunday issue of dailies. You can surely find an appropriate girl. I got to fetch the children. Bye. Now on, don't ever visit here.' She took out the keys to the car and the house and got up.

He looked at his watch. Still 2:15. It wasn't yet time to fetch the children. He understood that she had decided to pack him off. He felt that it was a brazen act to keep up the talk by contradicting her contradictions. He did not know how to make an exit. For some time, he sat confounded. Then he abruptly got up, swallowed the word 'alright', and picked up his helmet. She stood staring out of the window. He exited and gunned his scooter. The dogs started barking. Almost immediately, he killed the engine, parked the scooter again, and re-entered the house. Shutting the main door, he went into her room. She was still on her feet. He flung the helmet onto the bed, posted himself before her, and, raising his hand, struck her hard on the left arm. He then lifted his left hand and struck her on the right arm. Her eyes blazed with anger.

'Rascal, think you can fool around with me as you wish?' he struck her again.

'You are the one that is fooling around!' she yelled.

'You are the one that is mocking me despite me swearing in the name of God,' he lifted his hand again. In a flash that could never have been amenable to his anticipation, she slapped him once and followed it up by lifting her left hand. To ward her strike, he struggled to clasp both her hands. His first attempt going in vain, her hands struck him on the chest, back, and shoulders.

Hastening to debilitate her hands, he held her in a total clinch. She at once bit him hard on the left shoulder. As he could think of no other way of freeing himself, he impeded her right calf with his booted leg to secure a hold. Shoving his left shoulder that was slack from pain, she picked up her slippers from below the bed, one in each hand, and bounded at him. 'Kick me with your booted foot, will you?' she began smashing him left and right. By then, he realized his mistake. It is I that started this brawl by turning off the scooter and returning. I can continue to tackle her, floor her, and kick her over and over again with my booted foot. What will I achieve then! He stood immobile, submitting himself to her blows. After delivering eight, ten, twelve blows, unable to think of her next move, she stood her place, respiring like bellows. The next step was to be his. He that was soused in abashedness, wasted no time in pleading. 'Sorry. I left my brains at the mercy of ire. Henceforth, I will never cross the threshold of this house.' Collecting his helmet, he strode away.

~

He needed three full days to recollect what had actually transpired. This was not the first time that she had struck him. But on those earlier occasions, it was her ire that had caused such assault. I had chosen to remain collected and had endured the beating. Moral victory had been mine. But now, I allowed myself to be swayed by anger and sought her out for manhandling, not just out of indignation but fury rather. She countered similarly. I lost even in that. Balked halfway through. It wasn't difficult to physically overpower her. Impeding her leg to secure a hold and then grabbing her slippers would have seen the end of it. I was abashed and checked myself as I felt that it was a bestial act. She kept up with her fury. To sum it up – he began fuming within – I brought myself to merit that punishment.

In two days, another thought formed in his mind. Why not quit Mysore and return to Bombay? For what sake should I stay here? Sell the office premises here, clear the loan, take with me the remaining monies, and, like before, the Bombay life – dwell in some place, work in some other place, sweat profusely, and more bestial than a beast, rush in and out the doors of a metro train! He still felt that that was a better place. Mysore's open sky, calm streets, Kukkarahalli Lake, Gangotri, the hill – all lost their appeal. The direction of Lalitamahal is lost to me nonetheless. And the Chamundi Hill too. Mysore without the hill has no alignment. Why should I stay in this disoriented town? This disputation concretized in his mind. At nights, he would slip into sleep as soon as he lied down. But he would be awake in about two hours. Try as he may, he would get no sleep thereafter. Not always would her memories fill his mind. Except that last time when I surrendered my mind to anger, I have conducted myself righteously. And despite of this, if she disparages me, why should I fret about her? That consolation would surface naturally. Many a canvas rolled over in his mind, many a memory, which had no nexus with her whatsoever. Sleep remained elusive. Consolation pervaded him one night. Why should I quit this place just for reason of a relationship with a mad woman turning sour? Is she the pivot of this municipality? If I just let a couple of days or a couple of months pass by, her memory will fade on its own. Mysore will be as it ever was. But even while this consolation appealed vehemently, sleep eluded. By dawn, when it occurred to him that she was at the root of even such consolation, he was confounded again. She had, in no uncertain terms, declared that she was not in love with him, now and on many earlier occasions. Yet, he contemplated, why does my mind go after her as would a kicked dog after its master? But whatever unbecoming metaphor he thought of to describe himself, he couldn't free himself from the unremitting memories about her.

How about consuming a small dose of tranquilizer each night, say for a fortnight? He had an idea that if he retired early and was drawn into sound sleep till dawn, sleep would come on its own habitually without the need for the pill. How many Bombayites take a small dose of it each day! Or some whiskey? Never had alcohol abuse appealed to him. He recalled his earlier musing that to resort to alcohol was synonymous with defeat. Likewise, wasn't resorting to the tranquilizer a defeat? True, he reflected, not much difference there. Yet, he thought of consulting a physician. But what would he counsel? He will prescribe the pill. Or he will refer me to a psychiatrist. Is my present affliction psychosomatic? Many people would have had a similar experience. How can it be called an ailment? To call my state an ailment is to own up defeat. He made a mental note to delve into the root of the matter with a view to properly delineate the same.

One night, when he was abruptly awoken, he asked himself as to what was priority for a woman – her lover or her children. A mother that sacrifices everything for the sake of her children wouldn't think twice to sacrifice her lover. Her aunt cheated on her. Even her husband did. But he isn't an incompetent husband. Though he was funded by her money, he is a qualified engineer. I can lovingly tend her two children. But would they look up to me as they would their father? Down the line, they would probably incline more and more to that side. She probably has decided to distance herself having considered all this. Without letting my mind to get acrid, it would be wise on my part to look at it from her point of view and accept the situation accordingly. If it augurs well for her, well, sacrifice is characteristic of love. All of a sudden, he was swayed with feelings of magnanimity. Reflecting that it would be apt for him to distance from her, he once again thought, 'Shall I simply return to Bombay? Should I or shouldn't I inform her of my relocation plans? Why not inform her right now?' He got up, put on the light, and picked up the phone beside him. He had dialled no more than three digits before he replaced the receiver, for he was wary not to let such communication give a new start to the relationship. He recalled that he had expended ten grand to get that phone installed for her sake. Now even if he surrendered it to the department, they would not refund that amount. If she felt like calling, she would have. When she has exercised her prerogative and taken a stance, to accost her like a carnivore will only cause inconvenience to her as well as disappointment in me. Ceding to anger, it was okay to hit her, but I should not have sworn not to step in there thenceforth. Has she abstained from calling owing to that pronouncement of mine? Shall I call her myself, inform her that those words were uttered in a fit of anger and that they carried no meaning, and end the call at that? But if she countered it with her brand mockery! Trepidation set in when he recalled her propensity to barb her words by twisting their import. He rescinded.

When he abruptly awoke another night, he glanced at his watch. It was exactly midnight. Anon, her memories flooded his mind. Is she at home or at the ledge, the primed revolver in hand, to exterminate herself in darkness? Anxiety and trepidation set in. He didn't ruminate much. Sticking his arm out the mosquito net, he pulled the telephone in and hurriedly dialled. It started ringing on the other side. He held on, anticipating that she would lift it any moment, she will now, in another five seconds ... two minutes later, it still kept ringing. Has she already left for the hill by now? Or is she done with the terminal act of pulling the trigger? Grief billowed from within and caused a catch in his throat. Certain that a call at this hour would be none other than mine, is she checking herself from receiving it? Though that thought brought about dejection in him, he consoled himself that that would only mean she was alive. At that point, the call was received at the other end and, '*allo, allo,*' a male voice, a lackey's. He was perplexed as to what he should be asking. 'Who you, Sir?' the voice asked.

In five seconds, his mind gained composure and he asked, 'Madam is home?'

'She gone to her native place. Who you, Sir?'

'When did she go?'

'She will keep going, keep coming.'

'When will she return?'

'She said this time four to five days.'

'Well then, I will call after she returns.' He replaced the handset without disclosing who he was. Now everything was clear. Aunt's sermon has borne fruit. The couple has reunited. 'Shouldn't you have exercised discretion that you should not touch a married woman, a mother of two, and that you shouldn't play upon her impulses?' It was clear that this invective had caused that development. He felt comforted that she ultimately surmounted dilemma and anchored at her haven. Along came the feeling of being ditched. Very many times, she had said 'the genesis of the penchant for death is the fraud inflicted by my aunt and husband. After I befriended you, it developed into a great stress.' Now the stress might not be that intense; would have diminished even. In the entire episode, is the transgression mine? Weren't her compulsion and urge greater? Memories began rolling out.

No sooner had he slipped into sleep than the crows heralded dawn. He woke up at 7:30. Finishing his morning ablutions, he rolled out his scooter at 9. After breakfast, when he arrived in the office at 9:45, Neelakanthappa informed him, 'Jalaja Madam had called. You are to call her immediately. She wants to see you urgently.'

He very well knew why Jalaja had called him. The work of Dr Ramamurthy, the medic from America, is being delayed on my part. The contractor has finished land excavation for laying the foundation. The entire weight of the structure has to be borne by the columns. He would proceed no further unless the specifications and designs of the exact depth, the concrete bed, and the steel reinforcements were given. Prior to that, the soil examination should have been got done. That responsibility was mine. As of now, the work is two months behind schedule. Dr Ramamurthy had called him twice from America. In order to catch me on those two occasions, he had to make seven attempts. Once, out of frustration, he had even instructed Neelakanthappa to inform me to make a call collect. Fault is mine. All these cannot be handled by Neelakanthappa. The proposed structure is of such nature as requires my personal supervision. But I am lacking in concentration. I am unable to channel my attention to the work. My mind is stuck in her. He was not unaware that those involved in love affairs would lose interest in academics and career and would eventually be devastated. I am letting this happen to me too. He was heedful that it was on this count that he had balked the commission of Rajashekhar Shetty.

To call Jalaja is one thing. But if he had to earn back their confidence, he had to solemnly undertake that there would be no delay henceforth, that in three days he would be done with the design of the columns and should actually get the work underway right away. Presently, the phone rang. He picked it up. It was Jalaja. He told her that he was about to call and that she had pre-empted him.

'I want to talk to you for about ten minutes. When shall I see you?' she asked. 'Why should you? I will come myself,' he offered. But she cut him short, 'I am calling from the college. I am nearby. I will come myself. No more classes for me,' she said. He told her she was welcome right away. Somashekhar was not just venerable to her; she had utmost faith in him ever since he got her house built. On arriving, she sat opposite him and went silent for a while. He could understand her predicament at starting the conversation. In an apologetic tone, he informed her that he was aware of his slip-up, asked her to shed embarrassment, and tell him whatever it was. She then extracted a foreign envelope from her bag. He understood that it was Ramamurthy's. Taking out a bunch of sheets from the envelope, she withheld the first one and said, 'Ramamurthy's. Read on from the second paragraph.' He began reading.

> *I too am mystified about architect Somashekhar whom you so vehemently recommended. But as this is a million-rupee commission, besides confusion, I am angered too. Maybe he is honest. But he is languorous, lethargic. In my presence, he exhibited ample sincerity and responsibility, and like a gentleman, he assured me that the entire responsibility of this commission was his. Is it not cheating to go back on that when I return here after entrusting the work to him? Lying and embezzlement aren't the only dishonest acts. Not acting with responsibility as promised is also dishonesty. Such is the conception of equity of the peoples of this land. He continuing to act irresponsibly so, who is to make good the escalation in the cost of construction resulting from the delay? Nowhere else do prices spiral like they do in India. And a federal budget intervening, the levies on steel, cement, timber, paint, electrical cable, etc. would be hiked, the merchants making hay would raise it a bit more, and eventually if the estimates of my structure has to be revised upward from five to six or seven million, who'll have to make good the same? In America, it would be the onus of the person who causes the delay. If he doesn't make good the loss, he will be jailed. But the situation in India is entirely different.*
>
> *Since you recommended his work, creativity, reliability, and honesty to be of a high stature, I went directly to Mysore. Else, I would have got in touch with an architect in Bangalore and corresponded with him. I am not blaming you. Please do not mistake me. When*

> *I visited there, I found myself appreciating his work. Though he quoted his commission at four percent, I offered six and vested in him greater responsibility. Now, he is conducting himself poorly. As you informed me during one of our telephonic conversations, maybe he is troubled by some emotional issues. That is his personal matter. If I have to sympathize on such matters and give him leeway, who is to bear my loss? You meet him personally and resolve it categorically. If he doesn't work with application, dismiss him and call me. I will visit and engage an architect from Bangalore. Explaining my ideas and needs to the surrogate architect may call for at least ten days' stay. Add to it the travel time. Travel expenses. And the loss caused here to my profession all those days. Don't, for once, think that I am talking all economics. A conscientious person should be clearly able to see in this a question of ethics ...*

Family matters followed. Somashekhar folded the letter and, placing it before her, remained quiet. Jalaja looked at his face inquisitively. He felt discomfited. Abashed too. He also understood that she was finding it difficult to discuss the letter.

He said, 'Give me two days' time. I will mull it over, decide whether I can handle this commission, and inform you accordingly. I will call you myself.'

She now found it comfortable to start her debate. 'What do you mean by *whether or not*? You are ready with everything. All you got to do is release the required details to the contractor at various stages. Ramu himself has expressed that you are an intelligent one.'

'Interest in work,' he said, head hung.

'There is an allusion in Ramu's letter. I shared with him a speculation I had in the matter of your private life. Maybe, I should not have. I tell this to you as you are not a rank outsider. If you discuss your problems with a confidant, a solution would emerge. Later, you shall even evince interest in work.'

He did not lift his neck to look at her. He had no doubt in his mind that she was a well-wisher. Hence his discomfiture. 'Day after tomorrow is Sunday. Holiday for college. I will visit you at 9 am without fail. Please give me time till then,' he gave her no options. She got up. He escorted her down the stairs.

There wasn't much work at his desk. After shelving Rajashekhar Shetty's commission, he had not taken up any other work. He began contemplating in retrospect. Of late, I am not punctually attending my office. Prospects would have called. Unable to see me even after a few visits, they would have sought help elsewhere. Or, they would have been thus redirected by my own assistants. They would have attended to minor works themselves and made easy money. In any profession, were not the deputies wont to do so? If, in fact, Neelakanthappa and Nanjundegowda had done so, the fault is not theirs. After a while, sick of staying alone in his cabin, he picked up his helmet, exited, and, informing Neelakanthappa that he had some work, scaled down the stairs.

He could think of nowhere to go. After he stood by the scooter for about ten minutes, he felt like going to the suburbs and lounge beneath the green shade. He recalled that only in the solitude of greenery, shade, waters, and the hill are fundamental thoughts elucidated. He recalled that it was while lolling in the forests and the hills of Khandala did the thought of relocating from Bombay to Mysore occur and concretize. Checking the petrol in his scooter, he went to a petrol bunk, fuelled, checked the air pressure in the tyres, and drove in the direction of Brindavan. Oh, the beauty of the shade, the roar of the pounding waters, and the solitude there during daytime! Parking by the restaurant thereat, he went straight to the spot where the waters gushed with deadly force and created a mysterious world of foam and sprinkle. If I dived into this! He was charmed. He reflected that despite the awareness that the force of the swirl would engulf and mangle the body within no time, with the corpse floating two furlongs downstream, one's swimming abilities of no consequence, it still irresistibly tempts one to take the plunge. Besides, the pellicle that split sunlight into its constituent colours! For quite some time, he stood watching it. When the sun scorched his skull and his head seemed to ache, he went to the restaurant, had curd-rice and coffee, then descended the steps to the garden, discerned a cool pergola, and reclined on a stone bench. Body and mind soothed. Jalaja's suggestion to confide in her anything whatsoever coasted in memory.

He became aware of the paucity that in all these years since his arrival in Mysore, he had not befriended anyone. Would have had one if I had not come in contact with this woman. He recalled someone's oracle that there shall be no other friendships for one who is deep into a love affair. How will friendship with others establish in one who is juxtaposed to the lover or to the memories of the lover in all of mind and heart and time? Even an existing friendship would wither. He reflected that such was love's monopolistic force that it drew everything towards it. Now that it is done with, he reflected, he should earn other friendships, seek membership to a club. For a while, he felt that it was the right thing to do. Then another thought popped up. Visit Jalaja this evening and ease my heart by spilling out before her all phases of my relationship with Amrita. After losing contact with her in between, friendship didn't develop later. Nevertheless, the fact that she was a childhood acquaintance and a teacher's daughter lent justification. A woman can be appropriately evaluated only by another woman. To a man, a woman shall always remain an enigma. Much like grappling in the dark. Jalaja knows about it. Else, why would she have referred to it? A few more people in the college would be aware of it too, for she had made herself available all through the interiors of my office. He reflected that many more people would know of our intimacy through the construction workers, Neelakanthappa et al. What is wrong if I confide in Jalaja? While that resolve fortified, he had a misgiving if he was, at all, able to decide on his own without confiding in others, especially in a colleague of hers? Never confided in anyone about my Bombay affair. Not even when it fell apart. Even Amrita was apprised of it at a moment of exculpation that forbade advancement without sharing the truth. Didn't share her name and address though. The decision not to confide his personal matters in Jalaja without Amrita's permission finally won out.

By day after tomorrow, I must convey a decision to her. There wasn't much to be mulled over. If this commission were to be successfully completed, three lakh in fee, and in Mysore a building that is novel in form and amenities within a year or an additional three months. Thenceforth, such proposals will particularly seek me out. Dr Ramamurthy will recommend me to those in America who intend to relocate to Bangalore and Mysore. The horizons of my fame will extend to Bangalore. An assured income of eight to ten lakh per annum. If I walk out on this, that too will be well publicized. New commissions may not come my way. I will arrive at the nadir of my profession. Compared to sketching the lines of small houses, work of this sort is satisfying and fulfilling. When both arms of the balance thus emerged clearly, feelings of renunciation soon pervaded. What of fulfilment and handsome rewards? What of obliteration in career? When one has utterly failed in life, he reflected that it would be obstinacy not to accept defeat in career.

Till evening, he lounged there. The gush of water in the distant canal, the mortal pit of the Vishveshwaraya canal to that side, and a waterfall in between seemed to palliate his nerves. But his resolve did not change. Reflecting that there was enough time on hand till the day after tomorrow, he got up and started to leave. By then, visitors to the illumination park had started pouring in. He started on his scooter without even having coffee.

It was apparent that he had utterly failed. But he could not gather the why and how of it. Should failure befall just for having been spurned by a woman with whom a bit of fun was exchanged? That question began worrying him. Reaching Mysore, he ate whatever was available in some restaurant in Ontikoppal and went home. When he lied down, sleep overcame sooner than usual. And, as on the previous night, he was awake exactly at midnight. An arm stretched out the mosquito net by default and lifted the phone. Recalling that she was not in station, he replaced it, retrieved his arm, properly tucked the tails of the mosquito net so as not to admit mosquitoes, and reclined again. Since he was very sure that sleep would not come, he did not feign any attempt at begetting it.

As undertaken, he promptly called Jalaja at 9 am on Sunday. 'Please inform Dr Ramamurthy to appoint another architect. He has to visit here for that sake. I will hand him over all the designs and plans that I have done. I have also got the license from the municipal authorities. Over twenty-five percent of the job is done by now. I haven't asked of him any fee yet. Let him appropriate it against the expenses of his imperative visit. I have really no interest in work. On his visit, I will give an undertaking in writing as per his requirements.' 'Hear me … ' Jalaja countered. He cut her short, 'No more of this matter. I have really lost interest in work. I will meet you sometime.'

After having said so, he felt a sense of release and, in a greater measure, vanity too. Work held no meaning. Neither did staying away from it. No other resort seemed to be in sight. No enthusiasm to shave or bathe. He kept deferring breakfast by the hour – no urgency – and by 2, his body complained of tiredness. He drove his scooter and had lunch. He felt like going to Brindavan like yesterday and recline in the green shade, hearing the roar of the waters. But he recalled that tourists would start pouring in from noon. He found it difficult to decide where else to go. He returned home and lied down. Got some sleep. At 5, he went to Kukkarahalli Lake on foot, lounged on the bund for about two hours, walked into the town, supped, and returned home in an auto. By 10, he felt drowsy. As he slipped into sleep, well aware that he would be awake a little after midnight, a vague suggestion appealed to him that there probably was nothing else causative of his lack of professional interest other than just his mind's desire to unwind. By then, sleep overcame him.

He was awaken by the ringing of the phone. He picked it up in a flash, sticking his hand out the net. Even before he picked it, his intuition told him that it was she. But the moment he brought it to his ear, connection severed. He was very disappointed. Wrong call. Somebody's call to some number has reached here, he reflected, else I would have got some more sleep. Damn it! One of those demerits of the telephone facility. He tried to sleep again. Quarter past midnight. Is the mind discerning to unwind or has professional interest dwindled owing to my new-found feelings that there is no meaning to life? Surfaced again the poser that preceded the onset of sleep. It wasn't a new maxim though. While he recalled that it was just a variance of the feelings that had been ailing him for a few months now, he felt sure that this was no wrong call by someone some place. It was *her* call. She had dialled and, by the time I picked up, she changed her mind. Reflecting that her mind was in a state of turmoil, he got up, put on the light, and hurriedly dialled her number. It was engaged. He cut it and dialled again. Still engaged.

At this hour, who will she be calling? Who will call her? Getting up, he dressed, put on the shoes, picked up the helmet, locked the main door, and started on his scooter. A thought struck him – if, in case, her husband or someone else from her native place was visiting, and if, at this midnight hour, if he caused the gates to squeak or the dogs to bark, or if he sent wrong feelers by choosing to go over the gate and ring the doorbell? Nah! He was sure that she either was on her bed with the revolver in hand or the car would be scaling the hill. He drove speedily. When he approached her house, he slowed down but did not stop. Everything seemed calm. Accelerating, he drove in the direction of the hill. He recalled that he had never driven at this speed and felt that it was breakneck. But anxious that if he delayed any, it would be disastrous, he accelerated further when he hit the gradient. A little later, it was the hill proper, and the road clave through the rocks. The next curve took him higher and the one after that brought him to the ridge of the ravine to the left. In the distance, yes, the red dots of the rear lamps glowed from the light of the scooter's headlight. He urged the throttle some more, disappointed at the limitations of the scooter's acceleration. He was confident that she would have noticed the light in the darkness, that she would have recognized the sound as a scooter's and would have understood that it was me. He pushed the engine to its limits. The red dots gradually increased in size and the faded cream colour of the car came in view. *The* number ! She is seated at the steering. She has chosen not to put on the headlights, for she would then be recognizable from behind. Driving up and halting by her window, he killed the engine to cut off the sound and asked, panting, 'Why did you cut the call? And later keep the receiver off the cradle?' She did not turn towards him. Even in the dark, he could perceive that her sight was rooted in the yonder ridge and the ravine to the left. 'Why did you cut the call? Answer me.' Extending his arm inside the window, he held the back of her head and turned it towards him.

'So that you come running like a mad one. Why did you come here? Answer me,' inflamed, she shrieked. Even before he replied, she yelled again, 'I did not call anyone. Another of your girlfriends would have called. Instead of going there, why did you come here, like my karma of a previous birth?'

'I will tell you why I came. It is not proper to hold discussions here. Let's go to your house or mine. I will explain everything there,' he said calmly.

'I won't go anywhere. You say it right here.' She freed her head from his slackened hand and looked the other way.

'This is not a place for conversation.'

'Herein should be done what is appropriate for this location. You leave. I will commit it.'

'I am here to prevent just that.'

She turned towards him and cursed him in choice language. 'An irritant. Impeder. Sinner. My karma. You are a geek that is born to hinder my every move.'

For two minutes, he kept mum. The susurration of the wind that sheared past the foot of the hill was suggestive of the intensity of stillness. 'Reverse the car,' he commanded. Then he added, 'Come straight to my house.'

'Your house, *your* house! Is my house not yours?' her voice was even more exasperating.

'The children would be home. We would find it difficult to discuss,' he clarified.

'If that were the reason, you should have said Jayalakshmipuram house or Lalitamahal house. This is the second time you have differentiated *your house* from *mine*. I very well remember,' she said in triumph of raising a crucial point.

'Sorry, head for the Jayalakshmipuram house.'

'I need fear no kid. Let's go here,' she gunned the car. He got out of her path and waited, while she drove further till she found a wide patch for reversing. He followed her. Opening the garage door and parking her car in, she said, 'Park your scooter inside. By the time we are finished with our discussion, it will be dawn. You can then sleep some.' He complied without demur.

Inside the house, she gave him his dhoti. She closed the door and partially bolted it from outside so that they would be alerted if the children came out. Sitting beside him on the old cane sofa in the guest room and holding his hand, she said in cadence, 'I will get through with this preamble. Not in apology. Apology makes sense if I ensured that I would not commit a misdeed again. Such undertaking is indecorous of me. As to what happened that day, I could gather only after you left. I was biting into your shoulder. Unable to bear the pain, you impeded my calf with your leg to free yourself. Your shoes were on. Considering my state then, could all these subtleties have appealed to me? I hit you with slippers. Thirteen times. My memory will be alert even when my senses are wrecked. Know what mistake you committed that day? Let's see if you can decipher.'

'Yielding my mind to anger and battering you.'

'No. Rather relenting on your nerve and having checked yourself halfway through. Having started delivering the blows, you should have gone through it till I capitulated. I wouldn't have died. It is not in my good fortune to die from your blows. My fate, rather, is to die by shooting myself. Tell me, why you relented halfway through?' she awaited his reply. After a while, she continued, 'You had to cede, for you resorted to a method not characteristic of you. Bestial conduct is not typical of my kiddie. It is default in me,' she interleaved the fingers of his left hand with those of her right hand and gripped them firmly. She then placed her head on his chest and closed her eyes. With his right hand, he held her head in a hug. Both were one with silence.

His recent apprehensions as to 'the meaning of life' completely cleared of his conscious. He asked, 'What did you do after I left?'

'What I did after you left?' Recalling, she was introspect for about a minute. 'I haven't told you the situation before you arrived. Unaware of that background, how can you understand what I did later? Wait till I tell you. Have you had food? Looking at you, one would think that you have been consuming nutritious food three times a day,' she said, stroking his clavicle.

'You seem to be having it six times a day,' he brought smile to his face.

'Wait, let me bring something to eat. We need strength to speak.' She left for the kitchen. In a short while, she was back holding a tray filled with a dozen oranges, biscuits, two sliced apples, two big glasses of Bournvita, and drinking water. He went to the lounge and brought the teapoy. Sitting beside him as before and feeding him and herself two biscuits and two slices of apple each, she related in detail the aftermath of her aunt's visit. By the time they polished off their cocoa drink, she had related about her aunt's contrivance at winning over the minds of the children, quitting her job and staying indoors with a view to insulate their minds against such contriving, her strategy of packing off the aunt the very next day, and the sermon of the aunt that night on the eve of her departure.

'You shouldn't have resigned just because of the principal's tirade. You could have applied for sick leave for two more days. You acted rashly. It is not a question of income alone. I told you the other day that it was a means of keeping a part of your mind engaged.'

'Why should the college be engaging it? I vacated that section of my mind so that that too would be imbued by you.' Suddenly switching to an exultant mood, she chuckled and added, 'If this geek be away in college four hours a day, you would be rid of the annoyance to that extent at least. Is that not your intent?' Landing a feigned slap on his cheek, she continued, 'To tell you the truth, it was not possible for me to conduct the classes with utmost interest. I was not inclined to do a second-rate job and still draw salary. Else, do you think that I am not smart enough to counter that principal?'

He felt that this explanation was more close to the truth. She has lost interest in work. Though he felt that his state was similar too, he did not disclose the fact of shelving Dr Ramamurthy's commission. 'What happened next?' he asked.

'After aunt left, know how sullen I was? That's why I didn't even call you. I was under the influence of her words. A state of believing something to be true that was infallibly false. That day when you were here, my kiddie, I meted out untold torture on you. Have sinned much. Of them, will you pardon one great sin? If you say that you have, it will then be easier for me to go on,' she held his face in her palms and, looking in it, said, 'That afternoon, you came empty-bellied. That I fought with you is normal alright. But I sent you back without feeding you. You have pardoned me. But God won't. My conscience never will.'

He quickly cupped her mouth with his palms, 'Between me and you, there should never be any room for apology and pardon. Tell me what happened later.'

'Okay, I won't seek pardon. But I have lost my authority to consider you my kiddie. Beating and scolding aside, what sort of a mother is she who packs off a kid unmindful of its hunger? How then can I call you *kiddie*?' she began sobbing.

Muted, he just kept watching her face that was soaked in tears. He couldn't think of any words of solace to match the intense feelings. After a while, he cupped her face, wiped her tears, and said, 'Tell me what transpired later.'

'Next ...' recalling, she began relating protractedly, 'there's an adage that is prevalent in all countryside – *The eyes of the butcher are set on the heifer*. Didn't I so vent all my ire on you! My mind cleared later. I very well knew that this aunt was a great actor, a great liar. I resolved to ensure the veracity of her every utterance. Hadn't she told me that her daughter Leela was not happy, that her husband was an alcoholic, that he was on intimate terms with his secretary, and that she had saved me from such suffering by giving me away in marriage not to an alien but to her brother? I visited Chandrakala, Leela's close friend. Guilt surfaced on her face. She wouldn't talk to me properly. Reassuring her and without holding her at fault, I enquired about Leela casually. How was she? How was her husband's business? She began singing about her friend's good fortune. He had given his wife a new diamond necklace recently. Every summer, he takes her to hill stations. Often they visit his in-laws, that is, the estate of aunty. Last month, they toured Kashmir. She has sent photos taken at Kashmir to Chandrakala, which she showed me. I could notice intimacy on their faces. I got to know that at the very foundation of aunt's words was deception. I had no doubt that the aunt had arrived in Chandrakala's house a day earlier and had chosen the afternoon hours of the next day to visit me. There was really no need to ensure that by investigation. You and I hardly go out together. Almost nil. It is you who comes over here. Who would report this to aunt? I suspected that it was Chandrakala. How to probe this? I continued to chat with her cordially for some more time with a view to earn her goodwill. On my way home, I guessed that she would be in touch with my sons whenever they accompanied her daughter to her house, and at such times she would subtly quiz them now and then and gather all information. When we went to Bangalore, I had left the children in the custody of Susheelamma. She has then enquired them about me. They said that I was in Bangalore on examination work. She called the college to find out. Learning that in such an event, I should have been marked as "on official duty", but I was marked as being "on casual leave", she would have inferred that the Bangalore crap held no credence. She would then have called your office and discovered that you too were away in Bangalore for three days. A sly one, Chandrakala would do all this. My doubts were confirmed when, on returning home, I took my young one alone to the backyard and cajoled him. She would often ask of them such questions like – How's mother? Does uncle keep visiting? Do they know what time mom's college winds up for the day? She had, in fact, enquired about my Bangalore visit for examination work. I needed no more proof. She hadn't seen me on the eve of my Bangalore visit. Susheelamma was the one who saw me daily. I began to feel that it was possible for a shrewd woman to guess that I was pregnant by just one look at me. Could

Susheelamma have so inferred and discussed it with Chandrakala? When I returned from Bangalore, would she have noticed some variation on my face and reported that too to Chandrakala? No way of deciphering it. As far as I know, Susheelamma is a decent lady. But how can I know her inner mind? Aunt had done her homework well before visiting here and, on arrival here, has chipped in all her acumen while she debated with me. Without directly accusing me of anything, at the same time alluding that she knew everything, assuring that she would divulge nothing of it to my husband ... kudos aunty! I appreciated her for once. In those two days, she was also successful in distancing my children from me and drawing them towards herself and their father. All week, I kept ruminating on this. Should I keep on countering her at her plane by devising similar lies and manoeuvres? Or, should I ward her off in one stroke? In what way can I keep her at bay? Immersed in that thought, I decided that I should start the counter-attack from the very root of her deceit. Not just start, but categorically put an end to it all. Tell me what I would have done,' she began peeling one of the many Yemmedoddi oranges from the tray. 'Could I afford to stock these many fruits at home? Now my pantry has quite some stock. Can you guess how?' she looked at him. He could get nothing of it. She said, 'I will give you some more time. Think it over.'

He began thinking. 'Did you get in touch with your friend's father and sue your aunt?' he asked.

'Somu, you are a smart one. That day when you gave that suggestion, I went wild at you. Later, I felt that it was the right thing to do. Veerappa Gowda had earlier suggested that this called for a plaint. Taking the children along, I drove the car myself to the Jenkal Estate via Sakleshpur. Shveta is now in the USA. Her husband has a medical practice there. She is their only daughter. Seeing me, they were thrilled as if they saw their own daughter. After exchanging pleasantries and enquiring about Shveta, I informed them of my decision to sue my aunt to avenge the injustice perpetrated on me. I requested him to guide me, as I was not conversant with legal matters. Mr Gowda said, "Let me take you to the lawyer Malali Venkateshaiah. He is from our Sakleshpur and has his practice at Hassan. A lion of a lawyer he is. His fee is on the higher side. But he is not the type that drools after the carrot proffered by the defendants. He is rather faithful as to shove with the boot of his left foot even crore rupees that might be offered in inducement." I left the children with Mangalamma and went with Veerappa Gowda to Hassan. We met the lawyer. He said, 'Any more delay in taking legal action would have rendered the suit barred by time. Now we can bring about a plaint. Before that, you have to get me all necessary documents.' He sent along an assistant of his. We went to the sub-registrar's office in Sakleshpur to procure copies of the sale deeds of the estates that aunt had bought for her sons. It took all of three days. We then went to Tallam Venkataramana Shetty's shop in Hassan. At first, they were discreet. "A transaction of yore! We don't recollect." Veerappa Gowda threatened them, "Look, this is a matter of a suit in a court of law. You will be required to testify as witness." They then raked the old account books and evidenced that Mrs Jayalakshmi of Soogoor Estate had totally bought eight kilos of gold. Details of prevalent rates were also made available. The details of expenses of Leela's wedding, I was well aware of myself. The lawyer opined that all these could be bared in the cross-examination. He said that he would serve legal notice to the defendants and dismissed us. I was Gowdas' guest for five days. Later, I went to my estate with my sons, reflecting that when I was thereabouts, I rather pay a visit to verify accounts and also put the manager and others on tenterhooks. After two days' stay there, I returned to Mysore. I also reflected, why don't I stay back at the estate? What did Mysore hold out for me? Get it?' She saw him in the face.

He throated comprehension.

'Look, when I am overwhelmed with void, I may blurt out anything, scoff at you, swear and pledge solemnly, punch or slap you. None of it holds water. But you are not one that speaks without giving it forethought. And neither do you forget what you have uttered. How can I gather courage to speak to you, you who left the other day declaring that you would never step in this house again? I had resigned my job. You averred that you would never step in here again. Why should I continue to stay in Mysore? If I relocated to the estate, I would be engaged for a good part of the day, could even plug some pilferage. But it was impossible for me to leave Mysore. Know why? Guess.'

He thought over. Nothing crossed his mind. 'Nothing strikes,' he said.

'Hey, you are headlong. You are fond of being flattered. I stayed back with the faith that you shall come some day. If I vacated this place, there would be no prospect of meeting you. Know how many times I desired to call you? But fearing your rebuke, I would replace the receiver. Today, the sentinel informed that there was a call one midnight, and the caller promised to call back after *madam* returned, but did not disclose his name. Who else? I understood it was you. But by then, I was consumed by emptiness. It was 11 am when I arrived here. He reported this at 11:30.

'I had to pay a visit to collate more information for the plaint, and this time went alone. I was bored of driving the car. While returning by bus, I was already engulfed by feelings of void. I desired to die. If I saw an oncoming bus or truck, I aspired to come under its wheels and get reduced to pulp! Stayed with those feelings all afternoon – the allure of death! It is normal for me to get those feelings at late evenings. It gets intense late into the night when silence and inertia pervade everywhere. Today, I should have pulled the trigger. But I developed a desire to call you and hear your voice. Be it known that if I had not got the message that you had called one midnight, I would not have had the courage to call you. Hence I beg of you. I may order you out, may ask you to get lost, may punch you, may call it quits, but you should never order me out, should never walk off, should never declare that you and I share no relationship, that the relationship stands annulled, or that it has ended. Your words send a chill down my spine.'

His mind brimmed and got heavy. Holding her hand firmly, he said, 'Never will I say that again.'

'Clever one,' she pricked him. 'Never will utter it, but will stash it away in mind. Is that not what you mean?'

'Just stop distorting the meaning of everything. This time, why did you go alone?' he pulled the conversation back to the main point.

'Why unnecessarily subject the children to the travails of journey? Besides, they would miss their classes. I had lodged them with Susheelamma. One more matter. Veerappa Gowda's wife Mangalamma is a very compassionate woman, unaffected compassion without any trace of pretence. During my earlier visit, when I had left the children in her custody and was moving about with Mr Gowda in pursuit of the plaint, they got acclimatized to her. Their faces would bloom by the very mention of Mangalajji's name. Vikas once asked her why mom was moving about with grandpa. Vijai was also there when he asked that. Mangalamma clearly explained to them that their grandma had deceived them of the income from the estate and hence their mom was doing the rounds to the court to recover those monies. Vijai was very intimate with his grandmother. At first, he wouldn't believe. He sought clarification from me. Why should I beat around the bush? Recalling that she had charmed the children to devise a plot to trounce me, I answered in the affirmative. I also informed them that she had arrived one day earlier and stayed at Chandrakala's, but didn't disclose it. My mind pricked that to fill the children with these matters was to belittle myself. Nevertheless, I decided that it was entirely proper to keep them informed. So, on the eve of my latest tour, I cautioned them,

"Look guys, you should never go to Chandrakala aunty's house. She will ask about my tour and engagements. If you give out the facts, we will be let-down." I also conveyed to Susheelamma that I did not take a liking to my children getting in touch with that woman. I requested her to kindly exercise some caution in that matter.'

'Good. What about the suit? Have legal notices been served? Any response from them?' he enquired.

'I will tell you. My advocate is meticulous about every aspect. His standpoint is that legal proceedings should not be initiated unless we have all the documents ready and are thoroughly prepared, that we should abstain from blabbing even. Four days back, his assistant called and said, "Madam, please pay a visit. We may have to go to Tumkur. Please make yourself available for a couple of days." Without taking the children, I went alone to Hassan by bus. Aunt had got her brother an enrolment for an engineering degree at Tumkur. We had to probe into those details. Shivaramaiah is a wily one that is capable of milching information at the clerical level by greasing their palms. I was asked to accompany him just in case it necessitated deliberations with higher bureaucracy. Twenty thousand in donation was paid by demand draft in State Bank. One thousand three hundred plus in admission fee. We could get the numbers of the receipts. Ranganath stayed at a hostel. We looked for a bank nearest to the hostel back then, and enquired if there was an account in his name in their books. They had. And remittances flowed into it frequently from a bank in Sakleshpur. We recorded all the details. Returning via Hassan to Sakleshpur, we enquired with a clerk of the State Bank. The remittances were from none other than aunt's account. All transactions of my estate too were routed through that account. Shivaramaiah went through all the entries right from the date of opening the account till the estate was handed over to me. The dates of withdrawal of monies from this account clearly corresponded with those of purchase of the new estates. We returned to Hassan. I stayed at a hotel. In the evening, we met the lawyer and submitted the findings to him.

'By then, he had thoroughly verified the documents pertaining to the bank loan. He said, "Not just against your aunt and her children, we should sue even the bank. You being the title-holder to the estate, how did they disburse loan to your aunt without your consent? They have even sanctioned loan after you attained majority. This would not be possible without the corrupt bank manager being a party to it. You stop paying interest to the bank right away. I will cause the bank to puke whatever you have remitted, including interest. You have no more work here except making yourself available whenever I ask you to. Consider yourselves entitled to those two estates. You know, court proceedings are time-consuming. I will add one more contention – till this suit is decreed, the management of the two estates be vested at the hands of a manager appointed by the court, the defendants are not to stay there, the honourable judge to decide on the amount of monthly sustenance to the families till such time, and their right to the bank accounts be frozen in the meanwhile. We are entitled to all the profits that have accrued on those estates right from the day they were bought. I relate all this, for you should be aware of your plaint. Before you leave, sign here." He took one more signature of mine.

'When I started to leave, he said, "In this case, you will spend money. I will expend my brains. If we win, you will get thirty or forty lakh, and for me a sense of accomplishment. Win or lose, you will shell out my fee. Yet, I have to tell you this. In such family disputes, the defendants may threaten you of dire consequences, may beg at your feet, may bring pressure on you through mediators, or may pitch in God and divinity for effect. You should not let yourself be swayed by all that crap. If you relent and ask me to rescind on the case halfway through, for you have secretly arrived at a compromise, what will become of my status after having thoroughly gone through this much groundwork? Sue and see through till victory. Shouldn't rest even if it calls for moving on from district court to high court to Supreme Court. After victory, if you are moved by empathy, you can do a Bahubali act by donating the entire booty to your kin. But I will not take kindly to it if you backtrack beforehand. Malali Venkateshaiah is not a hunter dog that can be commanded to charge and be then held back by blowing a whistle. You may think it over again." On taking note of the bank transaction, I was seething at my aunt. I said, "Sir, I won't waver. I will not relent even if we have to approach the Supreme Court."

'Somu, you must meet Malali Venkateshaiah. A lion of a man he is. Will not rest until he has destroyed the opponent. I visualized his intent of meting out the same treatment to me if I checked him from doing that. Leaving, I rewarded Shivaramaiah with one thousand rupees for the pains he took for my sake, promised to recompense him in future too, returned to my hotel room, and slept. The lawyer's instruction to me to abstain from paying interest to the bank only meant an extra three and a half lakh liquidity. I had drawn on the estate maintenance imprest for incurring litigation expenses, and I felt relieved that my wallet crunched no more.

'I was awake at 3 am. In all, I had slept for four and a half hours. Even as I awoke, I was on the brink of feelings of void. Nothing new to me! I just lay. At dawn, I got up, bathed, had breakfast of two idlis and coffee, went to the bus stand, boarded the 8 am bus, and, when the bus moved and gained speed, I even got to know the genesis of the feelings of void. Somu, tell me the truth. Would you check yourself from mistaking me? If I confide in you everything that comes to my mind, I feel relieved,' she looked at him.

'Don't conceal anything. Tell me,' he reassured her.

'You may feel hurt.'

'Nah.'

'It would be untruth to deny before getting to know the facts. Rather, tell the truth that you would still grin and bear,' she growled at him.

'Okay, I will withstand whatever pain is caused. Tell me. And don't leave out anything,' he compelled her suavely.

'Ranganath incurred the expenses for his education from the money purloined from my estate and eventually landed up with a profitable career. You can't be very sure that only his sister was interested in my wealth that would accrue from our marriage, not he. Sister and brother share the same blood. Later, playing in tune with his sister's conniving, he impregnated me. Yet, I began to feel that he was after all my husband, the one who tied the hallowed connubial string to my neck. I'm mother to the children that he has sired and am in love with those children. I chastised myself for having embarked on the task of exposing the funding of his academics and pitting him against the talons of Malali Venkateshaiah. What sort of a femme was I! Not just compassion, I reflected that I was in love with him, am in love with him involuntarily. When the bus stopped at Holénarasipura, I had a compulsion to alight, return to Hassan, and inform the lawyer accordingly. Now tell me, are you not pained by this?' she looked at him.

Gathering that if he denied, not only would it be false, it would readily appeal to her investigating eyes, he said, 'I appreciate the nuances of your feelings nevertheless.'

'Somu,' she barked at him. 'Don't make a smart remark that sidelines the question. Your remark only means that you don't love me.' He was confounded. She then asked, 'Just tell me if what I said didn't cause jealousy in you.'

'It did,' as he said this, he cringed.

'Why cringe? You should be straightforward as to say, "You! You are mine. If you say that you love someone else, I will cut you up." Relenting your egotism, you have conceded that you did feel jealous. That's enough for now,' she neared him, put her arms around his neck, and planted an intensely conductive kiss on his lips. His response matched her feelings. Confidence descended on him that she was his, and he felt that there should be no room for such belittling feelings as jealousy.

She resumed her reporting, 'But I did not alight. Couldn't. The bus resumed its onward journey. I felt that I had no liberty to alight or to reverse the direction of the drive. The emptiness got intense. If the speeding bus hit a tree or fell into a gorge and I died on the spot, how nice! I would eye every other roadside tree and eagerly anticipate that the bus would crash against it. When, a little before K.R. Nagar, the bridge over the river Kaveri approached, I got eager again that the bridge would give away and the bus would drown in the water. Alas, nothing happened! Isn't the sinner long-lived? In retrospect, now I feel ashamed that in my eagerness to wish for my death, I ignored the lives of the fifty other people in the bus. Even after reaching Mysore, the feelings of void did not abate. They, in fact, got intense. After giving supper to the children and putting them to sleep, I started feeling that this was truly the last day of my life. If you had not called that night, if the sentinel hadn't reported it to me soon after my arrival, if you had not come running on properly interpreting my call, by now,' she consulted her watch, 'it would have been five hours since the consummation of my suicide. In five hours, how much would the essence, the ghost or whatever you call it, have traversed? They have computed the speed of light to be one lakh eighty six thousand miles per sec. What is the speed of the ghost?' She looked at his face. After a while, she said, 'Looking at you, I get the feeling that you consider this question to be senseless. But it holds sense for me. Well. Though I cause you untold torture and denigrate you much, why do you dote on me? Why did you rush to save me? Don't presume that I don't take kindly to your act of saving me. But I also get furious that you impede my death. Tell me, why do you love me so much? Must tell.' She squeezed his shoulders and tugged at him like an obstinate five-year-old girl.

He rummaged within himself. He felt it impossible to tender a reply that was acceptable to her. He simply said, 'You will rebuff whatever I say. Will ruthlessly lob it. Hence, I won't say anything.'

'Tell, man. Swear on me if you don't. I may not believe it. May rebuff it. But know how pleasant it will be to hear from you the words "I can't live without you, you are my life"? I think of staying alive just to hear such words. If I were dead, could I get to hear such sweet, though false, words?' While she said this, she kept anticipating and observing his efforts at containing the pain and anger induced. Presently, the crows began cawing. Outside the window, it had dawned quite some. She got up and tugged at him by his arm, 'Come on. Get some sleep. After you have retired, I will properly tuck the mosquito net and retire myself. Goodnight.'

~

He now thought of his life as purposeful, for the other day, endorsing his intuition that it was her call, he had driven up to the ledge and brought her back from the brink of death. He began feeling that if he rid her of the compulsion to commit suicide by which she was assailed frequently, he would be successful in life. Else, he reflected, he would be frustrated too. Now, it clearly appealed to him that zest and apathy in his life were equally entirely dependent on her. It was clear that other than understanding her, there remained no sensible endeavour in his life. But how to instil in her the love for life? At times, she will be of very pleasant disposition. She will especially buoy me on ripples of fondness. But, all of a sudden, she will turn hostile, austere. She will coin choice expletives, devise novel methods of torturing, and will experiment them on me.

Once, she said, 'Somu, when I am flooded by feelings of void, I will hate you more than I do anyone else in this world. Do you know that?' He was taken aback. He knew that she would go wild at him more than she would on anyone else. But anger is one thing, hatred is another. She even revealed the reason, 'If you weren't in my life, pulling the trigger and killing myself would have been unfussy. It would have been accomplished some two years back. When I reach the intense state of self-destruction, you invariably come to my mind. I get anxious as to who would tend you in my absence. Or I would develop a desire to inform you and take leave of you before ending myself. The disillusionment that my next step would be thwarted by this very anxiety and desire brings about fury and consequently hatred towards you. Hatred to the extent of shooting you, so that I would then be a liberated one and can die unobstructed! You pest, why did you get a phone connection at your residence? That makes it impossible for me to resist a compulsion to call you to bid adieu. If I do call, you will wind that cable around my heart and pull me towards you.' He felt that he understood her mind very clearly. Moved by empathy, he kept observing her face. 'The feelings of void that pervade me will be so venomous as to induce me to destroy anything or anyone that impedes its progress. The devastation is similar to the explosion of a nuclear bomb. Thus afflicted, I may not hesitate to point the revolver at you and jerk the trigger. Know what idea the mind pursues? If I kill you, it would be impossible for me to stay alive even for a moment. It would then be just a split second's job to shoot myself, for the obstruction would have been cleared from my path. I get this thought very many times. Somu, my kiddie, now when my mind is normal, I shudder at that thought. When I am assailed by void and am armed, please do not accost me. I will not be aware what my mind prompts me to do.' His heart swelled. He felt elated that he was the force that stood between her and her death. The next words flashed in him naturally and he said, 'So, it is in this state that you mouth the words *I don't love you one bit. That you do is just an illusion*?' When she said, 'You smarty! You can understand everything.' Besides appreciation, a sense of blest was explicit in her face. An idea flashed in his mind. He spilled it immediately. 'Amu, why don't you consult a psychiatrist? Let me enquire. Or I will make enquiries in Bangalore and get an appointment.' Antipathy surfaced on her face. She looked at him. In that sight, he could see that she was moving away from him further and further. In a short while, she became so mute that he felt she was so far away as to be nowhere in the vicinity. The glow in the sight waned too and finally petered out. 'Why? What is objectionable about it? Just like bodily illness, so is mental ... ' She cut him short and retorted in slander, 'You are fed up with this geek. You want to transfer it to a psychiatrist and be relieved. Right?' Acclimatized to the prick and tenor of her words by now, he said calmly, 'The constitution of the inner mind is better understood by them than us ... ' She cut in again, 'I know better than them. I know something else. That you are a coward, a chicken, one that feigns love. I will be fine the day when real love blossoms in you. And don't presume that I haven't consulted a psychiatrist.' 'What did he opine?' he enquired eagerly. 'He counselled that I would be alright if I took my mind off that sybarite who was feigning love,' she looked solemn as she said it. 'Never ever mention a psychiatrist. Get it?' she said as if in amnesty.

Arriving at noon, he would stay there till about 4. He would consider it his good luck if, in a week, she was amiable on one or two days out of six. He could just not fancy at what juncture she would suddenly flare up, would misinterpret what words, and hurl despicable accusations at him. After lunch, clearing the table and consigning the plates and glasses to the sink, she would mop the tabletop as he stood close by. On one such occasion, she said, 'Are you not ashamed of standing like an overseer and getting all the work done by me?' He felt disgraced. He contained it though. The next day, he took precedence in clearing the dining table. She was quick to say, 'So, are such acts your strategies of thawing my mind?' He did not speak. 'Silence is assent. Right?' He still didn't speak. 'Why this disregard? Isn't it your contention that I don't merit a reply?'

she asked, physically intercepting him, thereby suggesting that he could not escape without replying. He could truly not think of an answer. He said, 'Many a time, I can't think of anything to say. I really am not as intelligent as you think I am.' 'Don't you mean that had you been intelligent, you would not have got yourself into this trap?' He saw her in the face. Extending his arms, he held her shoulders and embraced her. 'I need none's mercy.' She wriggled free of him. Such events would occur at least five of the six days he visited her. Once the situation turned sour, it would not clear up till he exited. After departing, the intensity of the after-effects would be more on him. Though he would tell himself that her mind was torn asunder by contradiction, that it was ailing, wherefore he was not to let himself afflicted but to remain composed, the pain within would nevertheless pique. He would mollify himself by killing time alone on the bund of the Karanji Lake or in the park adjacent to the Hardinge Circle. At 11 pm usually, he would call her. Occasionally, she would reply cheerfully. She would amuse and josh him. But he could never imagine when such pleasant mood would morph to biting bitterness. But having resolved to stay calm whatever the degree of her sarcasm and anger, he would remain stoic. 'In spite of my expletives, you are not angered! Aren't my words blasé to you?' she would cavil him. At times, immediately on receiving his call, she would launch her tirade. 'Haven't you called now to check if I was dead? To verify whether I simply threaten to die or have lived up to my pledge?' Such talks through half an hour, three-fourths an hour, one full hour, or one and a half hours, scything the meat of life! On her part, she would not end the call. He would fear that she would be consumed with void if he chose to terminate it. If the call got disconnected in between, it was imperative on him to dial again. If he delayed an extra moment, she would call and accuse him, 'Did you cut the line to ward off this evil? Tell me the truth. You may swear by God in whom you don't believe.' Her anger intensifying, if at times she bangs the receiver, he would call two minutes later and wheedle her, 'Amu, I inadvertently commit very many mistakes. Now too, I have. Won't you pardon me?' The phone call would go on unto the small hours. When he retired after that, he would not get sleep. Many a time, being in an interim state that wasn't sleep, reverie, or quiescence, he would suffer from pain caused by the shredding of the canvas of his mind by the talons of a bird of prey. Descending at some indistinct hour, sleep would all through be characterized by tides of pain, unease, and anxiety. He would feel drained, disoriented, and drowsy and would keep yawning when he woke up the next morning.

When he arrived in office at 10 am, an envelope printed 'Shah and Shekhar' awaited him. Immediately on seeing it, he felt glad for having received a letter from a friend after long. Well, he too had not written to Naveen in a long time. He recalled the proverb that the friendships of one who was deep into the quagmire of love fell out like ninepins. Reflecting that his was the deepest of quagmires, he tore open the envelope. Naveen had written in his suave style. The industrial structure at Navasari was nearing completion. It should have been done some time back. Scarcity of cement caused some delay. Now he had landed new commissions – a textile mill and two other apartments in Bombay. If his hands would be strengthened by the presence of the likes of me, he would assume a few more commissions, etc. After cataloguing his professional advancements, he had written that the money loaned to me for acquiring the office premises was from Induben's natal estate. Now she intends to assist a sibling in trouble. All the same, she was sensitive enough not to ask me to repay it, as it might inconvenience me. She was aware that if the amount would have been mobilized, I would not have stayed from repaying it. He had ended it with a reference to Digant reminiscing 'Shekhar uncle', and an objection to his abstinence from visiting Bombay.

On reading the last matter, Somashekhar felt heavy in his heart. The matter of the loan had stayed off his mind. He would repay it surely, and there was justification for the delay that he would be paying interest. Now that Induben was projected, he began wondering if, in fact, the money was Induben's or Naveen's. In half an hour, everything became clear. As far as friendship was concerned, Naveen was a dear. When it came to dealings, he was a contractual party. He would not mix up the roles. By now, I should have remitted the interest and a third or at least a fourth of the principal amount. Had I mobilized properly, I could have repaid most or all of it by now. A politic that Naveen is, he has expected this. It was clear that this was the *first reminder*. What to reply? He applied his mind for one full hour. Shall I write that I have trouble paying him right now and he is to pay her on my behalf? He felt inhibited. It was getting to be noon. Climbing down the stairs, he headed to Amrita's house. Though there was no work, Neelakanthappa would be present in the office.

That day, Amrita was in a depressing mood. On such days, she wouldn't scoff at him. Neither would she speak. She would serve his meal silently and have hers equally quietly. Both would finish their lunch. When in that state of mind, she would wish to be left alone. Refraining from going to her bedroom, he would retire to the guest room. She would be unto herself in her bedroom. He, however, was not to depart owing to her desire for seclusion. Neither should he refrain from visiting at all. He should be in attendance, but she should be free to remain distant and aloof. It would be her prerogative to start a conversation, provided she veered to a congenial mood. Guided by the temper of her words, he would comprehend the disposition of her mind and then respond accordingly, as if nothing whatsoever had preceded. If she chose to speak jovially, he is to respond in the very same tenor and in equal measure. If he crossed the threshold even one bit and employed an affectionate word, she would bark at him, 'If I near you, do I send feelers that I am inclined to fornication and cause you to charge at me?' Or if she spoke amorously and if he gave just a plain jovial reply, she would seethe in disgrace, 'You! Aren't you indifferent as if I were a bitch that accosts over and over again shamelessly?' Notwithstanding the fact that his mind and heart were at their nadir, he would instantly respond and align himself in tandem with her mental state, at times even lying down dutifully, tempering his physical propensities.

Today as he lay, his mind was preoccupied with Naveen's letter. He thought it inapt to ask for more time. Naveen is progressing higher and higher in his career. I have bitten dust. Though the yardsticks of Bombay and Mysore are different, I have utterly failed by throwing to the winds the best of opportunities by the Mysore standards that came my way. Though I buy time, how can I repay when I am not in a state of mind to apply myself to my profession and earn a livelihood? More time only means more interest. It was a great favour that Naveen conferred on me by lending at a bank interest rate. Now, even that soft rate will be an unbearable burden. He contemplated if it were possible, even now, to evince interest in profession. Weren't it possible to have Neelakanthappa look for new jobs and bring them in? Depute him to meet with the contractors of Mysore and surrounding places, convey to them that for personal reasons I had sequestered myself, and that I was now available for any amount of work, induce him with a percentage commission... As his thought flowed thus, he reflected that it was unwise to have wrecked the nursing home commission. He recalled that he neither cared nor had the interest to get to know if Dr Ramamurthy had visited or whether he had made alternative arrangements.

At about 4 pm, he heard her take the keys to the car and the house and get ready to fetch the children. When she wore her slippers and began pacing, he got up, dressed, and left. She still was in no mood for conversation. In consonance with her mood, he exited and gunned the scooter. While he lounged on the bund of Karanji Lake, he reflected that he should be very cautious that night.

If I call, she will object to it that I disturbed her solitude. If I don't, the feelings of void will get intense and she will take hold of the revolver. He told himself that he should discern and be ready with a topic for tonight's conversation. Driving her car, by now she would have reached Susheelamma's house. Picking up her children, fuelled by the peripheral zing of her cringed mind, she would chat heartily with them. She would start by enquiring the day's proceedings at school. Returning home, she will narrate stories. She will recite from their books and explain to them. Within, she would be cringed too. Other details unfolded in his mind. After putting them to sleep, she would go static, as if her lips and mind were both sutured shut, and as if silence were her state and conduit. In this backdrop, a topic that would not incite her mind should be thought out for conversation. But the delineation of what would be instigative and what would be palliative do not readily appeal to him.

When he called her late into the night, she hurled accusations at him right away. 'Every moment your heart is wishing that if I am dead, it would be good riddance and you can rest contented. But on the outside, you are accustomed to lie that you are unable to live without me. Why this duality?' To refute it and placate her by means of cajoling, debating, and pledging, it took all of one and a half hours. Presently, he heard her yawn. She replaced the receiver only when he requested her to retire, and that he would be visiting tomorrow to resume the talk.

When he retired into the mosquito net, his mind began to think of a solution to Naveen's communiqué. By 3 am, an idea struck him. Anyway, there was no work. How about disposing of the office premises, clearing the bank loan, depositing the surplus in the bank, and live on two meals a day out of the interest earned? At once, he felt that many a burden was eased. Neelakanthappa was an honest assistant. He even thought of gifting him twenty-five thousand gratuity. Along with a succession of yawns, sleep overcame. When he woke up the next morning, acute void pervaded. To abandon an established profession, what a coward am I? He chastised himself. Getting up, he went through his morning ablutions. He was in no mood to have coffee and breakfast. He cautioned himself that if he let go of his profession, he would lose his gravitational locus. But how to arrange almost one lakh seventy-five thousand now? From whom to borrow? Who will lend? It made him once again cognizant of the fact that he had no friend other than her in this place. Neglecting his profession and landing in this situation was all because of that hook-up. Along came the memory of having borrowed from her to establish this office premise and then having repaid the same one afternoon by calling Naveen late night to get the money through telex. I probably hastened or had failed to understand her fully, but I had decided not to have monetary dealings with her. At times, he had even felt demure that she was footing his daily lunch. He began an exercise in self-analysis that if he let such thoughts rent his mind, what sort of love was his? Shall I show Naveen's letter to her? She may mobilize the monies and give it to me: 'Here, take this, remit to Bombay.' His heart unambiguously told him that she would definitely accommodate. The lawyer has advised her not to pay interest to her bank. In the coming harvest season, she will be netting three to three and a half lakh from the coffee harvest. Why not do so? After contemplating for about half an hour, he decided against it. But the whats and whys were not clear to him.

When he glanced at his watch, it was 12:05. He dialled her number. He did not volunteer to disclose if he was calling from home or office. She too didn't ask. 'Amu, I have some pressing work. You lunch. If I am done by 4, I will come over. Else, don't wait. I am taking the clients out for a treat. Okay?' He gave no room for continuance of the conversation. She did not reply immediately. He ended the call.

All through his drive to the restaurant and subsequent lunch, his mind continued to work. Can mortgage this office premise with a financier or a bank and raise loan. But how to repay it? When, during daytime, everyone is busy with one's professional tasks, I would be in her company for four hours each day. On exiting from there, my mind drained and in tatters from the onslaught, it would be impossible for me to apply myself to work. No proper sleep any night. I would be able to conduct my profession only if I completely severed my contact with her. He reflected that this wasn't a relationship that could be owned for life. By the time he finished his lunch, he sensed a suggestion to simply rid himself of it all. This was no mental affliction that could be cured. It is deteriorating by the day. True, because of me she has stayed from dying. I have saved her from death alright, but what next? Where is a haven for me? Though he knew that for love to be of a high order, it had to be non-restitutive, he felt that the practice of such an ideal was possible only by an emancipated sage. Any love between a man and a woman, intended for a protracted tenure, could be carried further only after reaching a consensus as to the mutual duties and rights, at least broadly. Wasn't the institution of marriage an established custom that fell in line with this delineation? In her relationship, there is nothing of these. I have not broached the subject of marriage. Even if I did, would it be possible to live under a single roof with someone like her? First of all, she should go into reparation. Post reparation, possibly, she would not need me at all!

Possibly, she would not need me at all! That thought made him feel empty. The question popped up that if he held no meaning in her life and was of no need to her, what significance would be his own life? A clear-cut answer emerged that his life would be meaningful if and only if he could lend meaning to her life, else it would be zilch. Lunch over, he drove straight to Brindavan. In the stillness of the afternoon, when he reclined in isolation on the same bench in the pergola he once before did, his mind cogitated calmly. Progress in career and earn four to five lakh a year. Naveen earns at least ten. Had I stayed in Bombay and slogged like him, I too would have equally prospered. But right from beginning, I was not so disposed. So I relocated to Mysore. Relocated and fell in her trap. Fell in her trap or landed an opportunity that held a great meaning? Every which way he thought it over, the feeling got denser that there remained no meaning without her. When it was dusk and a million lights came on, he got up and roamed the paths and the sub-paths of Brindavan amidst the flock of tourists. When his stomach stung, he ate tender cucumber and popcorn available nearby, and then as he kept looking at the fountain that, by turns, changed into seven colours, he reflected that with architects available by the thousands, his withdrawal would not hold up any civil engineering activity. Another – yet another – architect would be around.

Yet, when he set out to the broker's office the next morning, his mind was devastated. It was laden with feelings of defeat that he had failed in this town, and that he had acceded to failure. The broker who negotiated purchase and sale of houses and commercial structures was a professional acquaintance. When he proposed to him that he was winding up his profession and was seeking to dispose of his office premises, he felt wrung within.

~

At about 10 one morning, Amrita was washing her car. Puttamma was busy with her cooking. Mahadevamma was washing clothes on the stone slab in the backyard. The dogs freed within the compound were playing about her legs even as she attended to the washing. Suddenly, there was the sound of an automobile at the gate and the dogs barked and charged. Amrita craned her neck and noticed a car halt by her gate. As she kept looking, she saw the entire family of her aunt in the car. The car was driven by Jayarama, aunt's elder son of the same age as her. Seated next to him was the younger son Krishnamurthy. In the back row were aunt, Jayarama's wife Meenakshi, Jayarama's five-year-old son, and two-year-old baby girl. Grasping that they were here on being served the legal notice, Amrita was, for a minute, nonplussed as to how she had to conduct herself presently. As she strode up to greet them, the words of Shivaramaiah, her advocate's assistant, came to her mind. 'Madam, in such litigation, the moment legal notice is served, the defendants will approach you with ... ' She recalled his exact words.

By then, though all had alighted, none had opened the gate and stepped in. She walked up, opened the gate, and greeted them as if there was no warrant for any change in her. 'Welcome, wait, let me leash the dogs.' Holding Vikrant by his collar, she consigned him to the kennel at the fore and led Vishvas to the backyard. 'Welcome, Uncle. How are you, Krishnamurthy?' She showed them to the old sofa in the lounge. She did not take even the ladies beyond the lounge. She understood that even aunt was finding it difficult to come in and enact her pretentious love. She said, 'You would have started very early. Let me ask Puttamma to prepare *uppittu*. Will you have coffee first?'

'Until we are done with the purpose of this visit, we won't even touch holy water in this house,' chieftain Jayarama growled.

'Don't you say so. Visiting the house of your sister, you shouldn't say that you won't drink water, won't eat. She, too, has two lovely kids. Shouldn't they thrive?' aunt admonished her son.

Instantly understanding that this was aunt's default modus, deciding not to give much leeway to her, she said, 'I don't believe that my kids thrive only if someone eats, or they will perish if the guest returned empty-bellied. You are here to talk business. Go ahead. As far as I am concerned, there is nothing to say. Whatever I got to say is conveyed to you in the lawyer's notice. Anything else to be told in future, he will apprise you of it in the court of law. You too. Whatever you got to say, submit the same to the court through your lawyer. The courts are there for this very purpose, of settling disputes. Let us remain cordial as hitherto.'

Jayarama said, 'Do you pose a law point? I am not a bloke that will rest even if I need to go to Supreme Court. Law points are in our favour too.'

'Okay, bro. Who can check you from going to a higher court? So, do you admit that you will lose in the lower court?' That she had incited him into a brawl, she realized anon, for Jayarama got up, hollering, 'Let it be known that I have the capability to appoint a lawyer from Bangalore who can trounce your Malali Venkateshaiah.'

Amrita expected that his next step would be to assault her. But aunt intervened and pulled him down by his arm. 'Aunty, is Chandrakala fine? Hope you have visited her before coming here,' Amrita enquired immediately. Aunt was dumbstruck. 'I will not stay here anymore. I will rather fight it out in the court.' Jayarama got up. Krishnamurthy, an eligible groom, intervened brashly. 'A woman should always heed her husband. Aren't you intent on inflicting injustice to your natal household on being so directed by a paramour! Beware, this paramour will suck you dry and hand you the begging bowl.'

Aunt leapt towards him, smacked him on the back, and said, 'A kid that you are, what you got to do with raw lies?'

Amrita kept staring at Krishnamurthy's face. Her sight stayed glued to it for quite some time. Jayarama's wife Meenakshi got up and neared her, 'Your youngest brother always behaves brashly. You can very well understand my plight on having wed your brother and obtained lease of your natal household for life. Forget them. Come, let us talk about this privately,' she took Amrita's hand and tried to lead her inside.

A confounded Amrita shook off her hand and said, 'I won't discuss with anyone. I have already said that any debate will be in court. You may leave now.' She went inside.

There were murmuring sounds among them. She could hear the mother-in-law and daughter-in-law scoff at the brothers. Yet, uncle did not utter a word. Never was he a party to any matter whatsoever. He was no dunce, but his intellect had become blunt on being wedged at the hands of this super smart aunt, wherefore he had forfeited the gumption to take the lead in any matter whatsoever. Amrita overheard her aunt prod her husband, 'Why do you sit dumb? Speak up.' He blared out, 'Can I understand a thing? Jayarama seems to have rightly said that we shall win this in the court.'

Amrita sat at the dining table. After about five minutes, her aunt arrived there. Jayarama's wife Meenakshi was on tow. Seemed like she too was adept at smart-talk. Amrita understood that without being sourced from aunt's intelligence, Krishnamurthy wouldn't have had access to information regarding paramour and the like. She said to her aunt who neared her, 'Aunty, there can be nothing that you would say in private by oozing affection. I have instituted that plaint after giving it due thought. Whatever you got to say, you can relate it in the court.' She then got up, went to her bedroom, and locked herself in. After half an hour, the barking of the dogs and the gunning of the car were heard.

~

That afternoon, Somashekhar did not turn up for lunch. By about 3 pm, a feeling of revulsion swept her regarding her relationship with him. This is truly a bestial liaison. She felt that it was incorrect to correlate this with quixotic imports of love. It could have been called true love if it were just friendship without corporeal contact, without even mutual clasping of hands and not at all contaminated by feelings engendered in converse genders. In summary, it is my perdition. I have forfeited my ethical grit and authority. She began wailing. There was no need to control the sound, for there was none in the house.

Though she was aware that the sound of the wail pervaded outdoors and encircled the house, she still but wept uncontrolled. In between, she stepped up the punishment by striking her head against the frame of the bed twice. After the cathartic cry, as she lay empty-headed, she reflected whether Krishnamurthy's accusation – though stemmed from anger caused by possible loss of estate – could be faulted. Given that Ranganath is her husband, what else should this man be called other than *a paramour*? Friend, lover, and such are the terminologies that we tend to employ. This relationship could be called nothing but adultery. She again started weeping. After it subsided, anger took over. I should not blame anyone for this. I should punish myself. Not someone else, she decided, rather I that abandoned my husband who adorned me with the hallowed connubial string in the witness of *agni*, I that made available such adorned neck to be embraced by the arms of the paramour should punish myself. Not a token punishment of striking the head against the wall, but total punishment. The revolver surfaced in memory. Instantly, she drew the chest and took it out, but just sat holding it. In a while, more acute disgust overcame. She chastised herself that the moment of pulling the trigger is yet elusive to this doomed mortal. At 5, when she went to fetch the children, the moment she saw their faces, she recalled the fact of getting pregnant by adultery, of getting it removed, and was extremely grieved so as to cry then and there. Somehow, she contained herself. Bottling up the grief, she played shuttlecock with the children, narrated tales, and wheedled them. After supper, an idea took shape in her mind. In spite of such belittling feelings, why haven't I died yet? For the sake of the children? When I am dead, my in-laws would not stay from tending and educating them. He will definitely wed again. Will he persist with the court case on behalf of the children till the estate is won over? Or will he reconcile to the fact that the earnings from bribery was more than enough? Or has my inner mind resolved not to die till she, who defrauded me, was punished by the court? When she told herself that it could probably be so, the phone rang. Quarter to midnight. Picking it up, she blabbered, 'Look sir, I am okay. Got to finish some accounting. Am busy now. Henceforth if I don't call, you too don't. I will assure you that I will not harm my life. Please.' she replaced the receiver. In a while, a thought formed. Getting up, she went to her desk in the corner and wrote a letter.

> *We may fool ourselves into christening our relationship grandiosely. But truly, this is an adulterous relationship. You are a sybarite, I am your paramour. There is no reality to the exclusion of this. This reality is the cause of my sorrow. I cannot live in peace until I wipe it out. Hence, I request you to show mercy by staying away from me. Henceforth, do not hedonistically incite me by telephoning or any way else. Goodbye.*

She inserted it into a postal envelope, sealed it, immediately exited, locked the door, and with Vikrant on tow, she trekked the little distance and dropped it into a postbox.

On returning and retiring, anger was directed at Krishnamurthy. Were his words becoming of his age? She felt that she should immediately have thrashed him with her slippers. All the same, she recalled that she had resolved not to go wild, come what may. She ratified her act of not assaulting him. While returning from here, their mother apprised them of everything. Anger now turned towards the aunt. Didn't the eldest son mention the Supreme Court? She resolved that she too would not relent until she saw to it that they have had it. By about 3, sleep overcame. He did not visit next afternoon. My letter would still not have reached. Yet, why hasn't he come? She mulled it over for about an hour. Presuming that he was busy with work, she had her lunch. By midnight, the phone rang. After allowing it to ring seven to eight times, she picked it up and blurted, 'I was asleep. I am okay. Thank you,' and replaced the receiver. It did not ring again. She reflected that it was good riddance for him and for her as well. For one who has had a few women earlier, the thrill derived from me is not consistent enough. Let him rather free himself from me now, beget another partner, and live happily. That thought still made her fidgety. He didn't visit the next afternoon either. But he called. 'I got your letter this morning. I will never do anything that will burden your mind. But you may call at any hour during the night. I will be awake. Never call any afternoon. I will not be in office. If you give me your word on one matter, I will adhere to your words.' If she asked what that matter was, conversation would be furthered. If she didn't, he won't end it. She just grunted. He said, 'You should never commit suicide. Even if you are afflicted by anguish and agony, you should stay alive. That assured, I will adhere to your every wish. I will not even telephone you.' She remained silent, then heard him replace the receiver. She got angry with herself. Who is he to ordain me not to die? She channelled her ire at him.

One week later, she felt like visiting Hassan. Shivaramaiah had informed her that he would either write to her or call her about any progress, however small, in the plaint. Yet, she got eager to go and enquire personally. Presently, she wasn't otherwise engaged too. Besides, barring the eager anticipation of emerging victorious in this plaint, there was no other ambition in life. Entrusting the children with Susheelamma, she drove her car to meet Hassan. The defendants have retained the services of a lawyer. They have blankly denied all the allegations made by her. Showing her the reply sent in by the defendant lawyer, Shivaramaiah said, 'That lawyer is a dunce. He is just wont to shout in the court proceedings than getting to know the groundwork done by the opponents and to figure out their next moves. He has written to us that his clients have not embezzled a single paisa of ours and that they had other sources of income by which to acquire those properties, not in the least aware that he is assuming the responsibility of convincing the court, with proof, as to the sources of the fat sums of money. Our victory is hundred percent certain.'

She recited in mind, 'Wait till I'll show you the powers of an adulteress.' Shivaramaiah continued, 'By now, the plaint is registered in court. The ruling judge will take all necessary steps to see that there is no delay in the proceedings. He will bark at any party resorting to delay tactics.' She felt cheery. She saw Malali Venkateshaiah, conveyed her gratitude, and, from there, went to her estate. Inspecting the account books and the farm in the company of the manager, she stayed there overnight and drove to Jenkal the next morning. She could not stay from informing them of the progress in the plaint. Mr Gowda was not in station. He had left for Chikkamagalur a little while ago. Mangalamma was available. The lady talked to her cordially alright, but Amrita had a feeling that for some reason, the good woman had espoused discontentment towards her.

She knew too that Mangalamma was not the type that would bottle up what was in her mind. However, she took precedence in asking. 'Aunty, seems like you are peeved with me for some reason. Please do tell me. I will correct myself if I am wrong.'

Mangalamma too was tongue-tied. She took her to her bedroom, shut the door, and asked, 'Is it true that you have a paramour?'

She felt struck as if by thermal radiation from fire. For a moment, her mind went blank. But the next moment, it got into business, guessing who could have apprised this woman of these matters. She said, 'Shall I tell you who has told you this, or who has anonymously propagated these words to fall on your ears?'

'A smart one, you can easily guess that it is your aunt,' Mangalamma minced no words.

'Was she here herself?'

'The entire family was here to see my husband. They asked him to mediate a compromise and offered five lakh gratis. They have come to know that it was my husband who facilitated raking old records at Sakleshpur. "I have nothing to do with it. I had started for Sakleshpur one day when your girl visited and said that she had some work in the sub-registrar's office there and requested if I would help her out as she was not conversant with the procedures. After all, she was our daughter's buddy. I took her along, consenting to introduce her to the personnel there. I don't know what happened thereafter," he washed his hands off. Your aunt led me into this very room and related those facts.'

'Exactly what were her words?'

'She said, "She has also questioned the source of funds for the academics of her husband. Would a pious wife do so? The root cause of all these is that she has a paramour. He is inciting her to do so. Falling prey to him, she has abandoned her husband. If you can put her back on track, you will be a blessed one."'

She said immediately, 'You very well know that they have coined this smart-talk after I filed a suit against them in the court. Now you know what a vile woman my aunt is.'

'She says that it is seven years since you mated with your husband?'

'She told even that! Didn't she tell what injustice he inflicted on me? I feel abashed to confide all those matters in you. If Shveta were here, I would have related it to her. She is my buddy,' she concluded her talk. It was not in Mangalamma's nature to pry deep. The conversation ended.

Having lunch, as she drove towards Mysore, her mind was filled with the thought that she was an adulteress, a sinner. She felt that she should have brought out that plaint without falling into his company. She could then have countered more valiantly. Her mind heavy from being filled with distress, she drove speedily observing the numbers on the milestones. From that day, the intensity of void went haywire. She felt that there was no meaning to life and that only death made sense. Pulling the trigger seemed easy. Since then each night, she would hold the revolver in hand. In between, she would even visit the hilltop a few nights. But she had decided not to call him. Though she would think of him much and be compelled to just dial and disconnect the moment it rang at the other end, she would resolutely snub herself. As she analysed why it was getting impossible for her to end herself, she got the suggestion that probably her inner mind did not take a liking to death till the suit was won.

Before each monsoon, the roof had to be sealed with tar. She resolved that this time, she would directly approach the mason and get it done to the exclusion of Somashekhar. She knew that the mason's house was near Ganesh Talkies. One afternoon after visiting him, she was returning via Narayana Shastri Road. Midway on that road, a barricade was put up as repair work was being undertaken and traffic was diverted left towards a lane in Lakshmipuram. When she took that lane and drove further, she spotted Jalaja at a site where the construction of quite a large structure was in progress. As the traffic was moving slowly, they both fell in each other's sight. Amrita applied the brakes and asked, 'What's up?'

'Don't you know? My cousin's building.' Amrita noticed astonishment in Jalaja's face as she neared the car.

She recalled. A matter from the past. One year and a half would have elapsed since. Just the ground and the first floor is through. Unable to sidestep an ex-colleague whom she had met after long, she let the other vehicles pass by and drove up to the vacant space in the construction site only to spot Neelakanthappa. When their eyes met, he greeted her and walked up to the car.

After exchanging pleasantries with Jalaja, Amrita exclaimed, 'This is still at this stage?'

'Don't you know, Amrita? This is one big story. For getting myself into this, my blood pressure is stepping up,' she stopped abruptly as if she had bitten her tongue. While she guessed that it was some problem with Somashekhar, Jalaja instructed Neelakanthappa to do the rounds and that she would join him shortly. Getting hint of the suggestion, Neelakanthappa stepped away. 'This is a chance meeting, and I have met you after long. I don't know if I should be sharing this with you! Let not even my foe land in the predicament that I am now in. Hence, I exclaimed that this was one big story. Sorry.' Jalaja leaned against the car.

Amrita replied calmly, 'It's okay to tell me. I know nothing of it. Let's go some place and talk leisurely,' she held the door open.

When she parked under a tree in front of Crawford House, Jalaja related Somashekhar's loss of interest in profession, Ramamurthy's letter, her debate with Somashekhar, and then said, 'Don't know what has become of him. He wound up his office and sold the premises. I was told that he had to repay a loan to someone in Bombay. If he had seen through this nursing home, he would have earned three lakh. If he needed it, I would have paid him in advance. He had even gone through half of his work. The authority to sign cheques is vested in me. I had no qualms about paying in advance to an honest one like him. But he was not interested any more. So Ramamurthy flew from the USA and appointed an architect from Bangalore. They are not giving it due attention. After Somashekhar wound up his profession, Neelakanthappa was jobless. He has a small house in Mysore, and schoolgoing children. He was not in a position to relocate. He is now working as a technical supervisor for this architect from Bangalore. By going back on the contract, not only has Somashekhar ruined himself, he has caused great trouble to us too. Noticing what he, a pupil of my father and a childhood friend, has made of himself, I am touched.'

Amrita knew nothing of it at all. While relating all this, Jalaja's eyes were rooted in Amrita's face. Her shock was supplemented by a suspicion whether Jalaja was suggesting that she knew the reason for his downfall. She just said, 'I know nothing of it, Madam.'

'Know nothing!' It pierced her heart when Jalaja expressed surprise. 'How could I know of his Bombay loan? Neelakanthappa told me.' Jalaja changed the topic. 'Well, how are you, Amrita? For the likes of you, there is no compulsion to earn from employment. For us though, it would mean loss of two square meals if we quit.'

I would drive my car to the college. Even now, I move about in one. These people think that I am a wealthy landlady of a coffee estate. Though she knew that they were ignorant of the borrowings that offset the worth of the estate and the interest that weighed down the income therefrom, she related none of it. Recalling that it was the first time she was meeting her since resigning from her job, Amrita felt like sharing with her the grounds for sending in her resignation letter. But while relating that, she would have to divulge the backdrop of the situation. It would not be possible to just stop at describing the haughtiness of the principal. Even if she related just that, Jalaja would still say that I, being a rich one, could afford to do so, but someone as her had to hang on whatsoever. Thus forewarned, Amrita reacted none. She glanced at her watch. It was 1:30 pm. She offered to drop Jalaja at her house and gunned the engine.

Homebound alone, she felt dejected and downcast. Abandoning the commission worth three and a half lakh in fee! Would have happened some seven to eight months back. The office premises, I don't know, would have been disposed of some three months back. It is of late that I wrote to him to keep off, as I had no need for any relationship. Getting angry at the thought that though he visited her daily for lunch, he never informed of his downfall in profession, she recalled that he had telephoned her the very afternoon he received her letter and had informed her never to call him at afternoons for he would not be in his office at that time of the day. That was – she raked her memory – twenty days back. She understood that he had told her so, as he had already disposed of the premises by then. Back home, she felt disheartened. He has resigned a commission that would fetch him three and a half lakh in fee just for loss of interest in profession. Reflecting that he sold the office premises, she surmised that he who called Bombay overnight and got the funds by telex by 11 the next day would surely not share it with her if the Bombay loan was recalled. Obstinate, obstinate with me. Even his love for me is obstinate. In a whelming mood, at some intimate moment, he had declared, 'I love you.' He hung on to it obstinately. Within, he doesn't espouse real love. Else, before disposing of the premises, wouldn't he have informed me? Without informing me anything … she got very wild. She felt like going to his house right away, grab him by his tresses, and ask of him. But recalling the letter that she had written, she felt trounced. She ate just a morsel of rice and retired. She knew that sleep would not come. It turned out painful to lie down in any one particular position, so she kept changing sides – left, right, face up, face down, legs stretched, folded, and variously rolled over. He had probably distanced himself in the first place, and wishing for me to follow suit, he waited for me to take precedence in announcing it verbally. That thought kept returning.

By 4 pm, she had an idea. Neelakanthappa will be available at that site. Quiz him and learn all details of Somashekhar's dealings. Will he divulge? During the planning of the interiors of the office premises, he was very obedient and cordial with me. He will definitely be forthcoming. She perked up her confidence, instantly dressed, rolled a comb over her head, and left. Jalaja wasn't there. The workers were engaged in their work. Neelakanthappa was not among the builder's staff. He was there on behalf of the Bangalore architect, supervising just the technical finer points, wherefore there was no need for his presence there all through. She asked, 'Mr Neelakanthappa, got to talk to you some. Are you free? Or … ' He said, 'I too was about to leave, Madam. I am free.'

'Get in,' she held the front passenger door open for him. He felt hesitant to enter. 'Well, sit in the back seat,' she leaned over and opened the back door. Entering, he sat and pulled the door shut. Parking under the same tree opposite Crawford House as she had this afternoon, she said, 'I want some information. Without shying away, you have to tell me everything you know. I will swear on Goddess Chamundeshvari that I will not betray you for having divulged all that. You should not hold back anything.'

Neelakanthappa could guess what her query would be. He did not respond immediately. When insisted, he said, 'Madam, what is there that you do not know?'

She held the steering and continued to look ahead while speaking, for she reflected that if she turned in his direction and conversed with him face-to-face, diffident, he would stop short. 'You presume that I know everything. In fact, I do not know a thing. Why did he resign the commission of that American? When did he dispose of the office premises? Let me have all the details.'

He was surprised. She egged him to speak out whatever was, and without hesitation. He then said, 'He took to your friendship very seriously and lost all interest in life, in his profession too. That was what I thought. Not just I, even Jalaja madam and everyone else think so. Even the neighbouring business establishments exchange the same idea. *This love! See what it brings a man down to* – is what they say.'

'Will you believe this?' she asked him, turning towards him.

By then, he had got over the initial discomfiture at speaking. 'Neglecting his profession, wasn't he visiting you every day from noon to 5 pm? If we subordinates didn't mouth it, does it mean that we didn't know of it?' he came out candidly. She felt that he had offended her. For two minutes, she could not speak. Neelakanthappa continued, 'There is none professionally as capable as he. If he just gave broad instructions, I would have done the drafting. This Bangalorean is just a grand stallion. Voluminous business. Will get the works outsourced. They will not give attention to every detail like he does. He paid me a gratuity of twenty-five thousand and asked me to seek employment elsewhere. Prior to that, getting wind of his intent to dispose of the premises, I begged of him, "Sir, but why? Please don't do so." "When I am unable to evince interest in work, why carry on and annoy my clients?" is all I got in response. If he had the enthusiasm to work, it would not have been difficult to arrange a sum of 1.75 lakh. I think he had lost interest about ten months back when he backtracked on the American's commission. Najundegowda and I have much discussed as to why he went back on such a rewarding commission, why they were at loggerheads. Earlier, he had similarly resigned from Rajashekhar Shetty's commission too.' Neelakanthappa rested.

She could not think of anything else to ask. He too could not think of any more to relate. As evening fell, the sun was set to go down at the corner of Kukkarahalli Lake. The breeze swayed the neem trees. Neelakanthappa said apologetically, 'The neighbouring business houses, and me too, had thought that he was doomed because of you. But now I see that you are ignorant of it all. In fact, he may be in love with you; you might not be. Haven't we known of quite some lovers being doomed from such one-way love? Maybe, it is not your fault, Madam.' She felt as if struck on the head. She kept staring at the steering. 'Henceforth, if anyone asks of me, I will lay the facts bare before them. Till now, I was passive about it when anyone commented on it,' he opened the door and exited. 'I will go to the spot. My bicycle is there.' She continued to sit silently, unable to think of even offering to drop him back. He walked away apace.

~

She remained sitting, as if her brain was filled with piercing cold water. She didn't even realize when the sun set and dusk descended. After quite some time, she became aware of a torchlight swaying over the car. She craned her neck to see. *Khat khat* – the sound of boots. 'Whose car is it?' A police constable neared her from the direction of the district offices. Noticing her in the torchlight, he said, 'Why, Madam, are you parked here for quite some time?'

'The evening breeze. Was just enjoying it,' she stammered.

'Go home. Shouldn't stay alone here.' She gunned her car the moment he said so. Speeding past the district offices, and until she crossed the Lakshmibai Road, she was not aware that if she took this route she would have to drive through Devaraj Urs Road. If she drove through there, a little farther to the left on the first floor was his office premises and the board! She reflected that she had attended to the interiors and had got the board painted. Now what other board would be there! She did not want to take that route. She applied the brakes and came to an abrupt halt. She looked back. Traffic was heavy. She waited. When the traffic cleared, she reversed the car back and forth, re-entered Lakshmibai Road, and was homebound via Ramavilas Road. It was then she recalled that she had forgotten to fetch the children.

'Why late, Amma?' the children asked. She said that she had to attend to some litigation. She had already apprised them of their grandmother's and uncles' conniving and her plaint in court to avenge the fraud that they had perpetrated. She didn't talk to the children much. They too had understood that their mother would, at times, turn melancholic. After they slept, she sat on the sofa in the lounge for more than an hour, her head hung. The cause-and-effect relationship of the events that led to this development unfolded in her mind. When I got to know that he had borrowed from Bombay, I compelled him to repay it with my funds and then took a personal interest in the interiors. For more than a month, I personally attended to it, finally got the board painted, made all arrangements for the inauguration, and when the *homa* was being performed, my mind muddled and I slipped out of the venue and headed to Kannambadi to jump into the deadly sluice. All through the inauguration day, I was doused in thoughts of death and destruction. What else would become of an enterprise that was floated by such a character? Until I am dead, not just I, it is impossible that he too will beget contentment. The establishment was wrecked because I did so that day. She felt certain, akin to the enlightenment that Buddha attained, that this was precisely the cause and effect. Alongside flashed the remedy that obliteration of effect could be achieved only by obliteration of cause.

She did not waste a single moment. She got up. Locked the main door, took the car out of the garage, shut the gate, and drove downtown. It was 11:30 pm. She sped past the curve by the zoo, plied via Hardinge Circle, Sayyaji Rao Road, and Dhanvantari Road, and hit the road to Kannambadi. Ontikoppal went past. When she had driven past the sanatorium and the railway gate, and entered the crepuscular countryside, no dithering anymore, only the gush of the Vishveshwaraya canal will be heard; the potent force of the churning waters will not be visible. What with sighting it? No need to close the eyes even. Just take the plunge. Fifteen minutes at the most, she pressed on the gas. Driving speedily that she was, the fork where the road branched out to Srirangapatna pounced on her out of the dark and she had to apply the brakes abruptly to manoeuvre. The tyres complained. Still, the car made contact with the signpost and the bonnet lost shape. She alighted and inspected. Shouldn't have braked. All would have been done with this crash itself. My bloody foot! Stepped on the brake by sheer habit. To stay alive, there probably is no reason or justification other than just habit. That new precept flashing in her mind, she boarded the car, gunned the engine, swerved leftward in the direction of the dam, and drove as to cause the paddy and sugarcane fields on either side to scramble in the opposite direction. Though aware that the meandering road could cause another crash at that speed, she told herself that it was okay. Let it all be accomplished half an hour ahead of the appointed time. Mine isn't any holy resolve to end myself in waters only. Belagola is past. About one and a half mile more! She jacked up the speed a little more and, suddenly recalling something, she braked abruptly. The car came to a screeching halt. At nights, the main gate of the dam will be sealed and a sentry will keep watch. Nobody will be allowed inside. None, more so a lone woman! She would be suspected to have planned suicide and quizzed accordingly. Fury bubbled up from disappointment. She extended her arm to the left and fumbled about. Hadn't brought the revolver along. Since she had set out with the sole intent of leaping into the canal, the revolver merited no consideration. A doomed one whom even the summer rain wouldn't drench! Will not give up. Get back home. My emancipation is through my revolver only. The ledge on the hill is my emancipation site. Once she decided on that, she reversed the car and drove speedier than before.

The fork past. The mound past. The million lights of Mysore zoomed in. When she was past the railway gate and the sanatorium, a thought flashed through her – turn right into Gokula ahead and visit his Jayalakshmipuram house. Foot eased on the gas. Immediately, anger overcame. Should this sucker shamelessly return to him? She gave definite orders to her feet to jack up the speed, and by the time she went past Ontikoppal, she felt like plying via Devaraj Urs Road to see what other board was in that place. Turning right at the petrol bunk, she entered Devaraj Urs Road. She recalled her visit here and retreat of the previous nightfall. Foot stepped on the brake even now. She then took her foot off it, goading herself that she would still witness it before dying, would not dither, but would get to know the truth of the matter before dying. The spot on the upper floor to the left that was as familiar as her palm now displayed the board 'Hiralal Financiers'. An imaginary solution popped up in her mind – what if she had got to know of it, and if she had somehow bought it herself!

Even if I had bought it, he would not have set up his practice there. She felt that to him, her every paisa was synonymous with filth. Anger boiled up. Increasing the speed a bit, she returned home. Taking the revolver, as she exited, she instantly recalled his words during his last call. *If you give me your word on one matter, I will adhere to your words. You should never commit suicide. Even if you are afflicted by anguish and agony, you should stay alive. That assured, I will abide by all your wishes. I will not even telephone you.* He hasn't since called too. Who is he to instruct me to put up with anguish and agony and still keep myself alive? What authority is vested in him, he who has chosen to keep me aloof? I shall ask of him, right now, as to what authority he has. She returned inside, sealed the door, went to her room, and dialled his number. With two more digits to go, she cut the line and replaced the receiver, questioning the need of calling someone who had no authority. Revolver in hand, as she sat on the bed, she felt as if drained of all her vitality. Dead beat, she was unable to move her limbs or even cogitate. She reclined on the bed. Sleep overcame. Mahadevamma arrived in the morning for her duty and said, 'Madam, you have not parked the car inside the garage. You have left it outside on the road.' She then recalled that even the keys were left behind in the car.

~

While returning after dropping the children at the school, she recalled Neelakanthappa's words. *In fact, he may be in love with you; you might not be. Haven't we known of quite some lovers being doomed from such one-way love?* She began feeling that this might be true. While she bathed, she recollected that on visiting here, he would swallow the pain from my torture every day from noon to evening, and would also put up with my onslaught and goring during the late-night telephonic tirade. Could one ever own up such patience if one didn't nurse love! That thought made her go blank. She rested her face and shoulders against the wall of the bathroom. Her head reeling, she became aware that she would fall and become unconscious. For a minute, she felt that the entire universe was dead and nought. When she gradually regained consciousness, wail spewed from within. She cried, uncontrolled. Turning on the tap for the water to reverberatingly pool into the bucket so that Mahadevamma and Puttamma could not hear her cry, she permitted herself to three rounds of unregimented, cathartic cry. When she later rinsed her face, her mind stood eased. Wiping the moisture off her body, as she entered her bedroom, she felt that all her inner impediments had resolved and her future path appeared clearly. She wore whatever sari she could first lay hands on, combed her hair, put a dot of vermilion on her forehead, collected her bag with all the keys, and informed the women that she would be out for a while. Instructing them to shut the main door when they left for the day, she drove downtown. The rhythm of her drive was such that she would have arrived at her destination even if she had driven blindfold.

Opening the door in response to the doorbell, he was surprised. 'Come in, come in,' he greeted her. She observed his face. He was emaciated. But his personal hygiene had not suffered. He was orderly in shave, bath, and the way he wore his hair. The dhoti and vest he wore were fresh from the laundry. She left her slippers outside the door and entered his bedroom. A book on the bed. She picked it up. *Novel Concepts in Architecture*. She sat on the bed. He drew a chair before her and sat.

'How are you?' he asked.

'Can't you make out by just seeing me?' she laughed.

'Women have developed a new craze to reduce weight.'

'So with the men,' she repaid the compliment.

He just smiled. Presently, the cooker on the stove in the kitchen signalled. He got up, put out the stove, and returned.

'When did you start cooking?' she asked.

'About a month back.'

It was difficult for her to keep the conversation going. She had driven here in an enthusiasm to spill out everything, to purge him of everything. Now it seemed that there was a very thin glass partition between them. Everything is visible. But it was a state without touch, smell, and other such intimate rapport. She felt suffocated. Should smash it right now. Reflecting that any delay would only cause the tenacity of the glass to get more potent, she avidly resumed the conversation, 'I chanced on Jalaja. And Neelakanthappa. They told me everything. You resigning the nursing home commission as also other assignments, disposing of the office premises, clearing the Bombay loan. Everything. I had once before told you that I was destroying you. Why didn't you share with me that you were undergoing all this? If you had told me that your interest in your profession is slipping, my conduct would have improved.' He chose not to reply. He kept mum as if in assimilation of her words. 'Why didn't you?' she asked again.

'Would you really have improved? If it is just improvement in conduct, being exclusively propitious to me, I wasn't for it. I am not for it even now.'

It took some time for those words to sink in her. No apt reply formed. 'For how much net did you sell it? What are you doing for your livelihood now?'

'For three and a half lakh. I cleared the Bombay loan. I paid twenty-five thousand gratuity to Neelakanthappa. I cleared sundry other borrowings. I got a net profit of one lakh. I have invested it for interest. I will get one thousand per month. House rent is six hundred. I am living on the balance four hundred. That was why I started the kitchen fire. No other work too. That way, I can keep myself engaged.'

She could not contain her ire. 'You have assumed this poverty with the intent to torment me, right?'

'There is no warrant to persecute you. I am leading a life that my financial situation permits me. Compared to the condition of a good part of the people of our country, mine isn't poverty at all. Without working, if I am provided with two square meals a day and shelter, how can it be called poverty?'

'I vividly remember that once before, you had your friend remit money through telex and relayed the same to my bank. Yet, I ask. Why didn't you inform me even when you were compelled to dispose of the office premises? I would have arranged somehow. I would even have mortgaged the Lalitamahal house if need be. Distancing me from your mind! Love overtly! What is the meaning of love?'

He did not reply immediately. But his face revealed that he had mulled over this matter. She stared at his face as if exacting a reply. 'Look, I don't believe in easy money. Should work for it. To work, one should evince interest. If love for life is absent in you, how can it be present in me? When that is lacking, how will work be appealing? The root of my poverty is in here. Unless this is rehabilitated, not just from you, I won't accept a single *pai* from anyone.'

'What if this one thousand ceases to flow in? What if the landlord increases the rent of this house to one thousand five hundred, what will you do? Interest in work must sprout, right?'

'If I desire to stay alive, I must get back to work. Else, should stay inert and renounce food and life. Let's not discuss philosophy now. Come, taste my dish. Let me season the curry,' he got up and went into the kitchen.

She did not get up. In a short while, he emerged with two salvers, placed them on the teapoy by the bed, and pulled it closer. He went in again and brought drinking water. He had already put some rice and stew on the salvers. He now brought out the curry and a cup of curd. 'Don't laugh at the taste of my recipe,' he expressed civility.

She got up, washed her hands, and ate. A tasteless curry that lacked coriander or curry leaves and prepared from some nondescript curry powder bought from a store. While she ate, she could not think of anything to speak. Out of the four hundred that remained after paying rent, incur for electricity, cooking gas, groceries, vegetables, toiletries, milk, coffee powder, sugar, and, she reflected, a situation whereby nothing is left to buy any clothing. 'Will you cook both times?' she asked.

'What I cook for lunch will serve for supper too. There is that old fridge that I brought from Bombay.'

'Breakfast?'

'No exclusive breakfast. Brunch by noon and then supper late evening. Enough.'

After lunch, she washed the plate. He washed the vessels in which he had prepared food. 'No domestic help?' she enquired.

'Why do I need one? They will have to be paid forty or fifty per month,' he said casually.

She felt it difficult to stay there. 'I will leave. Call you later,' she said.

'You didn't relate the court matter,' he said.

'What has anybody got to do with that?' she said nonchalantly.

'If nothing else, I will be happy if I get to know that there is some progress in the proceedings. Do tell me,' he insisted.

She was in no mood for conversation. She felt hesitant to share this matter with him. 'I will tell you some other day,' she got up. While she wore her slippers by the door, he put on a shirt. He then followed her down the stairs, walked up to her car to see her off, and waved his hand to bid her bye.

~

By the time she arrived at her house, she was sure that he had mentally distanced himself from her. Reflecting that they were now poles apart, she got fidgety that she had no locus of existence. Feeding the dogs, she let them free and reclined on the sofa in the lounge. In a while, she recalled his words and felt that they were not merely pessimistic. *If love for life is absent in you, how can it be present in me? When that is deficient, how will work be appealing?* This love for life, can it be espoused just like that? Somu, you cannot understand the stimulus and proclivity inside me. I am not playing games. If you were fully aware as to how much I suffer in agony, unable to bear it when the stress of death sets in, you would not have laid the blame on me. Her eyes filled up. You may nurse love towards me, but you haven't the compassion to understand me. If you would have had it, you would not have been so harsh. She repeated this in her mind many times.

When she got up and went to her room, she resolved that she too would have just two square meals a day, that she would do away with breakfast, dessert, milk, et al. That insipid curry powder, she felt like giving him some home-made plain curry meal and vegetal curry meal. But she feared that he might refuse it. That was a sign of the genesis of fear towards him. When she changed and retired, she recalled that he maintained a physical distance throughout. I sat on the bed. He pulled a chair and sat opposite me. Did not even touch my hand. No cuddle or expression of love or any tender feelings. That reminded her of her letter and she recalled all the sentences thereat. *This is plain adultery. And that is the root cause of my agony*....Even after these many days, he still holds it vivid in memory and practices obstinacy. Where there is love, there isn't obstinacy, isn't harshness. She once again arrived at the conclusion that there was no trace of love in him. Even after she fetched the children that evening, she kept up with her musings. The words *where love is, there isn't obstinacy* that formed in her mind assumed the dimension of a postulate and rendered itself as a tool for warding him off.

When the children were asleep that night, she began mulling if, in consonance with her letter, he had resolved to nurse love to the exclusion of carnality. Love that excluded even the contact of hands!

That concept was not any new to her. When she recalled that she had read ample pertinent fiction, and was equally appreciative of it, her heart swelled and soared. She endorsed it. No dichotomy there. He is wise, she thought. He thinks well, farther than I do. When she thought of calling him and congratulating his stance, after spending the balance four hundred for every other effect, is he left with anything to pay for the phone bill? After abandoning his profession, why has he retained the telephone? For my sake, she told herself, for safeguarding me. Mind swelled in gratitude. Somu, Somu, what do you gain by persisting to possess me? Why should your love of life be dependent on mine? She felt like asking him, aspiring to fill her ears with his voice. She took the receiver, but was apprehensive of dialling. She replaced the receiver, reflecting that it was impossible for her to start the conversation once he picked the phone. To crave for carnality is a beastly conduct alright. But when minds have meld, the factitiousness of stubbornly keeping bodily desires at bay was nothing but cruelty perpetrated on feelings. She reflected that it was akin to the unromantic act of consigning a ready-to-ripen fruit into the refrigerator and retaining it raw.

~

One morning at about 9, the dogs were heard barking. Mahadevamma announced that there was a visitor. When Amrita came out, she saw Ranganath stranded to the other side of the gate with a small leather pouch in hand, frightened at the duet of the barking dogs that were set free inside the compound. She was embarrassed. It immediately flashed through her mind that he was here on behalf of his sister with a view to compromise settlement. While she consigned the dogs to their respective kennels, she let out a sigh of relief that he doesn't intend to stay overnight, for he has brought with him just a small pouch, no suitcase. After kennelling the dogs, she asked him to enter in a manner of according permission. Opening the gate, he came in. His hair was dishevelled as if from bus journey. Face reeked of sticky sweat. Showing him to a seat in the lounge, she went inside. Trepidation set in. What subject might he broach? What and how much his sister would have filled him on! She would have spilled everything. In about fifteen minutes, she regained her poise. Whatever he speaks, I shall counter it in just one sentence – legal affairs be restricted to the courts and those matters shall be dealt with by the lawyer. Resolving that she could so snub him, she emerged and sat on the sofa opposite him. She could gather that he too was embarrassed to speak. But she kept mum having resolved not to be the first to start a conversation.

After a while, he cleared his throat and said, 'Came by the first bus from Bangalore.' She nodded acknowledgement. At a loss for further talk, he stammered. He made another attempt at starting a conversation. 'Had been to Bangalore on official work.' She nodded acknowledgement once more. Again afflicted by embarrassment, he finally overcame it and said, 'It is the general transfer season now. My boss asked me to apply for transfer to a place of my choice. I would be posted there next month. I thought of asking you once before conveying to him.'

'What to ask me?' she questioned quickly.

He seemed to choke. 'I had informed him earlier on that I preferred Mysore,' he said.

Gathering that he hadn't the gumption to go ahead with securing the posting without her permission, the situation seemed a piece of cake. 'Are you aware that I have lodged a complaint against your sister in Hassan court?' she asked, staring at him.

Dodging her sight, he let his sight coast sideward and said, 'Yes, I know.'

'In the days to come, won't you side your sister and pester me to withdraw the plaint?'

'That is a matter of your ancestral property. In future, it concerns our children. I will not intervene. But for bringing me up, I have decided to send my sister five hundred rupees per month in gratuity. You should not object to that.'

She was taken aback. All her calculations went haywire and the restructured roles seemed beyond her comprehension. She felt the need for some time to think. 'Will you have something for breakfast?' she asked.

'I have had it already,' he replied.

'Let me get you coffee,' she went inside. By the time she had Puttamma prepare the brew and she re-entered the lounge with the cup, the constitution of all relationships was clear to her. After he polished off his coffee, she asked, 'Your sister would have related to you sundry matters about me. She, in fact, has. That aside, it is seven and a half years since you made physical contact with me. Since then, have you remained truly celibate? Tell me the truth.'

He floundered at this unexpected question that she posed, rooting her gaze in his face. He felt that if his tongue erred, his eyes and face would give him away. 'I will not question your past. Neither should you. If we can get straight henceforth, that should serve,' he said.

She replied immediately, 'Mr Ranganath, you are a government employee. If you get habituated to clandestine relationships at every place you are posted, it will tarnish your name. Get yourself a wife. You need one to run the kitchen too. I will sign all necessary documents. No need to contribute a single *pai* towards the maintenance of the children.' Crestfallen, he looked at her face. 'Go ahead, get yourself a posting to a place of your choice. That you are not going to indulge in such mean acts as visiting my children and instigating their minds against me, I very well know. Tell your sister that if she ever does that, I will take her to task.' She got up. He was perplexed. Though he could not think of anything to say, he sat his place unable to decide if he should leave. 'Consult a lawyer, get all the documents that I have to sign and courier them to me. Goodbye,' she said. She took precedence and went in. After a quarter of an hour, the barking of the dogs and the sound of the latch being turned on the gate were heard.

When she went into her room, tears filled her eyes. Shutting the door, she sat on the sofa and sobbed. After four to five bouts of sobbing, she felt that she had done the right thing. Yet, tears abound. Though she told herself that there would be no sorrow if the heart heeded the mind, her gloom did not ebb. In a short while, she heard a knock on the door. The cook Puttamma who had wound up for the day was there to take leave of her. In some time, Mahadevamma too left. An idea struck Amrita as she shut the door and went in. Immediately, she picked up the phone and dialled the number. 'Somu, it is me. Can you recognize the voice?'

He said *no*.

'You are in the reverie of some girlfriend. How can you recognize my voice? What's up?'

'I just came into the kitchen.'

'Got your scooter?'

'Sure. Why?'

'Else, I wanted to come over there in my car. Look, it is quite some time since you donned me with royal jasmine. I very much desire to wear it now. Will you go to the market and bring it now? Let's lunch here together.' He fell silent. After waiting for about five seconds, she said, 'Look, if you took very seriously some bloody letter that I scribbled, what distinction is there between you and me? That day when I had come over there, you didn't even touch my hand. Are you so obstinate as to resume it only after I seek pardon? Come soon. Got to share many matters with you. Who else can I confide in?'

'Be there in fifteen minutes,' there was enthusiasm in his voice. She knew that he wouldn't have had breakfast. Since she got to know of it, she too has been skipping breakfast. Just a cup of coffee. By 11 am, stomach stings and head reels from fatigue. Yet, she wouldn't eat anything. Quickly, she placed two plates on the dining table. She placed the food there. Water and glasses too. By then, the scooter was heard. Rushing, she opened the door.

'Shall I park the scooter inside the garage?' he asked. His face suggested gentleness. The royal jasmine peeped out of his trouser pocket.

She said, 'Leave it in the portico. Come on in.' When they sealed the main door, he removed the floral string from his pocket. She turned over and reclined on him. The royal jasmine that moved to her nape mellowed all emotions. Nobody spoke. Sans any need for words, they promenaded in synchronization of each other's steps in the perfect concordance of accompanists at a ballet. Both forgot their lunch. When their feelings meld tender like curd, her mind reflected that if they had not come together this day, their relationship would have been tainted of fornication. After quite some time, she caressed his stomach and said, 'Kiddie, your belly has gone shallow. If you don't eat, your head will reel. Get up.'

'Bring it here,' he said, but did not slacken his embrace.

After they had their lunch on the bed, she moved the dishes to the teapoy nearby and began relating the progress in litigation. Last in chronology was the episode of Ranganath's visit. By then it was 5:30 pm. 'Tomorrow, come at 11:30 in the morning. Let's talk some more. Wait, let me pack some supper. Let not your hands gather soot in the kitchen this evening.' She freshened up and got ready to fetch her children.

The children felt that mother was gleeful today. Instead of returning home, she steered in the direction of Lalitamahal hotel. Not only did she get them potato chips, badam-burfi, and ice cream, she roped them in for a game of tag in the spacious garden. Though she once tripped upon her sari and tumbled, not at all accepting defeat, she caught up with Vijai and Vikas. She matched them in running around, thereby panting and profusely sweating at the neck, back, and armpits. Though dusk descended and Vikas wanted to go home, she encouraged them for one more game, another, yet another, and when the toe of a slipper came off so as to render it difficult for her even to walk, she called off play and ambled up to her car. When Vijai jocularly remarked that her slipper snapped because she got snacks just for them at the restaurant, but did not help herself to anything, she concurred with him, 'True, kiddie.'

But her mind began to cringe from within. Cooking rice quickly, when she served their supper and put the children to sleep, feelings of void swelled so as to fully devour her. Darkness everywhere – within, without, and unto the future. She got restless as to where she was bound for and what was happening. The court, the sundry transactions, the big estate, two more estates that shall be won, these children, this love affair to top it all, each one unwieldy. Love ! A contra-attraction that dissects me in two, or a stress that corners and grinds me ! While these children are being tended, they are loveable. But once they grow up and question me as to why I have kept their father at bay, enemies. She felt that she should just commit suicide. No apt moment other than this. Never before was darkness abound above, below, behind, to the fore – in all eight directions. All those of this world who are dead have reached this state. She felt that there was no state more miserable than this. She told herself that today it would be certain and conclusive, not just a jolly ride to the ledge of the hill. What has to be done at the juncture of the hour of death ? She sat silently for two minutes reflecting on that thought. Then, something flashed through her mind. She got up, went to the bathroom, and washed her feet and hands. She then went to the worship chamber and adorned the idols of the gods with vermilion. She asked for pardon for any mistakes committed by her. For whose sake should she pray? Children? Ranganath will definitely care for their education and development. In my absence, they will surely get some other caretakers. They will grow. Now, Somu. If I am dead, it is a relief for him too. He would be rid of the bondage that he got himself into in a moment of animation of love. And while she consoled herself that he better wed a woman of normal disposition, she reflected that Vijai and Vikas will get some caretaker and grow, but there will be none for my kiddie Somu. With none to resort to, he will die an orphan without a custodian. She closed her eyes and prayed, 'God, at the moment of death, I have just one wish. Tend him well.' Prostrating before the deities once again, when she went to her room and picked up the revolver, she felt confident and smelt victory. She was about to pick up the keys to the car when the phone rang. She felt angered. She redirected the anger at herself, recalling that if she had not called him today and invited him, he would not have called now. She decided not to pick up the phone. If it was allowed to ring for many times, the children might be woken from their slumber, or Somu would get ideas and drive up here at breakneck speed. She leant over and picked up. but didn't speak.

He said, 'Hey, you. You told me about litigation regarding the estate. I have thought of a basic solution. This is not just court matter. It concerns you, which only means that it concerns me. I am coming now. I will explain everything.' She did not speak. 'Heard me? What's the matter?' he yelled.

'I am feeling drowsy. Is it okay to discuss in the morning?'

'I too am feeling sleepy. But I can't rest until I let this out. By the time I arrive, keep coffee ready. Let's have a cup of it and then discuss. I start now,' he replaced the phone. She sat dejected.

Some time passed. The sound of scooter was heard in the distance. She didn't want it to be parked under the portico outside at this hour. She left with the keys to the garage still in her hand. Vikrant growled. Following her instructions, he parked the scooter in the garage, shut it, and locked it. She was eyeing him as if she would burn him down. 'Why angry?' he asked. She did not reply. Nearing her, he turned her face towards him, holding her plait at the nape, and asked, 'Why are you angry, man?' The spark in her eyes had not subsided yet. He stood, eyeing so forcefully as to cause his sight to push hers back. In a short while, tears flowed from her eyes. Still holding her by her plait, he pulled her closer and put her face to his shoulder.

After a minute, she said, 'Let's go to the worship chamber. I got to show you something. Leave your slippers there and wash your feet.' Complying, he followed her there and stood beside her. She then said, 'Look here. Just now, I applied vermilion to the idols and the portraits. Today, I would definitely have pulled the trigger. Such an intense state had never occurred till now. Before setting out on it, I had never come here to offer my final prayers. A short while before, when I prayed, know what I thought of? Ranganath will tend the kids. No need to worry about them. But what would your fate be? If I were dead, who would you resort to? God, take good care of this kid of mine, I had prayed from the depths of my heart, knelt, and had picked up the revolver and the car keys. It was exactly then that you called.'

He was dumbstruck. He held her hand firmly even as he stood. She turned her face towards him and looked at him. There was a daub of tear in his eyes, enough to reflect light. For a while, both just stood so. Then she prostrated before God. He too. He then took a pinch of vermilion at the feet of God and put it on her forehead. She too followed suit. Hand in hand, they went to the guest room. When he sat on a cane chair, she walked up to the children's room, closed the door from outside, returned, and sat beside him. 'Why were there tears in your eyes?' she asked.

'For you have understood that I have no other resort if you are dead.' She did not speak. After a while, he said, 'I now have this feeling that now on, even if you suffer in agony, even if you are doused in feelings of void, you will not commit suicide. When that moment arrives, you shall invariably recall that I have no other resort.'

'It occurred to me once. Not necessarily it need appeal to me every time. You do not fully know the peculiarities of my mind.'

'You too do not know it fully. Do you know how deeply you love me?'

'Do you know how deeply I hate you?'

'I do. I also know the reasons therefor. That aside, I calling you at the very moment you praying as to what would be my fate if you were dead, and I feeling like coming over immediately! What do you make of that? I would normally have visited tomorrow afternoon.'

'I say that you better start believing in God,' she struck him on the shoulder as would a teacher do to an errant pupil.

'Amu,' he began recollecting, 'you very well remember what all you do, what all you say when the feelings of void get intense. Though I declare my love towards you in every which way, you snub me by retorting and giving negative rejoinders. Know what my feelings would be then? God, what should I do to instil faith in her? At least, you relay unto her the truth of my feelings. I do not know the truth or otherwise of God's existence. But it is not possible to express the intensity of love without the percept of God. I feel that to prostrate before God in your company is to give expression to the feelings of love.'

She beamed. Eyes got moist. For two minutes, both were one with silence. She did not wipe her eyes that were veneered from tears. Then, limbs folded, she squatted on the sofa and said, 'Kiddie, come on, put your head on my lap and recline. Know how much I desire to fondle you as if you were a kid?' He complied. Leaning over, she hid his face in her bosom and held him in embrace for quite some time. Then she asked, 'Said you had a suggestion regarding the litigation?'

'That's okay. Let me tell you that tomorrow,' he said, not wanting to forfeit the state of oneness with silence that his mind had attained.

'It is impossible for me to wait till tomorrow. Anyway, I won't get sleep now. Neither will you.' He was silent. She did not insist again. She continued to hold him in embrace.

After a while, he said, 'Sit up erect. I will continue to recline on your lap while I relate. But it will be easy to speak if I can see your face.' She straightened up and arranged her pallu so that it did not block their sights. He began relating, 'You have earlier apprised me of the litigation. I too kept mulling over it casually. When you related the developments this afternoon, I got a definite idea. Listen to what I say and think it over at leisure. It is right that you have brought about a plaint. That woman and the bank have to be taught a lesson. It is almost certain that the case will be decided in your favour. What will you do after that? What will you do with the booty? The children, what will they do with it? That apart, you have not fully grasped what your present situation is. All your acts are right, but their meaning has to be grasped in a different light. You have borne two children. By virtue of having born unto you, they have inherited the right to paternal and/or maternal estate. It is also your duty to maintain the estate till they attain majority. You are a trustee of that inheritance. Be just that. Resolve in your mind that you have no authority over it and that it is not yours. Legally, you are entitled to a third of the estate, right? If you so desire, retain that much. And even if you retain it, resolve to donate it and rid yourself of even that. Now for your sustenance. You just said standing before God that there was no resort for me if you were dead. That is enough to instil in me an interest for life. I can readily start earning. When you came that day, you didn't look to your right on entering. I have stashed away my drawing table, duplicator, scales, typewriter, office table, and chair. I disposed of none of them. If I utilized some twenty or thirty out of the hundred thousand in the bank, I can rent office premises downtown and start an office. If I just hint at it, Neelakanthappa will come running. He will get in touch with a score contractors in and around Mysore and bring in business. In a month's time, I can mobilize enough work as to earn ten thousand. In a year, my hands will be full. It is my responsibility to care for you. Swear unto you that barring what I give you, you won't eat one morsel out of the funds of the estate. If you feel that I should not slog it out alone, you too look for a job in some college. Or, didn't you attend to the interiors of that office? You had done a fine job. A pertinent academic course is available in Bombay. Enrol yourself for that, go there and do it. A six-month diploma. I will sponsor you. For the houses, offices, cinemas, shopping malls that I design or build, you attend to the interiors. In the same office, let us have your cabin. Let us name the combined office "*Amrita and Shekhar, Architects & Interior Decorators*." Let Vijai and Vikas stay with us. Let us spend the estate money for their care and academics. We should properly account the same. If we beget children, we should care for them with our own funds. When Vijai and Vikas attain proper age, tell them, "Look kids, though I had the complete authority, I haven't eaten one morsel from the estate funds. I have worked for my bread myself. In future too, till my death, I will work for my bread. For your sake, I have just managed the estate." Know how they will look upon you then? If nothing else, they will at least develop ethical fear.' He fell silent. Though she was looking at him, her gaze revealed that she was deep in thought. After a while, he resumed his speak, 'I could have informed you before disposing of my office premises. I knew that you would even arrange for the funds. But on knowing about your aunt and Ranganath, I was uncomfortable with the thought of mortgaging this house. It was another thing if you had savings from your income. I would definitely have asked you.'

She said, 'It was them who perpetrated the fraud. Estate is mine. This house is inherited from my mother.'

'Look, don't react to anything I said now. Don't reply. Just mull it over. Think it over at leisure. One more thing. Let's continue to stay in this forlorn house. This belongs to Vijai and Vikas. Till they attain majority, we are entitled to stay here as their guardians. Or, let's rent a house in the city and move there along with the children. I will be with you wherever you are. Let the dogs be. No need for more security than them. Surrender the arms license and sell the revolver. No need for that.' Attempting to utter something, she opened her mouth. He signalled her not to speak. After that, intense silence prevailed. After five minutes, he sat up and said, 'Isn't your thigh aching?' He looked at her. Her focus had drawn inwards. Then on, he too did not speak any. She was not at all present there. After half an hour, he asked, 'Get me a dhoti. Go and get some sleep. It is 3:30.'

She did not since bring up that topic before him. Neither did he. He would visit there by noon, have lunch, and stay till 5 in the evening. When he would take leave, she would pack the day's supper for him. Her talk had considerably reduced. She would always be unto herself, ruminating. Without disturbing her reticence, he would consign himself to her study and would chronologically read the books that she had marked for his sake.

Her anger was not subdued. 'Why come here just for the sake of restricting yourself to that room and reading? Can't you as well take the books to your house?' She got riled up. Once in her bedroom, he was engrossed in a book when she said, 'You hide your face in that book for you loathe seeing my face, right?'

Her mind had hit extreme depths and was occluded. Am I greedy, miserly? Didn't he take a liking to my initiating the litigation? Though he would be reclined on the bed beside her, she would contain herself from asking him, firmly resolving to find the answers herself. She even suspected if he was finding it difficult to come to terms with a woman of comparatively greater financial standing. She felt that it was very much possible. But after two days, she felt that that was also not a satisfactory explanation. Well before dusk, he would take leave. At nights, she would be awake as usual. Not infrequently, she would be assailed by the desire to die.

Whenever she reached for the revolver, she would recall his words: *I will be with you. Let the dogs be too. Surrender the arms license.* She felt that to touch the revolver was to be perfidious towards him. At times, she would take hold of the revolver and pull herself up, reflecting angrily that she would never be subservient to him, that he was not her lord. One night, she even took it along with her and drove to the ledge. After that discussion, he has not called her at late nights. He had said, 'I will not call. You call if need be, for I feel that you would be asleep.' A technique of meting out suggestion to my inner mind! Can't I get it? She smiled sarcastically. At the ledge, moonlight had pervaded. No darkness. For one who wants to shoot herself, what with darkness or moonlight? When she sought to so justify to herself, her mind subconsciously fancied the finer details of voluntary repudiation of all rights over the estate and living on vocational earnings. He may choose to suggest so, but why should I comply? Such contravention would also pop up. Returning after more than an hour's stay at the cliff, she would feel like calling him. He would not have slept. Would be just reclining with the book he took from here in hand? She would dial the numbers. The sap of love dribbles from the very tone of his voice, 'Amu!'

'Just called, dude,' concealing the fact that she had just visited the hill taking the revolver. 'I know that you would be reclined reading, that you wouldn't call me. Don't you know that at this hour I will be prompted to commit something? Or is it your divine disregard to let this greedy woman commit her death?'

'You are very well aware that if you are dead, there is no resort for me. You also know that thereafter, I too will not live. Therefore, I trust that you will rather suffer than commit suicide.'

'Kiddie, if I die, will you too commit suicide? Tell me the truth,' she asked affably.

'I swear on you. Suicide, meaning with revolver, rope, water, poison, wheels of a train, no, I shall not submit to any of them. My belief is that these are base acts. But without you, I will lose interest in life. Then life will be evicted from me in a couple of months.'

'Truly, dude?'

'Didn't I swear on you? If that is not sufficient, let me swear on God.' There would be tears in her eyes. She would sob and cry into the telephone. 'Amu, why cry?' he would ask.

Controlling herself, she would question, 'Why should you die for the sake of a lowly woman? Tell me the truth, do you know why you love me so much?'

'If I knew, I would be an enlightened one.'

'Which means love is a state of ignorance?'

'The enlightened one also loves. Loves more. Loves knowledgeably.'

'Don't fool me with vocabulary, you! It is not so easy to give me the slip,' she challenges him.

Eighth night since, the telephone rings at 8. Not his. Who is it at this hour? She picked up the phone and said hello. 'Should speak louder. Can't hear. This is Shivaramaiah, from Hassan,' he was shouting his lungs out. 'This is Amrita. I can hear you. Tell me,' she too yelled into the phone. 'Day before yesterday, interim orders were passed. Telephone lines were dead here, so I could not inform you these two days. Till this case is decreed, they are not to run the two estates. Since the residential quarters there are also part of the estates, they are to vacate them too. Their bank accounts too will be passed on to the custody of the court now. As both estates are nearby each other, the court will appoint a manager to manage the affairs of both. He has to manage the estates and submit accounts to the court. Both the plaintiff and the defendants have the authority to verify those accounts. Profits remaining after expenses shall be held by the court in suspense. Out of this fund, the court will pay a monthly sustenance of rupees one thousand to Jayarama, a family man, rupees five hundred to Krishnamurthy, a bachelor, and one thousand to the parents Jayalakshmi and Narasimhamurthy till this case is decided. Besides, it is decreed that the plaintiff Dr Amrita of Soogoor Estate need not pay interest on her bank loan till this case is decreed. Are you able to hear me?' She said yes. He continued, 'This order is very significant. It wouldn't have been issued if there weren't truth in our plaint. This is clear indication that we will win. When they heard the order, the mother and her two sons profusely transuded. Now, the court has to appoint a manager agreeable to both parties. Okay, then. How are you?' When she said that she was okay, the phone call was terminated at the other end.

She got excited. The first indications of victory have just poured in. They are to just walk out of the estate acquired from embezzled funds. Didn't he say he would go to Supreme Court! For now, let him go to a town and look for a rental accommodation. Besides, no need to pay interest to the bank. That means an annual surplus of three and a half to four lakh. She sensed contentment. In her triumphant mood, she could not think of what to do. She thought of sharing it with the children. But they were too young. She decided against such discussion with the children. She continued to be silently seated on her bed before the telephone.

Vikas came and said, 'Amma, I'm hungry.'

Entering the kitchen, she said, 'Give me fifteen minutes. I will prepare pudding.'

'What is special today?' Vijai asked.

'You know the case about the estate. We have won the first stage,' she put some cashews and raisins before him and asked him to winnow them.

The pudding with sugar and cardamom tasted fine. The children drank two glasses each. Thinking of Somu, she did not have any of it herself. He will be coming only tomorrow afternoon. Till then, keep it in the fridge. The very meaning of preparing it would be still and cold by then. Or shall I call and invite him? Let him come over when the children are asleep and we can together have the pudding....But why after the children are asleep? They too know that we are intimate, in future we have to live together too. Why don't I call him and invite him in their presence? But apprehension followed as to how he would receive this interim order of the court. He has prescribed complete detachment from the estate. Will he take a liking to celebrate victory by relishing the pudding? She was confused. The children supped and retired. She too ate. But she couldn't decide on tasting the pudding or otherwise. By then, it turned cold. If she left it at room temperature, the milk in it would coagulate. So she put the pudding in the fridge and went to her bedroom. I haven't the good fortune to savour the happiness that has accrued to me; never had it. She felt that none was as unfortunate as her. She sat on the sofa, her face hidden in her palms. Intense silence seemed to pool everywhere. In ten minutes, feelings of void pervaded. There isn't any meaning in this victory, in this life. She felt that if there was any meaning at all, it was only in death. She got up and pulled the drawer in the chest. *You very well know that if you are dead, I have no resort whatsoever. Wherefore I am confident that you will not commit suicide.* Though his words surfaced in memory, she reflected that there was no meaning in his words, in him too. Though she was impelled to end herself without any delay, something seemed to check her from touching the revolver and taking it out. For more than ten minutes, she stood watching it. Then, lifting her left leg, she kicked the drawer close with a bang. Is this the only means? Is there no other way? Reflecting that the nylon clothesline in the backyard was enough, she returned to the sofa and sat. In a while, she reflected that with the rope, this house was very convenient. The old roof is aloft. The hook of the ceiling fan … she began favourably aligning her mind with these provisions. By then, the phone rang. She felt angry. She thought that it was his and resolved not to receive it. She made an observation of the coincidence of his phone call with her attempts at suicide. Or – she had a doubt – is it that I develop a desire to die at the very hour he chooses to call? Apprehensive that he would come running in ten minutes if she did not receive the call, she pulled herself up and took the call.

Without even waiting for her hello, he said, 'I just finished reading Sri Srikantaiah's *Indian Literary Aesthetics*. A marvellous work. I could not fully grasp a few sections. You tutor me,' as if there was nothing else in this world other than the subject of that book.

'It is quite some time since I quit my teacher's job. You take tuitions elsewhere.'

'You fool, you resigned that job without conferring with me. If you have forgotten it, do some homework yourself, brush up your knowledge, and then tutor me. I feel like coming over right now to seek clarification of all the markings that I have made.'

She wanted to be unto herself. 'Bring it when you come tomorrow. I too have to read it once.' She felt impelled to relate the progress in litigation. 'By the way, look, the lawyer's assistant had called from Hassan....' She related everything.

'Kudos! Good. It means that the honourable judge is convinced that justice is on our side. It is right to evict them.'

She was taken aback. He who asked me to alienate myself from the estate is saying this! Maverick! 'Why do you congratulate me?' she asked.

'Nobody should gain anything from inequity. Seems like the lawyer you have engaged is a competent one. We should thank him.' She felt contented. 'Don't show any lenience. The stopgap sustenance awarded to them by the court is more than enough. And in appointing a manager, they may attempt at pushing their person. Guard yourself against that.' She felt like inviting him right away, informing him of the pudding she had prepared in celebration of the victory. But she checked herself as she felt that he preferred her to be detached from this victory.

~

At about 10:30 in the morning, the dogs started barking. Mahadevamma, the domestic help, announced, 'It is a lady from your native town. Calls herself Subbamma.'

Amrita could not immediately recall who she was. She went out only to see a paternal relative of her aunt. After Amrita's mother was no more, this aunt on establishing herself at the estate had dismissed the earlier cook and appointed this lady from her native town. Later, during the children's schooling at Hassan, she had stayed with the brood and taken care of them. When she recalled that she had heard that this widow now stayed in the Attikanu estate working for aunt and Krishnamurthy, her instinct told her that she was here as an emissary. 'Come on in, Subbamma, please,' she greeted her. Showing her a seat in the lounge, she asked her, 'Did you travel by bus? Where did you start from?' Amrita had a misgiving as to how this lady came to know the whereabouts of this house.

'Of late, there is a direct bus from Sakleshpur. I have to use the washroom,' she got up.

'Come this way,' after showing her to the bathroom, Amrita went to her room and called Somu. 'Don't come now. I will call you in the evening. There is a guest from the country. I still don't know a thing. She just arrived.'

'Whatever the matter, don't you relent,' he proffered more of his support.

Having washed her hands and feet, Subbamma emerged. Amrita handed her a cup of coffee. 'Let's lunch in half an hour. You too are hungry,' she led her to the lounge and, showing her seat asked, 'What's the matter?' She did not readily enquire about the well-being of aunt and her family.

'What shall I say? What is there that you don't know?' Subbamma grinned to reveal her teeth that had lost one of their members in the upper row and two in the lower row.

'What do I know, I who reside in distant Mysore and just ferry the children to and fro their school?' When Amrita thus underplayed, the lady, embarrassed at being handed the onus of taking the conversation further, once again grinned, only to display the same empty slots in her gums again. An untonsured widow, though she was elder to aunt by five or six years, her hair was black, almost like her complexion. Two solid gold bracelets on each wrist.

'Let's talk later. The cook and help are at home,' the lady said in cadence.

'Their work is almost over. They will leave now.' After they both left, Amrita laid the cuisine, appointed the table, and said, 'Let's have lunch. You would have started on empty stomach.'

Gobbling the curry-soaked rice and quenching her hunger some, Subbamma embarked on her errand. 'You have appointed a daunting lawyer. He can't even wait till the case is decided. He has ordered for immediate evacuation of the occupants of the residential quarters of the coffee estates. Though just a cook, I was serving you people. I have brought you up. I came here just to say a few words to you, my dear. Why should they be rendered homeless and evicted from their homes? Let the case take its course. Why should they be humiliated to the point of scampering for shelter?'

Subbamma's words were not unexpected from Amrita's point of view. It was but natural. 'Did they depute you just to tell this much?'

'What of them sending me? I came on my own. Why, haven't I the authority to advice you?'

'You surely have,' Amrita gave her leeway.

'And remember one thing. They are your brothers.'

'Brothers? Or cousins-in-share?' though she retorted, she held her voice gentle.

'Whatever you choose to call,' Subbamma said matter-of-factly and in an intimate tone. 'You would be aware. I am an outsider. It will be improper for me to relate. You surmise yourself and act accordingly.'

'What is it that I should be aware of? Why would it be improper for you and to relate what?' Amrita was taken aback at the hidden import. She got curious too.

'If you don't know, then I should not be uttering it. Let go,' Subbamma put her head down and resumed filling morsels into her mouth.

'Having ignited my curiosity, don't stop now. Reveal it fully. I won't disclose to anyone that you spilled this. If you wish, I will even pledge.'

After Amrita so assured her, the lady lifted her face and, looking at Amrita, said, 'You may choose to consider Jayarama as a cousin-in-share. But Krishnamurthy, look, don't you really know?'

Amrita's musings, which was groping in these directions, now hit the bull's eye. That day when they were here and Krishnamurthy exhorted her with talks of paramour and her conduct, the hazy thoughts that had come to her mind as she observed him from close quarters became clear now and, yes, she felt, his face resembled her father's. Behind came the justification that her father and uncle were, after all, brothers. If the progeny derived the physical features of an uncle, she reasoned, what was unusual about it? 'Subbamma, are you telling the truth? How do you know that?'

'Why shall I utter unfounded things and earn sin to my tongue? Not just me, all the labourers know discreetly. Who will speak openly about the personal matters of the lordship? After all, what wrong is there in this? Your father was a widower. Poor fellow, for your sake, he didn't marry again. Jayalakshmi's husband is a dunce. What compatibility? At least, I who got widowed at an early age didn't think of it as wrong. It seems you took serious exception to Krishnamurthy's mean outburst at you that day. Very angry, you have got the lawyer oust him from that house. Hence, I tell you this. However lowly he would have derided you, he is after all your own brother. Just pardon him. Don't utterly denigrate them so as to cause the court bailiff to physically evict them from the house.'

Not that she never got ideas as to whether her father and aunt would have had that sort of relationship. She has put to work all her memories from her younger days to ruminate on it. Not only the refrain from judgement then for lack of proper evidence, she understood that even now it was for reason of her disinclination to see her father in a bad light that she had stalled such assumption. She began mulling over. Yet, within, she felt aversion. Her gut curdled and she felt like retching into the sink. But she got cautious and contained herself, for if she vomited at this hour, Subbamma would get ideas and promptly broadcast them in the countryside. She did not further the matter. 'Have some more rice,' she just played a dutiful host. After lunch, she showed Subbamma to the small room by the back door, 'Get some sleep. You have got up early today.' She went to her room. She was disgusted at her father, rather disdainful, that he had handed over the reins to this aunt not just for the mundane reason of man's lack of enterprise in household matters, but for obnoxious reasons. She also felt that she would not have been so disgusted if her father, on the death of his wife, had rather kept a woman of some social order from the ghats below. The disgust with her aunt morphed to revulsion. She felt repressed. But alert, her brain kept up its meditation. Considering that unpretextual love without any consideration of benefits was impossible in this aunt, the revulsion aggravated and curdled her entrails further. As she continued to lie down for another half an hour, another idea formed in her, which, she reflected, could not be ruled out either. She got up and came out. Subbamma had just reclined, was not asleep. 'Why, didn't you get sleep?'

'No kiddie, I am not habituated to afternoon siesta,' she instantly sat up.

'Let me prepare some coffee,' she led her to the kitchen, and while they sipped their coffee, she asked, 'Were you at Sakleshpur last night?'

Unable to grasp the purport of the query, when the lady said 'no', she immediately added, 'Did Krishnamurthy see you off at the bus station?' The lady grunted in the positive. Amrita asked, 'My aunt sent you here, right?' She did not reply.

After they finished their coffee, 'Come here,' Amrita led the lady to the worship chamber, posted her before God, and, rooting her gaze in the lady's face, said, 'Subbamma, tell the truth. Is it not my aunt who sent you here? If you lie, God will get to know of it. I too.'

'Let go, kiddie,' Subbamma's reaction was unambiguous.

'One more thing. Aunt herself has asked you to convey to me that Krishnamurthy was born of my father. Else, you would not have exercised discretion on your own to put it across. Speak out the truth.' When she looked firmly at her face, Subbamma put her gaze down. 'You are standing before God. At least, in your next life, good fortune should be yours. Tell the truth.' When she insisted, the lady said conclusively, shaking off her responsibility, 'Have I ever assumed such lordship as to relate such things on my own? There is really no need to cause me to swear in the witness of God.' 'Okay, come over,' Amrita came out of the worship chamber. Subbamma followed.

In ten minutes, Subbamma's embarrassment increased uncontrollably. She went to her room. In another ten minutes, she emerged with her baggage and said, 'I will leave, kiddie. Drop me at the bus station. Why get involved in high-society matters, a country cook that I am.' As she observed the lady standing before her, Amrita understood that the woman was greatly afflicted.

'Why feel vexed, Subbamma ? Stay on. I will see you off tomorrow morning,' Amrita consoled her.

Amrita then retired to her room. Feelings of void. She slipped to a state wherein she felt that there was no meaning or enthusiasm in life, and to live on was nothing but a debilitating distress. She slept in that state till 5 and then went to fetch the children. She was one with the children, playing with them and enquiring about their lessons. At night, when everyone had finished supper, the children slept, and Subbamma retired to her room, an idea struck Amrita. One part of her mind vetoed against it. But another part endorsed it vehemently. When she called Somu at 11, she did not divulge anything to him too. She just said, 'Tomorrow, I am leaving for Hassan. Mostly, I will be back by night. I will call you after I am back.' Just in case she had to stay back overnight, she packed a day's clothing of the kids and retired.

Getting up early next morning, she woke up the children and attended to their toiletries. 'Subbamma, you too get ready soon. I will take you to the estate in my car. I got to visit there on some court work.' She asked Subbamma to sauté some *uppiṭṭu*, and after everyone had had their breakfast, she dropped the children at Susheelamma's, handed her their dresses, went to Mahadevamma's house, and instructed her husband to guard the house overnight in case she didn't return. She asked him to look after the dogs and then drove in the direction of Sakleshpur. Arriving there at 10 am, they brunched and drove straight to the estate of Elekanu where Jayarama lived with his wife and children. Jayarama was taken aback on seeing her.

'Jayarama, got to discuss a matter with you. Better if Krishnamurthy and your mother are present too. Let Meenakshi come too.' Jayarama listened to her subserviently. It was clear that the interim orders of the court had ruptured his guts. From there, he drove the car. Meenakshi sat beside him.

'All said and done, sister Amrita, these old model cars are ideal for these estate roads. This sturdy engine, sturdy chassis you can't find in modern cars,' he exhibited some affection.

Aunt and Krishnamurthy who saw all four arrive in the same car were taken aback too. Krishnamurthy still had a terse look on his face. Oblivious of any development in litigation, uncle greeted her. 'Whence, kiddie?' After enquiring about his health, Amrita said, 'Aunty, I am here to talk to all four of you.'

Krishnamurthy's room was on the first floor. The aunt climbed up the first. Amrita followed her. Meenakshi, Jayarama, and Krishnamurthy brought up the rear. After everyone had entered, Amrita shut the door and sat on the bed beside Krishnamurthy, her hand on his shoulder. Jayarama, Meenakshi, and aunt were seated opposite her on different chairs. She turned to Krishnamurthy and, without wasting any time, said, 'Look, Krishnamurthy, you should not interrupt my talk. You should give a patient hearing. If you give your word of honour, I will talk. Else, there is no need for any discussion,' she extended her right arm and held his right palm.

'Say yes, man. Your sister is here to tell something for your own good,' when his mother prompted him, he grunted compliance.

Amrita resumed, 'That day you accused me of bringing about this plaint by heeding the words of a paramour. You do not know the facts. I was then angry that you said so … '

Jayarama intervened, 'Don't take his words seriously, sis. He is one brat.'

'All of you first hear what I got to say. You may speak later,' she admonished him in the manner of a teacher and continued. 'That day, I was angry. But since yesterday, I have shed it, for I came to know that he is my own brother. That means he is not born to uncle, he is born to my father, your uncle. This fact is vouched for by your mother.'

Immediately, Krishnamurthy forcibly retrieved his hand and lifted it, 'You bitch! What are you driving at?'

'Krishnamurthy, I am not lying. Your own mother has declared so. Based on information from other sources, I too had suspected it could be so. Your mother has charmed my father and gained control over him to usurp my estate. This is a stale story. Aunty, any number of lies that you may be capable of creating, you just cannot deny this fact. This story is old by now. It concerns all three of you. Meenakshi, you being the daughter-in-law, I sought your attendance as I felt that you too should know the facts. Now hear what my plans are. I have developed an aversion towards this property. But I won't withdraw my plaint. If I do so, you will publicize that I was defeated. Jayarama, like you said that day, if need be, I will go up to Supreme Court and get my dues. After I have it all, legally I am entitled to a third of it. Two other shares belong to Vijai and Vikas. I will donate my share to both of you. I will make out a gift deed, donating the estate where Jayarama resides to him, and this estate to Krishnamurthy, a sister's gift of love. Spurred by self-respect, if you resign the donation, I will pass it on for some charitable purpose. I will not even touch it. What Vijai and Vikas, after attaining majority, will do of their shares is left to them. I have decided that I shall earn my bread from tomorrow. As per the court orders, you people must immediately vacate these two estates. I have already informed Ranganath to marry again and live happily.' She stopped at that.

While she related, Amrita kept looking at aunt, Jayarama, and Krishnamurthy. The three hung their heads as if there were a load of boulders over them. Meenakshi was glowering at her mother-in-law.

After two minutes, Amrita said, 'I nurse no more love towards Krishnamurthy than I do towards Jayarama and Leela just because he was born to my father. You both are my brothers. She is my sister. I don't discriminate. Bye, Aunty.' She got up, opened the door, and left. She climbed down the stairs apace. Subbamma, who was by the door, looked at her anxiously. 'Subbamma, if you find it difficult to continue here, see me. I will give you some gratuity. Deposit it in a bank and live on the interest. You would also be having some savings,' saying so, she walked on.

Uncle was seated on a bench. 'Kiddie, are you leaving! Without even lunching?' He got up.

'Uncle, I got some urgent work,' she bent over and prostrated at his feet, walked up to her car, gunned it, and steered away.

She drove steadily. She was in no hurry. The sable-green coffee plantations under the shades of silver oak trees on both sides drew her attention and she felt like parking and watching them. She did halt and watch intently. My kiddie should have been with me. She desired to view such greenery, hills, and woods in his company. Yet, she intermittently stopped to observe them, and reached Sakleshpur by 3. She went to a restaurant, munched a bellyful of assorted snacks, and topped it with coffee. She resumed her steady drive and arrived at Mysore by 7:30. Reclaiming the children, she was home shortly thereafter. It was 9:30 pm by the time she fed the children and supped. The children slept. She could not think of anything to do. After quite some time, she knew what to do. She dialled his number.

'When did you return?' he asked.

'It was 7:30 by the time I arrived at Mysore. The other day you told me about the interior decoration course in Bombay. How much will it cost totally in fee and overheads?'

'For all of six months, it may cost fifteen or sixteen thousand.'

'Look, now I haven't even a single paisa. The golden bangles on my wrist too are not mine. You must arrange for that much funds.'

For a long moment, he froze. Then he said, 'It is not necessary for you to seek that profession. Try in some college. The subject you have studied all these years ... '

'Know why? I should work at your office. What if I work elsewhere and you befriend some damsel in your office! Do you think I am not that cautious?' He laughed aloud. She continued, 'Should arrange for babysitting the children for six months. I will enquire tomorrow. When you come tomorrow, get me one hundred rupees. I haven't even a paisa for my personal effects. I'm feeling sleepy. I'll retire. Goodnight.' A yawn dilated her mouth.

ACKNOWLEDGEMENTS

To learn about the philosophy at the core of our traditions and culture, there is no resort other than the scholar Dr R. Ganesh (see back cover). I can't thank him enough. I am immensely grateful to Sri S.L. Bhyrappa for encouraging me to translate this novel, appreciating my work, and according consent for its publication. Thanks to the to the Editorial Director of Niyogi Books, Sri Nirmal Kanti Bhattacharjee, for his appreciation of the tale.